EVERY OTHER
WEDNESDAY

Books by Susan Kietzman

THE GOOD LIFE

A CHANGING MARRIAGE

THE SUMMER COTTAGE

EVERY OTHER WEDNESDAY

Published by Kensington Publishing Corporation

EVERY OTHER WEDNESDAY

SUSAN KIETZMAN

KENSINGTON BOOKS
www.kensingtonbooks.com

KENSINGTON BOOKS are published by
Kensington Publishing Corp.
119 West 40th Street
New York, NY 10018

All Kensington titles, imprints, and distributed lines are available at special quantity discounts for bulk purchases for sales promotion, premiums, fund-raising, educational, or institutional use.

Special book excerpts or customized printings can also be created to fit specific needs. For details, write or phone the office of the Kensington Sales Manager: Attn. Sales Department. Kensington Publishing Corp., 119 West 40th Street, New York, NY 10018. Phone: 1-800-221-2647.

Kensington and the K logo Reg. U.S. Pat. & TM Off.

eISBN-13: 978-1-61773-552-3
eISBN-10: 1-61773-552-3
First Kensington Electronic Edition: May 2017

ISBN-13: 978-1-61773-551-6
ISBN-10: 1-61773-551-5
First Kensington Trade Paperback Printing: May 2017

10 9 8 7 6 5 4 3 2 1

Printed in the United States of America

To women, and the confidence and relevance they seek.

And to Ted, as always.

ACKNOWLEDGMENTS

Thank you, Loretta, for your efforts at helping me find the most direct path. Thank you, John, for your care and expertise in editing my work. And thank you to everyone at Kensington who works very hard to make me look good.

To all who support me with your kind words and continuous presence, thank you for your friendship and love.

OCTOBER

CHAPTER 1

The calendar on the mustard colored wall of her kitchen confirmed what Alice Stone already knew; it had been two months since her youngest daughter left for college, and Alice was still baking cookies as if Linda were still at home. Every week, she baked two or three dozen, even though her husband, Dave, was running more and eating less, and even though Linda had long ago told her mother that teenage girls didn't eat cookies. It was a habit, this baking, that Alice had initiated when her three girls were young and looking for a snack when they got home from school. And it kept Alice busy for a couple hours, from the mixing of the ingredients she kept stocked in her cupboards to the baking of the dough. Baking cookies was a productive way to pass time, Alice had convinced herself, better than sitting on the couch and flipping through a magazine. And being productive at home was a good enough reason to be at home, to not get a job.

In some ways, Alice did want to work. Having a job would give her something to do, a new purpose in life, now that her girls were out of the house. And on some days, she longed for something to fill and challenge her brain, not to mention the extra money that Dave mentioned regularly. He certainly wanted her to work, so she could help with the "incredible expense of putting three kids through college"—although Hilary had just graduated and Cathy had been out of school for three years—something Alice was well aware of since she paid the bills. But, in terms of getting a job, she knew a lot more about what she didn't want to do than what she wanted to do. She didn't want to work at Fast Pace, the running store she and Dave had opened twenty-eight years ago when they had moved back to Connecticut, and when she was running as many miles in a week as Dave. And she didn't want to perform menial labor, though she had to admit that what she had been doing as a stay-at-home mom, the grocery shopping, meal preparation, driving kids to lessons and school events, and running errands, all fit squarely into that category. Working women liked to show their empathy by praising the honorable profession of mothers dressed in sweats instead of suits, by comparing the skill sets of the cookie baking, tantrum thwarting, coupon clipping moms to those of the team building, forward thinking, solution oriented corporate ladder climbers, but women at home knew better. If they were paid for what they did, it would be minimum wage. This had been okay with Alice, because, in addition to performing banal tasks, she had been caring for her girls. But if she tried to join the workforce now, she would be qualified for and have nothing but boring, inconsequential labor to define her days.

Dave told her this was crazy talk; she could do any number of things. She was a college graduate, with a degree in psychology that could be useful in many professions, including, he had said over the years, helping runners find the right gear for their style and activity level. But lately, since they had been talking about Alice working again, Dave hadn't encouraged her to join the team at Fast Pace. Perhaps he, like the rest of the working world, knew that someone who had been out of touch for as long as Alice had been making cookies would have trouble transitioning into the frenzied, twenty-four-hour, global, competitive employment arena.

The timer buzzed, and Alice pulled a sheet of peanut butter cookies out of the oven.

The sole thing Alice liked about the idea of returning to Fast Pace was the incentive it would give her to start running again. She exercised four or five days a week at the YMCA in town, but she hadn't run hard in several years and knew how painful it would be to push her fifty-five-year-old legs to move, as they once had, at a seven-minute-mile pace. She'd have to start at a ten- or eleven-minute mile. She might even have to settle for a twelve-minute mile if she wanted to run more than three. And at that speed, she might as well join the mall walkers. Alice shook her head at the thought.

Alice's body was still thin and toned; she went to the Y to work out more than to socialize. At five foot, five inches, she weighed one hundred and twenty-five pounds, which was what she had weighed in college. She could pull off wearing clothes meant for younger women, though she admitted to herself that she chose the popular, ubiquitous, oversized tops just as much to hide the loose skin around her abdomen as she did to be current. And she kept her blond hair long, down to the middle of her back, which helped her feel youthful and relevant. But looking like a runner and being a runner had nothing in common. And if Alice were going to actually be a runner again, she would have to train like she had in college. Would Dave run with her?

The clock in the hallway struck the hour, and Alice reached for the remote control to the Bose sound system that sat on top of the fridge. NPR was good company in the morning, giving Alice the news she needed to feel informed and the human interest stories that expanded her perspective. Her mind wandered during the news about the Middle East. Alice wanted to care more about events there, but her doing something that would matter to the Afghans, Syrians, Iraqis, or Somalians would look like what, exactly? She was making a mental list of her errands for the day when her thought process stopped. "...Shooting at William Chester High School in Southwood, Connecticut this morning." Alice grabbed the remote and rapidly pushed the up arrow button to increase the volume. "...Two confirmed dead in an apparent murder-suicide. Police have indicated that the shooting appears to have been targeted rather than random and that the students at William Chester are not in immediate danger. Still, school officials have canceled classes for the remainder of the day and are in the process of sending students home. The names of the deceased are being held until family members can be notified."

The timer buzzed, and Alice, her head heavy with the weight of the news, moved to the oven. She set the sheet of hot cookies on the countertop and then picked up her phone to text Linda. Less than six months ago, William Chester had been Linda's school— and Hilary's and Cathy's before that. Less than six months ago, Linda would have been in the hallways where this shooting occurred.

Did u hear about the shooting at Chester?

OMG—yes! Emmanuel Sanchez is dead! James Shulz shot him and shot himself!

James Shulz?

From drama—the sound tech. Never talked to anybody. Had a huge crush on Nanette Benoit. Emmanuel's girlfriend

Oh no!

I gotta go—too much going on right now. I'll call later

Alice put her phone down and reached for the spatula. She removed the cookies from the sheet, all the while trying to picture James Shulz in her head. Nothing came. She had no memory of him, even though Linda had been involved in the drama club since her freshman year. Alice did, however, clearly remember Emmanuel Sanchez, a star football player and scholar who had been in the newspaper just last week, smiling in a photo with a caption about recruitment offers he had received from prestigious colleges all over the country. Alice pulled a chair out from the kitchen table and sat for the first time that morning. She picked up her phone again and called Dave. He rarely answered his cell phone when he was at work, but she wanted to hear his voice.

CHAPTER 2

Joan Howard sat in an upholstered chair in the corner of her family room, her slippered feet on the matching ottoman, reading the newspaper. This was how she typically started her weekdays, or rather, how she had started them for a couple months now. She and her husband, Stephen, had moved Liz, the younger of their two daughters, into her college dorm in August, and Joan's mornings had been different, had been like this, ever since. She and Stephen had talked about what it would look like to live in a vacated nest, but they had stayed away from how it would actually feel. Their older daughter, Cassie, had been gone from the house for seven years now, graduating from college and settling into a communications job in Boston and into a rent controlled apartment with her boyfriend. Her departure from the house had been less disruptive for Joan, who still had Liz at home to nurture and protect. But now that Liz was gone, so was Joan's focus, as well as any possible reason for Joan to be sitting in a chair at eight in the morning with a cup of coffee on a nearby coaster. But here she was, skimming the headlines and glancing at the muted local news on the television instead of sipping from a travel mug on her way to another meaningful day at a fulfilling job.

Joan put the newspaper aside and got up out of the chair. She walked her cup to the kitchen, where she filled it for the third time, aware now of the slight buzz behind her eyes and at the base of her skull, thankful for chemical stimulation. She looked out the window over her kitchen sink to the deck and, beyond that, to the yard. The newspaper indicated it would be sunny and warm again today; perhaps she could rake some leaves before her two o'clock meeting of the Southwood Cancer Society. The SCS was one of several organizations Joan belonged to—but even though she still believed in the mission, the intention to do good, she had lately been restless, with her desire to attend meetings and events waning. Was this, too, a result of Liz's departure?

Joan looked at her watch. It was 8:20 a.m. Liz, if she were still living at home instead of at college, would be sitting in her first period class at William Chester High School. And Joan, wearing yoga pants that never made it to a studio, might be making Liz's bed or doing her laundry. Stephen had admonished Joan for "prolonging this dependency," and Joan understood his point. But she liked taking care of the little things for her daughters when they were home while she increasingly let them manage the big things. It beat exercising.

Joan had never been a particularly athletic person, finding skinny people's attraction to sweating, heavy breathing, and routine exhaustion mysterious. She liked to say that life was hard enough without the added misery of exercise. The only thing she liked about exercise was the soft clothing that most mornings tightly blanketed her body. She was only fifteen or so pounds overweight, according to her doctor, but felt larger due to today's continued cultural worship of slim, wrinkle-free women. At fifty-two, Joan had a limited number of options for eradicating the wrinkles around her eyes, but she could certainly lose weight. She dieted, along with, it seemed, every other member of her gender over the age of thirteen, but she was not particularly dedicated, and therefore not particularly successful. She liked fruits and vegetables well enough, but she liked meat and cheese and bread better. And even though her mother-in-law, Sandi, had passed along her best dieting secrets to Joan over the course of Joan's thirty-year marriage to Stephen, Joan liked to eat. Plus, Southwood needed a few chubby women to balance out the troops of fit baby boomers who jogged on the streets and lifted weights at the Y.

This was not to say Joan didn't have style. She dressed beautifully, with an especially good eye for color and accessories. Everything she wore complemented her black, chin-length bob, deep blue eyes, and smooth, blemish free skin, and she was often told how good she looked. Because she dressed so well, people didn't notice right away that she was slightly overweight. Only occasionally would someone inclined to say such things tell her that she carried her weight well. Was that a compliment?

It didn't matter. Stephen liked the way she looked. He was like her, in that he didn't exercise regularly. He went on what Joan called fitness kicks, as she did. But wherever they took place—in the pool at the Y, on a bike around town, along Southwood's running trails—these resolutions didn't last long. Stephen found his energy at the office, and Joan had always been able to recharge through her kids, and, to be honest (in spite of how it sounded), through her weekly manicures at Brenda's. But her battery had been depleted since Liz had left the house, and Joan knew that she needed more than a closet full of clothes and polished nails to move forward in life.

Joan finished reading the first section of the paper and dropped it to the floor. As she unfolded the regional section, she glanced up at the television and saw the words SHOOTING AT WILLIAM CHESTER HIGH SCHOOL in a banner at the bottom of the screen. She reached for the remote and turned on the volume. A Channel 10 news team reporter was standing in front of the main entrance, talking with a student. "No one really knew James," the student said. "He was quiet. He kept to himself. But until today, I would never have thought of him as a violent person, as someone who would take the life of another student."

"And tell us about that other student," the reporter prompted.

"Emmanuel? It's hard to know where to start. He was the star of our football team; everybody knows that. But he was a lot more than that, you know? He was a really nice guy who talked to everybody. He could have been really stuck up because he was such a talented athlete and a smart guy. But he was nice to everybody."

The young man's eyes started to fill with water. He blinked several times in an unsuccessful effort to clear them. The reporter put her hand on his shoulder.

"Thank you," she said. "Thank you for talking to us at this very difficult time."

"It's okay," said the student as he turned away from the reporter and walked out of the camera shot.

"To sum up what we know already, James Shulz, a senior here at William Chester High School, shot and killed fellow student Emmanuel Sanchez, a Southwood scholar and gifted football player, and then turned the gun on himself. The police have indicated they think this was a premeditated, isolated incident and that the other members of the student body here at the high school are not in immediate danger. Principal Sean Greeley has canceled classes for the remainder of the day, and the students were instructed to go home. As you can see behind me, the buses are pulling out of the main parking lot, transporting the students home to their families. Stay tuned for additional coverage as details become available."

Joan pushed the mute button on the remote and sat back in the chair. She remembered James Shulz as the student had described him, a shy, very quiet kid. But she also remembered his incredible technical abilities. Liz had been very involved with the drama department and had talked about James. Like many of the department participants, Liz hadn't known his last name, but she did know he was the one who routinely coaxed clear and consistent voices and music from aging microphones and an outdated audio system. He was the one who made everyone sound better than they actually did. All of the dramathletes, the moniker the head of the department had given her charges in an attempt at boosting their social status as well as enticing the booster club to contribute more money to her program, respected James. But none of them hung out with him between productions. He was exactly what so often is said about someone who does what he did—a loner.

The phone rang; it was Liz. When Joan answered the call, all she could hear on the other end was her daughter sobbing.

CHAPTER 3

This same morning, Ellie Fagen was sitting at her kitchen table, with her laptop open in front of her and a short stack of spreadsheets to the left of the computer. Today was the day to do something to rev up her bookkeeping business. Today was the day to find a new client. Today was the day to start making enough money so her husband, Chris, would stop talking about her getting another job—a real job is what he meant but didn't say, a job that would handsomely supplement his gym teacher's salary, a job that would help defray the cost of sending their younger son, Tim, to NYU. Ellie had been saying this to herself, giving herself a pep talk just about every day since Tim had packed all his belongings into his grandmother's hand-me-down Passat wagon and driven into New York City to start his freshman year in college, two months ago. In fact, if she were going to be honest about it, Ellie had been talking to herself about this very topic since her older son, Brandon, had driven himself and all his stuff eleven hundred miles from Connecticut to Northern Michigan University two years ago.

She knew why she was, as Chris said, dragging her feet. And she was resolved to work on this troublesome aspect of her personality—this tendency to think and talk about what she wanted in life, only to do nothing about it, zero follow-up. And while it was natural to talk about change rather than take the soul stretching steps to accomplish it, Ellie was particularly adept at procrastination, especially when it came to self-promotion, which was exactly what she had to do to find new clients. Selling herself was not a part of her makeup, her DNA, as someone on a television show about cops or doctors would say. Ellie had confidence in her ability to accurately and efficiently manage financial accounts; she simply had trouble telling people this, thinking it boastful and distasteful to do so. Wouldn't it be more convincing, more sincere to get promoted by others? Chris told her that no matter how good she was, her few clients had a multitude of things to think about rather than how they could help grow Ellie's bookkeeping business. He had told her so this morning, while they were eating toast with peanut butter, while he was looking at her over the top of his reading glasses. It was a look she had seen before, a look that said: *Are we really having this conversation? Again?*

Ellie was often on the receiving end of this look, whether it emanated from her husband, her father, her mother, or any combination of her six older brothers. In her excuse-making moments, Ellie blamed her large family for her inability to take charge, to do whatever she needed to do, because her brothers had, growing up, made decisions for her. If she had hesitated when asked a question, one of them had answered for her. If she had approached one of them with a choice she was facing, that one had chosen for her. And while her mother had taught Ellie to "stand on her own two feet," her brothers had, often without being asked, held her up by her elbows. Maybe this was why her *today is the day* resolutions often dissolved. Was she capable of changing her ways, of changing her life?

Ellie pushed back from the table and stood. She needed a walk to make sense of the jumble of thoughts and ideas in her head. She walked five miles a day, six days a week, often with her dog, but sometimes not. Today, she would go by herself, leaving the default two-mile loop with Buffy for Chris when he got home from school. She coated her lips for the second time that morning with the tube of balm she had in the pocket of her sweatpants and then strode to the back hall closet for sneakers, a windbreaker, and sunglasses.

She paused at the mirror hanging on the wall next to the back door and saw her mother's light green eyes looking back at her. Brigid Kilcullen hadn't hesitated one moment in her entire life—except, she liked to say at family gatherings, for a full minute after Ellie's father, Patrick, had asked her to marry him. Why couldn't Ellie be more like her mother? She took a coated elastic from her pocket and used it to put her barely long enough, wavy blond hair into a ponytail. She had been growing it since Tim left the house in an effort, and a very small one at that, at embracing change.

After a sixty-eight-minute walk, Ellie pushed through the back door. She filled a glass with water and returned to her computer. It was now close to nine. She told herself she would not get out of the chair again until she had a firm plan in place. But before she started in earnest, she decided to check the news. And as soon as she clicked on the bookmarked page for the local newspaper, she saw the headline about the shooting at the high school.

> Southwood—High school students, teachers, and administrators are reeling from the shooting at William Chester this morning that took the life of two seniors. The shooter, James Shulz, a barely known sound technician for the drama department, walked into a classroom during first period and shot Emmanuel Sanchez, a scholarly athlete, in the chest, and then turned the gun on himself. Physics teacher Bill Sanders said he led the students into the hall before returning to the classroom to check the condition of the boys.
>
> "Both of them were dead—I think instantly," Sanders said. "There was no opportunity for CPR or other life-saving measures. This is a horrible, horrible situation that took all of us by surprise."
>
> Principal Sean Greeley used the same word: *surprise*. "There has been no violence at the school in his twenty-year tenure," he said. In fact, he and other administrators had recently made the decision against installing metal detectors at the main entrance or ramping up security, in spite of shooting events elsewhere in

the country, and in spite of what happened in New-town. Greeley said that, "until today, danger dwelled elsewhere. We never saw this coming. We never thought this could happen in our small, coastal town in Connecticut." Greeley canceled classes for the re-mainder of the day—and potentially the rest of the week—and indicated counselors would be available to students upon their return.

Several students interviewed who knew James Shulz were less surprised. They called him a "techni-cal genius," but an "absolutely introverted outsider." One student described Shulz in the way other young men who commit violent acts are described: "He was always alone." Nanette Benoit, Emmanuel Sanchez's girlfriend, who was sitting next to him in class at the time of the incident, declined an interview but did say, "I don't know why he did this. James was not a bad person."

Principal Greeley, who said he was "heartbroken" over this incident, indicated he would send an e-mail to parents before the end of the day with more infor-mation.

Ellie got out of her chair and ran up the stairs to her bedroom for her cell phone, which was charging on the table next to her bed. There was a missed call from Chris and then a text message that he was on his way home. Phone in hand, Ellie ran back down the stairs and into the kitchen, just as Chris was coming through the back door. "Do you know?" he said, his face bearing the creased, pained expression of someone who is digesting sadness and shock.

"Yes," she said, walking to him, tears forming in her eyes. He wrapped his long arms around her and held her tightly.

CHAPTER 4

Alice pulled her green Subaru Forester into the high school parking lot only to find it full. She drove up and down the rows hoping to find a space that another driver hadn't seen, even though she already knew the futility of this exercise at an event of such magnitude. If she hadn't spent ten minutes posting pictures of her latest batch of chocolate chocolate-chip cookies to her Facebook account, she would be parked and walking toward the football field, where the candlelight vigil for Emmanuel Sanchez had just started. She drove her car back out onto the main road, where vehicles lined both sides, and managed to squeeze in between two others. After she shimmied herself out of the driver's side door, hemmed in by a large rock, she jogged toward the back of the school, now thinking it was probably too late to find a seat in the bleachers.

The field was ablaze with lights. As Alice got closer, she could hear Principal Sean Greeley's voice over the public address system. "...Senseless tragedy. Our presence here tonight cannot right the wrong. It cannot bring back Emmanuel Sanchez. But we can honor and cherish his memory. Our senior class has been handing out candles. If you don't yet have one, look for a student in a lime green T-shirt. These students will also light your candles...." Breathing hard from running, Alice slowed her pace when she reached the fence surrounding the field. She now had visual confirmation that the bleachers, like the parking lot, were full to capacity, meaning her best option would be to stand in the end zone with the other latecomers. As soon as she settled into a space, she was handed a candle by a girl who had been crying, her tears having smeared the letters *E* and *S* grease painted onto her cheeks. Alice closed her eyes in an effort to calm her heart and mind, both racing from what had been a hectic yet unfulfilling day of errand running and domestic chores, and to focus on the ceremony. She had not taken the time that day to register its import. Just as she opened her eyes, the overhead lights were cut off, leaving the assemblage in candlelit darkness.

"Alice?"

Alice looked to her right and saw Joan Howard, Liz's mom, a fellow drama parent. Liz and Alice's daughter Linda had been in three productions together. And Alice and Joan had helped with fundraising, set construction, and pasta dinners before performances. "Hi, Joan," said Alice in a whisper, and then she asked the rote question that shouldn't be asked on days like this one. "How are you?"

"I've been better," said Joan, keeping her voice volume low as well. "Can you believe this? Can you believe this has really happened, and we are all standing on the artificial turf that Emmanuel should be running on this weekend?"

Alice shook her head. "No," she said. "I'm in shock, actually. I'm having trouble processing this entire situation."

"A moment of silence please." It was Sean Greeley again, holding his candle aloft and bowing his head. Alice mimicked his stance for a moment and then opened her eyes and glanced over at Joan, who was rubbing her temple with the index and middle fingers of her left hand. Alice moved closer and put her arm around Joan's shoulder. Aside from Joan's quick intake of air, the stadium and its occupants were still; no one coughed, sneezed, spoke, moved. Alice conjured up an image of Emmanuel in her mind: a magazine cover, good looking boy, whose family had moved from Florida two or three years ago. Her daughter Linda had thought he was dreamy. And now he was dead. Alice didn't blame James Shulz as much as she blamed his mother, Kelly. What kind of parent doesn't lock up her guns?

Several minutes later the vigil was over. Principal Greeley asked that they all leave the field in a respectful manner and keep the Sanchez family in their prayers. Alice and Joan slowly made their way with the crowd back to the main parking lot. They stopped at Joan's car, parked in the final space in the last row.

"Putting all this aside for a moment, how are you really?" asked Alice. "How is Liz?"

Joan flashed a quick smile. "I'm good. And Liz seems to like Williams. Her roommate is from New York City, which Liz thinks is the coolest thing ever. I'm not sure she realized that some people actually grow up in Manhattan. How about Linda? Does she like UConn?"

"Loves it," said Alice. "My cell phone is uncharacteristically quiet. When she does call me, it's usually when she's walking to class and has six minutes to talk."

"Clever girl," said Joan.

"Hey, Alice. Hi, Joan." It was Ellie Fagen, Tim's mother. Tim had also been in the drama club and was friendly with Liz and Linda. Ellie, like Alice and Joan, had pitched in, with cast dinners and mural painting. Tim had played Henry Higgins in *My Fair Lady* and was now at NYU studying music and theater. The head of the Chester drama department, along with anyone who had ever heard Tim sing, thought he was bound for stardom. Ellie's Honda Fit was parked two cars away from Joan's car. Ellie walked past it to join Alice and Joan.

"Hi, Ellie," said Alice. "Tough night."

"Yeah," said Ellie. "Nice attendance though. Sean was good."

"He was," said Joan. "He can be such a blabbermouth."

Ellie smiled. "Not tonight."

"Thank God," said Alice. "How's Tim doing?"

"Great," she said. "He absolutely loves New York."

"Good," said Joan, "because he'll be living there when he's appearing on Broadway."

"Well..."

"Well nothing, Ellie," said Alice. "Your kid is talented."

"Thank you."

Joan opened her car door. "I'm going to run," she said. "What are you two up to tomorrow?"

"The usual," said Alice. "Nothing. I'm still trying to figure out this empty nest thing."

"I've got to balance some accounts in the morning," said Ellie. "And then I'm free."

"Good," said Joan. "Let's meet for lunch at noon at High Tide."

"I'm in," said Alice, backing away from Joan's car.

"Me too," said Ellie.

"See you then," said Joan. She sat down in the driver's seat and started the car. Before any of them had time to wonder about the invitation, discussed among women whose only social interactions had occurred when helping with drama productions, Joan shut the car door, pulled out of the parking space, and drove away.

CHAPTER 5

High Tide sat on the Southwood River estuary and routinely flooded when the full moon and Long Island Sound joined forces. The previous summer, however, new owners had raised the restaurant up out of the ground and set it on a sturdy looking system of stilts, some twenty feet above sea level, as well as gutted the aged interior. They replaced the crumbling stone retention wall that had done a poor job of holding back the water with a mass of reinforced concrete, resulting in a nearly dry parking lot, no matter what the lunar or tidal activity. And when it had reopened just after Labor Day, it was so popular that no one could get in without a reservation or an hour long wait. A month later, the initial buzz had diminished somewhat, but Joan still called to make a reservation, knowing the dining room would be filled with local business people and women's groups happy to have somewhere else to eat lunch.

Southwood had its fair share of restaurants for a town of ten thousand. But many of them served mediocre food, catering to the tourists who congested the streets in the summertime with minivans packed with family members headed to the nearby beaches or with Corvette-driving gamblers eager to try their luck at the casino just north of town. The less popular restaurants were simply worn out, with water stained wallpaper in their dining rooms and out-of-date bathrooms with rusting fixtures and loud overhead fans; and their faded menus featured dishes out of the 1970s: shepherd's pie, fried haddock and chips, mild chili. High Tide, with its roomy booths, martini bar, small plate offerings, and floor-to-ceiling windows overlooking the harbor, was everyone's new first choice.

Joan parked her Range Rover, a present from her husband for her fiftieth birthday, at the far end of the parking lot. Parking close to the front door was one of Stephen's pet peeves—and this included at shopping malls, airports, even people's houses. *When you're eighty,* he had told Joan more than once, *you can park up front. But until then, park away from everyone else's car doors and fenders.* Joan often scoffed at her husband's peccadilloes, but this one made sense to her. For the last two years, she had parked a distance from whatever building she was entering. She was proud of herself for making this gesture, even in bad weather. Her Range Rover had no dents or scratches, which Joan knew was not, she hadn't yet admitted to Stephen, merely an indication of luck. She hadn't asked for or even wanted the car—she had driven a Honda for years, much to the chagrin of the Howard family, who all drove either luxury cars or SUVs—but had grown fond of its sporty styling and automatic transmission.

This was another good weather day. Like the day before, the sun shone and the warm temperature made sweaters optional. Joan slid out of the driver's seat, locked the car, and strode toward the restaurant. Glancing at her watch, she was pleased to be five minutes early, which would give her a chance to check out the menu before Alice and Ellie arrived. Joan had skipped breakfast, a new dieting scheme that had not lowered her weight one ounce in the last forty-eight hours, and knew she wanted something with cheese. Starving her digestive system in the past had always increased her appetite. And this diet, touted by her mother-in-law, who put nothing in her mouth save coffee and seltzer water before noon and weighed what she had weighed in high school, was so far yielding the same result.

Escorted to a seat next to the large wall of windows, Joan couldn't help looking out at the water, with its colorful sailboats and inviting wooden docks. Stephen had talked about getting a boat to give them something to do, give them something in common, now that both girls were out of the house. Joan liked the idea of a boat, but not the commitment level it would demand. She enjoyed having in-laws with boats, her ticket to three hours of pleasure cruising that cost nothing more than sandwiches from the downtown deli and a six-pack of cold beer. Joan shifted her attention to the menu and was in the process of deciding between a chicken quesadilla and a BLT with Swiss cheese when Alice approached the table. She sat down, dropped her blue leather satchel to the floor, looked at Joan, and slowly shook her head. "Bad morning?" asked Joan, reaching for her water glass.

"Bad night," said Alice. "I think I slept for about an hour. I keep seeing Emmanuel's face. I keep trying to figure it out, to come up with a reason for this—other than the availability of the weapon."

"Meaning if the weapon hadn't been in James's mother's spare bedroom . . . What's her name again?"

"Kelly," said Alice.

"Meaning, if Kelly hadn't kept the gun in the closet of her guest room, this wouldn't have happened?"

"Something like that."

Joan cocked her head. "You don't think he would have found another gun? She has about two dozen of them in the house, according to the newspaper."

Alice took a sip of water from her glass. "Smart people lock up their guns."

Ellie, who had fast-walked across the spacious dining room, started speaking before she reached the table. "I'm sorry I'm late," she said. "I had to drop something off at the post office, along with everyone else." She sat down and looked at Joan and then at Alice. "How are you guys?"

"Exhausted," said Alice. "I'm so upset by the whole thing. What would possess a single mother of a teenage son to keep a gun where he could find it—and use it?"

"Why does she need a gun at all?" asked Joan. "This is South-wood, not Chicago."

Alice flipped half her hair over her shoulder with her right hand. "She's got every right to have a gun," she said. "That's not my objection. My objection is that it wasn't in a secured location."

"Who cares about the location?" asked Joan, leaning into the table. "The question of why she needs a gun at all still stands."

Ellie slipped her windbreaker off her shoulders and hung it on the back of her chair. "Well, she's got a right to have a gun. The Constitution gives us that right."

Joan crossed her hands in front of her face. "This is not a discussion on the right to bear arms," she said. "What I don't understand is the reason so many people think they need a weapon in the first place. To protect them from what—overpriced meat at the Corner Market? We live in an incredibly safe town."

The server approached the table, refilled the water glasses, and read them the specials. Alice got an arugula salad. Ellie ordered shiitake risotto, and Joan got the quesadilla.

"Not in the summer," said Alice. "The tourists bring all kinds of trouble with them."

"Like what?" asked Joan. "So there are some fender benders, some public drunkenness. What, are we going to shoot people for having too many cocktails?"

Ellie scratched her head. "This wasn't about a drunk tourist, Joan. It was about unrequited love."

Joan lowered her head for a moment and then raised it. "You're right, Ellie. And the fact that James had access to a gun turned what could have been a fistfight into a homicide/suicide."

"People have the right to have guns," Alice said, evenly.

"Only sane people," said Joan. "The problem arises when the screwballs have guns."

Ellie nodded her head. "Kelly Shulz may fit that bill. Do you guys remember her from drama club?"

"Yes," said Alice. "She was pretty creative with set design. But like her son, she kept to herself. I can't remember her ever talking, even to say hello or goodbye."

"Who can blame her?" asked Joan. "Her husband bonks just about every woman in town, producing children with several of them, and then has the gall to sue her for emotional distress while he's stalking her? I barely know the woman because, as you say, she was so quiet. But she does have my sympathy. She's got a very bad husband—ex-husband, I guess, now—and a dead child."

"I occasionally run into her at the dog park," said Ellie. "She's got two huge yellow labs who love to play with all the other dogs at the park. But Kelly stands over to the side, never mingling with other dog owners, never saying a word except when she calls her dogs' names."

"Why is that, do you think?" asked Alice.

Joan shrugged. "It probably has something to do with the jerk she married. My guess is his list of undesirable qualities is longer than adulterer and baby daddy."

"Here's the odd thing, though," said Ellie. "Her car is covered with bumper stickers. It's almost as if she lets them do the talking, so she doesn't have to."

The food arrived, and the women each took a bite of their meals.

"How do you know her car?" asked Alice. "Just from the dog park?"

Ellie nodded her head and then wiped her mouth with her napkin, which she returned to her lap. "She's Catholic, it seems, based on her 'I heart the Pope' and anti-abortion/birth control stickers."

"She has an 'I heart the Pope' bumper sticker?" asked Joan.

"She does."

"Well, even though I don't subscribe to the politics of the Catholic Church, I think that's kind of sweet."

"So does my mother," said Ellie. "She's the only other person in town who has one that I've seen—and hers is the only bumper sticker on her Mercedes."

"Tastefully placed?" asked Joan, smiling.

"Very."

Joan ate another bite of her quesadilla, chewed for a half minute, and then said, "I remember you telling me about your mother's social activism when we were working on the set for *My Fair Lady*. Is she still picketing the Planned Parenthood across the river?"

"Every chance she gets," said Ellie. "And she's eighty-four."

Joan laughed. "Where'd you and your liberal leanings come from?"

Ellie swallowed a forkful of risotto. "That's still up for debate," she said. "My brothers love to tease me about being a Democrat."

Alice's phone, on the table next to her bread plate, buzzed, and she looked at it. Ellie and Joan watched as Alice scrolled through the message. "It's from Linda," she said, smiling. "She got an A on her history test."

"That's nice," said Joan, wondering if this was the news Alice was waiting for, if this was the reason she had her phone on their communal lunch table. Joan understood the rationale for a handy cell phone for those expecting a call from someone with an urgent matter to discuss. But she thought people who put their cell phones on restaurant or meeting room tables were sending the clear message that whoever was trying to reach them through their slim, rectangular devices was more important than those present. Alice texted a response. "Did you talk to her about the shooting?"

"We talked last night," said Alice, still texting. "She's devastated."

Joan looked at Ellie. "Did you talk to Tim?"

"Not yet," she said. "He was in rehearsal last night. I'll call him this afternoon. And Liz?"

"We spoke briefly yesterday," said Joan. "I'm planning on calling her again later, after she gets out of her classes. Perhaps by then we'll have some news about the funeral. Though I'm sure she'll hear about it another way first; I'm sure the shooting is all over social media by now."

Alice nodded her head as she put her phone back down on the table. "Linda sent me a link to the Facebook page set up by the family. The funeral has not been scheduled, but it will probably be in the next day or so. Linda is already pretty sure she's not going to come. She's got a paper due and another test early next week."

"I don't know what Liz will do," said Joan. "She liked Emmanuel—everyone did—but she didn't know James very well."

"No one knew James," said Ellie. "Remember how he'd keep to himself during the drama department events? Whenever we'd do a fundraiser—even at preproduction dinners—James was always by himself. Tim approached him a few times, but he was always silently rebuffed. James, Tim said, had no interest in small talk."

"Yes," said Alice. "I had a hard time even remembering him at first." Her phone buzzed again, and Alice immediately attended to it. "It's Linda again," she said, reading the message on her phone. "The funeral for Emmanuel is on Monday. James's funeral is private."

"Do you want to go?" Joan asked, as spontaneously as she had asked Ellie and Alice to lunch. "I can drive."

CHAPTER 6

The pews in the nave of St. Mary's church in Southwood could hold almost a thousand people, which they sometimes did on Christmas Eve or Easter morning. On a typical Sunday, the parishioners numbered closer to two hundred at the ten o'clock mass, many hurrying in just a few minutes before the service began and sitting in the middle pews. A select few chose the first couple rows as their personal worship space, and the pews at the very back were typically populated by latecomers sliding in during the homily. On Monday, at nine thirty, a half hour before the start of Emmanuel Sanchez's funeral mass, the church was full.

Joan, Alice, and Ellie stood in the narthex with forty or so others, waiting for instruction. The word was they would be ushered into the adjoining parish hall, where the mass would be simulcast onto a large screen. True enough, a minute later, they were taken through a narrow passageway and into the capacious hall. The screen was already set up at the far end of the room, as were dozens of metal folding chairs facing it. The seating etiquette in church seemed to apply in the hall as well; most of the people, after shedding their dark-colored coats and jackets to reveal dark-colored clothing underneath, sat in the middle of the room, eschewing the front seats, looking to blend in with the other mourners. The parish hall, while built and routinely used for chatty coffee hours and other social functions, did not that morning have its regular anything goes atmosphere, produced by children, freed from the decorum of a church service, running in circles, or by enthusiastic parishioners at an Advent potluck dinner. The mourners, while a good distance from the nave where the formal funeral service would take place, were reverent, those choosing to talk doing so in lowered voices.

The three women draped their fall coats on the backs of their chairs and sat, purses on the floor underneath their seats and hands on their laps. They faced forward. It didn't seem right, somehow, to turn in one's seat and scan the room, as if looking for friends at a high school football game or in a movie theater. Alice took her phone out of the pocket of her coat, checked the time, silenced the ringer, and then set it down on her lap. Ellie briefly turned her head toward the back of the room and then leaned in and whispered to Alice and Joan, "They're still coming in."

"Incredible," said Joan.

"He was well liked," whispered Alice. "Linda said he was one of the nicest kids in the school—not at all conceited about his good looks or his abilities on the football field."

Minutes later, the mass began, and everyone in the room, like those in the church, rose from his or her seat. Once they were all standing, they were still, like military cadets at attention. Every pair of eyes found its way to and focused on the screen, on the image of Emmanuel's body encased by a shiny wood coffin making its way down the center aisle. "I am the resurrection and the life; whoever believes in Me shall never die," said the priest. The tears began shortly thereafter, starting with a girl several rows behind Joan, Alice, and Ellie, and spreading throughout the parish hall like fire through a dry forest. Joan, who always had tissues in her purse, had packed extra and handed them out to Alice and Ellie and to those around her, who in the last-minute rush to get out the door to the funeral, had forgotten the most useful thing. When the coffin reached the front pews, the mourners in the parish hall could see on the screen that the seats were occupied, two rows deep on both sides of the aisle, by football players in their jerseys. Some of the players kept their composure, shoulders back and arms hemmed in at their sides, while others openly wept.

"Oh my God," said the weeping girl at a volume that eclipsed the happenings on the screen. Everyone's eyes found her after this exclamation. "I can't take this." Those around her, other girls, moved closer to her, wrapped their arms around her, cried with her, but their tears did nothing to console their friend. They could not silence her sobs. And then she shouted, "I love you, Emmanuel!" before she collapsed, her kneecaps landing on the waxed linoleum floor. Two gray-suited ushers approached the group and, whispering words of encouragement, escorted the girl through the doors at the back of the hall to the sidewalk outside. Some of her friends followed, feeling noble perhaps in their mission, oblivious, as teenagers are, to the distraction their elevated voices had caused for the others. Ellie watched them go, and then turned her attention back to the mass.

Ninety minutes later, after several emotional tributes by family members and friends and an unexpectedly moving eulogy by Michael Hanes, the laconic, burly football coach, Alice, Ellie, and Joan filed out of the hall and into the sunlight. They moved off the wide front sidewalk and onto a grassy area, making room for the hundreds of people pouring out of the church. Many of the mourners appeared to be in shock, their collective countenance looking like that of someone who had just watched a disturbing movie. Others, who looked as though they had already recalibrated their thought processes away from the funeral inside the church and back to their own lives outside the church, jogged to their cars, now thinking about work or whatever their phone calendars dictated for the rest of the day. Those standing near Alice, Ellie, and Joan either talked quietly about the service or the weather. The morning clouds had lifted during the mass, a sign (those who discussed such things agreed) that Emmanuel was at peace in heaven.

Joan turned to Ellie and Alice. "Are you ready?"

"Yes," said Ellie.

They walked around the church to the back parking lot, which was busy with people standing and talking next to their cars, as well as others in their cars pulling out of their spaces and into the building line of vehicles waiting to get out onto the main road.

Joan led Alice and Ellie back through a gate at the far end of the lot and along the sidewalk that ended at a side street. They walked the length of the street and then turned onto another street, where Joan's car was waiting for them. They had already agreed that they would not go to the cemetery, even though the burial was open to the general public, and that Joan would instead drive Ellie and Alice home afterward. No one said anything until they were in the car and on Route 1 heading to Alice's house.

"That was a beautiful mass," said Ellie from the back seat. "I know that sounds cliché and stupid, but it really was an exceptional ceremony."

Alice turned in the front passenger seat, so she could face both Joan and Ellie. "From what Linda says, he was an exceptional boy."

"It's hard to believe he moved here just three years ago," Joan said. "His parents were both born in Mexico, immigrated to Texas, educated themselves, moved to Florida to be near relatives, and then moved here to further their careers."

"That's outstanding," said Ellie.

"Where did you learn all this?" asked Alice. "Linda never told me those things."

"Liz told me," Joan said. "I think she had a bit of a crush on Emmanuel last year."

"He was a very handsome young man," said Alice, turning in her seat to again face the windshield. "What seventeen-year-old girl wouldn't want him texting her in math class?"

Following Alice's directions, Joan pulled her car onto Alice's street, drove into the driveway of her expanded Cape Cod, and put the car in park. She turned in her seat to face the others. "I'm glad we went to the funeral. Thanks for going with me."

"I'm glad, too," said Alice, still buckled into her seat. "It would have been hard to go alone."

"I agree," said Ellie.

"What do you think about having lunch again?" asked Joan.

"I'd love to," said Alice. "Now that all three of my kids are out of the house, I have absolutely nothing on the calendar."

"I don't have a lot going on either," said Ellie. "And my book-keeping job takes up only so many hours in the week. I spent September cleaning closets."

Joan smiled. "Yeah, this new phase in life will take some getting used to."

Alice checked the calendar on her phone. "Can we do it next week? I'm in the middle of a painting project—and if I don't keep going, it won't get done."

"Sure," said Ellie. "Any day but Monday."

"Wednesday," said Joan, who kept her weekly calendar in her head. "Do you want to meet at High Tide again?"

Alice unbuckled her seatbelt. "That's the best game in town," she said. "Unless you want to go to the casino."

"Let's go to High Tide," said Ellie. "I want that quesadilla that Joan had last week."

CHAPTER 7

Alice pushed open the back door just off the driveway and walked down the short hallway into her kitchen. She set her purse and phone on the walnut table where she and her husband, Dave, ate all their meals. She glanced at the telephone answering machine that sat at the end of her granite counter, looking for a blinking light indicating a message; there was none. The only reason she had a landline was for Dave's parents, who called on the first day of each month to check in. They, like their friends and neighbors in their very small town, still thought cell phones were for jet setters. Alice shed her gray trench coat and walked it to an unoccupied peg in the back hall, the small space she had just walked through to reach the kitchen. She retraced her steps, walking back into the kitchen and then into the front hallway to climb the stairs to the bedroom that she had half-finished painting the week before. She studied the mango colored walls, again questioning the color that she had chosen. Was it too bright? As she walked into the adjoining bathroom and closet, she reached for the back zipper of the black dress she occasionally wore out to dinner but lately mostly to funerals and other somber or official occasions. A self-taught handyman, Dave had created this space a few years ago, after convincing Alice to move out of their twenty-year-old house in a subdivision and into a house built in the late nineteenth century. He was capable of plumbing, electrical, and carpentry work. And he was good at it. But he often ran out of time and typically lost interest in the task at hand when it was ninety-percent completed, meaning Alice had to either finish the job herself or find and pay someone who could. She was a good painter—she had painted just about every room in the house, save this bedroom and Linda's, in the four years they had lived there—but she knew nothing about pipes and voltage. She looked down at the wide planked floor beneath her feet, which she had yet to paint. She couldn't decide between forest green and dark gray. She slid off her shoes. Now that Linda was out of the house, Alice had more time to do projects like this. And Dave was so busy with the new store opening in January that she knew she would be doing most of the work by herself.

Alice and Dave had met in Oregon, where they went to college. Both had wanted to move far away from their Connecticut childhood homes for different reasons. Alice was on the losing end of an academic, social, athletic, and emotional competition with her only sibling. Her older and perfect (in her parents' opinion, Alice thought) sister, Carolyn, then a sophomore at Harvard bound for medical school, seemed to be always right about everything. And Alice was very motivated to put some serious mileage between them. Dave, instead of running from something, was running toward it—adventure! He had lived in a tiny hamlet his whole life, the town both his parents had grown up in and hardly ever left. And Dave, an only child, had loved spending his childhood there, where everyone knew everyone else and Dave always felt safe and well looked after. But at eighteen, he was looking for new faces. Dave and Alice met the very first week because they were runners and had both joined the running club. Dave had run cross country in high school, and Alice had run track. They both enjoyed the casual attitude of the club, whose members gathered at the student union every weekday afternoon at four o'clock for a five-mile run. On some days, just a handful participated. On the weekends, a dozen or so students usually showed up for an eight-mile run. Everyone was friendly, but they all ran hard.

Alice's and Dave's feelings for each other were platonic at first.

In the spring of their freshman year, however, those feelings had turned lustful and then romantic. By the end of their first year together, the passion had evened out, replaced by the desire to push their bodies to their physical limits outside the bedroom. They started competing in triathlons together, and they dreamed of earning a living through the promotion of good health and personal fitness. After graduation, they got jobs with Nike, which spawned the idea of opening their own footwear store, and they got married at the town hall, not telling either family until after the ceremony. Five years and a move back to Connecticut later, Dave and Alice opened Fast Pace, which catered to everyone from the casual Saturday jogger to the local and regional elite runners. They worked together six days a week until Alice had their first daughter, three years later. Their mutual decision for Alice to stay home for a while had turned into a twenty-five-year stretch. And now that Alice had the time to return to Fast Pace, she was not sure she wanted to.

She felt the same way now about running as she had in college—loved it—even though she had not run regularly for years. She had run through all three pregnancies. But Linda's birth was a complicated, unexpected Cesarean that had kept Alice off the trails for almost six months. When Dave had encouraged her to *get back out there,* the words he always used, she had explained to him that whenever she ran, it felt as if her insides were going to drop out of her. When Linda went off to kindergarten, Alice started running again. But she'd lost the competitiveness, the urge to push beyond mild discomfort, and she quit again, opting instead for step and spin classes and yoga, and lately Zumba and TRX. And this worked. But Alice was tired of classes. And with Linda's departure from the house, she was out of excuses. The only way to slim down and to build muscle before it was gone forever was to start running again.

After all these years, the women Alice had previously run with were no longer interested in running with her. They didn't come out and say this. Instead, their disinterest was evident in the tone of their voices—and also by the fact that they were never available to run whenever she wanted to run. Alice understood this. After all, she had been just like them, sprinting past less dedicated athletes who were stopped, panting at the side of the road halfway through

10K races. So she resolved to *get back out there* on her own. The afternoon of Emmanuel Sanchez's funeral, she changed into her high tech, moisture wicking athletic gear, laced up the lightweight running shoes Dave had given her the previous Christmas, and drove to the exercise trails over by the river.

Several other cars were parked in the lot when Alice arrived. She walked along the path to the trails, which, intended for cyclists as well as runners, were paved. They wound through a deciduous forest, with designated loops ranging in distance from one to nine miles. Dave, who ran five or six days a week, knew the system and distances as Alice once had. But she had forgotten some of the loops, and since she had left the trail map in the kitchen drawer, she decided to run a few laps around the shortest loop. She was also leery of going into the woods alone. While Joan was right that Southwood was a very safe town, one could never be too careful. Wasn't this the message, after all, that Alice continually preached to her three daughters?

A mile into what was supposed to be a three-mile run, Alice was already winded, and her knees hurt. No matter what anyone said, running was different from other forms of recreation. She could get through a forty-five-minute dance or spin class, but ten minutes of running had tired her out. She slowed her pace to a walk, realizing that all the running she had done in the past would not come back to her in one day. She would have to be patient and come up with a plan for getting back in shape that made sense. Alice jogged back to the car. She would ask Dave for a running regimen. He would be thrilled to know she was running again and to set something up for her. Maybe she could even talk him into going with her.

CHAPTER 8

Because she liked to be punctual and had been late to lunch the last time, Ellie arrived at High Tide seven minutes before noon. She was seated at a table near the windows and left with three menus and the promise of ice water. She shed her coat, took a small pad of paper and a pen from her purse, and then sat down to document what she had been running through her head that morning. It was a plan for this new stage in her life, a plan for the future. And while she had no answers to most of the questions she had asked herself as she vacuumed the family room carpeting, she did have a few ideas. Number one, she needed more clients. She had just written *new pet store* when Joan approached the table. "Hey," said Ellie, looking up from her task, pushing her thoughts aside. "Don't you look nice."

Joan smiled at Ellie as she sat down, not removing the gray suede jacket that covered a pressed, white cotton shirt. The jeans Joan had chosen for her outfit were definitely not from the Gap, where Ellie bought hers. "I get that a lot," said Joan, reaching for the water glasses that had just been filled.

"What, that you look nice?" asked Ellie.

"Exactly," said Joan.

"Is that a problem?"

Joan laughed. "No," she said. "It's just not an accomplishment, a life goal, something to be proud of. Anyone with enough money and too much time on her hands can look good."

It was Ellie's turn to laugh. "Sounds like you've been thinking about your life, just like I've been thinking about my life."

"Who's thinking about life?" Alice walked stiff legged to the table and sat, with effort, slowly.

"Are you okay?" asked Joan.

"I think so," said Alice, closing her eyes. "But I'm not sure." She opened her eyes and looked at Joan and then Ellie. "I started running again."

Ellie tapped the fingers of her right hand against the palm of her left hand several times and grinned. "We're all doing it. I'm so glad I'm not in this alone."

"Doing what?" asked Alice.

"Figuring out what the hell comes next," said Joan.

"What have you figured out?" asked Alice.

"Nothing," said Joan. "Although whatever it is, I think I have the right clothes for it."

"You always look so nice," said Alice.

"See?" said Joan, looking at Ellie.

Alice looked at Joan and then at Ellie. "What am I missing?"

"Let's order," said Joan, "and then we can start the process."

True to her hankerings, Ellie ordered the quesadilla; Joan got the falafel sliders, and Alice requested butternut squash soup and a side salad. Once the server left the table, Alice said, "Okay, so what's wrong with looking good all the time? I wish I had that problem."

"It's not a problem," said Joan, shaking her head. "It's what I have been focused on, other than mothering my children, for the last thirty years, and I'm pretty good at it. But, as I was saying to Ellie, it has not been a lifelong dream of mine to dress well."

"All right," said Alice. "I'll bite. Why do you dress well?"

"My husband wants me to dress this way." Alice and Ellie said nothing. "Because he's a banker. It's an image thing. He dresses well. His family of bankers dresses well. All the spouses dress well. So I dress well. It started when we were first married. Now, it's automatic."

"So what's your lifelong dream then?"

Joan looked at her watch. "We've been here, what, ten minutes, and you're already asking me one of the huge questions of my life?"

Ellie laughed and then leaned into the table. "Am I being too forward?"

"No," said Joan. She straightened her back. "But I'm going to talk about myself in a serious tone for another ten seconds, and then we are going to move on."

"You're going to tell us your lifelong dream?" asked Alice.

Joan took a bite from one of the sliders that had just been set down in front of her. She chewed and then wiped her mouth. "No. But only because I'm not sure I know what it is. You see, in addition to being told to dress well, I was also told not to pursue a career."

Ellie bit into her quesadilla, grateful for the melted cheese and barbequed chicken, grateful that she wasn't eating a salad like Alice's. "Really?" said Ellie. "Who would say something like that?"

"My mother-in-law, Sandi. She told me when Stephen and I got engaged that all the Howard women continued their schooling or volunteered until they had children, and then they stayed home with the children while their husbands worked. At the time, it sounded like a good plan to me. I had just graduated from college on a merit scholarship, and Stephen was happy to pay for me to get a master's degree, so that's what I did. After that, I thought about teaching—Stephen and I were having trouble getting pregnant, and having no children would have exempted me from the Howards' no-job-for-spouses rule. And then Cassie was born, and I have been home ever since."

"How many years?" asked Alice.

"Twenty-four and counting," said Joan. "I've been home and jobless for twenty-four years." Joan finished her water and asked the server for a Diet Coke. "Not that raising a family shouldn't be considered a job; I'd be doing a disservice to, and in hot water with, all stay-at-home mothers with that kind of talk. But full-time mothering is a *different* kind of job; it's a job away from the constraints and timetables of the working world. At home, you get to be your own boss."

"When your kids aren't bossing you around," said Alice.

Ellie picked up another quesadilla triangle from her plate. "Maybe you can explore getting a job now, since both your girls are gone."

"Maybe," said Joan.

Alice looked out the window. "This is the time," she said. "This is the time to do something with our lives."

"Is that what this running is all about?" asked Joan.

"Partly, yes. It's about recapturing who I once was."

"Please don't tell me you are trying to turn back the clock."

"No, Joan," said Alice. "No one can do that. But how can we move forward if we're unable to move?"

"Kind of like you are today," said Joan, smiling.

Alice laughed. "Look," she said, pointing a finger at Joan. "Six months from now I'll be a new woman."

"I can hardly wait," said Joan, looking at Alice over her glass of soda, "to see who you become."

"I'm doing it, too," said Ellie, pushing the too-large bite of food in her mouth into her cheek so she could talk. "I'm changing my life, too. I don't know what it will look like either, but this *is* the time to do it. This is the time to figure out who we are and who we want to be and how we're going to get there."

"Well, at least that sounds good," said Joan.

CHAPTER 9

In the fifteen years since the casino had been erected ten miles north of Southwood, Joan had been there twice: once for a birthday lunch with her sisters-in-law and the other time for a fundraiser for the Southwood Cancer Society, which Joan thought was ironic since the casino allowed smoking throughout its palatial buildings. The nonprofit apparently didn't sense or care about the irony, however, since the casino had been, again, chosen as the destination for its annual fundraiser. Last year, it had been an elegant dinner and a silent auction held in a ballroom, separated by floor-to-ceiling doors padded in leather from the hoi polloi parked at the slot machines, guzzling free house-alcohol drinks. This year, it was someone's idea to raise the price of the tickets, enabling the organization to rent the exclusive use of several roulette tables. Invitees were encouraged to wear tuxedos and long gowns, in an effort, Joan guessed, to class up the event and its surroundings. Joan had been surprised the previous year when she and Stephen walked through the casino to reach the fundraiser. Everyone she saw was dressed in very casual, sloppy even, clothing. No one looked like extras in a James Bond movie like Joan expected.

Stephen parked his Mercedes in the Red Maple lot, a short walk from the Rumbling Falls section of the casino. He hesitated a moment before opening his car door. "Are you ready?"

"As ready as I will ever be."

"You're a good person, Joan, to be on this board, to do this work. I know this casino event is not your idea of the perfect evening out, but it will raise a lot of money for the cancer society."

"Let's hope so," said Joan, looking at her reflection in the visor mirror to recheck the eyebrow wax job she'd had done that afternoon.

"Plus, all my banking buddies will be here," he said with a smile. "I'll bet you can hardly wait to see Jimbo."

"Believe me, I see enough of him at board meetings."

"Hey," said Stephen, opening the door. "You look nice tonight." Joan looked at him and smiled. "I know."

They walked briskly through the parking lot and into the elevator bank. Four floors up the doors opened into a well lit, high end retail area. Stephen took Joan's hand as they passed by Coach, Godiva, and Tiffany before moving onto earth-toned patterned carpeting and into much dimmer lighting. Joan stopped for a moment and scanned the room. "Ah," she said, pointing to the far end, "we're over there."

Stephen's eyes followed Joan's finger. "Yes," he said. "I see Harry and Jimbo."

As they made their way across the room, Joan again considered the name Jimbo, attached to a man who never failed to leave her with the same impression: He was an imbecile. In many ways, the nickname fit him. Jimbo was well over six feet, a head or so taller than Stephen, and he must have weighed two hundred fifty pounds. A former football player at a college for mediocre athletes and subpar students, Jimbo was now an investment banker, lending credit to the theory that moving money around didn't take a lot of brain power. It wasn't his intelligence, or lack of such, that poked at Joan's thoughts that moment; rather, it was his reluctance to jettison his college handle. Jimbo seemed like a good name for a beer-drinking linebacker, but wouldn't Jim or James be more suitable for a businessman in his late forties? A woman would never get away with that kind of playfulness by calling herself Bambi for

Barbara or Gigi for Gretchen in the professional world if she expected to be taken seriously. The old boy network was as relevant and robust in the twenty-first century as it had been in the eighteenth.

"Jimbo!" said Stephen, extending his hand toward his work colleague. "How's it going, big guy?"

Jimbo took Stephen's hand and pulled him in for a bear hug. He slapped him several times on the back before releasing him and shouting, "Outstanding, my man! Isn't this setup awesome? Joanie, how are you tonight, honey?" Jimbo leaned in to deliver a scotch scented kiss to Joan's cheek. "Are you ready for some fun?"

"I'm just great, Jim," said Joan. "It's good to see you. Is your wife with you?"

"She sure is," said Jimbo, wrapping his massive arm around Joan's shoulder and turning her body, while using his other arm to point a dozen yards away to a table covered by white linen and name tags. "She's over at the welcome table with the other girls, checking in. Why don't you head over there and say hello. I know she'd love to see you—and you can grab your badges so everyone will know your names!"

Joan flashed a smile at Jimbo and then turned to her husband and raised her eyebrows. "I'll just run along then," she said. "I'm hoping one of the girls has a laundry tip for getting lipstick off my dinner napkins." This attempt at humor was not lost on Stephen, who smiled and winked at his wife, but it didn't register with Jimbo, who laughed anyway.

"Oh, I'm sure you'll find what you're looking for. When you girls get together, all sorts of household problems get solved. It's beyond me!"

Most things are, thought Joan, amusing herself, as she made her way to the table. She had opted out of setting up this year, mostly because Jimbo had volunteered to "get 'r done." But Joan had to admit that he and his committee had done a good job, with crisp white linen, sparkling stemware, and gold goodie bags for invited guests. Joan approached the welcome table, surrounded by committee members and several bank executive wives, including Jimbo's spouse, Connie. Despite being married to a *Homo erectus,* Connie was more interesting than she first appeared, with her frosted blond hair and ample cleavage. She was getting a master's degree in political science, a relatively new passion for Connie, who had helped run the governor's successful reelection campaign. She spun around when Joan called her name.

"Joan!" said Connie. "How good to see you! You're looking fabulous, as always. I love your dress."

"That's what I do best, dear," said Joan, accepting a kiss on the same cheek Jimbo had chosen. "You're looking pretty good yourself."

"It's a nice change from jeans and sweaters," said Connie. "I love being a student, but we are not fashion plates."

Joan laughed. "How refreshing," she said. "How are your studies going?"

"I am having a blast," said Connie. "I'm the oldest one in the class by a couple decades, but no one seems to care. They all treat me like they treat one another."

"As they should," said Joan. "You may not be as young, but you are definitely as smart, if not smarter, than they are."

"Ha-ha!" said Connie. "I'm not so sure about that. Some of them appear to be pretty darned smart."

"But they're babies," said Joan, with a smile. "Their knowledge does not run deep like ours."

Connie laughed. "Oh yeah," she said. "People are always telling me how deep I am." She turned to the table to look for Joan's and Stephen's name tags. "I just saw your names," she said, scanning the tabletop. "Ah, here they are." She scooped them up and handed them to Joan, who hung hers around her neck by its gold cord.

"Where does a woman looking to have a good time at a charity event get a drink around here?"

Connie smiled. "Follow me," she said. "I could use a little something myself."

Drinks in hand, Joan and Connie circled back to their husbands. Jimbo was telling a story about the huge commission he'd made from a top quarter percent investor who traded stocks "like my kids trade Pokémon cards!" He turned to his wife. "Con, I think the commission check for last December's sale paid for half our house in Vail!" Jimbo guffawed at his own remark, while Stephen and Connie chuckled politely. Joan wore the pasted smile she employed at large social gatherings.

"So, what's the drill tonight?" asked Stephen.

"Okay," said Jimbo, rubbing his hands together. "Everyone plays roulette at one of the six tables in this section. Whatever you win goes to the cancer society."

"What if we lose?" asked Connie.

Jimbo gave his wife a sour look. "We don't lose, darlin'. This is for charity."

"But if we do?" she pressed.

"Well, then it's your money you're losing. You could consider it the price you pay for a wonderful evening out!" Jimbo seemed pleased with his explanation.

"Fair enough," Stephen said. "I'm going to grab a drink, Joan, and then we can get started."

"See you two around campus!" shouted Jimbo. "Good luck!"

As soon as they were far enough away from Jimbo that Joan was certain he could not hear her, she said, "How do you work with that man?"

Stephen laughed. "He is a knucklehead, as we've discussed. But he is also a pretty nice guy, too. Backward as hell, but a pretty nice guy."

"Don't tell me he'd give you the shirt off his back."

"Hell no," said Stephen. "He'd definitely *take* the shirt off your back if you didn't have the buttons done up. But if you were in a jam, a real jam, he'd help you out. Of course, he'd expect something in return. But he would definitely help you out." Stephen stopped and stood in front of the bar. He looked at Joan. "Do you want anything?"

She looked at her half glass of Pinot Noir; the warmth of the first few ounces had relaxed her shoulders and loosened her neck. "In a minute?"

Stephen nodded his head and then ordered a beer, even though his drink of choice, year-round, was a gin and tonic. He was very particular about how his drink was made, however—not only the brand of gin, which had to be top shelf, but also the booze to mixer ratio. He was one of the rare people who thought that a strong drink was a bad drink. He made himself, and Joan in the summertime, what he considered the perfect gin and tonic when they stayed home: lots of ice, a generous wedge of fresh lime, and a tonic to booze ratio of five to two. Because his drinks were so good and everyone else's were often bad, he rarely ordered one when they were out. Beer in hand, Stephen led Joan to the nearest roulette table. The expressionless croupier asked them how many chips they wanted. Stephen looked at Joan, who shrugged. "Two hundred dollars' worth," he said. When he handed the dealer four fifties, four short stacks of brown and white chips were pushed along the felted surface of the table until they were in front of Stephen. Neophytes, Stephen and Joan watched the other players place their chips on the numbers at the center. Stephen picked up ten of his forty chips and handed half of them to Joan. Just as they were getting started, Stephen's boss, Darren Cummings, approached the table.

"Stephen," he said. "Good to see you. Hello, Joan."

Stephen turned and shook Darren's hand. "And you as well, Darren. How's everything with you tonight?"

"Great, just great. There's someone I'd like you to meet. You don't mind, do you, Joan, if I take Stephen away for just a few minutes?"

Joan smiled at her husband's boss. "Not at all, Darren. Take him for as long as you need." Darren was ten years older than Stephen and Joan, but looked their age. He was fit, dressed in expensive suits, and had managed to keep all the hair on his head when most of his contemporaries were balding. The best thing about Darren was that he was good to Stephen. He confided in Stephen and trusted him, often choosing him, Stephen had told Joan, for the most sought after assignments.

"Courtney," Darren said, referring to his second, twenty-year-younger wife, "is chatting with some of the other wives. When I talk to her next, I'll tell her you're here. She enjoys your company, Joan."

"And I enjoy hers," said Joan. "These chips should keep me occupied for a while, so send her over." Joan watched Darren and Stephen weave through the crowded room until they reached a heavy man smoking a cigar. She then asked a circling server for a refill before returning her attention to the table and laying the five chips in her hand on five random numbers. The croupier flicked the small white ball onto the spinning wheel, and everyone watched as it circled the perimeter of the wheel several times before tripping through the numbered section and settling into the black ten. Joan looked at the board, confirming that she had, indeed, placed a chip on the black ten, and smiled. She let out a small "My!" and tried to remember the last time she'd won anything. Was it the math competition in high school?

"Ten black," said the croupier, who then pushed a small pile of chips in her direction.

Joan gathered them and then stacked them next to the others. She drained half her wine and then again placed five chips on five numbers. This time, she chose her and Stephen's birth months, as well as those of her daughters. The fifth chip she placed on number one, which was red.

"One red," said the croupier when the ball had stopped. He scooped up all the chips from the table and then doled out Joan's winnings. The next several rounds Joan used ten chips instead of five. She placed them on the numbers signifying additional birth months, as well as days marking anniversaries, holidays, and other happenings. She used some of her favorite statistics formulas to calculate her odds. By the time Stephen returned, she had four hundred dollars in chips sitting in front of her and a wide grin on her face. He handed her the glass of wine he had purchased for her at the bar on his way. Joan took it, deciding not to mention to him that she had served herself. At this point, her second glass was half gone, just as her first glass had been when Stephen had left with Darren.

"Well, well, well," he said. "Someone's on a winning streak."

"Stephen, this is so much fun," said Joan. "I'm using all kinds of numbers, and I've hit three times, even though there's only slightly more than a two-and-a-half percent chance of that happening."

"Lucky Southwood Cancer Society."

"How are you doing?" she asked, placing more chips on numbers.

"Okay," said Stephen. "We may have a new client."

"Stogie man?" asked Joan, looking now at the spinning wheel.

"Yes."

"And?" asked Joan, turning to Stephen when the ball stopped on someone else's number.

"He's a Colt. And he wants us to invest in his firearms manufacturing business in Hartford. They are in debt, and the regulations imposed by the state of Connecticut after Sandy Hook aren't helping."

"So you want to, what, help them bring back assault rifles?"

"No, Joan. We want to help them restructure their finances."

Joan took a sip of wine. "Meaning you don't care who your clients are. Emmanuel Sanchez was killed with a Colt gun."

"You know as well as I know how this works, Joan. Plus, manufacturing guns is not a crime."

Joan gave her husband a slight smile. "I know that."

"I'm not in a business that saves the world," said Stephen. "I'm an investment banker."

"A very talented, compassionate even, investment banker."

"But you," said Stephen. "Look at those chips. Tonight, you might very well be saving some cancer patients."

"Flattery always placates me," said Joan, giving her husband a studied look.

Stephen took his wife's chin in his hand and touched the tip of his nose to hers. "I know you better than that," he said.

NOVEMBER

CHAPTER 10

The women fell into a daily electronic relationship, group texting one another bits of information here and there, sharing random thoughts. So when they met the next time for lunch and Joan suggested they meet less frequently, Alice was confused. When she questioned Joan about it, Joan shrugged. "I don't know," she said. "I just don't want to turn into one of those women who do lunch all the time."

"What does that even mean?" asked Alice, sipping her water. They were again seated at a table near the windows at High Tide. Cheryl, the cheerful twenty-one-year-old who was working her way through college and who had served them their previous two lunches, had already poured their water, told them the daily specials, and taken their orders.

"You know what that means," said Joan. "It means that you have nothing to do, no ambitions, other than pampering yourself—treating yourself, as it were. If there is any word in the English language that is more overused by middle aged, nonworking women than the word *treat,* I don't know what it is."

Ellie laughed. "That is hilarious!"

"But true, right?" asked Joan. "The women I mingle with, the executives' wives, are always talking about treating themselves, whether it's a coffee or lunch date, a shopping trip, a pedicure, as if their entire existence isn't already one big treat." Ellie laughed again.

Alice, who didn't laugh, narrowed her eyes at Joan. "Wait, so you *are* one of them, but you don't *want* to be one of them?"

"Bingo!" said Joan.

"That makes no sense," said Alice. "Why don't you just be comfortable with who you are?"

Joan cocked her head. "I might ask you the same question."

"I have no problem eating lunch out," said Alice.

"Well, what's all this running about? I thought you weren't trying to recapture your youth. Why can't you be comfortable with who you are now?"

"I'm not necessarily that comfortable either," said Ellie, a remark that garnered no attention because Ellie, still amused by Joan's take on the word *treat,* was smiling ever so slightly. Her brothers' wives loved that word.

Alice ran her fingers through her hair. "As I've explained to you before, I'm *not* trying to recapture my youth. I'm trying to better myself," she said. "I'm trying to give my body the attention it needs, so it will serve me in my advancing years."

"That's exactly what I'm trying to do," said Joan. "Your emphasis is on the physical; my emphasis is on the emotional, the intellectual."

Alice narrowed her eyes again. "I'm not sure I agree we're talking about the same thing."

"You don't have to agree," said Joan.

"Agree with what?" asked Alice.

"Okay, you two," said Ellie. "What's our new plan?"

"I'm not suggesting that we go cold turkey—or have lunch just once a month," said Joan. "That's what charitable organizations and book groups do. I propose we have lunch twice a month, say on the first and third Wednesdays. It's already on our calendars; all we have to do is remove the second and fourth Wednesdays. Twice a month seems a little less indulgent than four times a month."

"I concur," said Ellie, who was thinking that—at fifteen bucks a pop—eating out each week was expensive. It would feel like more of a reward, or treat, as Joan put it, if they skipped every other week.

"Okay," said Alice, "fine." But it clearly was not.

Joan reached across the table and laid her hand on top of Alice's. "What's up, Alice? Are you upset about not meeting as often for lunch, or is there something else going on?"

Alice's lower eyelids pooled with tears that did not fall. "My knees hurt."

"Of course they do," said Joan. "You're pushing yourself too hard."

Alice slid her hand out from underneath Joan's. "Of course I'm pushing myself," she said in a voice that made no attempt to hide its bitterness. "When people get back into shape, they have to push themselves."

"You're right," said Ellie. "But maybe you don't have to push yourself as hard as you do?"

"I know I've kidded you, Alice. But I admire what you're doing," said Joan, leaning back. "I've never been physically fit, so I can only imagine the pain. But I know there is a big difference between being in our thirties and being in our fifties. I have no doubt that women in their fifties can run—and run fast—but I'm guessing it takes a bit longer to get there than it did when we were younger."

This was the kind of talk Alice had heard before. In fact, it was the kind of talk that Alice had proffered to others, when she had been in her thirties and the women she had been talking to were in their fifties. Alice tightened her jaw. She would not be pitied or advised on something she knew so much about. She would run through the pain. Cheryl slid their plates onto the table: a spinach salad for Alice, fish tacos for Joan, and the vegetarian quesadilla for Ellie. For a minute, they all ate in silence. And then Joan lifted her gaze from her plate to Alice's face.

"Go at your own pace, Alice," she said. "I know you know how to do this."

The tightness in Alice's shoulders eased. "Thank you," she said.

Ellie swallowed the piece of quesadilla in her mouth, and then said, "I have an idea."

"What's that?" asked Alice, the warmth returning to her face and voice.

"Along with our new lunch schedule, let's eat somewhere new each time."

"Where?" asked Joan. "Unless we get in a car and drive thirty minutes, we're stuck with the restaurants in town."

"We can go to the casino," said Ellie. "There are a million restaurants up there, and you told us what fun you had there at that fundraiser."

Joan, who had already been wondering how she could get back to the casino, smiled at Ellie. "That's not a bad idea."

Alice wrinkled her nose. "Isn't it smoky? I can't stand being in that kind of environment. I haven't been in a smoky restaurant in twenty years." She picked up her phone to read a text announced by a single bell-like sound.

"They do a pretty good job of filtering the air," said Joan. "Yes, my clothes smelled like smoke after being there for three hours. But if we spend just an hour or so there, we should be okay."

"Let's check it out," said Ellie. "If it stinks, we can go to plan B."

CHAPTER 11

Ellie finished her five-mile loop, breathing hard when she walked back into her kitchen. She downed a half cup of orange juice and a banana, and then called for Buffy. They got into the car and then drove through Dunkin' Donuts for a medium coffee with cream and sugar on their way to the dog park. Parked in the dirt lot, Ellie opened the back passenger door of her Honda and stood aside as Buffy jumped out and ran, panting with enthusiasm, to the park's latched gate. Buffy looked back at Ellie.

"Hold on, girl," said Ellie. "I've got to grab your leash, and then we'll be good to go."

Buffy sat at the gate and waited. "You are such a good girl. If only your brothers would mind me the way you do." She smiled at her own remark and the fact that she sometimes referred to her sons Tim and Brandon and her dog as siblings. As soon as Ellie opened the gate, Buffy took off to join the other dogs in the middle of the meadow. The dogs were supposed to be on leash, but it was an understood rule that dogs could be off leash if they behaved themselves and played well with the other dogs and owners. Ellie watched Buffy greet her canine friends, and then she turned her attention to closing the gate behind her. When she did, she saw Kelly Shulz's tired-looking black SUV pull into the lot. Ellie hesitated long enough to know Kelly had seen her, so she waited at the gate. A quick glance over her shoulder at Buffy told her Buffy was following the rules. Ellie looked back at the car. "Hi, Kelly," she said, when Kelly opened the driver's side door. Kelly seemed to make a point of looking at her, but said nothing. She opened the back hatch door, and out jumped Abbott and Costello, her seventy-pound yellow labs. They ran to the gate and immediately started wagging their tails at Ellie.

"They are such good dogs," said Ellie, as a means of initiating conversation.

"Some of the time," said Kelly, who had walked to the gate.

"Well, they're certainly on their best behavior here."

"They like it here," said Kelly, pushing through the gate into the open space. Ellie followed and then fell into step beside her. Kelly continued to look straight ahead.

"I'm sorry," said Ellie, "about James."

"Yes," said Kelly. "Everybody's sorry."

Ellie looked at the ground, as if she might find what to say next hidden in the trampled blades of grass. "He was a talented boy."

Kelly, who had moved a few steps ahead of Ellie, didn't turn around to face Ellie when she said, "Yes. He simply picked the wrong girl to fall in love with."

Ellie stopped walking. She had no adequate response to Kelly's comment because it was taking its time sinking into her mind. Is that what it was? Did he simply pick the wrong girl? If he had picked someone who loved him back, would he be alive and with her right now? And would Emmanuel be alive, walking the halls of William Chester High School, his arm casually draped around Nanette's tiny shoulders as they moved together from class to class? Teenage love, with its ardent feelings of complete and eternal devotion, had flirted with James Shulz and then cast him aside. Was there anything, at seventeen, more devastating than unrequited passion? Romantic rejection made people of all ages crazy. It made people with access to guns dangerous and deadly. Ellie watched Kelly walk toward the circle of dogs. She called for Abbott and Costello and led them away from the group. A minute later she and her dogs had disappeared into the woods.

Ellie slowly walked toward the group that Kelly had just left. She said a quick hello to the women with familiar faces and then called to Buffy. "We're heading off for a quick loop," she said, by way of explanation, as a reason for not staying longer. "Too much to do today."

One woman in the group, someone Ellie had seen only once or twice before, spoke. "I saw you talking with James Shulz's mom," she said. "God, she must feel awful."

"We all do," said Ellie, turning away and walking toward the same path Kelly had chosen. If Ellie had gone in the other direction, the odds of meeting up with Kelly and her dogs would have increased. Ellie took her phone from her pocket and texted Joan and Alice:

Just ran into Kelly Shulz at dog park. Made a fool of myself.

Alice, who had her phone with her all day and on her bedside table at night, replied: *I doubt it. I'm sure u were nice. These things take time.*

Ellie heard from Joan almost an hour later, when Buffy was at home sleeping on her bed and Ellie, freshly showered and dressed for calling on clients, was walking out the door.

Kelly is not easy to talk to, even in the best of times. Remember how quiet she was when we were all working together? Don't be too hard on yourself. Lunch next Wednesday, right?

Right, Ellie texted. *Thanks—I'm already looking forward to it.* Ellie put her phone in her cup holder and backed out of the garage. She pulled out onto the street, drove through Dunkin' Donuts for a second cup of coffee, and to the other side of town to Diana's Pet Supply. Even if Diana didn't need a bookkeeper, Ellie needed more dog food for Buffy.

Diana's Pet Supply was a freestanding wood building. It had been a fruit and vegetable market and then a craft store before Diana had opened the business at the end of summer. And while Ellie and her husband, Chris, had read about the pet store in the newspaper and agreed that they should patronize the local store rather than travel ten miles down the highway to the nearest PetSmart, they hadn't yet been there. Ellie had been thinking about approaching

Diana as a potential client ever since the first week she opened, but Ellie had, as she did with many things, put it off.

A pleasant-sounding electronic bell chimed when Ellie pushed through the glass door and walked into the shop. It smelled like a pet owner's home, like earth, grass, and slightly damp warmth. A woman who looked to be in her mid-to-late forties—although Ellie, who had just turned forty-eight, thought it was getting harder and harder to tell the vintage of others as she herself aged—smiled at her from behind a long counter. She was shorter than Ellie—maybe Joan's height—and had long brown hair that was pulled back into a pony-tail and light blue eyes that looked directly into Ellie's, making an instant, intense connection. "Hey," she said. "How can I help you this morning?"

Ellie approached the counter and thrust her hand into the space between them. "I'm Ellie Fagen," she said.

"And I'm Diana McGuire," said Diana, taking Ellie's hand in hers. "Nice to meet you."

"It's nice to meet you, as well," said Ellie. "I've been meaning to get in here since you opened in August."

"So, today is the day," said Diana, her lips pulling into a slight smile.

Ellie smiled in return, feeling a warm flush in her face, a flutter in her stomach. "It is, indeed," she said. "I'm actually here for two reasons. One is to buy dog food, and the other is to see if you need any help keeping your books."

"I can definitely help you with the dog food," said Diana, walk-ing out from behind the counter. "What kind of dog do you have, and what does he/she eat currently?"

"Buffy is a golden retriever," said Ellie, following Diana down a short aisle. "And she eats whatever my husband picks up on sale at PetSmart."

"Ah," said Diana. "We can certainly make some improvements to that game plan."

Together, they looked at the variety of dog food stacked on the pet store shelves. Diana talked about manufacturer reliability and guarantees, the balance between protein and fat, the essential vita-mins and minerals, and the difference in price. And then she asked

Ellie what kind of services she provided as a bookkeeper and how much she charged by the hour. Their conversation, which was interrupted three times by other customers, lasted almost thirty minutes. At the end of it, Ellie had bought a twenty-pound bag of premium, all-natural dog food, and Diana had expressed an interest in Ellie's managing the financial records and accounts for the store. Ellie whistled as she carried her purchase to the car. The sun was shining. The November air was warmer than it should have been. And at that very moment, Ellie felt content, alive, and confident. Had she been alone, she would have spun around in place. She hadn't felt this sure about herself in a long time.

It was not that Ellie was insecure; she simply did not possess the Kilcullen family confidence. She was not extroverted like her brothers, lawyers, all of them, and father, a retired lawyer turned state senator. When they all walked into church on Sunday mornings—they all lived either in or within a half hour of Southwood and attended the same Roman Catholic church they had been raised in—every head in every pew turned to watch the procession. It was a sight on many accounts: First, on any given Sunday, the Kilcullen clan numbered at least twenty; second, Ellie's older brothers were some of the most handsome men she knew. At church, they all dressed in blue blazers and subdued neckties; their wives, every bit as attractive as their spouses, dressed in skirts and heels, mostly, Ellie guessed, because that's what Ellie's mother wore. And the children were outfitted like their parents, especially noticeable in an age when jeans were acceptable everywhere. While Ellie was not usually impressed by the peacocks in the world, she loved the pageantry associated with the arrival of the Kilcullens at church, and she loved her family. As the youngest and the only female, Ellie was coddled by her older brothers, always had been, as well as her father, who, still, occasionally, bade her to sit on his lap for a minute at family gatherings. Ellie's mother, Brigid, would admit to only her husband that she loved her daughter just a little bit more than her boys—she had, after all, wanted a girl badly enough to have seven children. But she did not, like the others, spoil Ellie. Brigid was wise, politically active, and deeply religious, and she expected her daughter to be the same.

This was not an easy task for Ellie, who, in spite of her Roman Catholic upbringing, did not subscribe to the church's social agenda. Pope Francis was certainly shaking things up a bit, but the church had a long history of abuse and intolerance. Ellie had gone through a rebellious stage in college, when she refused to go to church. Drinking beer became her new religion, which was how she met her boyfriend turned husband. A rugby player on an unbeaten college team, Chris was always too busy celebrating on Saturday nights and hungover on Sunday mornings to attend church, even though he, too, had been raised in a Roman Catholic family. They went to church now—Ellie, Chris, and their two sons when they were home—but not with the same zeal as the rest of Ellie's family. Ellie did it for her mother, more than anyone or anything else, because she admired Brigid's unwavering tenacity, even if Ellie didn't always agree with her beliefs.

All the Kilcullen children were expected to be at their parents' large house on the river for dinner on the second Sunday of each month. Brigid had wanted them to come every Sunday, but her husband, Patrick, who had been sought out by his sons to intervene, had declared that one Sunday—in addition to all major holidays—was enough. Dinner was a midday event, with Bloody Marys at noon and the meal at one. The dress code, again at Patrick's insistence, was casual. Everyone wore jeans and sweaters in the winter, when Brigid made a large roast of some sort, mashed potatoes with gravy, green beans, and pies for dessert, and shorts and T-shirts in the summer, when dinner around two large dining tables turned into a picnic on the Kilcullens' expansive back lawn. True to her convictions and childhood traditions, Brigid, no matter what the weather, on Sundays wore a dress, conservative black heels, and her mother's string of pearls, an outfit she remained in until after the festivities were over and the dishes were cleaned and back in their storage cupboards.

When Ellie got home from Diana's Pet Supply, still feeling effervescent, she called Joan and then Alice and told them about securing a new account. As she expected, they told her how proud they were of her and how they could hardly wait to hear all about it at lunch. Ellie then made herself a cheese omelet, a brunch of sorts since she had not had much breakfast, which she ate while she read the newspaper. After eating, she took a large glass of ice water to her desk in the family room and worked for a few hours on setting up Diana's account. By three o'clock, she needed a break and a cup of tea. While she waited for the water in the kettle to boil, she called her husband, who did paperwork in his gym office at William Chester when his student interaction time was over. He picked up on the first ring.

"Hi, honey," he said. "What's happening?"

"Not too much," said Ellie. "Except I got a new account today."

"No kidding," said Chris. "The pet store?"

"Good memory. Yes."

"Well, good for you," he said. "It's been an absolute madhouse around here today."

"Yeah?" Ellie took a teabag from the drawer next to the stove and filled her favorite pottery mug with hot water. She dunked the teabag several times before setting it down in the kitchen sink.

". . . One month anniversary of the shooting."

"What?" Ellie said, reconnecting with the conversation that the school's poor cell service had partially erased.

"It's the month anniversary of the Sanchez shooting," said Chris.

"Oh God, I'd forgotten," said Ellie. "How could I have forgotten?"

"Well, two girls in one of my classes didn't forget. They came in crying, which might or might not have been a ploy to avoid participation in class. A few of the boys were upset, too. Unfortunately, the way some boys avoid exhibiting sadness is by acting like jerks. One of them hit the aggressive switch and whaled on everyone in dodgeball today. I finally had to tell him to take five in my office."

Chris had taught gym, or, as he called it, physical education, at the high school for nearly fifteen years. Some people, like Ellie's brothers, thought his job was a joke. But Chris took it very seriously, which made the Kilcullen family show him a modicum of respect. In truth, the Kilcullen boys might have been tough on Chris no matter what his chosen occupation, since Ellie's siblings thought no one was good enough for their sister. They had softened over

the years, with their impressions of a gorilla in Chris's presence oc-
curring now only once or twice a year. Chris didn't let it bother
him. In some ways, they were dead on. Chris was a big guy with
long, strong arms. He drank his fair share of beer, and he watched
a staggering amount of sports on television, from Irish rugby
matches to the men's downhill races in the winter Olympics. When
Chris was home, ESPN dominated the large-screen television in
their family room, which was connected to their kitchen. Ellie had
grown accustomed to the noise over the years. She was able to tune
out a lot of things.

"Dinner tonight?"

Ellie turned her attention to her grocery list on the kitchen
counter. "I've got to run out to the store. Um . . . how about fish?"

Ellie could hear the disgruntled look on her husband's face in
his voice when he said, "Didn't we just have fish?"

"We had crab cakes last week. I'm not sure that counts, Chris."

"Fine," he said. "But can you do something like put cheese on it?"

Ellie laughed. They both loved cheese, all kinds. "I might be
able to manage that," she said. Alice had e-mailed her a recipe for
fish, with mayonnaise, sliced onions, sliced tomatoes, and cheese. It
was the one fish dish, Alice had told Ellie and Joan, that her entire
family enjoyed. Ellie wrote the ingredients along with several other
items on her list. She grabbed her cloth grocery bags from the
kitchen closet and her keys from the set of hooks hanging over the
dog's food and water dishes, all the while replaying in her mind her
encounter with Diana earlier that day.

Chapter 12

Joan, who had researched restaurants at the casino and texted Alice and Ellie to meet her at Asian Fusion for sushi or a *ton of other choices,* was the first to arrive. She was shown to a black enamel table close to the host station and to three other tables, one of which was already occupied. Joan had to squeeze between two of the tables to reach the black padded bench against the grass cloth-covered wall. She shook her coat off her shoulders and laid it on the bench next to her and then picked up the menu she had studied online, not as a means to decide what she wanted to eat— she had already done that—but to block out the woman talking on her cell phone no more than five feet away. Joan focused on the print. The sushi was touted as the freshest in the state, and Joan, who hadn't been to a decent Japanese restaurant since her twentieth wedding anniversary dinner with Stephen in New York City, was excited by the prospect of cosmopolitan cuisine.

"... Is such a creep," the woman said into her phone. "He actually groped me at the table. No, we were sitting on the same side. Yes, and before I knew what was happening, he had reached over, squeezed my breast, and stuck his tongue in my mouth." Joan looked up from her menu and stared at the woman next to her. How, Joan wondered, could someone not know that was happening? The woman was in her early thirties, Joan guessed, with prematurely wrinkled skin, an inexpensive hair dye job, and heavily applied makeup. "I told him to fuck off. What did you think I did?" Joan scooted along the long bench she shared with the woman, reached over, and touched the woman on the shoulder. The woman wheeled around, looking both surprised and annoyed. "Can I help you?" she asked in an unhelpful tone. "I'm on the phone here."

"Yes, that's why I've approached you," said Joan. "I'm terribly sorry about the unexpected turn of events on your date, but I am not interested in hearing any additional details. And I would appreciate it if you would end your conversation now or take it outside the restaurant."

The woman widened her eyes at Joan. "I don't have to take orders from you, lady. You're not my mother."

"Thank God for that," said Joan, sliding out from behind the table and standing. She walked to the host stand, explained the problem, and returned to the table, followed by the hostess. "But you do have to take orders from her." Joan used her index finger to point to the hostess.

"I'm sorry, miss," the hostess said. "But there is no talking on cell phones in the restaurant. I let it slide a moment ago, but you now must end your call."

"Says who?" The hostess pointed to the sign next to her stand. "Bitches, both of you," said the woman, as she stood. "Carrie, I'm going to have to call you back. I've been shut down by the cell phone police. Yeah, I know. Some people really don't have anything to do except screw with other people." She gave Joan and the hostess a protracted stare and then grabbed her purse and coat from the bench. Using her free hand, she gave them both the finger before walking out the door.

"I'm so sorry," said the hostess. "We get all kinds here."

"Thank you for taking care of that," said Joan, turning her back on the hostess to return to her table. From her limited exposure to the casino, Joan knew the hostess was right; it did seem to attract all kinds of people. She thought back to the cancer fundraiser, when she and everyone else on the guest list had been dressed in formal attire and occupied a sequestered area. This was not the norm, Joan discovered today. For on her way from the parking lot to the restaurant, Joan had noticed that the great majority of people were dressed as if detouring to the casino halfway through their Saturday morning errands. They wore old jeans that had lost their shape, sweat pants and sweat shirts, tracksuits, tank tops, and T-shirts with slogans like "I'm with Stupid," or "Ain't Nobody Happy When I'm Not Happy." Apparently, casinos would take anyone's money.

And then there were the people with young children. Joan had checked her watch just twenty minutes ago, when, on her way to the restaurant, she saw a young mother with two elementary school aged–looking boys in tow. No school today? Did she homeschool the boys? What were they doing there at noon on a Wednesday?

And yet, as much as Joan wanted to dislike the casino, she didn't. Instead, when there she experienced—what was it?—a feeling of freedom, of escape, like she was far away from her normal life and set of expected behaviors. The people at the casino were so different from those she interacted with on a regular basis. The surroundings, the décor was distasteful to Joan; and yet it was intriguing, with its Native American themes and references to wildlife and nature. There were no clocks to remind people of what they were supposed to be doing, enabling them to get lost in this fantasy world. What was the harm—well, the potential of losing a bunch of money aside—in that? And as long as people could control their gambling, wasn't it just another form of entertainment?

"Penny for your thoughts," said Alice, taking off her coat. "I've said hello twice."

Joan laughed. "I was thinking about this place," she said. "What it stands for, what it means."

Alice smiled at her new friend. "And what have you discovered?"

"How deep do you want to go?"

"Within a half inch of the surface."

"Not a whole lot then."

Alice set her cell phone down on the table. "Speaking of lots," said Alice, "I definitely picked the wrong one. If we eat here again, Evergreen is not the place to park your car."

"Sorry, I forgot to tell you," said Joan. "Stephen and I have learned that lesson ourselves."

"Have you heard from Ellie?" asked Alice. "She's probably lost too."

"No," said Joan. "Call her."

Just as Alice was scrolling through her contacts, Ellie rushed into the restaurant. Coat still on, she sat down in the chair next to Alice. "Where did you guys park?"

Alice laughed.

"Red Maple," said Joan. "When you come for a meal at the casino, park in Red Maple."

"Now she tells me," said Ellie, smiling at her friends.

"I *am* sorry. The first couple times here, I was very confused."

"First couple times?" asked Alice, checking her text messages now that the phone was in her hand. "Do you guys come here a lot?"

"No," said Joan. "We were here for that fundraiser last month."

"Oh yeah, the Southwood Cancer Society," said Alice. "Dave and I were going to go to that, too, but we couldn't since he forgot to tell me about another obligation, a run in the woods, that night. Who runs in the woods at night?"

"Next year," said Joan, choosing to pick up her menu again rather than explore night running with Alice. She hoped looking at her menu would send a signal to the others to do the same, to order and then talk. When Alice and Ellie had lifted their menus off the table, Joan said, "As soon as we've ordered, I want to hear all about your new client, Ellie."

Ellie put her menu back down on the table. "She's wonderful."

Alice leaned in closer to Ellie. "You're blushing," she said. "She must have given you a lot of business."

Ellie shook her head. "No, it's not a lot of business. She's just a really nice person. You know when you connect with someone, when you can almost read the other person's thoughts? That's the way our first meeting went. We were in sync on everything."

Alice laid her menu on the table. "That's because she's a woman, not a man."

"I'm going to have some sushi," Joan said, her stomach announcing its hunger. She had had nothing to eat that day but a low-fat yogurt at seven o'clock.

"Me too," said Alice. "If there's a place to eat sushi, this is it."

"How about you, Ellie?" asked Joan, nodding at their server to approach the table.

"I'm going with Chinese," Ellie said. "I can't do the raw thing."

Orders placed and water glasses topped off, Joan said, "So, what's her name, this wonderful woman at the new pet store?"

"Diana," said Ellie, smiling. "Diana McGuire."

"Oh, no wonder you like her," said Alice, jabbing her left elbow into Ellie's side. "It's the Irish in both of you."

Ellie tilted her head slightly. "Could be."

"And you just walked right in there and asked for her business," said Joan.

Ellie grinned. "I did just that."

"Nice job," said Joan, raising her water glass in a toast. The other two lifted theirs and touched them to Joan's glass.

"The world needs more women business owners," said Alice.

"Something wrong with male business owners?" asked Joan.

"Yes," said Alice, squeezing her fingers into small fists and flashing a pained expression. "Or, at least, one particular male business owner. My husband is driving me crazy. He insists on hiring runners to sell our shoes. And I get that; they know what they're talking about. But they aren't always the best salespeople because half of their brains are always thinking about their next running opportunity." Joan smiled. Alice did not. "So, Dave is spending more and more time at the store—especially now that Linda is gone. He sees no real reason to be home in time for dinner, like he used to, to catch up with his youngest daughter, or, I guess, to be with me."

"Is the business in trouble?" asked Ellie.

"No—the opposite, I think. Although I don't honestly know because Dave is a lousy accountant," said Alice. "The new store in Kensington is scheduled to open on New Year's Day, but everything from shoe production to shelving units delivery is either behind or back ordered." Their food arrived: tuna rolls for Joan, California rolls for Alice, and chicken and broccoli for Ellie. Joan mixed some wasabi mustard in with the soy sauce she had poured into the small dish next to her plate, dipped a piece into it, and put the whole thing into her mouth. She closed her eyes. "Nirvana?" asked Alice.

"Close to it," said Joan. "This is fantastic sushi." She used the wooden chopsticks to pick up another piece, which she dipped and held in the air as she said, "So, are you going to help him?"

"Who, Dave?" asked Alice. "I don't know. Maybe. I've been toying with going back to the store, as you know. But I'm not sure I want to do it right now. I want some time for myself. And I know that sounds crazy—but having kids around the house for twenty-five years drained me. I'm not ready to work fifty hours a week for Dave at the new store. He'd be paying me out of our profits. Plus, I'm just starting to get back in shape."

Ellie speared a piece of broccoli with her fork. "How is that going? Are you as sore as you were in the beginning?"

"Not as sore, but sore nonetheless. It's not easy taking up running again—which is essentially what I'm doing—in your fifties."

"It's not easy taking up anything in your fifties," said Joan. "You're lucky you have a place to work if you want. Can you imagine the looks I'd get if I walked into William Chester High School this afternoon and asked them for a job teaching calculus?"

"You want to teach calculus?" asked Alice. "I flunked calculus. You can start with me."

"I can talk to Chris," said Ellie. "He can find out what positions might be opening next semester or next fall."

Joan picked up another piece of sushi and swirled it in her soy sauce. "I'll let you know," she said. "I'm not ready to talk to anyone yet, but I want to do something."

"What about your mother-in-law?" asked Alice. "What is she going to think of this plan? And how about Stephen—does he want you to work?"

"I haven't talked with either of them about it," said Joan, smiling. "However, if I'm going to change Sandi's or Stephen's mind, I'm going to need to develop a well thought out plan. These are not people you approach with half-baked ideas."

"Tell me about it," said Ellie. "When I was thinking about starting my own accounting business, my father and brothers grilled me for an entire evening."

"Hey," said Joan, turning to face Alice. "What about *your* family? You haven't talked about them. All I know is that you grew up in Connecticut and went to school in Oregon."

Alice bit into one of her California rolls. "I'll give you the short version," she said, chewing. "My only sibling, an older sister, is a neurosurgeon in San Francisco. And my parents moved out there twenty years ago to take care of Carolyn's kids while she changed the world. They, my parents, spend a week with us every summer, and that is that."

"Interesting," said Joan, a word she sometimes used when she really wanted to use something more negative.

"Very," said Alice.

"And your sister?" asked Ellie. "Do you see her?"

"Her family comes east every summer too. We all gather at one of those resorts along the Connecticut coast and pretend we're close to one another," said Alice, reaching for her water glass.

"What about Dave's family?" asked Joan.

"Oh, we see them," said Alice, moving her eyes to Joan's face. "As long as we're willing to go to them and stay no more than two nights, they're happy to be with us."

December

Chapter 13

When Dave walked into the kitchen on Friday morning, wearing his winter running clothes and yawning, Alice handed him a mug of black coffee. "It looks like you're heading out there."

"I am," he said. "Just for a quick one."

"Can I go with you?"

Dave gave Alice a blank expression for a few seconds and then spoke the words he might have been searching for during the pause. "It's icy, dark, and cold. Are you sure you want to go now? Why not go later when it's warmer and light outside?"

"Because you'll be at work then." Dave blew a stream of air out of the side of his mouth. Alice put her hands on her hips. "You have been telling me for two months that you'll run with me."

"I know," he said. "I know. And I think it's great that you're getting back into it. I just had a different thing in mind this morning. I was planning on doing four miles at a seven-minute pace."

"Never mind then," said Alice, turning her back on him and re-filling her coffee mug.

Dave walked up behind Alice and put his hands on her shoulders. "You're right," he said. "I haven't made time for running with you. If you let me off the hook this morning, I'll go with you tomorrow. It's supposed to be in the low forties, which will make it a lot more pleasant out there."

Alice turned around and faced him. "You're not working tomorrow?"

"I am," he said, "but only in the morning."

"What if you get busy?" asked Alice, who had been promised Saturday runs that never materialized. And the Christmas season was always crazy with people buying gifts or gearing up for their New Year's resolutions.

"I'll get extra help in the afternoon tomorrow," said Dave. He smiled at his wife, finished the coffee, and put his mug in the sink. He pushed several buttons on his runner's watch and strode toward the back door. "I'll be back in thirty."

Alice was tempted to change her clothes and follow him. She knew his route; she could start from the end and jog toward the beginning. When they met, she could turn around and finish the loop with him. She took a couple steps toward the hallway, toward the stairs, toward their bedroom, and then turned around, walked back to the sink, and squinted out in the darkness to check the temperature on their outdoor thermometer. It was twenty-seven degrees. "To hell with it," she said, heating her coffee in the microwave and then sitting down at the kitchen table. She read the newspaper's front page headlines, and then sat back in the chair and looked at the clock. She wondered how she was ever going to get back into the habit of running daily if she didn't have help.

Ellie had invited Alice to walk with her. Ellie walked just about every day at a—what was it?—thirteen-minute-mile pace. That was impressive, much faster than the mall walkers, who appeared to be more interested in window shopping than in exercise, or the mall talkers, who walked a mile and a half loop in forty-five minutes, who didn't come close to needing a shower before they parked their wide bottoms in a booth at the coffee shop for a whole milk latte and chocolate covered croissant. And these were women her age. Alice picked up her phone from the kitchen table and texted Ellie. *Are you walking this morning?*

Ellie texted back. *I am. In about an hour, when the sun is up! Do you want to come with me?*

Alice hesitated a moment, and then typed. *Yes. I'll drive to your house. I'll be there by 8. Text me directions?*

Perfect. It will be nice to have company—well, human company!

Alice finished reading the first section of the newspaper, focusing mostly on the news about the financial woes of Colt Defense, and then got up from the table to make Dave's lunch: a peanut butter and local honey sandwich on whole wheat bread, a Greek yogurt, a banana, and two of the oatmeal and raisin cookies she had baked the day before. She was tempted to send the whole tin of them to work with him; they didn't need cookies at home. But Alice had been baking cookies twice a week for two decades, and it was a hard habit to break. She was on her second—telling herself that eating cookies for breakfast once in a while was good for the soul—when Dave, sweating and breathing hard, came through the back door.

"How'd you do?" Alice asked the question that Dave wanted to hear, that used to matter to her too.

Dave looked at his watch, pushing several buttons. "Good," he said. "It wasn't as icy as I thought it would be. Each split was faster, and I finished the run in twenty-six minutes. I ran into Jeffrey on Main Street, so we did the last two miles together. He's fast. He pushed me."

"He's also twenty years younger than you are. He should be fast."

Dave removed his skullcap, releasing steam into the kitchen air. He walked to the sink, filled a large glass with cold water, and chugged it down. "It was incredibly invigorating out there this morning. Sometimes winter running is the most rewarding."

"Yes." Alice walked out of the kitchen and into the hallway. She called back over her shoulder, "Your lunch is in the fridge."

When Alice walked into Ellie's kitchen, Ellie was putting a leash on Buffy. "Hey," Ellie said. "Any trouble finding the house?"

"Nope," said Alice. "Your directions were perfect—much better than the smartass on Google Maps." Ellie laughed. "I like your house. This is such a pretty and private street."

"It is." Ellie grabbed her gloves from the kitchen table. "Are you ready to go?"

"Are you sure you want to take me on? I will slow you down."

"I'm not worried about that," said Ellie, leading Buffy to the back door. "We're going to shoot for a sixteen-minute-mile pace. And if that's too fast, we can slow down. I do this six days a week, so if we go easy today, I can always bust a gut tomorrow—or not."

Here was a surprise: someone who regularly exercised a certain way who was willing to alter her routine, willing to compromise. Runners, Alice thought, weren't like that. Once they reached a specified proficiency, they were interested only in moving forward, in getting better, faster. And they pushed one another in that direction. If they did slow down, take an easy run, it was intentional, this tapering; it was part of their training. Alice knew that Ellie was serious about walking, but she was nonetheless prepared to accommodate a newcomer.

The walking was more challenging than Alice anticipated. She walked quite a bit during the day, but it was typically only when she was doing errands, and it was always at a leisurely pace. She didn't walk for exercise because she didn't think of walking as exercise. Runners were convinced about the superiority of their sport, about the sheer stamina required to run at and sustain a predetermined pace, about the mental discipline needed to finish a long, hard race. Outwardly, they supported everyone practicing an active lifestyle. But inwardly, they thought their sport, for those who excelled at it, was the best. Alice managed to keep Ellie's pace for three miles, but then she asked Ellie to slow down. Alice's calves were cramping—they were still sore from running three times that week—and she needed to catch her breath. By the time they reached Ellie's house, they had slowed even more.

"I'm sorry," said Alice. "I think I ruined your workout."

Ellie shook her head. "You absolutely did not ruin my workout. Plus we got to catch up on the kids. I'm so glad to hear that Linda is enjoying UConn as much as Tim is loving NYU. The first semester away at college can be a real challenge for kids. Even when they think they are ready to be away from home, they don't know what that really means until their possessions are unpacked in their dorm rooms and they are living with strangers."

"Yeah," said Alice. "Cathy, my oldest, called us the first night and wanted us to come back and get her."

Ellie nodded her head. "Eighteen is such a tender age. High school seniors think they are adults until they have to handle adult responsibilities."

"Too true," said Alice.

When they were back inside Ellie's kitchen, Alice accepted Ellie's offer of a glass of water. They chatted for another five minutes or so before Alice announced that she needed to go. "Thank you," said Alice, "for taking me with you today."

"Anytime," said Ellie, even though she already had the feeling that another time was not likely.

On the way home, Alice decided that she didn't like walking for exercise. It took too long; that was one negative. And the engaged conversation they had that morning had certainly prohibited a serious, calorie-burning session. Of course, Alice admitted that she was not yet ready for a grueling workout. When she ran, it was at a ten-minute-mile pace. But the most compelling reason why Alice liked running better than walking was because running allowed both feet to be simultaneously off the ground. That suspension in the air, however brief, felt to Alice like flying. Nothing else—not yoga, not TRX, not walking—offered that same sense of controlled release. The human body, which Alice and Dave had marveled at and worshipped in college and continued to frequently discuss, was capable of much more than most people knew.

CHAPTER 14

They were back at the casino, this time at Tony's, a restaurant decorated as a throwback diner. Joan had been tempted to sit at the long chrome-fronted and Formica-topped counter, on a padded, spinning stool, but instead had chosen a booth. Once she decided what she was going to eat, she flipped through the musical selections in the small jukebox attached to the wall. She wondered if the jukeboxes in the other booths had the same offerings: Aerosmith, Frank Sinatra, Fats Domino, the Everly Brothers, Aretha Franklin, Prince. She was considering inserting a quarter and listening to the Rolling Stones' "Start Me Up" when Alice and Ellie approached the table.

"We came together," said Alice, taking off her coat and hanging it on a hook next to the booth. "We texted you, but you were already gone."

"Well, aren't you clever," said Joan. "Had I not been at the grocery store and running other seriously boring errands, I would have taken you up on it."

"And," said Ellie, plopping herself down in the booth next to Joan, "we parked in the Red Maple garage."

"Makes all the difference in the world, doesn't it?"

"Totally," said Alice, looking at her running watch. "We parked the car exactly four minutes ago. The last time we were here, it took me thirteen minutes to find the restaurant."

Alice and Ellie picked up the menus on the table, as did Joan, giving herself another opportunity to ponder the merits of the tuna melt over the burger. It was now clear to all of them that this was how it worked; they first chose what they wanted to eat, and then they talked. Joan already knew that Alice would give her some flack about having a burger and fries, but they would be worth the teasing. She was so tired of eating salads, which she usually had at home, and of women always ordering salad. Did any of them really like salad, or had they merely been expected to, conditioned to eat it? How many men voluntarily ate salad for lunch? Ellie put her menu down on the table. "I'm going to have a bacon cheeseburger and a chocolate milkshake."

"You're kidding," said Alice.

"We're at a fifties diner," said Joan. "Why would she be kidding?"

"Who eats like that anymore?" asked Alice.

"I do," said Joan. "Tell me you prefer a lunch of raw vegetables doused with low fat vinaigrette to a patty of meat covered with melted cheese, and I'll tell you you've got a screw loose."

"I love salads."

"Why? Because they taste good, or because you've been ordering them for so long you don't know how to order anything else?" asked Joan.

"Salads are good for you," said Alice. "That's why I eat them, Joan."

"Yeah, well, so is flax seed, but who wants to eat it?"

"I do," said Alice. "I put two tablespoons into my fruit smoothie in the morning."

Joan gave Alice a weary look. "Live a little. Get a burger."

Alice squinted her eyes and then glanced back at the menu in her hand. A gum chewing waitress who looked and dressed very much like one of Joan's mother's best friends, a professional housekeeper for forty years, appeared at their table, flip pad open in her hand, pencil poised. "What can I get for you girls?"

Joan and Ellie ordered their burger specials, which came with fries and shakes, and then turned to look at their friend Alice. "Ice water," she said.

The waitress wrote down the order and then looked at Alice. "Anything else, hon?"

Joan laughed.

"A plain burger," said Alice. "No cheese, no mayo, no bacon—just the lettuce and tomato."

"Fries or chips?"

"Neither," said Alice. "If you can give me a side salad instead, that would be great."

The waitress snapped her pad closed. "I'll see what I can do. You want Italian dressing on that? I got blue cheese and ranch. But you look like an Italian girl to me."

"Italian is fine," said Alice, who knew a request for balsamic vinaigrette would be met with derision.

"You other girls want water?"

"Yes," said Ellie. "Thank you." As soon as their waitress left the table, Ellie looked at Alice and said, "Good girl. I knew you had it in you."

"Why the hell do you even think about dieting at this time of year?" asked Joan. "It's over for me until January 2nd."

"Amen to that," said Ellie. "And as soon as the boys get home for the holidays, I plan on living in my flannel pajamas."

Joan smiled. "I like that idea."

"Not me," said Alice. "I plan on gaining no more than three pounds, and it will be gone by the middle of January."

"Not if you keep baking cookies twice a week," said Ellie.

Alice's serious expression momentarily disappeared, replaced by a relaxed forehead and slight smile. "That is resolution number one: no more cookies."

"Ever?" said Joan.

"Maybe once in a while," Alice said. "Dave said he'd leave me if I stopped baking altogether."

They all leaned back in their seats when the waitress returned with a circular tray holding three tall glasses of ice water and two chocolate milkshakes.

"So," said Joan. "Who's done with their Christmas shopping?"

"The only people who ever ask that question are the people who *are* done," said Alice.

"I'm not done," said Joan. "But I have made a bunch of lists. Tomorrow is my day to sit at the computer and get all the online stuff out of the way."

"You don't shop locally?" asked Ellie.

"If you tell me where to shop, I'm all over it," said Joan. "In the thirty years I've lived here—and you know what I'm going to say— I've seen the downtown go from a real downtown to junk shop city. Remember the sporting goods store, the pharmacy, the diner, the department store, and all the cute little shops run by local merchants? I bought everything downtown when the kids were little, save the Christmas and birthday treks to Toys 'R' Us. But now? What can you get downtown now? Other than a T-shirt with a black dog on it. There are only so many people who have black labs."

"Maybe we should open a store with mutt T-shirts," said Alice.

"I'm in," said Joan, raising her hand in the air.

"The bookstore is still there," said Ellie.

"Thank God for that," said Alice. "I love getting a good book as a gift."

"Me too," said Joan. "The bookstore is on my list for Friday. What do you think about a newspaper subscription for Liz? She's taking a journalism class and is expected to read the paper every day."

"She can go to the library for a newspaper."

"Excellent thought, Ellie," said Joan. "Another reason for her to go to the library is always good, right?"

The waitress set three large plates on the table and walked away. The three women picked up their burgers simultaneously. Joan looked at Alice before taking her first bite and said, "You are more than welcome to some of my fries. That salad looks like it was on someone else's plate yesterday."

Alice looked down at the clumps of iceberg lettuce that were browning around the edges. They had clearly come from a bag, along with the limp sliced red cabbage and desiccated julienne carrots. Alice reached over and took a fry from Joan's plate. "Hey," she said, chewing, "did you guys see the article in the paper this morning about Colt revving up its business in West Hartford?"

"I did," said Joan. "Stephen's met with the president of the company—but he doesn't think it's going to work out. The gun laws in Connecticut are becoming stricter, which makes Colt's job harder."

Alice dabbed ketchup from the corner of her mouth. "I didn't even realize that Colt still manufactured guns in West Hartford until I read about it in the paper."

"You don't get out much, do you?" asked Joan.

"As if you'd know anything about it if Stephen weren't involved."

Joan raised her eyebrows at Alice. "Meaning I wouldn't know about anything happening in the real world unless Stephen informed me of its existence?"

"God, you think too much, Joan," said Alice. "We're just talking. I know you're against regular citizens owning guns, and you know that I think people should be able to own them and use them with caution if they are inclined to do so. What I don't know," she said, turning to Ellie, "is how you feel about them."

Ellie took a big bite of her burger and chewed slowly. She had not, in fact, discussed her feelings about guns, or the laws surrounding their ownership and use, with her friends. And this was primarily because she had guns in her house. They were locked in an antique wood and glass cabinet in the family room: three rifles Chris's grandfather had given to him when Chris was twenty-one. His grandfather had taken Chris duck hunting when Chris was a teenager—so when his grandfather was looking to pare down his collection, Chris was a natural choice. Chris had introduced their sons to shooting, as his grandfather had done for him, when Brandon, their older boy, was thirteen, and Tim was eleven. They went annually, every October, into the northwest corner of the state for a weekend of what Chris called male bonding. Typically, they brought home eight to ten ducks, which they cleaned in the basement. Ellie insisted that they remove all the skin, to reduce the presence of contaminants, before they cooked the meat. It was then frozen and used in a variety of dishes throughout the winter. Ellie liked the taste of duck, actually, finding it flavorful and versatile rather than gamey and limited.

And Ellie liked that Chris was very careful when he was handling the guns. The night before their dawn departure for their hunting trip, Chris talked to the boys about safety and then quizzed them afterward. He employed their help in caring for the guns, so that they now knew as much about them as he did. He made it fun, Ellie thought, when it could have been a lecture or a chore. Tim and Brandon, who were now eighteen and twenty, seemed to look forward to this time with their dad. Ellie wasn't sure they told their friends what they were up to on their Columbus Day weekends, but they talked about it at home, boasting about who would bag the most birds. Brandon had missed this year's trip, unable to get home from school in Michigan. But Chris and Tim had talked about it with him over the phone, allowing him to experience the event vicariously. With both boys in college, Chris had just recently talked with Ellie about moving their hunting trip to Christmastime, maybe even having duck for their holiday meal.

Ellie swallowed the last bit of burger in her mouth and then reached for her milkshake. She took a long sip. What did she owe these women, Alice and Joan? Anything? She guessed they probably didn't know about the guns in her house. But they might know. Tim certainly could have said something to Liz or Linda—teenagers were anything but circumspect. Did it matter? Ellie never talked about her husband's small gun collection because she thought it wasn't anyone else's business. But she thought a lot of things weren't anyone else's business. She knew there was more that she could share about her life.

"We own three rifles," she finally said. And before Joan or Alice could ask her any questions, she launched into the story about how the rifles were manufactured by Colt in the mid-nineteenth century. That the rifles were given to her husband by a family member who had had the guns passed down to him. That they were kept in a locked case, with the exception of one weekend every year. And that safety was her husband's number one priority when hunting with her boys. When she was done talking, she put two fries in her mouth.

"That's a great story," said Alice. "I think it's really cool to have guns in your house."

"Why is it cool?" asked Joan.

"Cool in the sense that they are locked up. They are properly, lovingly even, cared for, and used for what guns were intended to do. Plus you eat what the boys kill. That makes it even cooler."

Joan cocked her head to the side. "You don't worry about the guns getting into the wrong hands? Into the hands of someone like James Shulz?"

"No," said Ellie too quickly.

"James Shulz didn't kill Emmanuel Sanchez because he had a gun," said Alice. "He killed him because he had mental health issues."

Joan put her hands on the table and leaned in. "So, if he didn't have the gun, he would have killed Emmanuel with his bare hands?"

"Maybe," said Alice. "Guns don't kill people; people kill people."

"That sounds like a bumper sticker. And it's completely inaccurate. It's crazy," said Joan, using her hands to push back from the table until she was up against the booth cushion.

Alice took another fry from Joan's plate and put it in her mouth. "Why? Because it's not what you think?"

"People use guns to kill people because killing someone with a gun is nothing like killing someone with a knife or with your hands. When you kill someone with a gun, you don't have to get too close. You don't have to touch the person. Gun violence is detached violence, which, I think, is why it appeals to so many people."

"Detached can be good, Joan. Let's look at this from the victim's perspective. Having a gun means the victim can stop someone—the thief or the murderer—before he gets his knife into her back or his hands around her neck."

"Point taken," said Joan. "But I still think it can happen too fast. It's an automatic rather than a visceral solution."

"I like this conversation," said Ellie. Knowing sarcasm when she heard it, Joan smiled at Ellie. "No," she said, registering Joan's amusement. "I'm serious."

"You are? What do you like about it?" asked Joan.

"I like it because we're having it," Ellie said. "Ten years ago, if we had known one another then, we wouldn't have been talking about guns or other topical issues. We were so busy with our children that we didn't have time for lunch out of the house or discussions that weren't about child rearing. And I like it that we can disagree. So many women I know seem to build one another up when they are together or online and then turn around and tear one another apart when they aren't. Being with you two is like being with my brothers. At our lunch table, everyone gives her opinion freely and knows she will be respected for it."

"That's because we're protected by the First Amendment to the Constitution," said Alice.

"Says the *Encyclopaedia Britannica*," said Joan.

Alice laughed. "I haven't heard the word *encyclopedia* in twenty years."

"I've got them in my basement if you're interested in reliving your childhood memories."

"No, no, no," said Alice, still smiling. "I prefer the Internet."

"Where you have learned all about the Second, and now, I gather, the First Amendment to the Constitution."

"Joan, knowledge is not evil."

"As long as it's balanced," said Joan.

"I couldn't have said it better myself," said Alice, taking another fry from Joan's plate. "I'll tell you another thing," she said. "You were right about the side salad. It sucks. And these fries are worth the calories. Thank you, my otherwise misguided friend, for sharing."

Joan laughed. "You, my overzealous patriot, are most welcome."

CHAPTER 15

They lingered in the massive hallway outside Tony's until their conversation was interrupted when Joan got a phone call. It was Liz, and so Joan answered it—her children and her husband were the only people she always picked up for—waving to Alice and Ellie as they walked away from her in the direction of the Red Maple parking lot. Liz didn't have anything major to report to her mother; she was simply using her, an expression they both employed, as a distraction while she walked from the dining hall to her first afternoon class. Joan was not much of a phone talker, so she was okay with this method of communication. She got to hear on a fairly regular basis what her daughter was up to, and Joan was able to catch Liz up on any interesting home news.' This eight-minute conversation, like all of them, was over as soon as Liz reached her destination. Joan put her phone back into her purse and checked her watch. She had done all her errands that morning and was not yet ready to go home.

Instead, she wandered in and out of several shops, where she half-heartedly examined several pieces of merchandise—a pair of smart black heels, a hand-dyed silk scarf, an oversized, cranberry colored leather purse—before setting them back down. Ten minutes later she was on the casino floor. It was the same section she and Stephen had walked through on their way to the cancer society fundraiser; she could see the roulette tables in the distance. *Why not?* she asked herself as she crossed the room. She approached the same table she had been so successful at during the event and put five twenties on the green felt surface, as if she did this every day, as if this behavior were normal for her. She ignored the flutterings of fear she felt in her heart and stomach. She disregarded the questions offered up by her brain. Instead, she settled into her chair, telling herself that what she was doing was fine. The croupier, a young Asian man with a gummy grin, pushed two short stacks of pink chips her way and, without making eye contact, told her good luck. Just as she finished placing her first bet, a young waitress carrying a small circular tray and dressed in what Joan could only describe as a Pocahontas outfit asked her if she wanted a drink. Joan's first inclination was to ask the woman if *she* had been drinking. But Joan quickly realized that, at two in the afternoon, people did, in fact, drink alcohol. Some people were on vacation and, having no one and nothing to report to, decided to relax with a drink. Others needed no excuse to drink whenever they felt the urge.

Joan's father, Gene Adams, drank because his workday was done. He had been an industrial electrician for fifty years, working at a car manufacturing plant near Detroit, where Joan spent her childhood. His shift, for almost the entire length of his employment, was from seven in the morning until three thirty in the afternoon, with a union imposed, timed half hour for lunch and two fifteen-minute breaks, one in the morning and one in the afternoon. Joan's mother, Brenda, was an aide in Joan's school. She drove Joan and her brother, Carl, to and from school every day, and waved to them every time she saw them in the hallways or the cafeteria. As soon as school was over for the day, Brenda drove the children home. They were expected to do their homework while she prepared dinner. Gene arrived at the house about thirty minutes after his family. He'd walk into the kitchen, kiss his wife as she prepared spaghetti sauce or tuna casserole or meatloaf, and then open the door to the fridge for a beer from the six-pack Brenda had picked up on the way home from school. He would take the first long drink in the kitchen and then set the bottle down on the counter so he could remove his coat. He'd have two more beers before dinner, which he expected to be served promptly at five thirty, and then he'd have three additional beers with and after dinner, finishing the six-pack. And then he'd stop. Later on, Joan surmised that the reason he stopped had a lot to do with the reason she and her brother sat in the car every weekday while their mother ran into the liquor store. Her dad watched television in the evenings, starting with the news. He was in bed and asleep by nine. And this routine seemed to work for him; in five decades, he never took a sick day.

Occasionally at the dinner table he'd ask his wife or Joan and Carl about her or his day at work or at school. But, for the most part, Gene kept to himself and appeared to think that his wife and children should do the same. Joan used to wonder what went on in his head. She never asked him, however. She hardly ever talked to him. She wasn't afraid of him, but she knew he preferred not to be disturbed, not to be spoken to unless he initiated conversation. The only time she was sure to get a few words out of him was when she brought home her report card. "My little ace," he'd say. "You got all the brains in the family." And then he'd put his arm around her shoulder and give her a quick hug.

Joan *was* an academic ace, which was the reason she was admitted on scholarship to the small, liberal arts college on the East Coast, where she met and fell in love with Stephen. She didn't meet him, however, until the fall of her junior year, which was coincidentally when she decided that drinking six beers a night wasn't, after all, a wise, healthy, or normal decision. Before that, Joan went to classes, did her homework, went to dinner, and then went to the campus pub. As expected, she met like-minded people at The Attic, a dimly lit, intimate bar on the second floor of the student union building. Her fellow students sat in booths, hunched over their two-dollar pitchers of Budweiser, discussing lectures, sports, the news of the day. From Thursday through Saturday night, The Attic was crowded, standing room only. But on Monday nights, the crowd thinned, giving Joan and her drinking companions the run of the place.

The spring of her sophomore year, Joan started drinking in the afternoon, before she did her homework, before she went to the dining hall for dinner. She thought this was okay, for a while. And then the students, the fellow drinkers she had been spending more and more of her time with, started talking about leaving school. They weren't, they'd decided one evening much like all the other evenings, getting much out of it. And Joan might have packed her things and left school, too, if she hadn't received in her mailbox a handwritten note from her mathematics professor, requesting a meeting. When they did meet, the professor told Joan that she was a gifted student—and then she told Joan that unless she started finishing the assigned homework, the professor would give her an F for the semester. Joan stopped drinking that day. A year later, when she started again, she decided that she would never have more than two drinks, or three when she could get away with it, when she had decided it was somehow warranted, and she would never drink before five o'clock. And she had kept that vow.

"No, thank you," said Joan to the casino waitress looking at her expectantly. Joan turned her attention back to the table, where she realized that the small white ball was sitting in eighteen red, the number she had put two chips on. The croupier moved two stacks of chips in her direction. She lost the next two bets, but won three in a row after that. The only other person at the table, a man in an outdated business suit with an amber colored drink at his right elbow, started to put some of his chips on the numbers she chose. The first time their number hit, he smiled at her across the table.

"Care to join me?" he asked, lifting his drink. "I don't drink the house stuff. I'll buy you a real drink."

"No, thanks."

"Wise woman," he said. "I always know an intelligent woman when I see one."

Joan looked at him for a moment and then flashed him an insincere grin before turning her gaze back to the table. She put eight chips on red and eight chips on black and then leaned forward to watch the ball travel around the wheel.

"Are you a faithful wife, wise woman?"

This time, Joan didn't make eye contact with the man. Instead, when she had collected her chips from the ball's landing on twenty-two black, she told the croupier she wanted to cash in, a phrase she had learned from Jimbo at the fundraising event. The croupier gave her a few larger value chips for her five-dollar chips, and Joan put them in her pants pocket.

"I didn't chase you away now, did I?" asked the man. Joan grabbed her coat from the back of the chair. "Now don't go away mad," he said.

Joan raised her eyes to look at him. "How can I be mad?" she asked. "I just won four hundred dollars." Not breaking eye contact with him, she put on her coat, buttoned up the front, and slung her purse strap over her shoulder. She then shifted her gaze to the croupier. She placed the two chips she had held back on the table and thanked him, and then turned her back to the other man and walked away.

"I love you!" called the man after her.

Joan smiled, knowing it was the alcohol and loneliness that fueled his remark. However, she also knew that because she was a sharp dresser, people thought she was more attractive than she actually was. Her clothing somehow hid the extra pounds she carried on her frame. Even so, Joan was no Alice, who was bone thin and in pretty good shape, especially since she had started running again. But Alice had the wizened face of someone five years her senior. And her long blond hair was, Joan thought, silly. Joan, who had been raven-haired since birth, suspected that women with blond hair that fell past their shoulders had a hard time letting it go. They had turned so many heads with that hair over the years. And yet there was something very frightening about viewing from behind a woman with hair down to the middle of her back and then having her turn around to reveal a face that looked like it had been underground for six months. *Tales from the Crypt*! At that thought, Joan laughed aloud. Giddy about her winnings, she felt like she *had* been drinking.

Joan stopped at the cashier windows to cash in the chips given to her by the croupier. The woman behind the bars gave her four crisp one-hundred-dollar bills, Benjamins her daughters called them. She put the bills in a separate sleeve of her wallet, thinking she would use the money to pay for something she normally would not buy. Or, she thought, walking toward the Red Maple parking lot, she could use the money if she ever felt like playing roulette again.

CHAPTER 16

Alice, Joan, and Ellie had discussed skipping their second lunch date in December, since life was so busy at holiday time. In the end, they agreed to meet for an hour instead of ninety minutes and to exchange Christmas gifts that cost no more than ten dollars each. To stick to the sixty-minute agreement, they decided to eat at a restaurant that could take their order and deliver their food quickly. It was Alice who suggested, to no one's surprise, that they try Sensational Salads!

She was the first to arrive at the brightly lit eatery, which featured a long display case of standard salad bar fare, like various lettuces, chopped vegetables, beans, and cheeses, as well as ready-mades like tuna, egg, and crabmeat salad, coleslaw, potato and pasta salad and the like. Customers simply chose the plate size they wanted and then, moving their cafeteria-style trays along the slide rail, told the two hairnetted, plastic gloved, tong wielding employees behind the counter what they wanted. Alice had just asked one of the employees if the chicken salad was made fresh that morning when Joan walked up behind her and said, "You must be in heaven."

Alice turned around to face her and smiled. "I do like a good salad."

"Believe it or not, I do, too. I'm just way too lazy to make anything that looks this interesting at home. So, a place like this is sheer genius. I may take something home to go with our dinner tonight."

Ellie, who double checked her watch to make sure she was on time, shed her coat and hung it on the back of the chair next to the one holding Alice's coat, and then joined the others at the rail. As instructed by Alice, Ellie grabbed a tray from the stack at the near end. As soon as she and her tray reached Joan, she gently bumped Joan's hip with her own. When Joan gave her an amused and questioning look, Ellie said, "I feel like I'm in middle school again."

"But this food looks a whole lot better than what we saw in middle school," said Alice. She asked for a bed of arugula greens, topped by a mound of chicken salad, a half dozen grape tomatoes, and six slices of avocado.

"It does indeed," said Joan, who ordered a mound of tuna, a scoop of pasta salad, a hard-boiled egg, and iceberg lettuce topped with blue cheese dressing.

"I liked that food," said Ellie. "Remember the veal cutlet and mashed potatoes?"

"Fake and fake," said Joan, paying the cashier.

"But good fake," said Ellie. "Hot lunches now are nothing but boiled hot dogs and reheated pizza."

"Served with a side salad, thanks to Michelle Obama," said Alice.

"I will miss Michelle," said Joan.

The three women took plastic ware and napkins from the dispensers at the table beyond the cashier and then walked to the restaurant's Hydration Station, where they poured water from a metal pitcher into eight-ounce plastic cups. When they reached the table, Joan took off her coat and sat across from Alice and Ellie. "Can I ask the Christmas shopping question now?" Joan asked Alice.

"You may," she said. "I finished this morning—well, except for Dave. All I have to do now is bake about a thousand cookies before the girls get home."

"When do they get home?" asked Ellie, spearing one of her cucumber slices with her fork.

"Tomorrow," said Alice.

Joan laughed. "Are you picking Linda up at school?"

"Yes," said Alice. "She's got her last exam in the morning. And she wants me there at noon on the dot. Hilary and Cathy, my working women, won't be home until next week. But they like my cookies every bit as much as Linda."

"You'll have to pull an all-nighter," said Joan.

"What smells like smoke?" asked Ellie. "Do you guys smell that?"

Joan wrinkled her brow and then smelled the sleeve of her sweater. "It's me," said Joan. "Sorry about that."

"Why do you smell like smoke, Joan?"

Joan could have told them the truth, that she had arrived at the casino at ten o'clock that morning and played roulette, that she had won, in the end, a hundred dollars, that she had hesitated for a long moment when the costumed waitress asked her if she wanted a drink. Instead, she said, "I left my dress gloves here the night of the fundraiser, and I got bad directions to the lost and found department. I wandered around for what must have been fifteen minutes before I found it. I guess I picked up the smoke smell in my travels."

The conversation went back to the children—starting with when Ellie's sons and Joan's daughters were due home and how long they could stay. The women then moved on to what everyone would be eating and where all the holiday festivities would be taking place. By the time they finished their salads, they had exchanged a few recipes and last-minute gift ideas for their husbands.

"Speaking of gifts," said Ellie, reaching for a bag beneath her feet, "I have something for the two of you."

"Yes, yes," said Alice, retrieving her large leather purse from the back of her chair. Joan, who had put her gifts for her friends under the table that Alice had saved with her coat, lifted her shopping bag off the floor and set it on her lap.

"Shall I start?" asked Ellie.

"Please do," said Joan.

She handed both of them red foil gift bags, with white tissue jutting out the top. "Open them together," Ellie said.

"Wow," said Alice, pulling a moss green scarf out of the bag. "I had no idea you were a knitter. And this color is perfect for me." She leaned over and hugged Ellie.

"This is absolutely beautiful," said Joan, draping hers, which was gray, around her neck. "I can't believe you never said a word."

"And we never saw you with the bag of knitting that all knitters haul with them wherever they go."

Ellie laughed, pleased with their praise.

"You are good, Ellie," said Joan, unwrapping her scarf and tucking it back into her bag. "I'm impressed."

"And she doesn't impress easily," said Alice, making a hitch-hiker motion to point to Joan.

"I'm glad you like them," said Ellie.

"And mine goes with my coat," said Joan.

"And your eyes," said Ellie.

"You are one of the last observant people in the world, Ellie Fagen," said Joan. "I'm double impressed."

"Me too," said Alice, smiling at Ellie. "Who's next?"

"You," said Joan. "I'm dying to see what kind of surprises you've packed into that suitcase you carry around with you."

Alice took two square packages, both wrapped in red paper and green velvet ribbon, from her bag and set them on the table in front of Ellie and Joan. "These boxes are pretty enough to be the gift," said Joan.

Ellie tugged at the green ribbon. Alice said, "I also want you to open them at the same time."

Joan and Ellie removed the ribbon and wrapping and opened the boxes to find a dozen petits fours layered inside, each decorated differently. "Tell me you made these," said Joan.

Alice smiled. "I made them."

"No wonder you've had no time to make cookies," said Ellie.

"They are exquisite, Alice." Joan held out her box. "Do you want one?"

Alice shook her head. "They are for you," she said. "My advice is to hide them in the freezer. Share only if you feel like it."

"I'm having one right now," said Ellie, biting in half one that was coated in green frosting and covered with red dots. The moist chocolate cake inside surrounded a cream filling. Ellie closed her eyes. "Incredible."

"Okay," said Joan, "now that we're done with the homemade portion of the celebration, let's move on to the store-bought category. I feel like a heel," she said, handing Alice a flat, rectangular box wrapped in candy cane paper and giving Ellie a short, square box wrapped in shiny, bright green paper. Both boxes were topped with a hunter green taffeta ribbon.

"You get points for the bow," said Ellie, untying it and wrapping the ribbon around her fingers. She set the coil aside and then removed the paper. Inside her box were three square bars of handmade goat's milk soap, which prompted Ellie to say, "How did you remember our discussion about nasty soap in my downstairs bathroom?"

In Alice's box were a reflective running vest and a Storm Whistle. Alice smiled at her friend. "After all the grief you've given me about running."

"Well, now that I know how dedicated you are, I want you to be safe out there."

"You went over the limit, pal," said Ellie.

"Says the woman who spent a month knitting us scarves," said Joan. "Plus, I didn't. The vest, while brand new, belonged to Cassie, who gave up running after her first run."

Alice laughed. "I know how she feels."

"And those whistles are supposed to be the loudest ones made," said Joan, pointing at the box in front of Alice. "You blow it on the running trails, and I will hear it at my house."

"I will wear this around my neck every time I run," said Alice, "starting tomorrow."

"No luck yet finding anyone to run with you?" asked Ellie.

"No," said Alice. "But Dave keeps promising."

"He'll go with you," said Joan, nodding her head. "And until he does, you've got the whistle."

"I do, indeed," said Alice, checking her cell phone on the table for the sixth or seventh time. "Hey, I've got to run. If I'm going to get any cookies done before I get Linda tomorrow morning, I've got to start the minute I get home."

Ellie and Joan stood as well. All three women put on their coats, stashed their gifts in their bags, and walked out of the restaurant. Neither Alice nor Ellie thought a thing when Joan peeled off from the group, saying she wanted to pick something up for Stephen. They all embraced and wished one another happy holidays. By the time Ellie had arrived at the pet store for her meeting with Diana, and Alice had creamed the butter for her shortbread cookies, Joan was down two hundred dollars and halfway through her first vodka soda.

JANUARY

CHAPTER 17

Ellie and Diana sat side by side at a small table in the tiny, organized office at the back of Diana's Pet Supply. They had gone over the numbers for the first few months of operations, as well as for Diana's start-up costs. Ellie told Diana her expenses were in line with her revenue, and that the business would be profitable by March. It was good news for Diana, who had used the profit from a house sale to finance the pet supply store; she was running out of cash.

It was just about noon when they finished their meeting. Diana asked Ellie to wait in her office for a minute while she checked in with her employee, who had been running the store by herself for an hour. Not that Diana was worried. Shawna was one of the most capable and confident twenty-six-year-olds Diana knew; she could do everything, from operating the cash register and restocking the shelves to accurately answering customer questions and anticipating what needed to be done next. Shawna gave Diana a two-minute summary and then told her boss, when asked, that if Diana wanted to have lunch with her accountant, it would be no problem.

Diana walked back into her office. "I've been given permission to take a lunch break," she said with a smile. "Are you hungry?" As

Ellie was thinking through her response, wondering if she, as Diana's accountant, should treat Diana to lunch, Diana reached under the table and produced a small cooler. She removed the lid and extracted the cooler's contents: two sandwiches wrapped in wax paper, two small Granny Smith apples, and a plastic container holding what looked like brownies. She stood briefly to fetch a large bottle of seltzer and two clean coffee mugs from the shelf behind her desk, and then returned to her seat and looked at Ellie expectantly. A picnic, thought Ellie, this is a picnic in January.

When Tim and Brandon were young, Ellie had talked Chris into Saturday picnics in the summertime. Chris much preferred eating at a table, but he had acquiesced, especially since Ellie said she would do everything. This meant preparing and wrapping the food of course. But it also meant finding suitable picnic spots, where they could play tag and explore their natural surroundings before their meal and quietly listen to Ellie read children's books afterward. They went to state parks, mostly, with their wide open green spaces, ponds, streams, and walking trails. Sometimes they were lucky enough to get a picnic table, but most of the time they all sat on the plaid wool blanket Ellie still kept in the back of her car. As the boys got older, their interest in Ellie's four-hour adventures had dwindled, unless they could bring along a friend. And Ellie had said yes, at first, and packed two more of everything. However, with friends in tow, it was no longer a family outing. The boys quickly ate what Ellie had prepared and then bolted from the table or blanket, leaving Ellie and Chris behind to look at their watches and think about what else they might be doing on a Saturday afternoon.

Diana unwrapped the sandwiches and, using the wax paper as a plate, slid one toward Ellie. It looked like something out of a cooking magazine. Ellie picked up a sandwich half and studied its contents. "This looks absolutely amazing," she said. "What's in here?"

"Grilled eggplant, sautéed mushrooms and onions, sundried tomatoes, goat cheese, and watercress."

Ellie smiled at Diana. "And you just whipped this up this morning?"

Diana picked up one of her sandwich halves. "I cooked the vegetables last night, so that everything would be cold when I assembled them this morning."

"You're a cook then."

Diana took a small bite of her sandwich, chewed, and then, shielding her mouth with her fingers, said, "I do like to cook."

"Well, I sure hope you have an appreciative family."

"I do," said Diana. "But my son is in Colorado, and my daughter is in Los Angeles, and my husband has a new wife now, so I don't feed him nearly as much as I used to." Ellie was feeling a tug of regret about the comment she had made when Diana said, "But my husband, my ex-husband, occasionally comes over for a home-cooked meal and a bottle of wine, which he provides, and he is most appreciative. His new wife much prefers to eat out than to, as she says, slave away in the kitchen."

"I guess I know how she feels sometimes," said Ellie. "I mean, I like to cook. But my family—when they are home—eats in six minutes what has taken me an hour and a half to prepare. They always tell me it's good, but I have a feeling they'd say the same thing about dinner out of a box."

Diana laughed. "I think my daughter eats out of a box or a bag most nights. On the other hand, my son, who is a ski instructor in Aspen, is a pretty good cook. He often prepares a hearty meal after a day on the mountain, and his wife, who is also an instructor, is very appreciative."

Ellie wanted to ask what had happened with the marriage, but she hardly knew Diana, and she knew her inquiry would cross the nosiness line. But it was hard to believe that anyone wouldn't want to be with Diana. From the limited time Ellie had spent with her, she could see that Diana was a kind, giving, and accommodating person—an ideal mate, yes? Of course, people got divorced for all kinds of reasons. Women liked to think that it was always the man's fault, that he was the one with the wandering eye, the one who had the affair, the one who wanted out. These same women, while quick to blame their spouses, were also reluctant to acknowledge the effect of their own actions and what role their demanding or controlling personalities might have played in the breakup.

Before Kelly Shulz's son had shot Emmanuel Sanchez at the

high school, everyone in town felt sorry for her. Her husband had had multiple affairs and even sired two children, according to persistent rumor, with other women. And Ellie agreed, when she bumped into the women who talked about these kinds of things, that this was a painful and cruel mockery of marriage. But Ellie felt differently about Kelly now. She, like Alice, blamed Kelly for having guns accessible in the house; she blamed Kelly for fostering in James an interest in guns—even though Ellie had to admit that she and Chris were guilty of the same things. Being nice to Kelly was, of course, warranted in the wake of the shooting, but it was even more forced and awkward than it had been before. Ellie's sympathy was tainted.

Ellie struggled with this because, in general, she was a sympathetic person. And every time she ran into Kelly, she fought the judgment she surely projected. It was too convenient, too easy to call someone a bad mother. Whenever a child throws sand at the playground or a tantrum in the grocery store; whenever an adolescent shoves a classmate up against the lockers or teases him in front of others, or smokes cigarettes in the girls' room, or resists authority, it is the mother's fault—for not setting limits, for not modeling positive behavior, for bad parenting. Sometimes a child does exhibit the behaviors of an ill tempered, inept parent. But most of the time, Ellie thought, a mother does the best she can. Diana, Ellie could tell by the way she talked about her children, was as concerned and connected a parent as Ellie and Chris tried to be.

"Tell me about your family," said Diana. "What do they do, other than eat quickly?"

Ellie started with her husband, telling Diana that he was a gym teacher at the high school during the school year and that he worked for her uncle's construction company during the summer. He enjoyed physical work and was therefore well suited to both occupations. Her older son, Brandon, Ellie explained, was in his junior year at Northern Michigan University in Marquette. He was right on Lake Superior, which made for brutal winters but superb summers—and he had chosen to live and work there after both his freshman and sophomore years. Ellie missed seeing and being with him, but she could tell that he was content with his choices, and she was pleased with his level of dedication. Her younger son, Tim, was a freshman at New York University, studying music and theater. Chris was worried about Tim's lack of career choices after graduation, his earning potential. But Ellie was convinced that if he didn't make it in the theater world, Tim could certainly teach others about music. There had been some talk at Christmastime about pursuing an advanced degree in music theory.

"And what about you?" asked Diana. "What do you like to do?"

It had been a while since anyone had asked Ellie that question, or since she had asked herself. She had fallen into the bookkeeping business because she was good at numbers, and it was something she could do from home, while raising the boys. Before the boys were born, she had worked in a bank as a credit analyst, and she was thinking about returning to that line of work full-time, but she'd had all fall to apply for positions and she had not done it. "Does that mean I don't want to be a credit analyst?" she asked.

Diana picked up the second half of her sandwich. "Maybe," she said. "The good news is it sounds like you have a choice: You can return to credit analysis; you can build out your bookkeeping business, which gets my vote, by the way; or you can do something completely different."

"Chris would like me to work full-time. He was very supportive of my staying home with the boys. But now he thinks there's no reason for me to be home. College is expensive, even with scholarships." Diana nodded her head as she chewed. "And I agree with him. I don't know why I'm hesitant to jump back in."

"Let's see," said Diana, wiping the corner of her mouth with one of the cloth napkins she had packed in with the food. "You've been a hands-on mother for twenty years, and now both your children are gone. Welcome to empty nest syndrome."

Ellie smiled. "Tell me *your* definition."

"Well, it's a time of discovery, isn't it?" asked Diana. "We will always be mothers, even when our children are not at home. We simply have more time now to pursue other interests. And it often takes time to figure out what those interests are, both in and outside of the working world. We can put pressure on ourselves to make this transition too quickly—or there can be pressures put upon us. When finances are a concern, we don't always have the luxury to figure it out. But if we can take the time, if we choose to take the time, this next stage in our lives can be a welcome change. Most mothers mourn when their children leave the house, but the smart ones also celebrate the freedom they now have to redefine themselves."

"Well put," said Ellie, thinking that she and Chris had discussed the empty nest syndrome a number of times and had not been able to put as fine a point on it as Diana had in a few sentences. Maybe this was because Chris was primarily concerned about their expenses, and Ellie, while certainly in agreement with him that the next several years would be very expensive ones, did not want to take on something she would regret. He wanted Ellie to get back into the workforce and was somewhat dismissive of her talk about an emotional transition. *The boys are off finding their way in the world,* he had said. *You've done your job, and you've done it well. Now it's time to get back to work.* There was nothing wrong with what Chris had said. It was the way he said it. This was typically the case when she and Chris talked about life's larger issues. They both spoke English, but employed it differently. Chris was pleasant, but also terse, direct, and, at times, unwilling to thoroughly discuss whatever topic stood between them, while Ellie was more exploratory in her thought process and wanted their conversations to include every possible option. However, no matter how it was said, Ellie knew Chris was right, knew that she should return to full-time work, that she was being self-indulgent. But because Chris was intolerant of Ellie's indecision, Ellie felt gypped. She yearned to discuss what was important to her with someone who would actively listen.

CHAPTER 18

Joan, five minutes late to lunch, quickly hugged both Ellie's and Alice's shoulders when she got to the table.

"What was that for?" asked Alice.

"Number one, I'm sorry I'm late," said Joan. "And number two, I haven't seen either of you in too long. I know we've been texting, but no matter what you say, Alice, that is not real communication."

"I politely disagree," said Alice, picking up her phone from the tabletop and showing the screen to Joan. "Linda just communicated with me."

Sorry she had brought it up, Joan flicked the air in front of Alice.

"I still can't believe the snowstorm we had a couple weeks ago," said Ellie. "Forty-eight hours without power, and I'm still trying to get warm."

"I wish you and Chris had taken me up on coming to our house," said Joan. "A generator makes all the difference." Alice nodded her head.

"He likes to be home in a storm," said Ellie, "to keep an eye on things. I told him it's a lot easier to keep an eye on things when they aren't frozen in their sockets."

Alice laughed. "Get him a generator—for his birthday or something."

Ellie smiled. "That would, actually, be right in his wheelhouse. I like that idea."

Joan studied the menu and said, "Do you two already know what you want?"

"We're sitting in a steakhouse," said Alice. "I'm going with steak."

"For thirty-six dollars?" asked Joan, checking out the steak options and their associated cost.

Ellie reached over the table and took the menu from Joan long enough to flip it over. "These are the lunch specials," she said. "I checked ahead of time so we wouldn't be looking at a $150 check."

"Good thinking," said Joan. She'd had just one vodka drink at the roulette table before lunch, but the alcohol had gone right to her head. She had skipped breakfast, so she needed to put something in her stomach to absorb the booze. When their server came to the table, Joan ordered a steak sandwich with French fries and a large glass of ice water. Ellie ordered a sirloin burger, and Alice requested the flank steak salad. "Now that that's done," said Joan, putting the white cloth napkin in her lap, "catch me up on your lives."

"Alice, you start," said Ellie. "I want to hear all about the new store."

"First, I want to thank both of you for coming to the opening," said Alice. "You were really nice to do that."

"It was fun," said Ellie. "My new walking shoes are incredible. And Dave was right; they're much warmer than what I wore to the store."

"I have yet to try my cross-trainers," said Joan, "but they look beautiful in the box."

Alice smiled at Joan. "I think things are going well. Dave has been pleasantly surprised by the customer turnout because he cut back on advertising to save money. The kids who work for the store told Dave they'd spread the word via social media—and so far it seems to be working. Have you seen the new Facebook page?"

"Not yet," said Ellie.

"Here," said Alice, again reaching for her phone. "Let me show it to you." It took Alice less than a minute to sign on to the casino's wireless network and to find the Fast Pace Facebook page. Alice handed the phone to Ellie, next to her, who looked at it and then handed the phone to Joan.

"This looks good," she said. "And look, you already have eight hundred likes." Joan didn't have a Facebook page, mostly because she thought social media was a tool developed for her daughters' generation. She'd seen the Facebook pages of her bankers' wives friends, who routinely posted girls-night-out pictures of themselves and then, in the comments section, congratulated one another on their cute outfits, for looking so hot or young, or for being so much fun! Boastbook is what Joan thought it should be called. She did, though, see the merit in using it for business promotion. From the limited exposure she'd had to the platform, Joan thought Facebook users were the best self-promoters out there.

"Any more thoughts about working there?" asked Ellie.

"Yes and no," said Alice, sitting back in her chair while their server placed her steak salad in front of her. "I'm not sure I'd enjoy it the way I did before the girls were born. And Dave isn't pushing me. I mean, he's pushing me to do something, but he's not pushing me to do something at the store. He seems to be happy with the kids on his team. They have weekly pizza meetings now, in addition to running together twice a week."

"Is this something you can do with them—the running?" asked Joan, shaking salt on her fries.

Alice shook her head. "They're way beyond me. I could never keep up. And even if I tried, they would resent my slowing them down."

"Really?" asked Ellie. "These great kids that you keep telling us about would treat you like that?"

Alice put her hands up, palms facing out, next to her shoulders. "Hey, I get it," she said. "I know how they feel. When you get to a certain stage as a runner, you only want to look and move forward. I used to be like that myself."

"But it still kind of stinks," said Joan, lifting her sandwich to her mouth.

"I'm getting used to running alone," said Alice. "And I'm always on the lookout when I'm on the trails for my next running buddy."

"You can always walk with me if you get too lonely," said Ellie. "I know it's not the same as running, but it's nice to have company."

"Thanks," said Alice.

"So, Joan, what about you?" asked Ellie. "What are you doing to keep yourself out of trouble? Any more thought about teaching calculus at the high school?"

"Oh God, did I actually say that out loud?" said Joan. "I'm not sure I want to do that. I'm not sure I even have the ambition to pursue that. I'm so out of practice. Do I really want to start a career now, in my early fifties? Or am I just talking?"

"Talking is good," said Ellie. "If we don't talk about this, explore what's next for us, then we run the risk of making uninformed choices or doing nothing at all. Doing nothing at all, making no change, is fine, as long as that's what we want to do. Do you want to make changes in your life, Joan?" Ellie was surprised and pleased to hear these words, based on Diana's ideas, coming out of her mouth.

Joan ate a fry that she had just dredged through the mound of ketchup on her plate. "It's complicated," she said, chewing. "First, Stephen doesn't want me to work—mostly, I think, because his mother doesn't want me to work. She's a charming woman, but she's enormously big on that keeping up appearances thing, even though she's eighty-three and doesn't need to keep up with anyone. She would be embarrassed if I got a job because then all her friends would think that Stephen wasn't making enough money to support his family. The notion that a woman might want to work, might want to realize her intellectual potential, might want to make her own money, is absolutely unfathomable to the Howard family. Why would a woman work, when she can shop for nice clothes, attend her children's daytime recitals and sporting events, and volunteer at church and in the community instead?"

"That is such backward thinking," said Alice, shaking her head. "Do they think women should vote?"

Joan laughed. "As long as they're voting according to their husbands' wishes."

"So, what are you going to do?" asked Ellie.

"I'm going to take it slowly," said Joan. "As long as I don't make any rash moves, nobody gets hurt!"

"Let's hope you don't die of boredom in the meantime," said Alice. "If I weren't running, I'd be completely crazy by now. I've cleaned out and organized the girls' rooms, the attic, and the basement, so I'm now on a first name basis with Jacob at Goodwill. And I've helped at the store here and there, when Dave was short a worker, and for the opening of the new store, of course. But every time I'm there, at one store or the other, I'm thinking that I belong somewhere else. Maybe I'm just out of practice, too."

"Maybe," said Ellie. "But maybe you haven't found the right thing. Is that what you're thinking?"

"Yes," said Alice. "But I've got to find *something*. Time is suddenly hanging heavy. Ellie, you've got your bookkeeping to occupy and challenge you. Joan, what are you doing to stop you from losing your mind in your empty house?"

Joan swallowed the bite of sandwich in her mouth and gently wiped the A.1. sauce from her lips. "Who says I haven't lost it?" Alice and Ellie smiled at her, thinking, Joan guessed, that she was kidding. But the remark was more truthful than humorous. In the last month, she had been at the casino three or four times a week. She'd spent three hours each time at what had become her favorite roulette table, sipping no more than two vodka drinks, followed by a large glass of ice water and two cups of black coffee. And, if her calculations were correct, she'd lost a thousand dollars. The croupiers and pit bosses called her by name and hit on her almost as much as the solo businessmen did. She had not had such attention paid to her since her drinking days in college.

"You'll figure it out," said Ellie. "As my mother says, 'You've got a good head on your shoulders.' "

Alice drizzled more dressing from the small pitcher that had arrived with her salad onto her greens. "Do you ever wonder if you're more lonely than crazy? I really miss having Linda at home. She and I were more like friends than mother and daughter."

"I feel the same way," said Joan. "While Liz certainly had her own friends, my relationship with her was much more easygoing than my relationship with Cassie. I was very regimented, very strict with Cassie, in terms of what she could and couldn't do. I was tougher on her than I ever was on Liz. So when Liz left the house, it really did feel like I was losing a companion. Did you feel the same way about your boys, Ellie?"

"In some ways, yes. Like you, Joan, I was harder on Brandon and easier on Tim. But they also gravitated toward Chris as they moved through high school. I know he misses them as much as I do."

"And what about your relationship with Chris?" asked Alice. "Has that changed?"

Ellie reddened. "What do you mean?"

"I don't know," said Alice, spearing a piece of steak with her fork. "I can't really put my finger on it, but I feel like my relationship with Dave is different."

"How is it different?" asked Joan, who'd had similar, yet undeveloped thoughts run through her head.

Alice chewed and swallowed the steak in her mouth. "I hear some women talk about how the period after their kids leave the house is like a second honeymoon. I'm not feeling that. I feel like Dave has moved ahead without me. I feel like he's got expectations for who he thinks I am. But how can he think he knows who I am at fifty-five when I don't even know who I am? And I feel like he's impatient with me, or just too occupied with his own life to help."

"Because he's so busy?" asked Ellie.

"Maybe," said Alice. "I've dropped to fourth place on his list of priorities, behind the business, his beloved employees, and way behind running."

"Okay," said Joan, "but to take the other side for a moment, where was Dave on your list of priorities when you were raising the girls? And let me answer for you—somewhere between fourth, after Linda, Hilary, and Cathy, and tenth, after doing whatever it took to stay in shape, getting your errands done, baking, etcetera. We are lost right now because we feel like our husbands have turned their backs on us or moved ahead without us. But, in reality, didn't we turn our backs on them first?"

"Point made," said Alice. "But someone had to take care of the children. And our husbands are grown-ups who can take care of themselves."

"I'm not sure that I did turn my back on Chris," said Ellie. "I've given him attention all through our marriage. I've worked hard at it. My problem is that it wasn't reciprocated. To be clear, Chris has always been attentive to me. But it's in a way that pleases him rather than pleases me."

"What do you mean?" asked Alice.

"Chris is a big doer, but he's not a big talker—even though he said we'd have more time for conversation once the kids were gone. Tim has been gone for four and a half months, and nothing has changed. I try to talk with Chris, and while I do think he's making an attempt to talk back more than he used to, he's not talking in the way that I want him to talk to me. Am I doing something wrong? Am I expecting too much?"

Alice leaned in toward Ellie. "No, you're not. Maybe you're not making yourself clear? That's what Dave always tells me. I think I'm saying one thing, but he seems to be hearing another."

"That's exactly what it is," said Ellie. "How do I fix that?"

"Good question," said Alice. "If you can solve that problem, you can run for president, and every woman in America will vote for you."

FEBRUARY

CHAPTER 19

When Alice heard the weather forecast on the radio, she decided to postpone her run until the afternoon, when the sun would be out and the temperature would climb to the mid-thirties. Lately, she had been running in the morning, after Dave left for work and before her day got started. And, because she owned two running stores, she certainly had all the gear for winter running. But, unlike Dave, Alice didn't enjoy running in freezing temperatures; she preferred running in the spring and fall, on a crisp day, under a startlingly blue sky. Dave loved running in any kind of weather. In the winter, he'd walk back into the house with a grin on his face and often say, "It feels good to be alive."

And so, after eating a late breakfast and doing a few errands, Alice changed into her running tights, long-sleeved shirt, jacket, socks, and shoes. She grabbed a lightweight hat, a pair of gloves, and the whistle Joan had given her for Christmas from the basket that held such things in the back hall, and walked out the door. Six minutes later, she was parked in the empty lot adjacent to the head of her latest favorite running trail, which the town plowed and salted as needed in the winter. On it, she could run along the river for a mile before turning into the woods for a two-mile loop and then returning to the same section of trail to end her run. She was now up to four miles, about half of what she had run on a regular basis when she was younger. She ran it in just over forty minutes; she had run the eight miles in her mid-twenties in just over fifty-five minutes. At first, this new, much slower time was hard for her to accept. But Dave had commended her progress, telling her to focus on the future instead of on the past. Plus, it was winter, she told herself. Once spring came, she could run in shorts and a T-shirt, in perfect fifty-degree air, and her mile-per-minute ratio would improve.

She got out of the car and stood next to it for a moment to perform what she called an assessment. This was the time to decide about the hat, gloves, and jacket because she didn't like carrying anything in her hands while she ran. She always had her phone with her, but she could zip it into the back pocket of her pants and barely notice its existence. She brought it along for a few reasons: One, she would be available if one of her daughters called; two, she could use the phone if she got injured and needed help; and three, it stored her music. She had made herself a dozen running playlists, ranging from a cappella singing and acoustic guitar to hip-hop and rock. She chose to run without her hat, but with her gloves. And Bruce Springsteen's *Born to Run* would serve as her inspiration.

Alice turned into the woods just after Bruce had finished jamming through "Night" and was wailing the lyrics of "Backstreets." Her legs were fully warmed up and her knees, which routinely gave her trouble, felt better than they had all week. It was the warmer temperature, she thought. It was kinder to her joints. Her hair, normally held captive by a coated elastic, flew untethered behind her. She felt strong as she ran along the narrow section of trail bordered by thick evergreen trees; her breathing was easy, normal even. A split second later, shoved from behind, she was facedown on the trail, with blood spurting from a flattened nose and something on top of her. "Get off of me!" she screamed, not turning her head to see what she was certain was a bear. There had been news reports of a black bear near the trail. Runners had been advised to make noise along their route. When Alice reached for her whistle, the thing on her back lifted her head by her hair and smashed her cheek back down on the icy pavement. A flash of light exploded behind her eyes, and excruciating pain filled the right side of her face. Blood was now pouring out of her nose. "As soon as you give me what I want, bitch." Alice's heart, a cable-snapped elevator, dropped into her stomach. It was not a bear or another wild beast; it was a man, a rapist. Her breathing quickened; her heart rate soared; sweat soaked her armpits. She told herself to calm down, but her body didn't listen. Her bladder released a tablespoon of urine. He pushed himself up off Alice, but quickly put one knee on her back, keeping her pinned to the ground. He put his mouth to her ear and kissed it. He whispered, "You're going to make this nice and easy, sweet blond baby." Alice used her hands to push off the ground, but he used his to shove her back down. She closed her eyes, focusing on the whistle around her neck. Because it had bounced up and down on her chest when she ran, she had tucked it into her jacket at the end of the river section of the trail. "I'm going to spin you over onto your back, so I can get at what I want." And when he flipped her, she instantly understood the formidability of her foe.

Dave was five foot eleven, one hundred sixty pounds; this man was taller and bigger, maybe fifty pounds heavier. He was dressed in oversized black jeans and a very large, puffy black coat. He had red hair and green eyes and very white skin, with no trace of pink from the cold. He had no facial hair, except for two thin lines of short hair that served as eyebrows. He looked to be in his late twenties, maybe early thirties. She willed herself to stare at his face, to remember details that she would be questioned about later. She wondered for a moment if there would even be a later, or if this man would rape her and then kill her. "You think I'm handsome?" he asked her, his calloused hand wrapped around her neck. He leaned in closer. "You staring at me because you think I'm handsome, pretty lady?"

Alice's heart thundered beneath her jacket, beneath her whistle. She had no saliva; her breathing was shallow and rapid, like it had been when she gave birth to her daughters. She felt nauseous. But she forced herself to look into his eyes, to concentrate on what was happening. She had thought about this moment, all women did, about what it would feel like to be overpowered by a man with evil intent. And she had seen this kind of scene played out in movies and on television, and she had thought, at the time, that she would be like all the strong women, who were able to ward off their attackers with fast talk and quick knees. Instead, she said, "Take off my pants."

A slight smile spread across his lower face, not reaching his eyes or his forehead. "You want it, don't you? Your man don't satisfy you like I can. You want me, baby, like I want you." As soon as he removed his hand from her throat, as soon as his massive body was in motion, shifting its focus, its weight, from her face to her chest, to the waistband of her tights, Alice slowly reached into her jacket for her whistle. She got it into her mouth just as the man was using both hands to pull her running tights down to her knees. Alice used her abdominal muscles, strengthened by daily core exercises in her family room, to lift her upper body into a sitting position. She leaned forward, her head close to his, and blew as hard as she could on the whistle, which was three inches from his ear. His hands flew from her bare thighs to his head. Alice scrambled to her feet. Breathing hard, she kicked him in the groin and then pulled up her pants and ran back toward the river. Ten yards down the trail, she looked behind her. Her right eye was swollen shut, but her left eye could see that he was still on the ground. She ran faster, blowing her whistle every time she exhaled. Another thirty yards from him, Alice stopped to vomit. She looked back to see him getting up from the ground, and she started moving again, running even faster, intensifying the pain in her throbbing face and sending more blood out of her nose. She was crying now, blowing the whistle, running as fast as she could, looking back over her shoulder every twenty yards. He was not following her.

As soon as she got to her car, she grabbed the key from the top of the right rear tire and used it to open the driver's door. She launched herself inside and used her left hand to push the automatic locking device and her right hand to direct the key to the ignition. She missed twice, the trembling in her fingers, wrist, and forearm preventing her from inserting the key, from getting farther away. She steadied her right wrist with her left hand and was able to insert the key and start the car. She yanked the shifter into reverse and stepped on the gas pedal. The car flew backward, stopped by a towering snow bank. Gasping for breath, she pulled the knob into the drive position and roared out of the lot. As she drove, she pulled her phone from the pocket of her pants and called Dave. When she got his voice mail, she shouted, "I've been attacked on the running trails! Dave, please help me! I'm going to the police station!" and hung up.

The female officer she spoke to at the Southwood police station apologized for the fact that she had to take photos of Alice's face. Afterward she helped Alice, still shaking involuntarily, clean up in the newly constructed, handicapped-accessible bathroom. Alice remembered reading in the newspaper about the renovations to the police station, thinking them excessive at the time. Now, she was thankful for the large sink, the bright lighting, and the bench, where she could sit comfortably while Officer Walsh, who told Alice to call her Marilyn, gently washed her face with a soft cloth. "I'm sorry to say I think your nose is broken," Marilyn said. "But it's a good break, meaning I think it will heal nicely. You will not forget this day, but a month from now you will not look like your nose was broken."

Unable to act brave for another second, Alice started to cry, her teetering composure crumbling. "I'm sorry," she said, tears spilling out of her eyes.

"I'm the one who's sorry," said Marilyn. "I'm sorry this happened to you. I'm sorry you're sitting here right now. But as soon as you're all cleaned up, we'll start the process of catching the animal that did this to you."

Sitting in a chair next to Officer Walsh's desk, Alice told the story of what had happened to her on the running trails. She described where she was attacked, the approximate time of the attack, the physical details of her attacker, as well as what he said to her. Marilyn asked her to describe his voice: Did he have an accent? And she asked Alice to focus on his face: Was there anything other than the paleness of his skin? Birthmarks? Scars? Tattoos? What would distinguish him from all the other bad guys out there? What would help the department catch him? Marilyn asked Alice to close her eyes, and when she did, Alice was startled when an image of the man popped into her head. "His lips," said Alice. "His lips were red, almost as if he'd been wearing lipstick and had rubbed it off, leaving a residue. They were like blood on snow."

Marilyn nodded her head as she continued taking notes. "That's helpful," she said, handing Alice another tissue from the value-sized box on her desk. As Alice dried the fresh tears from her cheeks, she again checked her phone, which was sitting on Officer Walsh's desk, and had also sat on the bench in the bathroom. There was still no word from Dave. And while Alice knew that he wasn't always accessible and that he was bad about checking his messages, she was angry that he had not called her, had not somehow known she was in trouble. "Anything?" asked Marilyn.

"No," said Alice.

"That's the funny thing about cell phones," said Marilyn. "We have them so we can be in constant contact—but that hardly ever happens. The battery dies. We forget that we switched off the ringer. This kind of thing happens all the time."

Alice gave Marilyn a slight smile, even though it hurt to do so. She knew the officer was trying to make her feel better about the fact that she had nearly been raped and her husband was still un-available, for whatever reason, to comfort her. Dave was short-staffed that day; Alice knew this because he had texted her that morning. The flu was running through his young employees, the twenty-somethings who didn't get enough sleep and didn't believe in getting the flu shot, who still thought themselves invincible even though they got sick twice as often as people twice their age. When Alice had asked Dave if he wanted her to come in, he had told her he actually welcomed the opportunity to get out of his office and onto the sales floor. Working directly with the customer was the best way, in his opinion, of getting feedback. Online surveys had their place, but there was nothing like a face to face encounter to know if a product was good, bad, or, even worse, average. The de-sign and materials used to construct shoes that half the people liked and half the people didn't were the hardest to tweak.

And so Alice sent a group text message to Ellie and Joan, asking if they could come to the police station together so that one of them could drive Alice's car home. Officer Walsh told Alice that she had been able to drive her car to the station on pure adrenaline, but that it wasn't a good idea for her to drive home. And within seconds, both women said they would be there in ten minutes.

When they arrived at the station, they were escorted through the locked door next to the reception desk. Ellie and Joan had stated their names and their purpose through the perforations in the bulletproof glass that separated them from the officer asking for their information. On the inside of the glass, of the locked door, they were greeted warmly, taken directly to Alice, and asked if they wanted coffee. Ellie's hands flew to her mouth as soon as she saw her battered friend.

"Oh God," said Joan, using the exact words that would have come out of Ellie's mouth had her hands not been in the way. Joan reached down and gently hugged Alice. Ellie did the same. Joan then turned to face Officer Walsh. "What can we do to help?"

The officer told them to take Alice to the emergency room for an evaluation. "Her nose is broken, and she probably has a concussion," Marilyn said. "As you can see, she's already developing a nasty contusion on the right side of her face, as well as having more superficial cuts and scrapes on other parts of her body. After that, take her home and stay with her until her husband gets there." Marilyn spoke to Alice. "Are you ready to go?" Alice nodded her head.

Joan and Ellie helped Alice into the front seat of Joan's Range Rover, and then Ellie took Alice's keys from her and said she'd follow them in Alice's car. At the hospital, they learned that the officer's suspicions were correct; Alice had a broken nose, a hairline fractured cheekbone, a concussion, multiple cuts and scrapes, and emerging bruises. She was given a prescription for pain medication and told to avoid aspirin products, restrict physical activity for at least two weeks, rest as much as possible, and schedule a follow-up visit with her primary care doctor. On the way from the hospital to Alice's house, Alice's cell phone rang.

"Alice, honey, it's me. Are you okay? What happened?" Instead of being reassured, calmed by Dave's voice, Alice was angered.

"Oh, so you got the voice mail that I left for you"—she looked at her plastic watch that was still clocking her run—"three hours ago?"

"Shit, I know. I just listened to it. I'm sorry. It's this damned midwinter blowout sale," he said. "I've been on the floor with customers nonstop all afternoon." He waited. Alice wondered if he expected sympathy from her. She said nothing, concentrating on her breathing. "Where are you now, sweetheart?"

Alice took a moment to select her words. "My friends Joan and Ellie are taking me home. They've been with me at the police station and in the emergency room—every step of the way, they've been with me. I have a broken nose, a broken cheekbone, a concussion, and a banged up body. My friends have further offered to be at home with me, since we had no idea what the hell you were up to or when you'd show up."

"I just turned the car onto the highway," said Dave. "You know I was at the Kensington store today. I'll be home in thirty minutes. I'm so sorry this happened, Alice, and that I didn't respond to your voice mail sooner."

"Me too." Alice pushed the end call button on her cell phone.

As soon as Joan and Ellie heard Dave's voice as he came through Alice's back door, they stood and put their coats on, hugged Alice and, after very quick hellos with Dave when he found them all in the family room, made their way out of the Stones' house. Dave looked at his wife on the couch and said, "Oh my God! Alice, I had no idea you were so beat up. Honey, are you okay?"

"No," said Alice, her voice rising. "I am not okay! I hurt everywhere, and I am furious—more so at you than at the monster who attacked me!"

"Honey," said Dave, approaching her.

"Don't touch me!" screamed Alice. "Don't come near me! You, Dave, are why this happened! It's your fault! I've asked you a hundred times to run with me, and each and every time you turned me down. What kind of husband does that?" Dave opened his mouth. Alice held up her hands. "I'll tell you what kind of husband—a shitty husband! A self-absorbed husband! A bastard!" Dave lowered his chin, lowered his gaze to the floor. "Yes, that's right," said

Alice. "Bow your head in humiliation." When he raised his head, there were tears in his eyes. "It's a little late for that," said Alice, arms folded tightly across her chest.

"What can I do for you, Alice," asked Dave, submissive, subdued.

"Nothing," said Alice. "I want nothing from you."

Dave removed his coat and hung it on the back of the desk chair in front of him. "I'll run you a tub," he said. "And I'll help you out of your clothes."

"Just get out of my sight," said Alice. "Get the hell away from me." She closed her eyes. And when she opened them, Dave was gone.

Chapter 20

Alice cut her last piece of butternut squash filled ravioli in half and dragged it through the remaining pesto sauce on her plate. "I feel unsettled," she said. "If I can put a name on it, that's what I feel—unsettled."

They had talked about her blowup at Dave, which both Joan and Ellie said was completely justified. And they talked about all the physical ailments, her nose, her face, her head injury, the scratches, the cuts, the bruises—all of which were healing and were, aside from the concussion which had never been visible, much less prominent. Alice hadn't left the house much the first week after the incident. She had referred to herself as a freak show and had not, she told Joan and Ellie over coffee in her kitchen on the first Wednesday instead of meeting at a restaurant for lunch, wanted to force her ugliness and its accompanying trauma on the people out there who were simply trying to shop for groceries or wander the aisles of the hardware store. She did not want to have to endure their lingering stares, their probing questions, or their sympathetic countenances. Although what happened on the running trails would be stored in her memory for as long as she lived, she was tired of telling the story—even though she knew it should be heard.

Joan reached across the table and gave Alice's bruised right hand a very gentle squeeze. "Of course you feel unsettled," she said. "How can we help you?"

"I wish you could help," said Alice, reaching for her water. "But I think I have to do this myself. I have to get better and feel stronger on my own."

Joan shook her head. "No, you don't. This is what friends are for," she said. "Push the social lunches and text messages aside, and this is what friendship comes down to—being present when you are needed."

Alice's eyes brimmed with tears. She had been overly emotional since the attack, quick to tears and flashes of anger. She had yelled at Dave that very morning for spilling his coffee on the kitchen floor that she had washed the day before, telling him that he would never understand the difficulties and challenges of being a woman. She knew afterward that the connection between the spilled drink and the gender issues was an emotional response. But it was real for her. She had been thinking about what women have suffered at the hands and minds of men for centuries—and the spilled coffee seemed to illustrate this power struggle perfectly. Men sometimes didn't know what dicks they were, how little they paid attention to what seemed to be the little things in life, which were, in fact, representative of much larger questions. "And I want you to be present," said Alice, making eye contact with Joan and then Ellie. "But I also increasingly feel that I need to do this alone."

"What do you need to do?" asked Joan.

Alice hesitated a moment before saying, "I need to feel strong and safe." She reached into the bread basket at the center of the table. Alice rarely ate bread, but she took a piece and slid it through the last puddle of pesto sauce still on her plate. She held it in front of her mouth as she said, as casually as if she had been commenting on Joan's new handbag, "I'm thinking about getting a gun."

The silence was instant, as if someone had muted the conversation. No one moved. They were barely breathing, until Joan said, "Alice?"

Alice held up her hands in front of her. "I know what you're going to say, Joan. I understand your viewpoint. Mine is different. It always has been, but it is especially so after what happened to me."

"Tell us more," said Ellie.

The tears returned to Alice's eyes. "I don't know what else to do," she said. "I don't know what to say to my daughters. I'm terrified that something like this might happen to them. And I don't know what to do with my husband. Since I screamed at him, Dave has tried to be sympathetic and caring. But I can tell he thinks, deep down, that this will go away. It's like he's nursing me through the flu. He doesn't understand that the problem is systemic."

Joan momentarily closed her eyes. Alice had been spending a lot of her time at home on the Internet, researching women's rights groups, reading about gender inequality. And a number of the articles Alice had shared by e-mail with her and Ellie made sense. But it was easy to claim the world was run by men, that men had all the power. The historical relationship between men and women was a lot more complicated than the versions offered by zealot Web sites; forward movement certainly did follow radical action, but only if accompanied by deep reflection, uncommon levels of patience, and long spans of time. And Joan did not think that owning a gun was part of the solution, of any solution.

"I can't change the world," Alice said, as if reading Joan's thoughts. "But I can change mine."

"Will you really feel safer with a gun?" asked Joan, as gently as she could.

Alice raised her eyebrows. "Of course I will, Joan. With a gun, I can run again. With a gun, I can walk through a dark parking lot at night with confidence."

"With a gun you can win arguments?" asked Joan.

"I don't think that's what Alice is talking about," said Ellie.

"And I understand that," said Joan. "But what happens when emotions surrounding an event escalate? If you'd had a gun the day of your attack, would you have shot the man who tried to rape you?"

"Absolutely," said Alice.

"I don't think it's a yes or no question," said Ellie. "There is a lot of in-between ground, Joan. If Alice had had a gun on the trail, she might have just pointed it at the man. She might have frightened him off."

"Yes," said Alice. "And if that didn't work, I would have shot the asshole."

"There are repercussions. There are consequences to that, too," said Joan.

Alice shook her head. "I can't believe you're fighting me on this."

Joan breathed in through her nose and exhaled through her mouth. "I'm not fighting you, Alice. I'm worried about you. I'm worried about what might happen. You're emotional right now. Sometimes our emotions can cloud our reasoning."

"Yeah, I'm emotional," said Alice. "I came close to getting raped two weeks ago. Jesus, Joan."

"I'm sorry, Alice," said Joan.

"I'm not an idiot, Joan," Alice said. "If I get a gun, I will learn everything about it. I'll keep it locked up when it's not on my person. And I'll probably never use it. But owning one and carrying one when I need it will help me no longer feel afraid. I can't count on Dave to save me. I've got to save myself."

Their server, who had left them alone for ten minutes, eased up to their table and asked if he could get them anything else. "The check," said Joan.

CHAPTER 2 1

Joan was determined to win the money back, even though Stephen didn't know it was missing, and, therefore, hadn't questioned her about it. She had been taking cash withdrawals from a bank he was not associated with, from an account she had opened the year before in secret. Since she didn't have a job with a paycheck, the only deposits she made were the weekly checks Stephen wrote to her. He gave her five hundred dollars every Sunday night to do with as she wished. The money was not for groceries, bills, or other household items; it was for her. She could use it to buy clothes, take an educational or creative class, or eat lunch out with friends. All the Howard women got weekly allowances for their amusement. They were all discouraged by their husbands from talking about the amount they received, but Joan, a numbers person since early childhood, had figured out what her sisters-in-law, mother-in-law, and various Howard cousins *made,* based on their purchases and conversations. At two thousand a month, Joan was at the lower end of the scale. This was not because Stephen was stingy. It was more because, although he complied with the practice, he thought the idea of a twenty-first-century husband writing weekly checks to his spouse was archaic. He had long ago told her to put whatever she needed on her credit card.

And while Joan thought the issuance of the weekly checks from a husband to a wife was insulting, she cashed them. She put up with a number of Howard traditions because she had been raised to do as she was told, because she knew her protests would be misunderstood, because her opinion would always be outvoted. The Howard women liked their role in the family. They enjoyed preparing and serving their communal meals. They took pride in their appearance, presenting to the world freshly made up faces and snappy, if a bit conservative, clothing. The Howard women were involved with several local charities, including one to benefit Southwood Hospital and another to send underprivileged kids to summer camp. They lived comfortable lives, the Howard women, and made no apologies to those who judged their existence as anything less than exemplary. Over the years, Joan had come to admire them. This was not because they could make a cheese soufflé without a recipe or collected thousand-dollar scarves like others, less financially fortunate, collected shapely pinecones or smooth beach stones. It was because the Howard women knew who ran their households—and it was not their investment banker husbands. They were an intimidating force, and when Joan was amongst them, their influence was palpable.

Before her losses amounted to real money, Joan's bank account balance had been close to six thousand dollars. It was money she was planning on using to pay for a vacation for Stephen's fifty-fifth birthday. And while she still had two more years to save, she knew that a top-notch holiday for a family of four—one worthy of Howard approval and, perhaps, envy or imitation—would cost at least double that amount. And now she was down to four thousand. Plus, she needed to buy a dress for Stephen's cousin's black-tie wedding, and that would cost at least a thousand. On her way from her car to the casino, Joan again analyzed her gaming strategy, tried to figure out why she was losing. At first, she had played only numbers that meant something to her: birthdays, anniversaries, and other dates; phone number sequences; even meaningful highway exit numbers. And then she had branched out to random, chance numbers that popped into her head or had been successful for others at the table. There had been no pattern. She had been winning, and now she was losing. She had fleetingly thought about trying another game, blackjack or craps. But the former seemed to require more knowledge of card playing than Joan possessed at the moment, and the latter involved throwing dice, which Joan had decided was juvenile. Plus, it had a distasteful name.

There was an elegance to roulette that appealed to Joan—the noiseless spin of the wheel; the long seconds the ball traveled around its track; the *pink-pink-pink* sound of the ball bouncing from one number to another. The statistics that ruled other games—what were the chances of rolling a seven or an eleven?—didn't seem to apply to roulette. All things were possible. This was exactly what was running through Joan's mind when she took her normal seat at her normal table in the section of the casino she had long ago learned was called Earth. Chaz, her favorite croupier, winked at her when she sat down. He was attentive to her needs and just flirtatious enough to give her the confidence she needed to play longer than she knew she should.

"Red or blue today, Ms. Joan?" he asked when the demands of the previous bet had been satisfied.

"Green."

"Mixing it up a bit? I like that," said Chaz. "How many?"

"Five hundred," said Joan, pulling five crisp bills from her wallet.

"I like that too," said Chaz. "A bold move. Are we imbibing this afternoon?"

Joan looked at her watch. She had four hours before she had to be home to start the pasta dish Stephen had requested for dinner. "Sure," she said.

Three hours later, she finished her second cup of coffee. The buzz from the back-to-back vodka drinks she'd had when she sat down was gone, replaced by fatigue. The coffee had perked her up, but it had done nothing to stifle the sense and scent of dread that pervaded her brain and body. The adrenaline that had been pumped into her bloodstream had run its course; she was fed up and anxious to get home. And she was down another thousand dollars. She tossed her last chip at Chaz, a tip for his kindness, and stood. "I'm off."

"Bad luck today," he said, dropping the chip into his shirt pocket. "You played well. I'm surprised by the outcome."

"Me too," said Joan, wrapping Ellie's gray scarf around her neck.

"Are you coming in tomorrow?" Chaz had just spun the wheel. Joan watched it, as she had all afternoon.

"No," said Joan, breaking eye contact with the wheel and making it with Chaz. "Maybe on Friday."

"I work ten to six on Friday," he said. "Come see me."

Joan gave him a weak smile before she turned her back. The uneasy sensation had moved from her head to her chest to her stomach, an unwelcome companion to the iced vodka and hot coffee. She suppressed a burp and then quickened her pace, knowing from experience that the next eruption would contain liquid as well as gas. She walked quickly into the ladies' room just outside the Earth casino. She burst into a stall, dropped to her knees, and vomited her lunchtime egg salad sandwich and then, eventually, bile into the toilet bowl. Afterward, Joan slowly lifted her exhausted body, moist from perspiration brought on by retching a half dozen times, off the floor. Standing but wobbly, she braced her arms against the stall walls for balance. She made her way to the sink, where she wet several paper towels and used them to dab her face, to regain cognizance and composure.

"Are you all right, honey?" It was a voice coming from behind the closed door of the stall next to the one Joan had just vacated.

"Yes," said Joan. "I'm fine. Thank you."

A brief hesitation followed by, "Are you pregnant, dear?"

Joan laughed. "If I am, call the national news station."

The woman in the stall did not laugh. "It's the drink then," she said.

Joan looked at her face in the mirror. Her mascara and lipstick were smeared. She had a coffee dribble stain on her white cashmere sweater that she was sure Chaz and everyone she had passed on the way to the bathroom had seen. Her face was ashen. "Yes," said Joan. "It's the drink."

CHAPTER 22

Joan, who had won two hundred dollars that morning and not had one sip of vodka in the process, was humming when Ellie approached the table. "I'm not sure I've ever heard you hum," said Ellie.

Joan looked up and smiled at her friend. "No?"

"And if I have, it was definitely not Bachman-Turner Overdrive."

Joan laughed. " 'Takin' Care of Business' is definitely in my top ten," she said. "What's going on with you?"

"Not much," said Ellie, shedding her coat and sitting across the table from Joan. "Chris pulled a muscle in his back shoveling snow over the weekend, which means I've again got a child living at home."

Joan shook her head. "Aren't they the worst? Stephen comes running to me when he's got a splinter."

Ellie laughed now. "We've done the cold packs, the heating pad, the ibuprofen, the massages. I think I've pulled something in my back taking care of his." Joan smiled. "I know it's painful. I haven't had back issues, and I hear they are awful—and so I feel for him. I do. But the neediness level is off the charts. I mean, this guy was an athlete. He should know how to take care of himself, right?"

"Why take care of yourself if you can get someone else to do it for you?" asked Joan.

"Hey, I meant to tell you that I'm glad you suggested we squeeze in two lunches this month, even though we're off schedule. I think it means a lot to Alice."

"I think so, too."

"Before she gets here, I've got something to tell you," said Ellie, leaning in toward Joan, who mirrored Ellie's movement. "Alice is moving forward with buying a gun."

Joan sat back. "Shit."

"Wait a minute," said Ellie, tilting the left side of her face toward Joan, as a mother might when making a listen up point to a child. "She's doing research. She'll take lessons. She's getting all kinds of advice about how, when, and if to use a firearm. She's not taking this lightly. And I'm only telling you because I know how you feel about it. But you might want to take it down a notch because you and I haven't been through what she's been through."

Just as their server was filling their water glasses, Alice strode up to the table. "Hey," said Joan, making eye contact with Alice. "You look really good. How's the head?"

"Clearer," said Alice, hanging her coat on the back of her chair. "And the headaches are less intense."

"I'm so glad," said Joan.

Alice looked at Joan for a moment before shifting her gaze to Ellie. "You told her," she said.

"Told her what?" Ellie picked up the menu and looked at the lunch specials.

Alice looked back at Joan. "You told her about the gun."

"Yes, yes, yes," said Joan. "She told me about the gun. Now sit down, and you tell me about it."

Alice sat down in the chair next to Ellie, her back rigid against the wood slats it barely touched. "I'm just about ready to purchase a Glock 42; it's a semiautomatic pistol," said Alice. "I'm going to learn how to use it, and I'm going to carry it on my body when I feel like I need protection. End of story."

Joan picked up her menu, but she didn't open it. "It sounds like the beginning of the story to me."

Alice picked up her menu, but stared at Joan. "If you think I'm receptive to an uninformed discussion about guns today, you're wrong. Every once in a while, Joan, you're wrong."

"Why are you so defensive about this?" asked Joan. "Why are you so angry?"

Alice dropped her menu, her eyes wide open and a vein visible now on her left temple. "Are you kidding me?"

"Hey, hey, Alice," said Ellie. "It's okay. It's okay. We're friends here. We're supporting you." She looked at Joan.

"Yeah, well, one of you is supporting me a whole lot more than the other."

Joan had never been very good at backing down from an argument that mattered to her. She could easily keep silent when it didn't matter, which was often the case with whatever topic arose at Howard family get-togethers. They discussed interesting things—local and national politics, sports contests, ethical questions—but in a low-stakes, jocular way. No one switched sides or was perceptively moved by these discussions. Everyone's mind was made up and firm; the conversation was just that, conversation. Joan participated in these family chats, but she didn't fervently express her opinion, simply because it didn't really matter. Whether or not Alice bought a gun did matter, not only to Alice, but also to Joan. She made eye contact with Alice. "I understand what happened to you. . . ."

"No!" said Alice, her voice rising. "No, you don't understand what happened to me—unless, of course, you've had a near-rape experience and haven't shared it with us."

"I understand what happened to you," Joan started again, "was extremely upsetting. I understand you were terrified. And I understand your need to feel protected, to stop this from ever happening again. What I don't understand is how you know you're ready to take someone else's life."

"Joan," said Ellie. "Alice isn't talking about taking someone else's life. She's talking about taking lessons, getting a permit, and buying a gun."

Joan sipped her water. "Same thing."

"It most certainly is not the same thing," said Alice. "There are many gun owners who never fire their weapon."

"And there are many who do," said Joan, "like the trained police officers we continue to hear about in the news who fire their weapons at people who have nothing in their hands but a cell phone or a toy gun or an imaginary knife. Now if a trained police officer does that—let's call it panicking—what do you think a frightened housewife is going to do when she comes face to face with danger?"

"With a gun, Alice will be less frightened," said Ellie.

Joan turned her attention to Ellie. "So you're totally okay with this? This is because you've got three rifles in your house, and you think owning guns is a great idea? This is because you think there's no way Alice could shoot someone unless she absolutely had to? What makes you so sure this is a good idea?"

"And what makes you so sure it isn't?" asked Ellie.

Joan opened her mouth to retort just as their server approached the table. The women, who had each glanced at the menu and had a vague idea of what they wanted to eat, quickly ordered. "I've made my best argument," said Joan. "Accidents happen all the time. Parents take their children to firing ranges, and somebody ends up dead. Children find guns in their homes when their parents' backs are turned and shoot themselves. Just the other day, in the newspaper, there was a story about a four-year-old boy, in Alaska, I think, who was shot by his mother's gun when it fell out of its holster and fired. A misguided, mentally unstable high school student shoots his rival in physics class."

"Let's not cheapen what James Shulz did by turning this into a discussion about him," said Alice.

"It *is* a discussion about James Shulz!" said Joan. "It's a discussion about what happens each and every day in a world that tolerates—no, encourages!—every Joe and Jill to protect themselves, to assert themselves with guns. You've got to tell me, Alice, that owning a gun scares you as much as not owning one. If you can tell me that, we have more common ground than you think we do."

Alice leaned in toward Joan. "Of course I'm scared," she said. "I'm crazy scared. But I am resolved. I will do whatever I need to do to not experience what I experienced ever again." She leaned back in her chair. "Linda tells me . . ."

"What does Dave tell you?" Joan interrupted.

"Wait," said Ellie. "I want to hear what Linda had to say."

Alice looked at Ellie. "Thank you," she said. "As I was saying, Linda tells me she knows two women at school who carry guns."

"Why?" asked Joan, in as measured a voice as she could manage.

Their server carried a large circular tray on her shoulder. She lowered it onto a stand several feet from the table and then carried Joan's grilled cheese on homemade sourdough, Alice's Cobb salad, and Ellie's French onion soup to the table, and set them down. "Be careful," she said to Ellie. "The soup is hot."

"Why?" asked Alice. "Because one of the women was raped after a party, and the other one, who Linda says comes from a misogynistic neighborhood in South Boston, carried a gun all through high school for protection."

Ellie blew on the spoon of soup she held three inches from her mouth. "Boy, I'm not so sure allowing guns on college campuses is a good idea," she said.

"What?" asked Alice. "You think it's okay to carry a gun in the, what, real world, but it's not okay to carry a gun on a college campus?"

Ellie chewed the melted Swiss cheese in her mouth. "There's a difference," she said. "College campuses are populated primarily by eighteen- to twenty-two-year-olds. They think they are adults, but they are most decidedly not. They are immature. They routinely make bad decisions. And they drink too much alcohol, which leads to even more bad decision making."

"What she said," said Joan, biting into her grilled cheese.

"What recourse does a young woman have when she's been raped by a classmate?" asked Alice. "Joan, you've told us all about the news you've been digesting, so I'm sure you've also heard about the lack of response to women telling their college administrators that they've been raped, after being drugged, by the captain of the football team and six of his best buddies."

Joan nodded her head in agreement with what Alice was saying. "It's a problem," said Joan. "It's a big problem. But dead football team captains are also a problem. When is it okay to take someone else's life?"

Alice forked a cube of chicken into her mouth. "It's okay when you feel like your life, your person, is in danger."

"It may be all right at that very second," said Joan, "when you pull the trigger. But then you have to live the rest of your life questioning, justifying your actions as a killer."

Alice looked at her phone, which had just buzzed. "It's a text from Linda," she said. "She's going to a Women in Power meeting on campus tonight after dinner."

Joan swallowed the bite of sandwich in her mouth. "Have you told Dave about any of this?"

Alice looked down at her salad. "No," she said. "And I don't plan on doing it anytime soon."

MARCH

CHAPTER 23

Ellie pulled her car into the parking lot of the dog park just before Diana drove in. They parked next to each other, waved, and then got themselves and their dogs out of their cars. Buffy and Lily, Diana's mixed breed puppy, sniffed at each other and then bounded, Lily chasing Buffy, to the gate.

"She is adorable," said Ellie. "You must be thrilled to have a dog again. But how do you get anything done with a puppy in the house?"

"I don't," said Diana, smiling, opening the gate. "We play for at least an hour at the end of the workday—and we play most of the day at the store. We are definitely fast friends."

"How old is she?"

"She's three months old," said Diana. "I've had her for one month."

"And you're loving it?"

"I am," said Diana, choosing the path on the right, the longer loop. "Now that I live alone, she's good company."

The women walked several steps without speaking. The snow was gone, but the ground was still frozen. The dogs ran ahead, on the path and off the path and into the wooded section that buffered the park from the street. The entire park was surrounded by chain-link fencing, but most of it was hidden from view, giving the impression of wide-open country rather than suburban planning. All the dogs seemed to care about was that they were free to run unencumbered.

"It's so funny that I haven't run into you around town," said Ellie, initiating conversation, breaking the quiet between them.

"Well, I haven't been here that long," said Diana. "I moved here from West Hartford about a year ago. And I've been pretty focused on the store."

"Why West Hartford, and why here?"

"We lived in West Hartford because my husband, my ex-husband, works in Hartford. He's an insurance agent, and I was a dutiful housewife."

Ellie called to Buffy, who had taken Lily to the stream for a drink. The dogs ran back toward their owners. "What is it about the word *dutiful* that implies reluctance?"

Diana laughed. "I *was* reluctant! I loved being a mom—I still do—but I didn't like everything that went along with being Phil's wife. I am not a good corporate spouse. I'm not good at schmoozing. I am not good at polite but irrelevant conversation. I frustrated Phil because I was not like the other executives' wives. I didn't dress like them. I didn't act like them. I didn't always do as I was told." Buffy approached Ellie, who gave her a piece of kibble from her pocket. Buffy then ran back to where Lily was standing, waiting for her companion. "Aren't you smart," said Diana.

"Not at first," said Ellie. "The first few times I brought Buffy here, she chose playing with the other dogs over me. I had the hardest time getting her to come to me, getting her to get back in the car. She comes pretty well now that I have treats in my pocket."

Diana reached into her pocket and held up a piece of kibble. "I'm starting early," she said. She called Lily, who came to her only after she squatted and held the kibble in an outstretched hand.

They continued walking. "I'm envious of your independence," said Ellie. "I feel like I've lived my entire life doing what others have thought was best for me."

"Oh, it hasn't always been that way," said Diana. "As I said, I was very dutiful for many years. I became less so when I uncovered who I was and what I wanted."

Ellie stopped and looked at Diana, who had stopped and was looking at her. "Is 'uncovered' a therapy word?"

Diana laughed. "Oh yes," she said. "It took me two years to even say that word."

"Well, it rolls off your tongue very nicely now."

"Why, thank you."

They rounded the corner to the far meadow, where the dogs were frolicking in the tall, brown grass. "What did you uncover?" asked Ellie. When Diana said nothing for several steps, Ellie said, "I'm sorry. That's your business, not mine."

Diana shook her head. "It's okay," she said. "I brought it up. And I hardly ever bring it up, so it must be something I want to tell you."

"Only if you want to," said Ellie, slowing their pace, looking at the side of Diana's face.

Diana stopped and faced Ellie. "I'm gay," she said. "That's why Phil and I are divorced. That's why I'm doing this pet store endeavor on my own. That's why I'm alone and need a puppy for company." Diana started walking again, and Ellie followed her, even though she was suddenly having a hard time lifting her feet. Her legs felt like they had doubled in size and weight. For several minutes, the women said nothing. When they turned the next corner and were, again, surrounded by woods, they were met by two women with black Labrador retrievers. Diana told them how beautiful the dogs were, and the women, in turn, complimented the good looks of Buffy and Lily. Ellie, typically friendly with everyone she met, couldn't find any words to say—they were all swirling around in her mind, sweaty and bumping into one another in the presence of this brave woman who had just confessed she was gay. Was that what it was, a confession?

"Are you okay?" asked Diana, when the other women and their dogs had left them and she and Ellie still hadn't moved, hadn't spoken.

"Yes," said Ellie.

"I've upset you?"

"No, no," said Ellie, refocusing, looking into Diana's eyes. "You haven't upset me; you've inspired me."

"I have?"

"If I can ask," said Ellie, "how and when did you know that you were gay? When did you discover this?"

"Hmmm," said Diana. "That's a good question. On one level, I think I've always known that I was different from other girls, from the elementary school girls who chased the boys around the playground and from the high school girls who pushed themselves up against the male athletes. My romantic crushes, in junior high and high school, were on girls as often as they were on boys, probably more on girls. In college, I had a relationship with another woman, and it was very satisfying, until she broke my heart by dumping me for a guy." Ellie nodded her head, continuing to process the information Diana was sharing while encouraging her new friend to continue. "And then I followed suit and dated a man, Edward was his name. He was very scholarly and not much interested in sex with me—so we were perfectly matched. If I had to guess, I'd say that Edward was gay, too."

They started walking again, back toward the near meadow, back toward their cars. "Then what happened?" Ellie asked.

"I dropped out of college and hiked the Appalachian Trail."

Ellie stopped again. "Really?"

Diana laughed, nodding her head. "Really! I was completely lost and felt I needed to get away from Edward and everyone else. My parents were not impressed, let me tell you. And I shouldn't say I dropped out—my father made me finish the semester. After that, I hiked for eight months, and then worked for four months to pay my parents back. I went back and finished school, and was accepted after graduation into an insurance training program, which I pursued partly because I saw so many ill prepared, accident prone people while I was hiking and mostly because I had no idea what I wanted to do. That's where I met Phil. A year later we got married, started having kids, and I didn't question any of it. Well, I didn't until about three years ago."

They were at their cars now. The dogs were in their respective vehicles, and Ellie and Diana were standing next to Diana's car. Ellie didn't want to go, didn't want to stop the conversation. "What happened three years ago?" she asked.

"I fell in love with a woman and told my husband I was gay."

"Holy shit," said Ellie, her head rocking back.

"Indeed," said Diana, a slight smile on her face. "It was a very interesting time in my life."

Ellie nodded her head, hesitated a moment, and then said, "Are you interested in a cup of coffee?"

Diana checked her watch and smiled fully at Ellie. "Yes. But just because we are prolonging our time together by having a cup of coffee does not mean we need to continue this conversation."

"I absolutely want to continue this conversation."

"All right," said Diana. "I told Shawna that I'd be in around noon, so I do have a little more time—not that she needs me. That young woman could run the store with absolutely no supervision."

"Follow me to my house," said Ellie. "Chris got me a cappuccino machine for Christmas. It has turned me into even more of a caffeine addict than he is. But I don't need to drive to Dunkin' Donuts anymore."

Over coffee, Diana continued her story. The woman she had fallen in love with, it turned out, was bisexual. She and Diana were together for six months, but then the woman returned to her husband. Diana, whose conviction that she was gay was nothing but reinforced by this relationship, did not even consider returning to Phil. Although, by then, Phil had filed for divorce and started dating.

"Was he angry?" asked Ellie, pushing the plate of Vienna Fingers closer to Diana. Diana took one and bit into it.

"I would say he was more disillusioned than angry," said Diana. "But I was also—about our relationship, who I was, and who he was. In the end, however, he was remarkably civilized. While I'm not sure he suspected, he told me he had, several times, over the course of our marriage. When I asked him to explain, he couldn't, however. I don't think he really did suspect I was gay, because I really didn't know myself. I mean, I did know, but I had buried it for so long that I wasn't sure what was going on. I was resolute and conflicted at the same time—if that makes any sense."

"It does," said Ellie, nodding her head, listening and thinking, thinking and listening. "It does make sense."

"I think because Phil was so good about it—because we both

tried to make our separation as painless as possible—the kids were good about it. We are still a family. Phil and I just don't live together anymore." Diana finished her cappuccino and set the cup back in its saucer. "And I don't really know why I'm burdening you with all of this. It's the anniversary today of the day I told Phil. It's on my mind. I'm sorry."

"Don't be sorry. I'm glad you told me."

Diana cocked her head. "Are you? Why are you glad I told you?"

Ellie took a cookie from the plate between them. "Because it makes sense," she said. "I understand it."

"You seem to understand it," said Diana.

Ellie said, "Yes. I do."

CHAPTER 24

Ellie and Joan sat across the table from each other at Casa Maria. Their chicken quesadillas had just been set down in front of them; their chips and salsa were gone. And even though they had tried to not make Alice's absence and what it signified the topic of conversation, they had failed. She had e-mailed both of them the night before, telling them how sorry she was to be missing lunch. But she had decided to attend a Well Protected Women's meeting in Hartford. It was a group of gun-carrying women she'd learned about on the Internet—and they met the first Wednesday of every month. Alice had not acknowledged or addressed the potential future conflict. If she continued to attend these meetings, she would no longer be able to meet for lunch on the first Wednesday of each month. This meant, Ellie and Joan had discussed, that Alice would either ask them to reschedule their lunch date, or she would simply join them on the third Wednesday only.

"We're jumping ahead," said Ellie, scooping guacamole from a plastic cup onto her quesadilla. "This is one meeting, one missed lunch we're talking about here."

Joan nodded her head in agreement. "I know," she said. "But I'm worried about her nonetheless."

Their server approached the table and asked them the obligatory question all experienced servers ask five minutes after they have delivered meals to their customers: "Is everything all right?" Both women, who had each taken one bite, indicated that their quesadillas were delicious. Ellie asked for more salsa.

"You're worried she's taking this too seriously, that she's getting in too deep."

"I know she's taking it too seriously," said Joan. "And I do have to admit that, if what happened to Alice happened to me, I'd be serious about protecting myself, about feeling safe. What I'm worried about is her interest in, no, her obsession with guns. I know you don't worry about it, Ellie. But I do. She hasn't even told Dave yet."

Ellie dumped one of the two plastic cups of salsa that had just been set down on the table over the layer of guacamole she had spread on the browned tortilla. "Just because you and I have different views about gun ownership doesn't mean I'm not worried about her."

Joan finished chewing the bite in her mouth. "You're right; I'm sorry. So what do we do? What do we say?"

Ellie shook her head. "I have no idea. She's pretty fragile right now. But she's not looking for a lot of advice."

"Point delivered," said Joan. "Maybe I've been too vocal. But I feel like she is being pulled into a dangerous world that she is looking at from only one side. She thinks owning a gun will give her security, keep her safe from harm; I think owning a gun will do just the opposite. Somebody is going to end up dead. It may be an accident. It may even be justified. But it will be permanent."

Ellie smiled at Joan. "Do you think there's the slightest possibility that you're overreacting?"

"Of course I'm overreacting," said Joan, not returning Ellie's smile. "If I don't act as a counterbalance to Alice, who will? Her daughters applaud their mother's behavior, telling her she's brave and strong. Dave has no idea what his wife is up to. And these women in Hartford are going to make her feel like a hero for fending off her attacker and like a scholar for getting a gun. Where is the voice of reason in all of this?"

"It's not unreasonable to have a gun."

"No, it's not," said Joan. "But Alice is thinking differently from how she used to think. She has crossed over to the gun carrying side. And you have to admit, Ellie, that having your grandfather's shotguns in your house and hunting once a year is not the same thing as carrying a pistol on your body every moment you are outside of your house. What is going to prevent her from thinking that she not only has to protect herself, but that she also has to protect others? She might stumble upon some trouble out in the world and think, because she's got a gun, she's got the answer." Joan put her fork down on her plate and sat back in her seat.

"Joan," said Ellie. "Joan. This is one meeting. She doesn't have the gun yet. She's gathering information. There is time for her to calm down."

"I'm not sure she wants to calm down, Ellie. I think she's on a mission here, to right her wrong and the wrongs of women everywhere."

"We don't know that," said Ellie. "Sometimes people talk big because they need to convince themselves—or their friends. You have been critical of Alice's interest in guns."

Joan had not yet returned to her lunch. "What kind of friend isn't?"

"Meaning I'm not a good friend, Joan?"

"No, Ellie. You've been supportive of her because you know that owning guns is legal and, in some circles, accepted, celebrated even," said Joan. "Even though I would never have guns in my house, I can certainly understand why people do—especially those who hunt. What I object to is gun ownership by people who have issues, agendas, criminal intent, debts to settle, etcetera."

"Oh for God's sake, Joan. You've just described every member of the human race."

At this, Joan's face, neck, and shoulders relaxed. "Perhaps I have," she said, reaching for her fork and cutting off a large bite of quesadilla, which she lifted to her mouth. "Do you love it when I get on a roll?"

"I actually do love it," said Ellie. "You have convictions, and you're not afraid to share them, and I admire that."

"I share them with you and Alice," said Joan. "I certainly don't share them with just anybody."

"That's because you're smart," said Ellie.

"Smart or not, that's enough grandstanding for one day. Tell me about you. How's the bookkeeping business?"

Ellie smiled at Joan and said, "It's good. I'm busy. I'd like to be busier, but I know I can find more clients if I actively look." Ellie took a sip of water. "It's the looking part that's hard for me. I want people to somehow find out about me and then call me and give me their business."

Joan smiled in return. "I don't think it works that way."

"It most definitely doesn't work that way," said Ellie. "But I am such a lousy salesperson. I don't know the first thing about promoting myself."

"So promote what you *do*," said Joan, "promote your services, your expertise, your experience."

"I do that," said Ellie. "But I also have to convince my prospective clients that I am the right bookkeeper for the job."

"You are totally the right bookkeeper, for any job out there."

Ellie laughed. "How do you know that? You don't know anything about my business."

"But I know you," said Joan. "People have to trust their accountants. And I think people can see that you're an honest, hardworking person the minute you walk through the door."

Ellie forked the last bite of quesadilla into her mouth and said as she chewed, "You are a good egg."

Joan pointed her finger at Ellie. "Did your father used to say that?"

"Still does."

"My dad said it, too—sparingly. God, he was a man of carefully chosen words. And when he did say it—that someone was a good egg—it was always in reference to one of his work buddies, never about family members, friends, or neighbors. I'll bet that's what that pet store woman thought about you when you first talked to her. What's her name again?"

Ellie blushed and then said, "Diana. Diana McGuire."

"That's right. How is everything going with her?"

"Well," said Ellie. "Things are going well." And she stopped there. She was tempted to continue, but she didn't know how to proceed. Her relationship with Diana was evolving, from a business relationship to a personal relationship, one that mattered more to Ellie than many of her established relationships. And Ellie was struggling, in a sometimes pleasant way, to reconcile this fast friendship with her typical method of finding and keeping friends. Ellie was a friendly and engaging person, but she was quiet at first, often taking in what others said before offering her opinion, if she offered it at all. Perhaps this was because she was the only daughter, and her brothers always had dominated and continued to dominate the conversation at home. But this had not been the case so far with Diana. That very first day, Ellie had been able to talk to Diana as if they had known and understood each other for years rather than minutes.

"So what do you need—four, five more clients like Diana?"

There were no clients like Diana because there was no one like Diana. Being with her was for Ellie like being with a long-lost sister. Except she did not want to be Diana's sister. They were so like-minded, the two of them. Was it because Diana was gay? A tingling sensation emanated from Ellie's heart and spread out through her circulatory system until her entire being was warm, alive, ready—a sprinter just before the race. Yes, Ellie thought. It was because Diana was gay, and because she had the courage to proclaim her homosexuality after decades of consciously and unconsciously hiding it. She was exactly who Ellie wanted to be because Ellie knew at that exact moment that she, too, was and always had been attracted to women more than men. And that if she were going to be at peace like Diana was at peace—no matter the upheaval it would take to achieve this—she had to come out, too. "Unbelievable," Ellie said aloud.

"What," said Joan, looking at the check, calculating the tip. "The four or five more clients? That may sound like a lot, but I think you could find four new clients next week. Have you tried the mall or the casino? How about the appliance store on Canal Street? Everyone there is definitely collecting Social Security. I'll bet they're dying for someone to take over their books." Ellie grinned at Joan, but not in relation to anything Joan was saying. Ellie had not been listening. "What?"

"Nothing," said Ellie, looking at her watch. "I've got to get rolling." She could not get to the pet store fast enough. "What do I owe you?"

"It's my treat," said Joan, feeling magnanimous since she had won three hundred dollars at the roulette table that morning.

Ellie stood. "You really are a good egg."

Joan laughed. "Go," she said, flicking the backs of her fingers at Ellie. "I'll take care of this."

Ellie put on her coat. "We didn't talk about you at all. How are you doing in your quest to find the meaning of empty nested life?"

"I'm working on it," said Joan.

CHAPTER 25

As soon as Alice got home from the meeting of the Well Protected Women in Hartford, she grabbed the laptop she kept on the kitchen counter and parked herself at the table, pushing the newspaper that sat underneath Dave's cereal bowl aside. Seconds later, she had found the Web site her new friends suggested she consult for more information about gun safety and handling classes. "Of course, we can tell you everything you need to know," Jamie had said after the meeting. "But if you're anything like me—and I can already tell that you are—you'll want to do the research yourself."

As it turned out, Alice was indeed something like Jamie. They both had daughters, and they both had nearly been raped. Jamie, who lived just outside of Hartford, had gotten a flat tire after dark in an economically depressed section of the city. If a woman who kept a handgun in her purse and held it like she knew how to use it hadn't happened by, Jamie said she would have become a statistic like all the other non-armed women of the world: raped, dead, or both. Two men, with their pants already around their ankles, had her pinned against the side of her car parked under a faulty streetlight. Cindy, another member of the Well Protected Women, lived in Springfield, Massachusetts. She had been held up at knifepoint outside a shopping mall at Christmastime. The thieves stole all the presents she had bought for her children and the credit cards and cash in her wallet. Both Jamie and Cindy lamented about the tragedy, their word, of women experiencing violence before they thought or sought to prevent it from happening. Both Jamie and Cindy also knew women who had not been as "lucky"—they both used air quotes when talking about their good fortune—as they had been: One woman in the group had been stabbed in the back and lost a kidney, and another woman, who'd had no money or presents for her children at the time of the attack, had been raped and beaten severely enough to warrant a two-month hospital stay.

Jamie and Cindy had asked Alice to tell them her story over a cup of coffee during what the organization president called sharing time—a twenty-minute break midway through the meeting when members were encouraged to get to know one another—and she did, starting with the incredible feeling of peace she'd had on the run when she started out that afternoon and ending with the fear and anger that had not left her since. She told them about her assailant. She told them about the police investigation that had so far turned up nothing but footprints in the snow, now gone. She told them about her whistle. She told them everything, except her instruction to the man to take off her pants. She had relived that line in her mind, over and over, and still had no idea why she'd said it. It made her sound like a willing participant rather than a victim. She was ashamed and had said nothing to anyone, not even to Ellie or Joan. Jamie and Cindy nodded their heads, scribbling their cell phone numbers on scraps of paper, telling Alice to call them any time of the day or night. Alice thought all the way home about how they had treated her, how everyone at the meeting had treated her. No one challenged her story. No one appeared to doubt the veracity of the details. No one forgot her name. No one put her needs ahead of Alice's, or half listened to Alice's story until she could segue into one about her own experience. The Well Protected Women were the most supportive group of friends (and Alice had already decided they were friends) she had ever met.

Alice signed up online for the classes and the instructors the women had recommended to her. She knew she would be able to apply for a permit only after she'd taken the classes and fired a gun, and that the wait once the application was filed was up to eight weeks. Alice counted the weeks in her head; she could be carrying a weapon by Memorial Day. She closed out of the registration Web site before walking to the stove to make a cup of tea. She thought about baking some cookies; she hadn't baked anything since the incident. Just as she was getting the flour and sugar from the cupboard next to the oven, Dave walked in the back door.

"Hi," he said.

Alice turned to face him and briefly smiled, a reflex more than a pleasant response to his presence. She looked at her watch. "What are you doing home at three o'clock on a Wednesday?"

"Going for a long run with Brad," said Dave. "He's off today and called the store to see if I could sneak out for a quick ten miler. I don't often get to run with Brad, and I'm flattered that he asked me. So here I am."

"That's interesting," said Alice, half full bags of flour and sugar on the counter, hands on hips. "I can't remember the last time you left work early to run with me."

"Hey," he said, approaching her, wrapping his arms around her unyielding shoulders.

Alice backed away from him. "Hey what?"

Dave looked at his watch. "Look," he said. "I have to meet Brad in fifteen minutes, so I've got to move. But let's sit down tonight after dinner and come up with a plan. You are absolutely right. I have been neglectful about running with you. And we've talked about it a lot. So let's get something on the calendar."

Alice turned away from him. "It doesn't really matter anymore, Dave." She put the flour and sugar back in the cupboard, her desire to bake gone.

"Of course it matters," he said.

"No, it doesn't," said Alice. "Because I've got something else I can run with now."

"That's great!" said Dave. "You found someone to run with?"

"I said something, not someone."

Dave's forehead wrinkled in incomprehension. "Something?"

Alice turned around to again face him. "Yes," she said. "A gun. I'm in the process of buying and learning how to use and carry a gun."

The wrinkles on Dave's forehead moved up, as his eyes widened. "Alice?"

"Don't give me that look," said Alice. "Since you have chosen not to run with me, not to protect me, I've got to protect myself."

Dave hesitated for a long moment before taking his cell phone out of his back pocket. He entered some data and then held the phone to his ear. "Brad? Yeah, it's Dave. Hey, something's come up, and I just can't make it today. Yeah, I know. I'm disappointed too. But let's shoot for next week. Wednesdays are typically a pretty good day for me. And I'm open to going early in the morning, if that suits you. Okay, good. Thanks. And have a good run." He put his phone down on the kitchen table. "Let's sit down, Alice, and talk about this." As soon as Alice complied, Dave said, "Start from the beginning."

And so Alice told him everything that she had shared with the Well Protected Women—that she had been afraid since the attack, that she was having trouble sleeping, that she was frustrated by the lack of progress made by the Southwood Police Department, that she was hurt by Dave's lack of interest in her physical and emotional health. "I am over the fact that I had to rely on two friends to meet me at the police station and take me to the hospital," said Alice. "I know that you often don't have your cell phone on your person, and that you don't use it nearly as much as I do. So I have chosen to accept your story that you were on the floor at work that day and that you didn't get my message until long after I needed you."

"It's true, Alice. You know that. And I have apologized many times for my absence."

"That you have," said Alice. She took a sip of tea. "And you took good care of me when my injuries were fresh."

"Well, you're nice to say that. I think the long weekend that Linda was here caring for you was the most helpful. She is a good caregiver," said Dave. "She takes after you."

Resisting her natural instinct to soften whenever Dave paid her a compliment, Alice said, "What you have to realize—what you have failed to realize—is that this is not over." Dave's quizzical look returned. "In fact, it's just beginning." Alice went on to explain that her new goal in life was to never feel vulnerable again. And that she had to rely on herself to feel secure.

"You can rely on me, Alice," said Dave, leaning forward to take his wife's hands in his. "I will do whatever you want me to do to help you feel safe."

Alice pulled her hands away and shook her head. "You say that, but you don't really mean it. I'm not saying you're not trying. On some levels, you are. But it's not enough—it will never be enough—because you don't understand how I feel."

Dave nodded his head. "I do," he said. "I do understand how you feel because you've explained it to me. You are afraid. You feel vulnerable. You feel alone in this. What I don't understand is how a gun will alleviate your feelings of fear."

Alice sat back in her chair. "Because having a gun will negate my feelings of fear, of being inadequately protected. And once I feel sufficiently protected, I will be able to handle my vulnerability. When I carry a gun, I will never be alone."

Dave stood and walked to the sink. He took a glass from the cupboard and, after testing the temperature of the water with his index finger, filled it. He drank all the water right there and then set the glass down in the sink. He gazed out the window to the backyard, where the half inch of snow that had fallen last night was gone except for underneath the large pine trees that served as a natural boundary between their yard and their neighbor's property. He turned around and, pinning his hands with his back, leaned against the counter. "You may not be alone, but you will be in danger."

Alice gave him a tight smile. "You're going to have to explain that statement."

"The mere fact that you've asked me to explain it tells me you haven't thought about this gun ownership from anyone's angle other than your own."

"Meaning what?"

Dave removed his hands from behind his back and crossed them over his chest. "I'm guessing you've done all your homework on how to handle, shoot, acquire, and carry a gun. But I'll bet you haven't done all your homework on what the National Rifle Association sponsored Web sites don't mention. What about accidental discharges that could injure you or someone else? What about getting shot and killed by someone you've pulled your gun on who happens to subscribe to the adage of shooting first and asking questions later? And how are you going to feel if you shoot someone—either on purpose or by accident? If there's one thing that can ruin your life in an instant, it's taking the life of another."

Alice put her feet up on the chair Dave had vacated. "That won't happen."

"Are you kidding?" asked Dave. "It happens all the time."

"But it won't happen to me."

"And why is that?"

"Because I won't let it happen."

Dave raised his hands into the air. "Until it does."

Alice took her feet off the chair and stood. She pointed her right index finger at Dave. "That's a bullshit argument. That's like saying you shouldn't drive a car because you could get into an accident. Or that you shouldn't take a walk because you could fall and break your wrist. Or that you shouldn't eat steak because you could choke on a piece and die. You don't live your life that way, so I have no idea why you expect me to."

Dave ran his fingers through his hair, pushing it away from his forehead, holding it for a moment at the peak of his scalp before releasing it. He had Raggedy Andy hair, brown instead of red, that flew when he ran and gave women aged twenty-five to sixty-five a reason for a second look. "It's a bad idea, Alice. In your heart, you know this is a bad idea."

"It's the only idea I have as a way to feel safe again," said Alice. "You let me know when you come up with a better one."

Chapter 26

"I know you think I'm crazy to be doing this," said Alice, setting her chopsticks down on her plate of Drunken Noodles and looking at Joan. "But I'm a really good shot."

Joan gave Alice a half smile. "Yes, I do think you're crazy to be doing this, but I am pleased to know you are a really good shot."

Ellie looked at Joan. "I do believe you're softening."

Alice laughed. "Oh yeah, she's getting soft all right. The next step will be going to a Well Protected Women's meeting with me."

"That," said Joan, "would indicate an unprecedented level of softness."

"Thank you," said Alice, serious now, "for not berating me today."

"My pleasure."

"So, Joan," said Ellie, spearing a piece of chicken in her pad Thai with her fork and lifting it to her mouth. "The last time we were together, when you paid for my lunch, we agreed to talk about you."

"We did?" asked Joan, straightening her back.

"We did."

"Yes, let's definitely talk about Joan's life," said Alice. "God knows I've been in the spotlight long enough."

Ellie picked up her water glass. "Alice is working on becoming a sharpshooter. I am growing my bookkeeping business. What are you up to, other than trying to impress your mother-in-law?"

Joan laughed. "I've actually booked a trip to visit *my* mother."

"In Detroit?" asked Alice.

"Very close to Detroit," said Joan. "She lives in Livonia."

"Is your brother still there?" asked Ellie. "What's his name again?"

"Carl," said Joan. "No, Carl got the hell out of Livonia when he turned eighteen. He lives in Sedona with his partner, Aaron. Stephen and I try to get out there every couple years. I routinely invite Carl to Southwood, which he calls Mayberry, but he'd much rather have us come there. And I can certainly see why. Once you spend any time in Sedona, you never want to leave."

"Your brother has a partner?"

"He does," said Joan. "He and Aaron met at the University of California at San Diego. They broke up before leaving college, but got back together after running into each other—oh, ten years or so ago—at a grocery store in Sedona. They are both outdoor enthusiasts, spending every minute of their nonworking, nonsleeping time in the pursuit of physical excellence." Joan laughed. "When Carl sees me he just shakes his head."

"How come you never said anything?" asked Ellie.

"About Carl's being an outdoor enthusiast?" asked Joan, looking amused.

"That he was gay," said Ellie. "I had no idea he was gay."

"Well, when I first mentioned him a minute ago, you were hard pressed to even remember my brother's name," said Joan. "I don't talk about him a lot, but I am close to him. We try to talk on the phone every few weeks."

"Is he married?"

"They are thinking about getting married. Arizona is a tough state to be gay in," said Joan. "But Sedona is very different. They love it there."

Ellie sat back in her seat and stared at Joan. Finally she said, "I just can't believe I didn't know that."

Joan laughed. "There's a lot you don't know about me!"

Ellie gave Joan a confused look, before saying, "But isn't this kind of a big deal?"

Joan shrugged her shoulders. "Not to me, I guess."

"Wow," said Ellie.

"Wow, what?" asked Alice, who set her cell phone back on the table after sending a text to Hilary, whom she routinely referred to as her middle daughter rather than by name.

"It's a big deal in my family," said Ellie. "Either we're not talking about it, or we're talking about it big time. The Kilcullen family has a strong opinion about homosexuals."

"Which is . . ." said Joan.

"That it's a sin," said Ellie. "That homosexuality is a sin, and that homosexuals should repent."

"Is that what you think?" asked Joan.

"God no," said Ellie. "But I still go to a Catholic church."

Joan shook her head. "The Catholic Church is going to have to get its head in the game on this one," she said. "Gay rights have exploded in this country. And if justice has its way, things will only get better—as Obama used to say."

"I'm blown away," said Ellie.

"Why?" asked Alice.

"Because I just assumed most people felt the same way as my family members."

"Do you read the newspapers? Do you listen to NPR?" asked Joan.

Alice said nothing.

"Yes and yes!" said Ellie, laughing. "I'm just so pleased that a regular person like you feels this way."

Joan said, "There is nothing regular about me, dear."

"You can say that again," said Alice. "But we got sidetracked—tell us about your upcoming visit with your mom."

Joan took a sip of her tea. "She will run me around like she always does. The woman is nearly eighty years old and has a social calendar that rivals that of the Kardashians. We'll go shopping. We'll have lunch. We'll play euchre with her friends."

"Euchre?" asked Alice.

"It's a card game," said Joan. "If you live in Michigan, you play euchre. We might even go bowling."

"Your mother *does not* bowl!" said Ellie.

"Oh yes, she does," said Joan. "She's in the Sweet Seventies league."

Alice and Ellie both laughed. "It must have been fun growing up in your house," said Alice.

Joan cocked her head. "Not really," she said. "I mean, it was okay. But my mother didn't really come alive until after my father died. Their marriage was much more functional than blissful. And my mother functioned well: She kept the house, prepared the food, worked full-time in the school system, and raised my brother and me. My father was the provider, but he didn't provide much outside of his paycheck. He didn't pay much attention to my mom, my brother, or me. One day was much the same as the next. We did as we were told. We kept to ourselves. When my father died of a massive heart attack, work friends and family gathered to mark his passing. But the women in the group that day were quietly celebratory, about my mother's opportunity to live life on her terms. And she has been making every day count since."

"Why didn't she get divorced?" asked Ellie.

"Because it wasn't done back then, except in dire circumstances—and even then, it happened without official comment; it wasn't talked about. But to divorce because you were unhappy in your marriage was unheard of, mostly because it was regarded as incredibly selfish. What about the children? What about their happiness? I think a lot of my mother's friends had the same kind of marriage she had. They all married young, as they were expected to, and didn't have a good idea of what they were getting into. And if they did decide that marriage was nothing like what their mothers told them—the same mothers who were trying to get them paired up and out of the house, off their financial books—it was too late, meaning the young housewives had two or three small children and no income. They were reliant upon their husbands for financial support. Because my mother was able to talk my father into paying the bills while she raised us, she didn't get a job until we were in school. He wanted her to work, but he approved only of what he called "invisible" work, meaning whatever she chose to do had to be done without inconveniencing him. He wanted her to make money and to continue doing everything else as well."

"It sounds like he was tough on her," said Alice.

"He was a whole lot better than some of her friends' husbands," said Joan.

"Well, then she sounds like an amazing woman," said Alice, moving her focus to her phone, which had just buzzed.

"She is, indeed."

"So, when are you going?" asked Ellie.

"Next week," said Joan. "I'm flying out next Thursday morning, and I will be back on Sunday night—thoroughly exhausted!" Alice again reached for her phone. "What's happening, Alice? You've been looking at your phone for half of the last hour."

"I'm sorry," said Alice, who rarely apologized for paying as much or more attention to her phone than to Ellie and Joan. "My girls all seem to need me today. Linda will be getting out of a test in"—Alice again looked at her phone—"five minutes. Hilary is stewing about upcoming vacation plans, and Cathy is displeased with the erratic behavior of a work colleague."

Somebody has an ingrown toenail, Joan thought in response, *or a bad haircut.* Alice had trained her daughters to call her any time of the day or night. She would pick up immediately, and she would pause whatever was happening in her life, so she could jump into theirs. "What's the vacation drama?" asked Joan, half kidding, half annoyed.

"Oh, it's typical middle daughter," said Alice. "Hilary and a bunch of girls are going to Florida for their first official vacation from their jobs, and middle daughter is not happy with the hotel room assignments."

"Aren't they all friends?" asked Ellie, more tolerant of Alice's phone habit than Joan.

"Well, sure they are," said Alice. "But you know how you can be closer to some people than to others." And the story was launched. The topic of conversation had moved away from Joan and back to Alice. Joan was thankful, actually, that Alice was talking about something other than pistols. Like the beginning of most love affairs, Alice's relationship with guns was intense. And Joan, for the moment, had stopped trying to break them up.

CHAPTER 27

Joan walked away from the cashier's window, grinning as she recounted the thirty-six hundred-dollar bills that had just been pushed her way underneath the glass that separated the patrons from the money. It was not enough to replenish her vacation account, but it was a good start, a very good start. It was almost noon, and the effects of the double vodka and soda she had consumed at ten thirty were fading, leaving her with a slight headache and very hungry. She thought about getting something to eat in one of the casino food court restaurants, but opted instead to go home for a grilled cheese followed by a short nap. She had promised Stephen her mother's meatloaf that night for dinner. It was one of his favorite comfort foods, which he routinely sought to combat the pressures and stress of his job. There had been talks at the bank about cost cutting, in an effort to counterbalance the price tag associated with stricter federal regulations. And even though Stephen thought his position was secure, it was an uneasy time at the office. He knew already that two of his colleagues would be let go at the end of the month.

The two glasses of water and cup of coffee that Joan had chased her vodka with were making their presence known in her bladder. She'd have to use the restroom before returning to the garage for her car. Being familiar with the casino, Joan chose to wind slightly out of her way to use the slightly out of everyone's way women's room. It was a four-stall bathroom fashioned out of pink stone, porcelain, and tinted glass, located next to a florist shop that had been closed for a couple weeks for renovations. This particular bathroom was always clean and usually empty, like the lavish facilities in high-end hotel lobbies. And it was quiet, which was a refreshing change from the hum of the casino floor.

Joan set her coat down on the long padded bench in the mirrored alcove and then locked herself into the third stall, hanging her purse by its strap on the door hook. Less than a minute later, she heard the door to the women's room open. The sharp clap of leather boot soles on stone stopped after not more than a dozen steps. The person did not enter a stall, choosing instead, Joan guessed, to check herself out in the mirror. This was, after all, what many women did in the bathroom; they relieved their biological urges, washed their hands, and then gazed at their reflections. Some were shy about it, conscious of other women around them, and took no more than a half minute to comb their hair or reapply lipstick, making an effort to look at themselves only long enough to get the job done. Others, either more vain or not cognizant of the judgmental opinion of competitive women, spent multiple minutes checking themselves out. Did they not have bathroom mirrors at home? Joan had wondered, since she could walk into the restroom, urinate, wash her hands, rub cream into them, brush her hair, and walk out while these women, typically good looking enough that they had little if not nothing to correct at the mirror, contemplated their visages.

And so this was the kind of woman Joan expected to see when she emerged from the stall, purse slung over her right shoulder. Instead, she was met by a young woman with greasy brown hair that fell to her biceps, jeans that had holes due to wear instead of by design, and an oversized pea coat, unbuttoned to reveal a stained and wrinkled T-shirt covering what looked like a belly that was six months into a pregnancy. Joan gave the woman a quick smile, as she had been taught, as she always did when she encountered another person, on her way to the sink. She turned on both faucets and put her hands underneath the stream of water. "You were pretty lucky out there today," the woman said.

A surge of adrenaline quickened Joan's heart rate. Joan used the mirror to meet the woman's eyes. "I beg your pardon?"

"At the roulette table," she said. "You've had a rough time lately—well, since I've been watching you. But today, I'd say you cleaned up."

Joan washed her hands and slowly dried them on a paper towel from the dispenser. She could leave her coat on the bench if she needed to leave in a hurry. "You've been watching me?"

"I watch a lot of people on account that I spend a lot of time here. But I'm especially interested in well-dressed housewives on a winning streak."

"Oh?" asked Joan, trying to sound casual, even though she now knew there was something very wrong with this young woman. "Why is that?"

The woman reached into her coat with her right hand and pulled what turned out to be a gun out of the waistband of her jeans. She pointed it at Joan, a wide smile creating clown-like circles of flesh under her glassy eyes. She laughed. "Why, it's because you fancy, amateur gamblers sometimes get lucky—like you did today." Joan raised her hands in the air, which made the woman laugh harder. "This ain't the old west, lady. I just want your cash." Joan closed her eyes. "And I got no time for a prayer session, sister. I want the money you won at the roulette table this morning. I want your credit cards. I want your rings and your diamond earrings. And I want them now." She raised the gun, so it was level with Joan's face.

"Okay," said Joan, "okay. I'll give you what you want." Joan un-zipped her purse and looked inside. And for a moment, the woman with the gun faded out of focus. If Joan had subscribed to Alice's gun-toting philosophy, she would be looking at a gun right now, nestled in between her package of travel tissues and her hairbrush. And she would simply reach into her purse as if going for the wad of hundred-dollar bills and come out with a gun instead of the cash.

But what then?

"If you can't find what I'm looking for," said the woman, who had moved two steps closer to Joan, "I can always search your purse after you are lying on the floor in a pool of your own blood."

Joan looked at the woman, who was clearly engaged in their conversation but seemed to be unaware of their surroundings, of the fact that someone else could walk into the restroom, as unlikely as that might be, or that Joan could, indeed, have a gun in her purse, which, of course, she didn't. Joan wondered, again for a small fraction of a minute, what would happen if she charged the woman. Instead, Joan pulled the crisp bills out of the side pocket of her purse and handed them over. She frowned at the woman, who asked her again to remove her rings and diamond stud earrings. And then, when prompted again, Joan handed over her credit cards.

"Here's what we're going to do next," the woman said. "You're going to head over there to the far wall and sit down underneath the hand dryers. You're going to close your eyes and count to thirty—and I will know if you do not count to thirty—and then you are going to walk out of this lovely bathroom and directly to your car. If you even think about going to casino security, I will find you the next time you're here, because I know you will be back, and I will shoot your rich head off. Do you understand?"

"Yes," said Joan, walking slowly to the designated wall, holding her cashless purse with her naked fingers.

"Now sit down—no, face the wall. Close your eyes and start counting." Joan heard the door at three. She kept counting as she opened her eyes and spun on her bottom so she was facing out instead of in. At twenty, she stopped counting, leaned back against the wall she had just been facing, and took three deep breaths before she attempted to stand. When she was able to stand, she walked to the sink and splashed cold water on her face; she retrieved her coat from the bench; and she walked to her car and drove home, checking the entire time to see if anyone was following her. When she got home, she called the police, who took her information over the phone, and then she called Stephen. His administrative assistant told her he was not yet out of a meeting he had been in all morning.

* * *

When Stephen got home at three thirty in the afternoon, Joan knew something was wrong. Stephen, and the rest of his banking cohorts, routinely worked until six o'clock. Working ten-hour days was a badge of honor at First Federal, almost as important as their titles. Joan went along with this, even though she didn't agree with it. She hid her skepticism from the Howard women, who stood by their financial industry men, picking out their conservative suits and power ties, telling one another how hard their husbands worked. And over the years, Joan had fallen into this pattern, perhaps to fit in with them or to please her mother-in-law. But, in truth, Joan had been resentful of Stephen's prescribed hours—not so much now, but certainly when the girls were younger. Joan had lost track of the number of recitals, concerts, plays, and sporting events that Stephen and all the other banking dads had missed over the years. He had apologized for his absences, but Joan wasn't convinced of his sincerity. As the breadwinner, Stephen thought what he did was more important than anything else. This included everything his daughters were involved with that took place in the afternoon, everything that happened before six thirty, when Stephen could rush in, wearing his work clothes, and show the rest of the working people who had taken time off to cheer on their children that what *he* did for a living was on a different level from *their* day jobs. His services were indispensable. Yet Joan knew that the banking industry would carry on—its ability to move money unhampered—if everyone left the office at five, if not earlier.

Because Joan had continued her education rather than sought a job after college, she couldn't talk in absolutes about the working world, but she had her suppositions about what it was like—and it was not, she was sure, as arduous as those who were in it made it appear. Yes, there were long days and difficult projects and hard-to-please bosses and clients. But there were also catered lunches and weeklong training sessions that included inspirational speakers and afternoon golf. There were business trips and customer dinners, team meetings and group outings. There was more time in the day than many would admit, she thought, filled with industry chatter, shooting the business shit. And Joan received the greatest number of forwarded humorous e-mails from the few friends of hers who worked, and they were always sent during the business day. Joan had talked to Stephen about this one day when he had not only missed the girls' soccer games, but had also electronically sent her a series of particularly good *New Yorker* cartoons. He had balked, and she had changed the subject of their conversation— but not because he said something to alter her point of view. Rather, she came to the realization that the captains of finance had more interest in their comradery, in themselves and their world, than they did in their families. And that nothing she could say would convince her husband that his long hours at the office were more habitual or ritualistic than necessary.

In spite of this code of conduct, Stephen had been an attentive father in the evenings. After he'd changed out of his suit, he'd played with the girls while Joan got dinner on the table. And he'd played whatever they wanted to play—silly, childish board games, dolls, Beanie Babies. He had also introduced them to other things: Lego, K'NEX, Lincoln Logs. As they got older and more coordinated, one of their favorite things to do with their dad was to draw. Stephen would put an object in the middle of the family room floor, and the three of them would have to copy the image into their sketch pads. When Liz and Cassie were in high school, he had helped them with their homework after dinner. Joan, too, had helped, with the addition and subtraction in elementary school, and then with the algebra, geometry, and calculus. These sessions around the cleared table were when Joan felt very close to her daughters and her husband—more so than during the family meal, which everyone, including Joan, ate quickly. Sitting with Liz while she did her homework was one of the activities Joan missed the most, being bent over a particularly tricky problem with her daughter, their heads almost touching, their brains in sync.

Stephen took off his overcoat and slung it over the nearest kitchen chair. Joan, who was standing on the other side of the table, near the wall phone that she refused to get rid of even though her sisters-in-law had told her several times that *no one* had a landline anymore, looked at him. He locked eyes with her. "They fired me," he said. "They fired Darren, John, Roger, and me."

Joan stood still, knowing that Stephen thought sympathy was for the weak. "Darren's group," she said.

"And that's just the beginning. Sit down, Joan." Joan sat, opposite her husband. "I've made bad decisions based on the advice of risk-taking colleagues and, as a consequence, I've lost a lot of money. I've lost a lot of our savings. I think when I go over everything with you, you will reach the same conclusion I have."

Joan swallowed. "What conclusion have you reached?"

"I think we need to sell the house."

He was overreacting. Joan knew he was overreacting. He did this in a crisis. He jumped to the most dismal, but in the end least likely scenario. It was his way of processing bad news, which was not well tolerated in the Howard world. But if he threw himself into the darkest corner of the pit, there was only one way to go. Joan had long ago realized that Stephen, when adversity struck, needed, at first anyway, to wallow in it. He did not want to be told that everything would eventually work out for the best, or that they would certainly not have to sell the house. So, she simply said, "Okay."

APRIL

Chapter 28

The Well Protected Women were not meeting because the Hartford school system was on spring break, so Alice was available for lunch. After they ordered their meals, Alice updated Ellie and Joan about her increasing accuracy at the shooting range. All the instructors called her a natural. And Ellie told Joan and Alice that she had secured the business of Seashore Ice Cream, the most popular of the three parlors in the downtown area. It was Diana, Ellie told them, who introduced her to the owner. They were about halfway through their Southwestern chicken salads, the special that day, when Joan told Alice and Ellie that Stephen had lost his job.

"What the hell happened?" asked Alice, her fork and its attached lettuce leaves stopped on its way from the plate to her mouth.

"It's one of those bullshit reorganizations," said Joan. "And they decided to cut from the top instead of from the bottom."

"I can't believe it," said Ellie. "How long has Stephen been working there?"

"At First Federal? Almost twenty years," said Joan. "He started there right after leaving Morgan Stanley in the late nineties."

Alice used her front teeth to remove the lettuce from her fork. She chewed several times and then said, "I know you must be worried, Joan. But, from what you've told us, Stephen is really well connected. I don't think he will have trouble finding another job. His record shows that he is loyal. He has a ton of experience. Two months, maybe three tops, and he will be sitting behind a bigger desk at a better bank." Ellie was nodding her head as Alice was talking.

"I don't know," said Joan, taking a sip of her water. "He's fifty-three years old. He makes a very good salary. And he was planning on working only another four or five years."

"He's the perfect hire," said Ellie. "He can walk confidently into any number of financial jobs due to his vast experience, which means he can hit the ground running, no tedious training required. He can probably *lead* whatever training needs to be done and run several departments while he's doing it. Stephen's resume is worth something."

Joan shrugged. "What you say sounds good, Ellie. And it makes sense. But whether or not it will actually happen is another matter. Stephen doesn't want to move—all his family is here. His choices are limited."

"How far is he willing to commute?" asked Alice.

"We've talked about that," said Joan. "It's hard to do much more than an hour each way and have any kind of quality of life. The super-commute is an option, but that brings its own challenges. I think he could easily get a job in New York—but he'd have to find a place to stay three or four nights a week. And that's financially prohibitive unless his new employer wants to include that in the deal."

Alice shoveled a forkful of black beans into her mouth. "Does this make you think more about working?" she asked, chewing. Since they had decided to meet over lunch, the three friends had long ago abandoned the good manners rule of not talking with one's mouth full of food.

"Alice," said Joan, "what kind of job am I going to find where I could make even one twentieth of Stephen's salary?"

Alice shook her head. "I'm not talking about being the bread-winner here. I'm talking about contributing. And I'm talking about having some independence."

Joan poured more dressing onto her salad. "Go on," she said.

"It's something I have been thinking about," said Alice. "It's past time for me to get out of the house. And I'm still not sure I want to work at one of our stores. Lately, I've been thinking that maybe I could be a security guard—find some kind of job in which I could use my newfound skills and interest in guns."

"And you have talked about teaching," said Ellie, moving the focus back to Joan. "Maybe you could get certified this spring and summer and start in the fall."

Joan offered a slight smile. "You two are crazy."

"We're not," said Ellie. "I work because it would be hard to live on Chris's salary alone. But I also work because I really like earning money."

Joan frowned. "I'm not sure I know how to work."

"That's only because you don't work," said Alice. "I'm dying to work again, once I find whatever it is I want to do. It's so nice to earn an income, to have a little bit of financial independence."

"I love it for that reason alone," said Ellie. "I help with our utility bills and groceries, but I have money left over for myself."

"Which you never spend on yourself, I might add," said Joan.

"Sure I do," said Ellie. "I'm wearing new pants even as we speak."

Joan bent down and looked under the table. "They're very nice pants," she said, after she had lifted her head.

Ellie lifted the corners of her lips. "I know you think I'm being silly, but it really is true. There is something to be said about earning your own money, whether you need it or not. If I didn't have a job, I'd feel guilty about buying stuff for myself, about going out to lunch every other Wednesday."

"The Howard women have absolutely no trouble spending money on themselves."

"But maybe you do," said Alice. "And now you have the perfect excuse."

"I don't think so," said Joan. "I think Stephen would be humiliated if I wanted to work, especially now."

"Yeah? When's the last time you talked about it?" asked Alice.

The server came to the table to clear their plates. Joan and Ellie ordered coffee, and Alice asked for green tea. As soon as the server left, Joan said, "I'm not sure we ever have."

"You're not serious," said Ellie, eyes wide, a small smile on her face.

"Oh, I am, indeed, serious," said Joan.

"That," said Alice, "is ridiculous."

Joan reached for the cream so she could put it in her coffee as soon as it was set down in front of her. "Welcome to the Howard family."

"You have got to shake things up a bit, Joan. Seriously, I think the Howard women would thank you."

Joan stirred her coffee. "The Howard women would think I was out of my mind. And they would be pissed at me for messing with their sweet deal."

"So, none of them wants to work?"

Joan hesitated. "I don't think so. At least working has never been discussed when we are together."

"So they enjoy being kept women?"

And while Joan didn't think any of Stephen's family members would consider themselves kept, it was easier to agree than to explain. "I guess so."

"Well, think about it," said Ellie. "I think you'd be an awesome teacher." Joan shifted her gaze to Ellie and, for a moment, considered telling her friends about the robbery in the women's room. She had not yet told Stephen she was robbed, mostly because he was absorbed in his own problems. The money she had lost was a considerable sum, but it was play money, meaning it was Joan's to use at her discretion. Stephen didn't ask her how she spent it. Although he had just the other night told her to consider operating without a weekly allowance until he found another job and to start wearing the clothes she already had in her closet.

CHAPTER 29

Since she had revealed to Diana at the pet store the day after her lunch with Joan that she, too, was gay, Ellie regularly fantasized about what it would be like to live with Diana, to be with Diana all the time. They would share a house with enough room for the two of them and their two dogs—and there would be additional bedrooms for visiting children. They would do everything together, from gardening, raking the leaves, and other household chores to walking the dogs, meeting new friends, and talking about their communal goals. And they would sleep in the same bed. As Ellie pulled her car into the pet store parking lot, she stopped thinking about a life with Diana. She knew how foolish, and dangerous, it was to daydream about something that could never happen. Ellie would never leave her husband. He might forgive her, but her family never would.

Just the previous Sunday, the Kilcullens had gathered for an Easter celebration. It had been a mild, sunny day, and the grandchildren, who ranged in age from five to twenty-six, spent almost an hour searching for colored hard-boiled eggs hidden, as tradition dictated, by the Kilcullen sons. The eggs had all been dyed pastel colors by the wives, who had also carefully written the names of the dozen grandchildren present on six eggs each. The age of the child determined the difficulty of the hunt, meaning the eggs assigned to the five-year-old were out in the open and easy to see, and those intended for the older grandchildren were harder to ferret out: of the stones that comprised the boundary wall surrounding the property or in the knotholes in trees. The men even buried some eggs, forcing those in their teens and twenties to look for signs of fresh ground disturbance. While the children searched, the grown-ups sat on the Kilcullens' huge sun porch, drinking Brigid's Bloody Marys, and discussing whatever casually came up in conversation. They were talking about baseball, Ellie remembered, when two of her nieces, one six and one seven, ran, holding hands, to their grandfather, the hunt scorekeeper and rules master. One of her brothers had pointed out the scene as *pretty damn cute,* and another, who was on his third drink, called the girls, neither one of them his, future lesbians. The men all laughed, even Chris; Ellie was silent.

"What's the matter, El?" asked Sean. "You got no sense of humor today?"

"I don't think your remark was funny."

"He's just horsing around," said William. "He doesn't really think Sophie and Brady are gay."

"No," said Sean. "And anyway, the lesbians don't start licking each other off until they get to high school." Aiden spit out his drink and guffawed. Ellie stood and left the room. She walked through the living room and into the dining room that held two long tables she had set when they arrived at the house after church. Ellie walked into the kitchen, where her mother, apron on the minute after she had shed her camel hair coat, was stirring the hollandaise sauce that was warming on the stove top.

"Can I help you?" asked Ellie, kissing her mother's cheek and pushing the conversation on the porch into the back of her brain.

"You have already been a big help," Brigid said. "Now, if I could only get your brothers to help, I could finally put my feet up." Ellie smiled at her mother, knowing what she had just said were just words. They had been said before; they would be said again. Brigid had waited on her sons from the moment they had expectations of her to do so. To be fair, she had attended to Ellie's needs for a while, too. But Ellie, having what her father called a kind and generous soul from early childhood, had refused Brigid's help midway through elementary school, and, instead, had offered hers. And so it had been some time since Brigid had fussed over her daughter. She liked to cook alone, Brigid did, but she was pleased to have help transporting the food from the kitchen to the warming units on the dining room sideboard. "Where are we on the hunt, Ellie?"

Ellie looked at her watch. "I think we'll be wrapping up in another ten minutes or so."

"Good," said Brigid, on her way to the fridge. She reached in for a freshly made pitcher of Bloody Marys. "Why don't you head back to the porch, refill glasses, and let everyone know the meal will be served as soon as the hunt ends." She handed the pitcher to Ellie. When Ellie got back to the porch, her brothers were gone, having joined their wives out on the lawn to witness what they always called the photo finish. Once the grandchildren had all their eggs, either in their hands or in a basket, they had to sprint to their grandfather and touch his outstretched hand before they could be declared the winner. The brothers had forgotten all about Sean's comment on the porch because it had had no impact on them; what he had said was no more incendiary than an offhand remark about the weather, for everyone on the porch, except for Ellie.

Shifting her thoughts to the present, Ellie parked and got out of her car, and then walked through the pet store door, triggering the electronic bell. She waved at Shawna, who had looked up from her paperwork behind the counter and smiled, before walking to the back of the store and into Diana's office. Diana, who was on the phone, waved Ellie in, and then held up the index finger of her left hand to indicate that she would be off and available in a minute. "Of course, I'm disappointed," Diana said to the person on the other end of the line. "We love your product, and our customers love your product. Do you have any suggestions for an alternative?" Ellie removed her coat and sat in the chair facing Diana's desk. She studied Diana's face, framed by soft hair that was not bound at the back of her head as it normally was. Her lips were gently stretched into a slight smile as she talked. And when she looked up from her paperwork and again made eye contact with

Ellie, the same jolt that Ellie had felt the day she met Diana—that she felt every time she was with her—fired up her heart rate. "I see," said Diana. "Well, the best of luck to you in your retirement. I'm sorry you couldn't talk your children into taking over for you. Yes, the world is a bigger place now. Thanks, Fred." Diana hung up the phone and smiled at Ellie. "How are you today?"

"From the sound of your conversation, I must be better than you."

"Oh, it's not that big a deal, really," said Diana. "Fred is one of our suppliers. He makes incredible dog food—all natural, reasonably priced—and he's closing down his production plant outside of Hartford at the end of the month. The man is seventy-five years old. I can hardly blame him."

"Boy, I hope I'm not working when I'm seventy-five."

Diana closed the manila folder that had been open in front of her and set it aside. She leaned back in her chair and stretched her hands over her head. She smiled at Ellie. "What do you want to be doing when you're seventy-five?"

"I don't know," said Ellie. "But whatever it is, I'd like to be doing it with you."

Diana's smile quickly faded as she lowered her arms and righted herself. "Ellie?"

Ellie closed her eyes for a moment and then opened them. "I know what you're thinking. You're thinking that I just told you that I'm gay, and that I now want to completely change my life, so that I can have a relationship with the first lesbian I've ever known."

"Actually," said Diana, "I was thinking how nice it would be to be with you. I know we haven't known each other very long, but I do feel like we are kindred spirits."

Ellie shook her head. "It can never happen."

"Because of your husband and sons?"

"Because of my mother, father, and six brothers."

Diana stood. "I'm going to get another cup of coffee. Would you like some?"

"I'd love some," said Ellie. "Cream and sugar."

"I remember," said Diana. "I'll be right back."

Ellie had surprised herself by her response to Diana's question. Most people considering quitting their marriage would be most concerned, she guessed, with those directly involved—in her case, with her husband, Chris, and her sons, Brandon and Tim. But they were not the first obstacle that came to mind for Ellie; instead, it was the Kilcullen family, with its Roman Catholic conservatism and political profile. As a state senator, her father had always voted alongside the right-wing Republicans, espousing fiscal responsibility and family values. What would happen to him, to his political gravitas, if he had to reveal to his like-minded colleagues that his only daughter was gay? Ellie knew what would happen; they would turn their backs on him. And his Republican, born-again Christian constituents would vote him out of office. He would end his tenure in the senate not as a champion of morality, but as a disgraced failure, as someone who couldn't keep his own house in order.

Diana walked back into her office carrying two mugs of coffee, both emblazoned with Diana's Pet Supply logos. She set one of the mugs down on the desk in front of Ellie, and she walked the other one to the other side of the desk and sat down in her chair. "So," Diana said, "why do you feel like you cannot tell your extended family?"

"I can't tell anybody," said Ellie, wrapping her fingers around the coffee mug. "I'm not like you, Diana. I can't do this."

"Ellie, it's okay. We're just talking. You don't have to do anything today."

"And I won't be able to do anything tomorrow or the day after. I will never be ready to do this."

"If you are resolved to tell your family, you will be surprised at your strength and ability to do so. It's the depth of your conviction that will see you through this," said Diana, reaching for her mug. "When you are ready, you will do it. When you can no longer live the life you are living, you will have the conversation that you have rehearsed a hundred times in your mind."

"That's so easy to say."

Diana raised her eyebrows at Ellie. "It may be easy to say, in your opinion, but it isn't easy to do. I've done this, Ellie. I've done what you are contemplating. So I have a little bit of experience here."

"I understand that," said Ellie. "But your family is not like my family."

Diana sipped her coffee. "Maybe, just maybe, Ellie, your family will be more reasonable than you think. From what you tell me, from the stories you share, I can tell there's a lot of love in the Kilcullen family."

"It's conditional love," said Ellie. "There are rules that have to be followed."

"So then it's up to you to decide if you are able to stretch or even break the rules in the pursuit of happiness."

"I cannot break the rules," said Ellie, standing and reaching for her coat. "I will never be able to break the rules. I cannot be with you. I cannot be gay. I'm sorry, Diana. I have to go." Ellie rushed out of the office and out of the store, and once in her car, out of the parking lot. All the way home, she told herself that she would carry on with her life as she had been living it. She would be a straight mother to her boys; a loving wife to her husband; an obedient daughter. But by the time she parked her car in the driveway, she admitted that, at this point, she wasn't sure she could continue to live a lie, now that she had defined it. She had been doing it for too long, denying her true feelings for too long, going through the motions for too long. There was only one way to go now, and that was forward, even though she was terrified of doing so. Tears came to her eyes, and her hand trembled as she unlocked the back door. At that very moment, she was convinced that, if she had to continue living a lie, then she would rather not continue living.

CHAPTER 30

"Just the fact that he's had three interviews is amazing," said Ellie. "Is he using a headhunter?"

"He is," said Joan. "That and social media. Cassie has helped tremendously with his LinkedIn page."

"Social media is such a good way to make quick connections," said Alice. "Remember what it did for our Kensington store opening? He'll be back to work in no time."

"I sure hope so," said Joan. "Because having him around the house is definitely messing with my mojo. I feel like I need to entertain him all the time when all I really want to do is get my own stuff done—and to be alone."

"He must be spending some time on the computer," said Ellie. "And then he's had these interviews."

Joan sipped her cold tap water, a poor substitute for the peppery taste of vodka. Since Stephen had been home for three weeks and, had therefore, been aware of her comings and goings, she had spent considerably fewer hours at the casino. She had been back since the robbery in the women's room because she had convinced herself that changing her behavior as a result of the incident would prolong its effects—a specious theory. She went back to the casino because she loved playing roulette. So, she had gone three times in that span, citing a list of errands on her way out the door, instead of three or four times that amount. And she missed it. She missed the confidence, the sense of independence that the casino instilled in her. She missed nurturing, giving in to her resurrected attraction to risk and adventure. She missed the gambling. She missed the drinking. Sure, she and Stephen sometimes had a drink before dinner, but it was so calculated, so measured. At the moment, he was overly mindful of keeping his head clear, so he was drinking just one gin and tonic. Opportunity could present itself, he had said more than once, during an evening phone call. "Yes," said Joan, responding to Ellie. "He's on the computer and making calls in the morning. But by late morning, he emerges from the study and wonders what I am up to. It doesn't feel right, somehow, to be sitting on the living room couch with a novel in my hands. If I'm balancing the checkbook, that's fine. But he doesn't seem to understand my leisure time. In fact, he asked me the other day what, exactly, I did each day to fill my time. 'When is it,' he asked, 'that you do something productive?' "

"Wait a minute," said Alice. "Didn't he put you in this position in the first place? I mean, he doesn't, or didn't, want you to work, right?"

"You are absolutely right, Alice," said Joan. "And that was all fine and good when he didn't have to witness my goofing off."

"So get out of the house," said Ellie. "Make up some errands."

"I do get out of the house," said Joan. "But he questions me upon my return. Where were you? Who were you with? And staying away from my house for no reason seems ridiculous."

"He's being ridiculous," said Alice. "Has he always been like this?"

"God no," said Joan. "He has been wrapped up in his banking world since he left college. The only thing he really cared about on the home front was that the girls were well looked after and that dinner was served at seven."

"That stinks," said Alice.

Joan shook her head in an attempt at refuting Alice's implication that someone else, namely Stephen, had joined Dave in the doghouse. "Look," she said. "I'm making this out to be a bigger deal than it is. Stephen has always been very supportive of my doing whatever leisure and volunteer activities I choose. He's simply at a loss now that he is not working. As soon as he gets back to an office, his scrutiny of my life will cease and desist. He will have a bunch of new people to manage."

Ellie bit into the second half of her Very Grown-Up Grilled Cheese, which featured four kinds of cheese, pesto, pine nuts, and spinach leaves. "Have you talked to him about getting a job?"

"No," said Joan. "He is definitely not in the right frame of mind for that discussion." Joan had also not yet had a conversation with Stephen about the robbery at the casino. She'd told him she'd left her wedding rings in a restaurant bathroom, after taking them off to rub lotion into her hands. And when she realized she had walked out of the women's room without them and raced back, the rings were gone. The jewelry was insured, so it was not going to be a problem to replace them. But Stephen had been surprised by and disappointed in her carelessness. He had not asked about the earrings, since Joan hadn't worn them every day. But she had worn the rings every minute since Stephen had given them to her, and her finger, her hand, still felt odd without them.

"Hey, where are your rings?" asked Alice, as if she had been inside Joan's head. "I don't think you had them on at our last lunch either."

"How would you know that?" asked Joan.

"Because your engagement ring is huge and gorgeous. It's hard to miss, especially if you're a ring gawker like I am."

"They're being reset," said Joan.

"Yeah? I'd like to reset mine," said Alice, "to something much bigger! I mean, there is something sentimental and sweet about having the engagement ring that your husband-to-be gave you when he was young and broke. But there is something fantastic about having a huge ring that everyone looks at."

"That comment out of your mouth surprises me," said Ellie. "Until now, I thought you didn't really care about jewelry."

"That's because I have no jewelry worth caring about," said Alice, laughing. "I really don't care. Big rings, I've learned from the Well Protected Women, are a target for robbers, who know that because a woman has big rings, she probably has a bunch of credit cards and cash, too."

"The rings are not being reset," said Joan. "They were stolen."

"What?" said Ellie. "When?"

"Last month," said Joan. "Here."

"What happened?" asked Alice.

"I went to the bathroom on the way to my car, and I was accosted by a woman in the bathroom."

"What?!" said Alice. "Did she have a weapon?"

Joan made eye contact with Alice. "Yes," she said. "She had a gun."

Alice ran her fingers through her hair. "God, Joan—this is what I'm talking about!" she said. "This is why I'm doing what I am doing! Because the world is a dangerous place filled with nasty people—and the only way to fight back is to arm yourself!"

"I'm so sorry," said Ellie. "Are you okay? Did you get hurt?"

"Of course she's not okay," said Alice, shooting a loaded look at Ellie. "She was robbed at gunpoint. She was defenseless. Joan, if you'd had a gun, you could have fought back."

Joan sighed. "Alice, if I'd had a gun, the thief or I could be dead right now."

Alice shook her head. "That's not the way it goes down," she said. "If you had pulled out your gun, the woman would have realized you were no longer the easy mark she made you out to be, and she would have run from the bathroom."

"I'm not sure," said Joan. "She didn't look like she had it together. She might have been on drugs."

"So then you pull the trigger," said Alice. "You shoot her in the thigh."

"She was pregnant," said Joan. "Plus, I'm not going to shoot someone over three thousand dollars and my wedding rings and a pair of earrings."

Ellie put down her sandwich. "What were you doing with three thousand dollars? Do you always carry that kind of money around with you?"

Joan reached for her water glass. Here was another chance to tell the truth, to tell her friends that she had been coming to the casino for months to gamble, that she often sipped vodka as she did so. Alice and Ellie both looked at her expectantly. "I had the money in my purse to pay a contractor who only accepts cash."

"That's bad timing," said Ellie.

Neither Ellie nor Alice asked Joan about the timing of the robbery, about whether it had occurred on a day they'd had lunch together.

"Come with me to the meeting next month," said Alice. "You don't have to make any promises to me about arming yourself. But at least you will be educated by people who know what they're talking about."

"We'll see," said Joan, choosing to table the discussion rather than continue it. Alice had become enamored with the Second Amendment to the U.S. Constitution, the National Rifle Association, target practice, everything having anything to do with carrying guns. And like most people with a new passion, she needed very little encouragement to talk about it.

"And, of course, you're welcome to come, too, Ellie," said Alice. "It's an extremely welcoming group." Joan was tempted to say that she thought the Reverend Jim Jones had probably been pretty damn welcoming as well.

"You're nice to ask, Alice," said Ellie. "Chris is fairly savvy when it comes to firearms. And every year, when he and the boys are getting ready for their hunting trip, I do get a bit of an earful."

"Well, you can't talk about it enough," said Alice. "People try to sweep the right to bear arms under the rug along with all the other human rights out there. As a member of the Well Protected Women, I need to do whatever I can to educate the general populace."

Joan looked at her watch longer than it took her to read the time. "Well, I've got to get rolling," she said. "I promised Stephen a stew for dinner, and if I don't get it in the oven in the next hour, we'll be having takeout—which would prompt yet another discussion about how I spend my days."

"Oh, I love stew," said Ellie, pushing back her chair and then standing. "Send me that recipe, will you?"

"I will when I get home; I've got to run an errand first," said

Joan, taking her coat from the back of her chair. "Cassie's birthday is coming up, and Stephen wants me to get her something special from Tiffany."

"Must be nice," said Alice.

Joan got a ten and a five out of her wallet and handed them to Ellie, who was calculating the check. "So, I'll see you two later."

"Yes," said Ellie, setting the check and the bills down on the table. "Wish Stephen good luck on the job front."

"I will," said Joan. "Thanks."

Joan walked to the restaurant entrance, turned, and waved at Ellie and Alice, who were still watching her, and then walked out. She would have to remember to e-mail Ellie the recipe for the Howard stew, which had served as an excuse rather than an accounting of how Joan would be spending her afternoon. She hadn't made the stew in years. Stephen, in fact, didn't like it very much. Perhaps, she thought on her way to the roulette table, she'd better write a reminder to herself. Alice had recently taught her the benefits of using the notepad feature on her phone.

"I hope she goes with me," said Alice, standing next to Ellie, who was putting on her coat.

"She may," said Ellie. "Keep in mind that you know where Joan stands on gun control. Just because she had this incident—that thankfully resulted in nothing but missing jewelry and money—does not mean that she'll suddenly want to carry a weapon."

Alice shrugged her coat onto her shoulders. "How can you say that jewelry and money are nothing? They were Joan's property, taken from her without consent simply because one person had a gun and the other one didn't."

Ellie nodded her head as she slipped her fingers into her gloves. "I hear what you're saying, Alice. Joan certainly knows your offer is genuine."

Alice looked into Ellie's eyes, searching for signs of derision. Seeing none, she said, "Thanks, Ellie. Anything you can do to encourage Joan to take action would certainly be appreciated."

Ellie patted Alice's shoulder with her hand and said, "Have a good afternoon now," before walking out of the restaurant. They had driven in separate cars to the casino, as Alice had come directly from target practice.

Alice picked up her phone from the table. She texted her friend Jamie from WPW.

My friend Joan was robbed at gunpoint at the casino last month.

Jamie, who, like Alice, thought anyone with a cell phone had an obligation to check it frequently and respond to messages immediately, texted back.

OMG! Do you need an intervention? Can we get her to a meeting?
Working on it.
Let me know what I can do to help!
I knew you'd say that. I appreciate your support.
I've got your back, girl. So does the rest of the organization.

Alice sent Jamie a smiley face emoticon, and then slipped her phone into her pants pocket.

CHAPTER 31

Alice didn't tell anyone about the march on the state capitol, not Dave, not her daughters, not Joan, not Ellie, no one. She drove herself to Hartford and met Jamie and Cindy from Well Protected Women in a commuter parking lot. When she drove her car into the lot, Jamie and Cindy, recognizing Alice's Subaru from the picture of it Alice had sent in a text earlier that morning, broke away from the WPW crowd gathered and approached the car. As soon as Alice turned off the ignition and unlocked her doors, Jamie, who had been hovering outside the driver's side, opened the door and leaned in. "Good to see you, Alice," she said, giving her a hug.

"It's great to be here," said Alice. "I had no idea that this many of us were going to show up."

"Oh yes," said Cindy. "As you are probably beginning to learn, we are a motivated group. It doesn't take much to get these women out of their houses and offices for some First and Second Amendment exercises at the state capitol."

"I'm impressed."

"Well, we're impressed you're here," said Jamie. "You never know who's really committed until the activism starts. It's one thing to attend civilized meetings, discuss policy, and pay dues. It's another matter altogether to participate, to effect change. Unfortunately our president is out of the country on business, or she would be leading the charge. She asked Cindy and me to organize the march."

"So," said Alice, grabbing her purse from the passenger seat before getting out of the car. "What's the plan?"

"It's an ambitious one," said Cindy. "We're going to march to the state capitol and attempt to walk into the building with our concealed weapons."

Alice hesitated a moment. "I thought weapons aren't allowed in the capitol."

"That's correct," said Jamie.

Alice wrinkled her forehead. "Then why are we walking in with them?"

"Because we think they should be allowed everywhere in Connecticut—in the state capitol, on college campuses, in municipal buildings, wherever," said Cindy. "That's the very point we want to make today!"

"But . . ." Alice started.

"No time for talking right now," said Jamie. "We've got to get moving."

The three women walked from Alice's car to the other side of the lot, where fifty or so women were standing. On this mild morning, most were dressed in jeans and brightly colored Well Protected Women T-shirts, free to all members. Some held disposable cardboard cups of coffee from Dunkin' Donuts and Starbucks. Others held plastic bottles of water. When Jamie and Cindy approached the group with Alice, every set of eyes in the group was upon them.

"Okay, ladies," Cindy said in an outdoor voice. "Jamie and I want to thank you all for being here on this beautiful morning. We know you could be doing a million other things—but you are here. And that tells us a lot!" A number of women applauded. Cindy held up her hand, and they immediately quieted down, like second graders practicing good behavior in exchange for extra recess. Cindy waited a dramatic moment and then looked at her watch. "In a minute or so, we are going to start our walk to the capitol." She took a revolver from her belly belt and held it in the air. "For those of you with weapons, please carry them in the place you normally carry them—in your purse, in your bra, wherever. The point is not to *show* anyone our weapons. The point is to be able to walk into the state capitol *with* our weapons. Our intention is to go through the front doors and proceed to the governor's office."

"Any last-minute questions?" shouted Jamie.

"Aren't there metal detectors?" called a woman from the group.

"Good question," said Cindy. "Yes, there are metal detectors. We are going to attempt to walk through the metal detectors and to the governor's office."

"Won't they stop us?" asked another woman.

"They can try," said Cindy. "But I would encourage you to keep going. Jamie and I will go first and try to talk some sense into the state police."

Alice had an unsettled feeling in her stomach. She was not sure if she had misinterpreted Cindy's e-mail announcing the rally, or if she had simply chosen to read what she wanted to read because she was so excited about the prospect of participating in something that mattered to her. But it had been her understanding that the women were simply going to march to the capitol and hold an awareness rally outside the west visitor entrance for maximum visibility. How could they get into the capitol building with guns when it was illegal to do so?

"Ladies!" cried Cindy. "Grab your signs, and let's march!" As the crowd started moving, Alice could see the signs leaning against the chain link fence behind them. Some of the women stopped and picked up a sign. Most of the signs looked handmade, constructed from white poster board, taped or stapled to wood yardsticks or broom handles. The signs, Alice could see as they were lifted above the heads of the marchers, featured large letters written in colored markers: GUNS PROTECT US! ALLOW GUNS EVERYWHERE IN CT! WE ARE NOT AFRAID! WE HEART THE 2ND AMENDMENT! Alice fell into step with the other marchers. Not asking Alice to join them, Cindy and Jamie had moved to the front of the crowd to lead the way.

It was a very short march, just over a mile, Alice calculated with her runner's brain. Along the way, the women walked on the sidewalks. Some of the people in cars along the same route sounded their horns in allegiance, resulting in bursts of applause and shouts of approval from the group. Alice was silent, wondering if what she was doing, if what all of them were doing, was an idea with merit. She believed that most causes needed leaders willing to make personal sacrifices—but she was not sure she was a leader. Hadn't she made her sacrifice when the man attacked her on the running trails? Hadn't she taken action by applying for a permit and learning how to shoot a gun? Was she now expected to further the political goals of the Well Protected Women? Did she really care if guns were allowed in the legislative buildings? As she was formulating the answers to these and other questions in her mind, Cindy and Jamie were suddenly again in her presence. They linked their elbows with her and brought her to the front of the group. Cindy yelled "Onward!" and they marched through the doors of the Connecticut State Capitol. Within seconds, the metal detector alarms sounded, the state police were upon them, and Alice was quickly facedown on the floor with her hands cuffed behind her back, feeling not like a hero but instead like a victim, like she had felt that day she was attacked on the running trail. Cindy, who had called an officer a "fucking pig" before spitting in his face, had been hauled off the floor and into an adjoining room.

Four hours later, Alice drove home. She had been frisked, questioned, and released because she was not carrying a weapon, and, therefore, was doing nothing illegal. But she had been given a stern warning by a member of the state police, who told her that guns in the capitol building were perceived as a threat to the governor and the legislative process. And that if he, or any other member of the state police, found her again amid a group of armed women in the capitol, she would be treated in the same manner as the others and arrested.

Alice's only other brush with police had been in college. Before she had started dating her husband, she had a brief romantic involvement with a student political activist named Rodd Hamilton. Rodd had come from an affluent California family and had enjoyed a privileged upbringing that included private schooling, lavish vacations, pretty girlfriends, popularity, and the self-entitlement and hubris that can accompany such economic and social status. At

Reed College, Rodd did what people later referred to as a one-eighty. He severed all ties with his family, renounced what he called the entrapments of wealth, and emptied his substantial bank account with a single check to Greenpeace. In fact, caught up in the controversy about commercial whaling, he not only joined the organization, but he also volunteered to be their Reed College representative. Alice, looking for something other than a keg party to pass one Saturday night, walked into one of his meetings—and was immediately taken in. It was not the Greenpeace mission that necessarily spoke to Alice, although she was concerned about what her biology professor had called the deterioration of the planet; but, rather, it was Rodd himself. He was a strikingly handsome young man, with the clear complexion, full head of wavy hair, brilliant eyes, and towering stature of American nobility. There were fifteen or so people in the room, sitting on couches and in stuffed armchairs, listening, raptly it appeared to Alice, to Rodd talk about Russian whaling vessels. Encouraged by Rodd with a hand motion to join the group, Alice sat in a vacant seat and spent the next hour staring at his made-for-the-movies face and listening to his plan to end the slaughter of innocent creatures. When the meeting ended, Alice chose to walk out of the room rather than approach him like the other, mostly female, members of his audience. Twenty minutes later, he found her drinking coffee in a booth at the student union and asked her if he could sit down.

Their subsequent four-month relationship was much more superficial than Rodd's cause. He was two years her senior and, in Alice's opinion, the best-looking guy she had ever seen; he thought she looked like Joni Mitchell. The sex was frequent and fantastic, as was their conversation, because Alice, like many lovers at first, was enamored with everything Rodd said, and he was impressed by her quick grasp of his theories and strategies. It was one of those strategies—the idea to place himself in a Zodiac inflatable boat, physically between a Russian whaling vessel and its prey—that drew the attention of the local and state authorities. And since Alice was on the beach with Rodd and two other Greenpeace activists the designated day of the intervention, she, too, was transported to the state police headquarters. It was then that she decided she was either not a natural born leader like Rodd, or that she was simply not interested enough in the cause to risk arrest and a disruption of her studies, her student life. Rodd, who was disappointed in her lack of conviction, broke off their relationship. A month or so later, Alice's romance with Dave heated up, and she soon after forgot about Rodd, as well as Russian whaling—until now. Her stake in the Second Amendment was much more personal than had been her interest in whales. But the two activist events in her life were linked, by her initial attraction to people and ideals, and, in the end, by her unwillingness in each instance to commit to the all in, fervently felt, against the law if necessary ideology and tactics required to further a cause.

MAY

CHAPTER 32

"How does he feel about the super-commute?" asked Alice, lifting a forkful of spring greens lightly dressed in balsamic vinaigrette from her plate to her mouth.

Joan finished chewing the bite of flank steak and caramelized onion sandwich in her mouth. She would have to remember to make the sandwich at home, when the girls were around. All four of them loved steak, and Stephen was very capable at grilling. He had little interest in the preparation of food in the kitchen. But give him some beef tenderloins, a marinated pork loin, a butterflied chicken, homemade burgers, anything destined for the grill, and he was eager to help. "He's okay with it," said Joan. "If the bank is willing to put him up in a hotel three nights a week, it's hard to say no."

"Are you okay with his working from home on Fridays?" asked Ellie.

Joan smiled. "I am already rearranging my schedule, so that I will be gone most of the day on Fridays." She wiped a bit of horseradish mayonnaise from the corner of her mouth. "We will need to update his home office with whatever he needs for this new role, but that should be relatively easy. He will be traveling some, too, in this job."

"How do you feel about that?"

Joan raised her eyebrows at Ellie. "Are you kidding? I can't wait. Stephen and I have had a whole lot of quantity time lately; we could both use a break."

Ellie took a sip of water. "Chris and I have never spent a night apart from each other since we were married."

"What?" asked Alice.

"I know," she said. "It's hard to believe, isn't it?"

"No weekends away, out of town funerals, business travel?" asked Joan.

"Nope," said Ellie, studying the sweet potato chip she held between her thumb and index finger.

"Not a single day," said Alice, who, after checking her phone for messages, set it back down on the table.

"Not a single day."

"I can't believe you haven't jumped off a cliff by now," said Joan, a smile on her face.

Ellie's somber face brightened. "Oh, believe me, I've thought about it."

"I can't believe there's no gym teacher convention in, say, Boulder, Colorado, where they could all climb a mountain while discussing childhood obesity," said Alice.

"He went to Hartford for a couple days last year, for the first Connecticut Physical Education Teachers' Annual Meeting—but he came home at night, preferring to commute instead of spending the night in a hotel."

"Well, that's kind of sweet," said Alice.

"Not really," said Ellie. "He likes routine. He likes knowing his schedule. He likes eating what he wants to eat. He likes the coffee at home. Chris is not big on change."

Alice scooped the last bit of tuna salad on her plate onto her fork. "I'm not sure any man likes change," she said. "Dave is so settled into his pattern—if he poops a half hour after his normal bathroom time, he's in a mood."

Joan laughed. "Stephen likes to pour his coffee into his travel mug at exactly seven thirty. God forbid the coffee is still brewing when he needs it in his mug."

"Why seven thirty?" asked Ellie.

"Because he walks out the door at seven thirty-two."

"So how is your man, who doesn't like change any better than our men do, going to swing this job in New York?" asked Alice.

Joan finished chewing her last bite and was instantly sad that her sandwich was gone. "He's making lists, charts, diagrams—the man has never talked about Microsoft Office until two days ago. And now that's all he talks about."

"Sounds fascinating," said Alice, a grin on her face.

"Yeah, shoot me now," said Joan, who quickly regretted the words that had just slipped out of her mouth. She made eye contact with Ellie instead of Alice.

Alice picked up on Joan's evasive move. "You can look at me, Joan," she said. "I'm not going to bend your ear about Well Protected Women."

Joan sat back in her chair. "Why not?"

And Alice told her friends about the march on the state capitol, about her near arrest, about her wavering conviction. She was still interested in guns and planned on owning one as soon as her permit was approved. But she was less enthralled with the group, particularly with the leadership. They were zealots, she said, and she was not. "Does this make me a softie?" she asked. "An uncommitted amateur? An equivocal housewife?"

"No," said Joan, almost too quickly. She was so relieved to hear that Alice was having second thoughts about the Well Protected Women, especially after hearing about their attempt to storm the state police metal detectors. What was it about people with one track minds? "Backing away from stupidity sounds pretty smart to me."

"I think I know what you're asking, Alice," said Ellie. "Are you wondering how we define ourselves if we have no strong convictions, if we have allegiances to nothing?"

Alice looked at Ellie and then squinted her eyes. "I think I am, Ellie. I think that's exactly what I'm wondering."

"Me too," said Ellie. "I've been wondering that for some time now."

Joan exaggerated a blink. "Educate me."

"It's just another way of asking what we are doing with our lives," said Ellie. "Now that our children have left the house, and we are no longer day to day mothers, what are we?"

"So," said Joan, closing one eye, "being a member of a group that breaks the law to further their personal agenda is a good thing?"

"No," said Ellie, "but it's something. I'm talking about having convictions—or at least having interests. For so many years, we put whatever interests we had aside so that we could raise our children. And now we have an opportunity to rediscover these interests or to find new ones. Alice had—still has—an interest in her own protection with firearms. And she was charged up by being part of a movement. But now that she is questioning that movement, she is questioning herself. Here it is, May. Our children have been gone for almost nine months and what do we have to show for it?"

"You're serious," said Joan.

"I'm quite serious," said Ellie. "If a man has a midlife crisis, he buys a sports car and has an affair. We should be able to go a little nuts too. But because we are so sensible and practical from mothering our kids, we do nothing. Or, if we're kind of adventurous, we use ground turkey in our meatloaves instead of beef."

Alice smiled. "I've used ground turkey all along."

Ellie put down the bite of sandwich she was holding in her hand. "You can joke if you want to," she said. "But I'm close to fifty years old, and, in some ways, I feel like my life hasn't even started yet."

Joan rested her head on her intertwined fingers, elbows on the table. "How would you start it, Ellie? What do you want to do?"

Ellie sat back in her chair, not knowing how to even start the conversation, not knowing how to say aloud that she wanted to leave her husband to pursue a lesbian relationship—even though such an announcement, not to mention a follow-through, would anger, confuse, frustrate, and disappoint everyone in her immediate and extended family. She had since childhood put everyone else's needs before hers. "What if I want to move my needs and wants from the back of the line to the front?"

Alice, who had just responded to a text from Linda at UConn about a care package of cookies for final exam week, put her phone back on the table. "Is that even possible for a mother?"

Ellie pointed at Alice with the index finger of her right hand, a gesture both she and Alice had learned from Joan. "This is my point! We are mothers, yes, but not in the same way we were when our children were still home. They don't need us like they used to. They are moving forward with their lives, which means we have an opportunity to move forward with our lives. Are you moving forward, Joan? Alice?"

Joan looked at the check that the server had placed facedown on the table. "No," said Joan, looking at Ellie. "I'm not."

"I thought I was," said Alice. "I was getting my house in order, getting organized. And then I got attacked—and that changed everything."

Joan, who knew she should be more sympathetic to Alice, but had wearied of her friend's near-rape story and handgun firing chatter, quickly said, "So, the question is still on the table, Ellie. What do you want to do?"

Ellie breathed in and out slowly, finding and then losing her courage. "Too much," she said. "I want to do so much, but I don't know how."

CHAPTER 33

With Stephen gone during the day—for four days at a time now—Joan was able to resume her regular schedule at the casino. But after she had spent several nights in a very quiet house reading in their company-ready living room under dust free lamps or watching unsatisfactory television, Joan decided to try the casino in the evening instead of in the morning or afternoon. She promised herself she would drink only two drinks, like she always did, followed by water and coffee so driving home would not be an issue. Plus, she would not drink on an empty stomach, something she had been better about lately. On this particular evening, she made herself a roast beef and cheddar sandwich, which she worked at eating slowly while reading the newspaper until the six chimes of the clock in the hallway told her it was time to go. If she left home at six, she had discovered, she could play, drink, and talk with strangers for a couple hours, and be home by nine.

When Joan had first started to gamble regularly, she didn't talk much with the other players at her favorite roulette table. But as she had become more familiar with the game, she didn't need to think as much. And some of the people who sat down next to or across the table from her sought conversation. She would give a one sentence response to the first few queries posed by fellow gamblers, but if they persisted after that, it seemed rude not to engage, at least on a superficial level. It was easy for Joan to do this, not because she was a superficial person, but because she understood the social world. The Howard women had prepared her well for casual chatter with almost anyone. The trick was to get the person to talk about herself or himself, and that was not much of a trick at all. Given the chance, and the encouragement, most people could and would talk about themselves for long periods of time, often without asking polite reciprocal questions, often without even realizing this omission.

Occasionally someone versed in the art of conversation did his or her best to draw Joan out, either as a means to avoid revealing intimate details of his or her own life or for amusement. Those in the latter group were rarely disappointed, since Joan was well-read, witty, opinionated, and a convincing liar. Her lies were not malevolent, and she, more and more, did not even consider her stories to be anything but just that, stories. She swapped the details of her life for those of the lives of friends and acquaintances. Sometimes, she made things up—nothing farfetched or grandiose, and absolutely nothing she could get caught in. It would be bad but not impossible luck, she decided, to portray herself as, say, a skydiver to someone who had actually jumped out of a plane. She kept it simple, believable, light.

When she sat at her usual table that evening, she barely had time to purchase chips and order a drink before a suited man in his fifties with the bloodshot eyes of someone who likes hard alcohol joined her. He sat across from her, nodded a greeting, and then ordered a single malt beverage from the waitress who had been hovering next to his right elbow. As soon as she had written his order on her rolled-top pad, she was off, fringed suede sweeping her upper thighs as she walked. The man looked at Joan. "They like to keep the booze flowing," he said in a voice indicating that the drink he had just ordered was not his first. "Gets us to loosen up, gamble more." He bought a thousand dollars in chips from the croupier and set six of them on the layout, all even numbers. Joan had already placed her bet, also even numbers. "What are you drinking? Vodka?"

"Yes."

"You look like a vodka drinker. It's the ladies' choice, you know," he said. "A subtle buzz when consumed in moderation. No odor on the breath." The ball landed in seventeen black, and the croupier, whom Joan didn't recognize, leaned out over the table and swept with his hands their chips into the felted hole in front of his station. "So," said the man, setting another half dozen chips on even numbers, "what's a nice girl like you doing in a place like this?"

Joan had heard this tired question before, more than once, yet she was consistently surprised by the way it came out of a man's mouth, him thinking, perhaps, that its utterance would produce a smile, an opening. Joan shrugged her shoulders and then launched into a story. "My husband is a comedian," she said. "He's in the Fox Den Theater, starting at eight." She looked at her watch.

"No kidding," said the man. "You going to see the show, or is he one of those guys who doesn't like family in the theater?"

"I'll watch him," Joan said. "For a while."

"How's his language," the man asked. "Does he have a foul mouth?"

"Pretty much comes with the territory," said Joan. "He doesn't talk that way at home. But on stage, he gives the people in the audience what they want. Seems the *f* word never loses its comedic appeal. My husband tells me that's because it's so versatile."

"Is that right? I can take or leave it myself."

"Then you probably wouldn't like his show." Suddenly bored with her own tale, Joan stood and cashed in her chips.

"You leaving already?" asked the man, finding Joan's eyes.

"Yes," said Joan, turning her back and leaving the table. She had no idea who was actually performing in the Fox Den that evening, but she was betting that watching whoever it was would be more interesting than passing the next hour with an over-served businessman. The theater, when she reached it, was closed. The show featuring a comedian Joan had never heard of didn't start until nine, and the doors didn't open until eight thirty. By then Joan would be on her way home. What to do for an hour, she thought. As she continued down the main corridor of the casino, she passed by a sports bar illuminated with large-screen televisions suspended from the ceiling. Seeing Red Sox players on the screens, she turned around and walked in. She'd had just one vodka soda at the roulette table; she would have her second here. Within a minute of Joan's settling onto a barstool and rooting through her purse for her wallet, a middle aged man with thick, graying hair combed back on his head sat on the vacant stool next to her. He was dressed in tight-fitting jeans, a black turtleneck, and black leather shoes, looking part European and part like a man who had read in a men's magazine what clothing women in their forties and fifties find attractive. Five minutes later, he had bought her a vodka soda made with Grey Goose and told her he was a Porsche, pronouncing it "porsha," representative scoping out the area for a dealership.

He, Phillip, no surname offered, was tall and lean. He moved slowly, with the subtle gestures of someone who has charmed other women: leaning in to listen to Joan; casually touching her elbow, her knee; buying her this delicious drink. Stephen, too, was tall, but his trimness came and went. He was not like this man, this Phillip who sold expensive cars. Stephen had the—what was the word? Doughy was too harsh. Soft?—look of someone who shunned regular exercise. He'd go on what Joan called fit kicks: run three miles every day for thirteen days and then quit; lift weights with his brothers on Saturday mornings (when it was convenient); use the TRX strap hanging in the basement that their daughter, Cassie, had given him for Christmas. It was always temporary, his interest in exercise, started with gusto and abandoned with excuses. As a result, he looked much better in clothes than naked. Joan didn't fault him for this; after all she hardly exercised, and when she did, she was much like him, into something for a few weeks, and then out of it completely. This man, this Phillip, was not like Joan or her husband. Whatever he did to work out, she could tell that he did it five or six days a week; exercise was as much a part of his day as showering or eating. She could see his developed biceps spreading the ribbing of his shirt sleeves. His thighs filled the fabric of his dark wash jeans. Joan could tell that without clothes he would look like a marble statue of a Roman god. And she wondered what it would be like to have sex with this man.

She had rarely thought about sex with a man other than her husband in the thirty years she had been married. She had an interest in a well built male body, but more in an aesthetic than lustful way. The fit runners that sprinted on the streets of Southwood didn't turn her head, for instance, but the image of their taut, muscular arms and legs in motion stayed with her for a few moments after she drove past them. There had been just one man, at a bank convention ten or twelve years ago, who had tempted her. He was attractive, kempt, and fit, but what most attracted Joan to him was the attention he paid her. This came at a time when Stephen was on the fast track at the bank, which meant he not only worked long hours, but he also had a magnified sense of self-importance. At the convention, he was more interested in smoking cigars with the boys after dinner than in dancing with or talking with Joan. Terry Sullivan was interested in both dancing and talking. He was a divorced, single man at an almost exclusively married event and was grateful, he said at the time, to be seated next to such an intelligent and lovely woman the very first evening. By the second evening, Stephen had spent no more than an hour or so in the company of his wife, and Terry looked at her like she was the only woman in the room. He never solicited her, but Joan knew that if she had initiated an invitation to an intimate encounter that Terry would have eagerly consented. Now, in this sports bar, many years after her glorious three days of undivided attention from Terry, Joan again felt singled out, felt special in a world in which that very word had long ago lost its meaning.

Abruptly aware of her appearance, Joan excused herself and went to the restroom. Looking into one of the mirrors over the row of sinks, she reapplied her lipstick and brushed her hair. She checked her teeth and removed with floss from her purse the tiniest bit of roast beef that had lodged itself between her right incisor and canine. When she walked back to her place at the bar, Phillip smiled at her. Did he know she had been preening for him? Was that what she had been doing, making herself presentable, as her mother-in-law would say, for a stranger? Joan settled onto her stool and took a long drink of her vodka. It was important to the Howard women, and thus to Joan, to be presentable. She had been making herself so every morning before she left the house since she had been engaged to Stephen. She smiled at Phillip and listened to him tell stories about the famous people he had sold cars to—the latest being the young British actor who had just won an Oscar. This led to a discussion about movies, what both of them had recently seen and what they thought about the various actors in the films. It wasn't until Phillip changed topics, asking Joan what she did to occupy her time, other than go to the movies and watch the Red Sox in casino sports bars, that Joan lost her focus, feeling as if she had been plunged fully clothed into a swimming pool. She pulled her gaze from Phillip's face to her drink, which now looked like two drinks. She tried to stand, but she had to lean against the bar for support. In a slow-motion flash, Phillip was at her elbow. He wrapped one arm around her waist and grabbed her coat and purse with his free hand. She looked at him as he steered her toward the exit, but she was not able to find the words to ask him where they were going. She was floating now, on the surface, feeling warm, calm, so relaxed. She was trying to remember how much alcohol she'd consumed, but she could not put a number on it. She faltered in front of an elevator.

"Are you okay?" he asked.

Joan brushed away the hair that had fallen from her forehead into her eyes. "I'm not sure," she said. "I think the alcohol . . ."

"It's the Rohypnol I put into your drink."

"What?".

"It's a relaxation drug, meant to, well, relax you, Joan. I'm taking you to my room, where I'd like you to be able to relax."

"Help," said Joan, in a voice no louder than a whisper. "I need help." The elevator doors opened to reveal a casino security guard, who looked at Joan and looked at Phillip.

"My wife's had too much to drink," said Phillip, reading the concerned look on the guard's face. "I'm just taking her back to our room."

Having seen a thousand drunk women in his ten-year tenure, the security guard was not convinced that Joan was merely drunk, or that the man supporting her was her husband. Plus, there was something familiar about the woman. "Let me help you, sir," he said.

"Oh, we're okay," said Phillip, dragging Joan into the elevator and pushing the button for the eighth floor. "I've got it from here. Thanks for your kind offer."

"It's no trouble at all," said the security guard. "I'll ride up with you." In the several seconds the elevator took to ascend to the eighth floor, the security guard remembered how he knew the woman, how he knew Joan. She was a local who gambled in the afternoon. And she'd been robbed a few months back by a druggie in a women's room. Haywood? Hollings? Howard! Her name was Joan Howard. As soon as the doors opened to the eighth floor, the guard walked off the elevator with Phillip and Joan. "Let me hold her for a minute," he said. "I'd like to see some identification, Mr. Howard."

Phillip heaved Joan's body at the guard and bolted down the hallway. The security guard set Joan, now unconscious, onto the carpeted floor and propped her back against the wall. He then unhooked the radio attached to his belt. "It's Ernest," he said. "I have a woman with me who I suspect has been drugged. Yes. I'm on the eighth floor of the tower, A bank elevators. Can you send someone up with a wheelchair? Good—thanks. Yes. The guy who I suspect did this to her ran from the scene. Middle aged, gray hair, black jeans and turtleneck, blue eyes." Ernest looked at Joan, who had not moved, and then checked the time on his watch. He was only an hour into his shift on what was already proving to be an interesting night. No matter what anyone thought or said about his occupation, being a security guard at the casino was never boring.

Ernest's coworker, Glenn, arrived with the wheelchair, and both men lifted Joan into it and strapped her in place with the seatbelt. They rolled her into the service elevator and pushed the LL button, which would take them to the underground level, where the security department monitored the hotels, restaurants, shops, casinos, and parking lots twenty-four hours a day.

She did not remember either elevator ride, the ambulance trip on the highway, the examination by the doctors, or the intravenous needle going into her arm. When she next opened her eyes, it was light outside. She was in a hospital room, and Stephen was sitting in the chair next to her bed.

Chapter 34

"Rohypnol's effects include sedation, muscle relaxation, reduction in anxiety, and prevention of convulsions. However, Rohypnol's sedative effects are approximately seven to ten times stronger than those of Valium. The effects of Rohypnol appear fifteen to twenty minutes after administration and last approximately four to six hours. Some residual effects can be found twelve hours or more after administration," said Alice, reading from her phone. "Jesus, Joan. I can't believe a middle aged man slipped you a roofie. Linda sent me a text saying that women have to be on their guard at school parties. She never drinks anything she hasn't opened or poured."

"I didn't open or pour my drink," said Joan, a headache forming at her temples, "because I didn't anticipate this would happen. I don't really know why I was in the bar in the first place, let alone accepting a drink from a stranger."

Ellie lifted a slice of thin crust pizza to her mouth. Alice had balked at the idea of eating a "greasy, fatty, high calorie lunch," but she had been pleasantly surprised by the healthy offerings. Ellie, who had suggested the pizza place, ordered a personal size, four cheese pie with fresh diced tomatoes; Joan got mozzarella and sausage; and Alice got the veggie special, covered with broccoli, sautéed mushrooms and onions, red bell peppers, and a sprinkling of cheese.

Alice had downed two slices before Ellie and Joan had finished their first. Ellie took a bite and, chewing, looked at Joan. "What *were* you doing at a bar in the casino on a Tuesday night?"

This was the very question Stephen had asked Joan, after she was discharged from the hospital, had a shower at home, and was sitting on the couch in their family room. And she had shared her story with him, shared her feelings of loneliness and confusion about her role as a mother, shared her frustration at using her brain for nothing but domestic chores, shared her anger at his lack of perception about what an empty nest meant for a woman who had done little outside of tending its inhabitants. Stephen, who had taken the day off from work, who had "cleared his calendar," listened attentively, lovingly even, before apologizing and telling her that they would work through these issues together, that he, too, had felt somewhat adrift since Liz had left the house.

And because Joan had broken the dam when she confided in Stephen, she saw no reason to hold back now. She told Ellie and Alice about the roulette table, about the vodka drinks, and about her decision to walk into a bar alone and accept a drink from a man she didn't know. When she was done, Alice and Ellie were both looking at her as if they had just been told about a good friend of theirs getting into a horrendous car accident.

"God, Joan," said Alice. "What the hell? Why didn't you say anything?"

Joan raised her eyebrows at Alice. "Why didn't I confess sooner to being a problem gambler and daytime drinker? Alice, this is not a good story. This is something to be ashamed of, to hide from those you care about. It's embarrassing. No, it's more than embarrassing; it's pathetic. Middle aged bored housewife turns to gambling and booze when her youngest child leaves the house? Can you see the headline? I haven't told you, Alice, or you, Ellie, because this reads like a story about someone with an unspeakable upbringing, a perilously low level of self-esteem, and an absolute lack of connection with reality."

Ellie shook her head. "No, it doesn't. This kind of thing, this derailing, happens to all kinds of people for all kinds of reasons. As we grow up, Joan, we define ourselves by how others define us. It isn't until we reach middle age that we take the time to wonder who we really are."

Joan laughed. "So the real me is a drunk gambler?"

"No," said Ellie, smiling at her friend. "The real you is *temporarily* a drunk gambler. You are simply in the midst of discovering who you are. If Stephen and Alice and I have anything to do with it, your drunken gambling days are behind you—and you will have a clean slate to figure out what's ahead."

Joan took a sip of water. "It's the clean slate," she said, "that terrifies me."

Alice nodded her head. "Good point, Joan."

Ellie's face broadcast confusion. "I don't get it."

"The slate is clean, and I can now do anything I want to do, right?" said Joan. Ellie nodded her head. "Number one, I have no idea what I want to do, and number two, I'm afraid of failing at whatever I try. We've talked about my interest in teaching math. And in theory, Ellie, that's a great idea. But actually doing it—getting certified, finding a job, standing in front of a classroom of seventeen-year-olds and acting like I'm in charge—terrifies me. I might be able to start a lesson. But five minutes in, all I'd want to do is tuck my textbook and planner under my arm and walk out the door, apologizing along the way for being a complete fraud."

"How do you know you'd feel like that?" asked Ellie. "And why do you think you'd fail?"

"I *don't* know," said Joan. "But the prospect of failing at fifty-two is a whole lot different from failing at twenty-two. We expect young people to fail."

Alice took a broccoli floret off one of her remaining slices and put it into her mouth. "I don't think you'd fail," she said. "If you decide you want to teach and you put as much energy into it as you did raising your girls, I don't think there's even a remote chance of failing. You're too smart. And you care too much. Any kid would be lucky to have you for calculus."

Joan smiled. "I feel like I'm in the midst of an intervention."

"You are!" said Alice. "Look, if you can't turn to your friends in a time of crisis, then what good are they? Who took care of me after I got attacked? Who took me to the police station and to the hospital? Who brought meals to my house? Who sat with me while I cried at my kitchen table? Who listened to me talk about myself for hours without ever once looking at their watches? You two did. It wasn't my husband. It was you, Joan, and you, Ellie."

"Yeah, well, getting attacked is a legitimate cause for alarm, for intervention," said Joan. "I'm a rich woman who doesn't know what to do with her newfound spare time. If one of my sisters-in-law ever confessed to me what I've confessed to you, I'd tell her to grow up."

"No," said Ellie. "You'd help her. Because an issue that's invisible to those around you, even though it consumes you, can be a much harder problem to solve than one people can see."

"You," said Joan, pointing her index finger at Ellie, "should have been a shrink."

"I've thought about seeing a shrink," said Alice.

"What stopped you?" asked Joan, smiling.

But Alice was serious. She shrugged. "I haven't made a definite decision yet. But I do think that if I ever did start seeing a psychologist or a psychiatrist, I would never want to stop."

"What do you mean?" asked Joan, even though she suspected she knew the answer to her own question.

"Can you imagine how nice it would be to walk into someone's office every Thursday morning and be able to—no, be encouraged to—talk about yourself for an hour? And the doctor would do nothing but politely nod her head, jot down a few notes, and ask questions you'd always hoped your husband would be insightful enough to ask. And she would never try to *solve* anything. Dave thinks he has to solve my problems when all I really want him to do is listen to them."

Joan nodded emphatically. "God, yes," she said. "Is it biological, this need men have to fix women's issues, as if we are not capable of fixing them ourselves? Okay, so I screwed up with the gambling and drinking thing, but eventually I would have figured it out, right?"

"Definitely," said Alice.

"And I really love your version of seeing a head doctor."

"Well, maybe you and I should think about it," said Alice, switching her gaze to Ellie. "You, Ellie, as the poster woman for well adjusted, middle aged women, don't need a shrink. You have a part time job that you are good at and that requires brain activity. So, you can check that box. You have incredibly talented and gentlemanly sons, successful mother box checked. You have an obedient dog, check. And your husband does not drink excessively or cheat on you, check. All your boxes are checked."

Ellie looked down at the table. She was, seemingly, not amused the way Alice thought she would be. "Not every box is checked," she said.

"Yeah? What are you missing?" asked Joan.

Ellie made eye contact with Joan and then with Alice. She looked, briefly, up at the restaurant ceiling and then back at them. "I'm missing the biggest box of all," she said.

Both Joan and Alice said nothing. They knew Ellie was referring to a tangible, explainable thing. They also could tell that she wasn't ready to tell them.

CHAPTER 35

Ellie sat at her kitchen table, sipping a cappuccino from a ceramic mug and looking over the Excel spreadsheet she had created for Tip Top Car Wash. The owner wanted to shave five to ten percent off his expenses and had enlisted Ellie's expertise to suggest possible solutions. Labor was Joseph Milligan's biggest line item, but Ellie was hesitant to cut it. Everyone went to Tip Top, Ellie included, because the service included a thorough hand-dry for each vehicle by four or five workers committed to wiping every drop of water from hoods, doors, and windows. When customers drove out of the Tip Top lot, they were pleased with their sparkling vehicles, as well as with the coupon for three dollars off the cost of their next visit. Ellie decided Milligan's customers would rather see an increase in the cost of the wash than lose the coupon. When her cell phone rang, Ellie dug into her purse, which was hanging from the back of the chair she was sitting in. When she saw Diana's name, she silenced the ringer.

Ellie had not spoken to Diana in more than a week, even though Diana had called three, now four, times. Ellie had been confused by their most recent discussion, during which Diana had told her that they shouldn't rush into anything. Those were her words: *Let's not rush into anything.* These had been devastating words to Ellie, not only because they indicated that Diana was not as interested in pursuing a relationship as Ellie was, but also because they meant that Diana thought *rushing* was even an option. Ellie had been gay for almost fifty years and not told a soul, except for Diana. And the fact that she had done so, had confided in Diana, had confessed an attraction for her was interpreted as rushing? Sure, when talking to Diana, Ellie had been excited, words pouring out of her mouth like water from an unkinked garden hose. But this was only because it was suddenly safe to do so. And, of course, Ellie thought Diana would understand. When she didn't, or at least when the look in Diana's eyes changed from warm and caring to what Ellie perceived as cool and detached, Ellie shut her mouth, feeling instantly foolish for thinking of Diana as anything more than a client.

But she *was* more than a client, much more, and every time Ellie thought about her, which seemed to be every ten seconds, her heart ached. Ellie hadn't felt so crushed since college, when her feelings of closeness, of tenderness toward a chemistry lab partner had been harshly rebuffed. The lab partner, Molly Bennett, had also lived in Ellie's dorm. They were fast friends, sharing lab notes and meals together. And Ellie thought she'd discovered what it was like to have a sister. They were studying one night, lying next to each other on Molly's queen sized bed, when Ellie had the urge to kiss her—not in an urgent, passionate kind of way, but rather, in a familial way, on the cheek as an expression of affection. And yet when Ellie leaned in and kissed Molly's cheek, Molly flew off the bed, and accused Ellie of being a lesbian, of making untoward sexual advances. When Ellie found herself in the hallway outside Molly's room minutes later, her euphoric feelings of intimacy and compatibility instantly replaced by sensations of shame and confusion, she decided that it must be better to squelch any expression of love or attraction she might have for another woman. And she had done so from that night forward. She was so good at it that she had convinced herself that her lack of interest in sex with her husband was because she was asexual and not homosexual.

When the phone rang again, Ellie answered it. "What is it,

Diana?" she asked in a voice that did not manage to mask her fragile emotions.

"I'm glad you picked up."

"Why?"

"Because I have been trying to reach you," Diana said. "I want to talk to you."

"I'm not so sure we should be talking. I wouldn't want to rush into anything." Ellie knew saying such a thing was childish, but she could not stop herself from inflicting hurt on a woman who had so deeply hurt her.

"I think you misunderstood me."

"Oh?"

"When I said I didn't want to rush into anything, I meant that . . ."

"You meant what?"

"I meant that I didn't want you, Ellie, to rush into anything." When her comment was met with silence, Diana continued. "I didn't want you to come out to your husband and your sons and to your entire family, thinking that you would be able to put that part of your life on a shelf, and assume that everything would be okay, and that we could move in with each other the next day and have a fairy tale life."

Ellie pushed the Tip Top paperwork away from her. "I wasn't thinking that."

"Okay," said Diana. "It seemed to me that you were thinking like that. I didn't want you to think that this would be easy."

"Who said anything about thinking this would be easy?" asked Ellie. "Diana, when I learned you were gay and I told you that I was too, I was exuberant! I could finally talk to someone who understood what I was feeling, what it was like to be me. If you interpreted this as my thinking telling anyone else would be anything but devastating, then it was you who misunderstood me."

Diana paused a moment before saying, "Fair enough."

"I love it that the U.S. Supreme Court supports us. And I think it's great that a bunch of movie and TV stars and professional athletes are telling the world that they're gay. But no matter what anyone says, I know this won't be easy, Diana. Why do you think I haven't told anyone but you?"

"What do you want to do, Ellie? How do you want to proceed?"

"I'm not sure," said Ellie. "What I do know is this: I've got to have a plan. This is not something I can blurt out after an extra glass of wine at the dinner table. That may fly at nineteen, but it doesn't work when you've made commitments, when you've lived a lie for more than half a lifetime."

"I agree," said Diana. "I'm sorry, Ellie, if I doubted that you were thinking carefully about this."

"I *have* to think carefully," said Ellie. "I'm scared out of my mind. I have no idea how my husband and sons will react when I tell them, and I greatly fear how my parents and brothers will react. I have no idea where to begin. I feel liberated because I told you, but I feel utterly unable to tell anyone else, to tell the people I love the most."

"I understand."

Ellie refilled her coffee mug. "So, what made you think that I was taking this lightly?"

"When we are in love, we take everything either heavily or lightly. There is nothing in between."

"You think I'm in love with you."

"Are you?" asked Diana.

"Why do I suddenly feel like I'm in the seventh grade?" said Ellie. "Look, I appreciate your concern and your friendship. But just because you've gone through this yourself, do not presume you have the answers for everyone facing an unlocked closet door. And because I'm not in seventh grade, I'm going to say goodbye before I hang up the phone. Goodbye, Diana." Ellie pushed the end button on her phone, set it down on the table, and leaned back in her chair. She closed her eyes.

An unlocked closet door. Was it unlocked? Had she unlatched the bolt by telling Diana? Was she free to walk through it? Ellie sipped her coffee. Of course, she was not free. And she would never be free—not unless the entire Kilcullen family in a highly un-likely act of nature disappeared from the earth forever.

"God," said Ellie aloud. "I'm being a bit dramatic, aren't I?" If she told her parents and her brothers, there would be plenty of drama: arguments, yelling, name calling, protracted and weighty si-lences, shunning. Was this what was stopping her from becoming her true self? Could she survive being ostracized by her family? Could she survive acting straight for the second half of her life?

JUNE

CHAPTER 36

When Alice approached the table, Joan could tell she was wearing her new gun. It was not so much its slight visibility underneath Alice's navy blue shirt and pink cardigan sweater. It was more that Alice walked like a cop now, with her arms three or four inches from her sides, looking like she was ready for a shootout. "So, how does it feel to be holding?" asked Joan.

"You can tell?" asked Alice, sitting down.

"Only because we know you," said Ellie, who was thinking that Alice now walked like Chris.

"What's different?"

"You carry yourself more like a gorilla," said Joan, breaking into a smile.

Alice, who by this time had learned that if she took everything Joan said seriously that Joan would not be her friend, smiled back. "So, I look tough then?"

"Totally tough," said Joan.

"How does it feel?" asked Ellie. "Are you getting used to the bellyband?"

"It is surprisingly comfortable," said Alice. "I feel very powerful." Joan took a sip of water. She knew this was not the time to poke holes in Alice's new gun toting confidence. "What are you guys eating?"

"Burgers," said Joan and Ellie in unison.

Alice shook her head. "Does the word *summer* mean anything to either of you?"

"Yeah," said Joan. "It means hot weather and cool drinks." Ellie laughed.

"I'm talking about bathing suits."

Joan put her napkin in her lap. "Bathing suits matter only to people who allow them to matter. At fifty-two, I'm not trying to compete with the twenty-year-olds on the beach. And I would suggest that those middle aged women who do try—no matter how good they may look—are simply going to come up on the losing end of that competition."

The server appeared at the table, and Joan ordered a cheeseburger, with sautéed onions and mayonnaise; Ellie ordered a hamburger, with lettuce and tomato; and Alice ordered a garden salad topped with grilled salmon. "I'm not competing with twenty-year-olds," said Alice.

"No?" asked Joan. "Then why mention summer and bathing suits—if you don't care?"

Alice shifted in her seat. "I do care about how I look," she said. "We all do, Joan. You know that better than anyone. Like you, I like to look good. And I also like to feel fit."

"And you do look fit," said Ellie.

"As do you," said Alice, returning the compliment.

"And I'm fat and happy," said Joan.

"You are not fat," said Ellie.

"I'm not skinny," said Joan.

"I thought you didn't care," said Alice.

"Good point," said Joan. "Let's get back to the gun. You like having it, I presume." It was a surprise to her, but Joan felt more interested in discussing guns now that Alice had one.

"I do," said Alice. "It's been two weeks—and I've run seven times."

Ellie nodded her head. "That's a good thing, Alice. Joan, you have to admit that Alice's return to running is a good thing."

"It is a good thing," said Joan. "Even though she brings a bad thing with her."

Again, Alice chose to smile. "You're just jealous of my freedom."

Joan laughed. "Maybe you're right!"

"Are you bringing it everywhere?" asked Ellie. "I know you were trying to decide if you should have it with you, on you, every time you leave the house, or whether there would be times that you would leave it behind."

Alice nodded. "I'm taking it everywhere right now. I want to get used to having it next to my skin, so it feels like part of my body, rather than a foreign object."

"And the target practice?" asked Ellie. "Are you still doing that once or twice a week?"

"Twice a week," said Alice. "I will do that forever, I think, because I love it. At this point, I'm a pretty good shot."

"I feel so safe in your presence," said Joan, not bothering to hide her sarcasm, ready now to poke holes.

"You should," said Alice, ignoring it.

"Do I want to ask what Dave thinks?" asked Joan.

Alice slid back in her chair when the server placed her plate of salad in front of her. She put her napkin in her lap and lifted her fork. "Dave is a sore subject right now."

Both Joan and Ellie let Alice's comment sit for a minute. They knew from their common, as well as individual, conversations that Alice increasingly felt abandoned by her husband, who was absorbed by his work and his race schedule. Now that spring had settled in, he was traveling every weekend to races throughout the region. He trained with his employees, proud that he could keep up with them, that he was, at his age, injury free. He hadn't acknowledged Alice's gun, preferring, Alice had said, to keep his mouth closed rather than to talk about it. She thought that this was because if he had the conversation Alice wanted to have, he would be forced to honestly evaluate her choice. And that would mean that he could conclude only that Alice had a gun because he could not—would not—keep her safe. Joan had decided after a particularly lengthy discussion with Alice that one of the biggest differences between women and men was that women thought too much.

"Anything new?" asked Ellie.

"No," said Alice, stabbing a grape tomato with her fork. "We live in parallel universes, and I seem to be the only one who knows it."

Joan cut her burger in half and took a large bite. Any thoughts she occasionally had of becoming a vegetarian like one of her sisters-in-law dissipated immediately when she had a piece of meat in her mouth. "I hear what you're saying," she said, chewing. "And I know you've had your unique issues. And what I'm about to say is not meant to discount what has happened to you and how you are feeling. But"—she swallowed—"I do think that a bunch of women in their fifties feel the same way. We are doing our own thing, and our husbands are doing theirs."

"I totally agree with that," said Ellie. "Chris and I can go days without having a conversation. We talk—chitchat about the weather or what's on tap for the day—but we don't discuss anything meaningful. And, from what I can tell, he's totally okay with that. Or, to be more accurate, I'm not sure he notices."

"Same with me," said Joan. "Of course, Stephen had me under a microscope for two solid weeks after my roofie experience—as he should have—but now? Everything has returned to its pre-roofie state. At the end of the workweek, he is more interested in watching or playing golf than catching up with me. And I don't think, by the way, that this is the case because he doesn't love me. He just doesn't think about me the way he used to. And, to be fair, I'm not always thinking about him."

Alice wagged her index finger at Joan. "But I'll bet you think about him a lot more than he thinks about you. You have to. You run the household, and he is a part of it—so he must figure into your plans, if only when you are at the grocery store. But do you figure into his plans when he is making golfing dates? Does he call and ask your permission? Dave has no trouble filling our calendar with his races every Saturday. In the last two months, he has not asked me once what I might like to do on a weekend—not once."

"You blame Dave," said Ellie.

Alice shook her head. "I do. I do blame him, for being self-centered, for being myopic."

"This might sound like I'm making excuses for the male gender, which I'm most definitely not," said Ellie, squirting ketchup onto her French fries. "But aren't they all a bit that way?"

"No," said Alice. "I don't think all men care only about themselves. And I'll tell you why I say this. I have a college friend who is married to the most attentive, caring, generous man in the world. He puts her needs before his. He does whatever she wants him to do without complaining or telling her she's trying to change or control him. He lives to please her."

Joan took a bite of her burger and chewed for a few seconds before saying, "Give us another example."

Alice looked at the space above her head. "Hmmm . . . I don't think I have another example."

"Exactly," said Joan, wiping mayonnaise from her bottom lip. "Your college friend? She's got the only considerate one in the entire world."

Ellie laughed. She then said, "I think it's a societal thing. Why do you think colleges now offer courses, majors even, in women's and gender studies? Because it has been so one-sided for so long. And the only way to change things is to broadcast to the world that we exist and that we are every bit as important as they are."

"Or become a lesbian," said Joan.

"I could definitely be a lesbian," said Alice, "except for the sex. Then again, I'm not having a lot of sex with the marathon man right now, so maybe that wouldn't really matter."

"Are you kidding?" asked Ellie, feeling warm.

Alice put a piece of salmon in her mouth and chewed. "Yes, I am kidding," she said. "But doesn't it seem like life would be easier if we could live with a woman instead of a man?"

"As in men are from Mars and women are from Venus?" asked Joan.

"Exactly," said Alice. "And I'm serious here. Don't you ever feel that your life would be easier—better even—if you lived with

an empathetic, sympathetic, like-minded, caring, considerate, un-
selfish woman?"

"Sometimes," said Joan. "Absolutely."

Alice turned to Ellie. "How about you?"

Ellie blushed. "All the time," she said. "I think about it all the
time."

CHAPTER 37

Alice received a phone call from the Southwood Police Department when she was in the produce section of Stop & Shop. Thinking it was the second phase of the fundraising appeal that she had read about in the newspaper, Alice let the call roll to voice mail and finished her shopping. It wasn't until she was loading her groceries into the back of her Subaru that she again looked at her phone and saw that she had a message.

Alice, this is Officer Marilyn Walsh with the Southwood Police Department. We think we've got the guy who attacked you on the running trails. Please call me back when you get this message, so we can schedule a lineup.

Alice slowly moved the phone from her right ear to her right pants pocket, her thumping heart marking microbursts of panic, her breathing labored, as if she had run a road race rather than walked the aisles of the local grocery store. It had been, she counted on her fingers, four months since what she had for two months been calling "the event." At first, when she told her story, Alice thought it was important to use the word *attack,* to accurately portray the violence and to engender feelings of outrage from those listening.

But for the last two months—since the Well Protected Women's march in Hartford—Alice had begun to feel differently about what had happened to her. She was still very angry, but she also felt partially responsible. She could not erase from her memory the fact that she had told her assailant to take off her pants. Even though doing so had enabled her to get away from him, she was ashamed of herself for not thinking of another way to distract him, for not talking him out of hurting her. In her most serious moments of self-doubt, she wondered if she had, in an unnamed way, brought this upon herself. It was wrong to think like this, and she knew it. But she felt guilty nonetheless. She had not shared these feelings of insecurity and embarrassment with anyone, and she had said absolutely nothing about this to Officer Walsh.

When Alice got home, she unpacked the groceries and made herself a cup of tea. She sat down at her kitchen table with a yellow legal pad and a felt tip pen and called the police department. When Officer Walsh picked up her extension, Alice had to hold her breath and pinch the bridge of her now-healed nose to keep herself from crying. Alice listened as Marilyn Walsh explained the process, ending with the suggestion that they schedule the lineup for that very afternoon, if Alice was available. When Alice told her three o'clock would be fine, she knew that she could not do it, face this man, alone. When she got off the phone, she texted Ellie and Joan, who told her they would certainly go with her and that Joan would drive. Alice didn't tell Dave.

When they arrived at the police station, it was quiet, as one would expect a small town police department to be on an otherwise ordinary Tuesday afternoon. But as soon as Marilyn Walsh escorted them into the viewing room, the pleasantries ceased; the business at hand became the single focus. She again explained the process, emphasizing the security of the one way mirror. She then asked Alice if she was ready, a simple and also complicated question. Of course she was ready to put an end to this. But she did not feel ready, would perhaps never feel ready, to again see the young man who had violently forced his way into her life. Alice simply nodded her head. Ellie and Joan flanked her, their hands on her back.

And there he was, the fourth from the left of five redheaded young men lined up against the wall in front of her. The speaker in the viewing room was on, allowing Alice, Ellie, and Joan to listen to the instructions: face right, face left, face front. He was six foot, two inches. His hair was longer than it had been that day. And when he opened his mouth to speak, Alice heard his words before they came out of his mouth. "She wanted it," he said. "She told me to take off her pants." The officer in the room with the men told him to shut up, and he did, all the while looking intently at the glass, sending what Alice interpreted as a message of hatred and certain revenge as if he were still speaking. Officer Walsh rushed through the door next to the mirror on an urgent mission to get the speaker turned off. When she came back, she apologized and told Alice to focus on the faces of the young men. Ten seconds later, Alice identified him—Greg Anderson—and told Officer Walsh that yes, she was sure. They were ushered back into the administrative area of the police station, where Alice completed twenty minutes of paperwork and was thanked for her willingness to prosecute. With any luck, Officer Walsh said, Greg Anderson would admit his guilt—even though he had already done so when he announced during the lineup that Alice "wanted it"—in exchange for a reduced sentence. Alice would never have to see him again.

"Does he know my name?" she asked.

Officer Walsh shook her head. "No. And he will never know your name."

"If he does plead guilty, how long will he be in jail?"

"That depends," the officer said, "on his record and on the tenacity of the prosecutor."

"Does he have a record?" asked Ellie.

Officer Walsh's gaze never left Alice's face. "He's done this before."

"Why did you have the speaker on in the room?" asked Joan.

"That was an oversight," Officer Walsh said. "The speaker was turned on earlier today for a training session. I do apologize."

As soon as they were back in Joan's car, Joan started it, pulled out of the parking space and onto the main road, and then said what she had wanted to say to Officer Walsh. "That's a pretty big oversight. You shouldn't have had to listen to that."

"It's okay," said Alice. "I deserved it."

"You deserved what?" asked Ellie from the backseat.

"I deserved to hear what he said."

"What—that you wanted it? That you told him to take off your pants?"

"Yes," said Alice, her voice barely above a whisper.

"Why do you think you deserve that?" asked Ellie.

"Because I said it," said Alice. "I did tell him to take off my pants."

Joan took a right at the very next stop sign, turning her car onto a side street. She parked on the side of the road, switched off the engine, undid her seatbelt, and shifted her body so that she was facing Alice. "What in God's name are you talking about?"

The tears that had been filling Alice's eyes spilled over her lower lids and onto her cheeks, where they ran in parallel lines down to her jawbone before dripping onto her exposed collarbone. "I told him to take off my pants."

Joan rested her back against the locked driver's side door. She inhaled deeply. "Start from the beginning," she said.

And so the incriminating information Alice had been keeping to herself was made public. The words explaining how she had encouraged this man sprang forth from her mouth, the gate swung open, the dam burst. The more she talked, the harder she cried. Not only had she encouraged Greg Anderson with her words, but she had also worn alluring clothing. From the backseat, Ellie kept saying it was okay. Joan leaned over the center controls to wrap her arms around Alice's sagging shoulders. As soon as Alice pulled away, Joan sat back in her seat and started in. "Look," she said, "there are plenty of men out there who think that women ask for whatever they get. But, as a woman, Alice, you've got to stick up for your right to run on a trail in the same high-tech, skintight clothing that men wear when running."

Alice's crying jag had given her the hiccups. "But you know what I mean, don't you? I don't really believe it, but I sometimes think about it, like I am right now."

"You're wondering if you were dressed provocatively, and if being dressed that way sent an inviting message," said Ellie. "And you're wondering if you made that invitation concrete by telling him to take off your pants."

"Yes," said Alice.

"No and no," said Ellie. "You were dressed as all runners dress. And, by the way, you can dress any way you like, running or otherwise. Plus you had a plan. You encouraged him to focus on your pants, so you could get your whistle out of your jacket and use it to deafen him."

"Couldn't I have done that without asking him to take off my pants?"

"Maybe, maybe not," said Joan. "It's not like you had any more than three seconds to think about it. You were under attack, Alice, and you did the best you could under incredibly stressful circumstances. I happen to think you did the right thing."

"You do?" asked Alice.

"I do," said Joan. "And it worked. And you got away. And now the guy's going to prison. This is a job well done. And this is the beginning of the end of this horrible chapter in your life."

Although Alice was not as sure as Joan seemed to be, she nodded her head, signaling that it was okay for Joan to start the car, that it was okay to end the conversation. They were quiet for the few minutes it took to get to Alice's house. When Joan pulled her car into the driveway, Alice thanked her friends for going with her, for supporting her throughout the entire ordeal, the event. She could look at this differently now because the man who had assaulted her was going to be locked up and because she had a gun to protect herself. As soon as she walked into the kitchen, she made herself another cup of tea and decided to make peanut butter cookies for Linda, who would be home at six from her summer job at a clothing store downtown. Just as Alice was finishing creaming the butter, her cell phone rang. Greg Anderson, Marilyn Walsh was sorry to report, had overpowered another officer and sprinted out the back door of the police station and into the woods. Alice staggered backward against the counter. The bowl of butter shattered on the kitchen floor.

CHAPTER 38

Joan, Alice, and Ellie were back at High Tide. The warm weather was conducive to having lunch outdoors on the deck. Plus, Joan was trying to stay away from the casino. Stephen had told her the best way to curb her gambling addiction was to not put herself anywhere near where it was happening. And he had used the word *addiction*. She had, at first, denied that she had a problem. But when Stephen presented her with the very facts she had shared with him—that she went to the casino four days a week for the specific purpose of gambling; that she had become accustomed to, comfortable with even, winning and losing large sums of money, thinking that she would either win back whatever she'd lost or win more; that she was drinking during the day, which, he said, could signal an addiction to more than just gambling; and that she had kept it a secret—she had admitted that he was right. It had been the secrecy, more than the winning, losing, and drinking, that had convinced Joan. There were many reasons to keep secrets. But one of them, the most compelling in Joan's case, was so that someone (her husband) wouldn't find out what she was up to. Because what she was up to, she had known all along, was questionable.

When the server set Joan's chef's salad with blue cheese dressing on the side down in front of her, Ellie asked her if she missed the casino. Joan looked up at her and smiled. This was happening more and more often as the three friends became closer, this ability to read one another's minds or at least the appearance of doing so. "That would imply that I haven't been back," she said.

"Have you been back?" asked Alice, lifting a spoonful of cold cucumber soup to her mouth.

"Do you want me to be honest?"

"Does that mean you haven't been honest in the past?" Alice swallowed the soup, the cream in it coating her throat on its way to her stomach.

"Well," said Ellie. "There is the dishonesty that is associated with telling an outright lie. And then there is a murkier area, a void created by lies of omission."

"Like not telling you I gambled four days a week and drank while I was doing so." Joan speared a hard-boiled egg quarter and dipped it into her ramekin of dressing.

"Yes," said Ellie, "exactly like that. You weren't being dishonest. You simply weren't being truthful."

"I like that interpretation."

"Getting back to the question at hand," said Alice, digging into her garden salad.

"Which was?" asked Joan, knowing what question Alice was talking about, as if it were written on a piece of paper that was sitting on the table in front of her.

"Have you been back?"

"Yes."

"To gamble?" asked Ellie.

"Yes."

"Are you justifying this?"

"No, Alice," said Joan. "I'm answering your question."

Ellie dipped her quesadilla triangle into a small bowl of salsa. "Tell us more," she said before biting into the cheesy tortilla.

Joan poured her dressing over her salad. "When you have something you like to do—an addiction, some would call it—it's not always over when someone declares it over. I am looking at it differently now. I go once a week. I limit myself to a hundred dollars. I don't drink. But, yes, I've been back."

"Is it still fun?" asked Ellie. "You know, with all the restrictions?"

"That," said Joan, "is such a cool question. Stephen would never look at it that way. For him, it's black or white, yes or no, under control or out of control. Gambling is still fun, but not as much fun as it used to be. When you gamble in a measured, clear-headed way, the adrenalin rush turns into more of a trickle."

"Are you tempted to return to the highs and lows of unrestrained gambling?" asked Alice.

"I don't know, Alice," said Joan. "Do you like the highs and lows, the power and the peril, of wearing a pistol strapped to your abdomen?"

"Hey," said Alice, holding her hands up in front of her shoulders. "I was just asking a question. There is no reason for you to jump down my throat."

"It was a loaded question," said Joan. "It was an unpleasant question. And so I simply asked you one in return."

Alice sipped her iced tea. "I'll continue to be an avid gun owner and carrier as long as Greg Anderson is running around town."

Joan closed her eyes and then opened them and looked at Alice. "You're right," she said. "I'm sorry."

Alice shook her head. "It doesn't matter," she said, even though it did.

"Yes, it matters," said Ellie. "Have you had any news this week from Officer Walsh?"

"She called me yesterday to tell me they think he's still in the area, and that they are doing their best to track him down."

"So, that's reassuring," said Joan, trying to make up.

"Not really," said Alice, not ready to give her friend a pass. "I'd rather hear that he's on a bus headed for Mexico."

"Of course you would," said Ellie.

Joan forked a cube of turkey into her mouth. She looked down at her plate as she chewed. And then she looked back up at Alice. "Are you afraid?" she asked.

"Yes," Alice said. "I'm terrified." She told them that she hadn't slept well; that she locked the doors and windows of her house and her car, even when she was home; that she hadn't gone for a run since the day he escaped, even though she had a gun; that she looked for him everywhere; and that she was tired of her husband's patting her hand and telling her the police would find him, as if Greg Anderson were a lost pet rather than the man who had attacked her. "And yes," she said. "I'm back to calling it an attack instead of an incident or event."

"How do the police know he's still here?" asked Joan. "Maybe he is long gone."

Alice shook her head. "His aunt lives here. Neighbors have told police they have seen him—twice—in the last week. His aunt denies it, of course, telling police that it was another nephew visiting, that the people of color on her street think all white people look alike. But one of those neighbors, a retired photographer with an expensive camera and a powerful zoom lens, snapped his picture. He was there on Sunday afternoon."

"He's not looking for you, Alice," said Joan. "And even if he were, he would not know where to find you. He doesn't know your name. He knows nothing about you."

"But what if I run into him?" asked Alice. "What if I am minding my own business and I run into him, crossing the street in front of me while I am in my car?"

"You can run him over," said Joan. Alice allowed herself a slight smile. "I'm joking, Alice, but that doesn't mean I don't take this seriously. I understand your fear, and I wish there were something I could do, that Ellie and I could do to help."

"You are already helping by listening to me," said Alice. "Being listened to means more to me than you may realize." This was a reference to Dave. And Joan and Ellie were fully aware that he was not listening, had not been actively listening since the beginning.

"Hey, how is Linda's job going?" said Ellie, knowing Alice would be pleased with a shift in conversation topics, especially if the new topic was one of her daughters. "Is she getting any more hours at Just Looking?"

Alice's slight smile grew to a grin. "No, but she just got a job delivering pizza four nights a week. Her Honda has a SOUTHWOOD PIZZA—SIMPLY THE BEST! sign affixed to its roof and magnetic signs stuck to the driver and front seat passenger doors. She has been working for the last three nights and said she is rolling in dough. Pun totally intended."

"Does she like working at night?" asked Joan. "Liz wanted to work during the day so, as she put it, her evenings would be free for social interactions."

Alice laughed. "As far as Linda is concerned, her evenings *are* free. The pizza place closes at ten. Last night, she was home at ten thirty and out the door again ten minutes later."

"Do you remember those days?" asked Ellie. "I had so much energy back then. Midnight felt like noon."

"Yeah," said Joan, "but you weren't getting up at five thirty, six days a week, to fast walk five miles."

"Too true," said Ellie. "It's easy to stay up until three in the morning when you sleep until lunchtime."

"Speaking of sleeping until noon, raise your hand if your kid is drinking alcohol," said Joan. All three women raised their hands. "How do you two know?"

"I can smell her breath when she comes in at night," said Alice. "I don't really care if she has a few beers. I just don't want her driving afterward."

"Our kids are much better about that than we were," said Ellie. "They take drinking and driving much more seriously."

"I hope they do," said Alice.

"They have to," said Joan. "When we were growing up, there were no drunk driving laws. There are consequences for the driver now. People get prosecuted. People go to jail."

"And, at the very least, they lose their driver's license for six months to a year," said Ellie.

"Thank God for that," said Joan. "But do you care about the drinking? Does it bother you?"

"No," said Alice. "Don't you think it's part of the growing up process, of transitioning from high school to college, from dependence to independence?"

"I don't know," said Joan. "Maybe it bothers me because I abused alcohol in college, and I wonder if Liz will do the same."

"She probably will," said Alice. "I think most kids do. But she will come out of it, just like you did."

"Have I come out of it?" asked Joan.

"You are emerging, Joan," said Ellie. "Plus, you know and communicate with your daughter. She's not far away. Continue to talk and listen to her. If she's in trouble, you will hear it in her voice."

"I hope so."

Alice sipped her water. "A lot has changed, hasn't it? It was so hard to say goodbye to them—but now that they're back home, I can see that it was time for them to go."

"Does this mean you like the empty nest?" asked Joan.

"No," Alice said. "At least, I'm not particularly enjoying the bird I now share it with."

"This will change," said Joan, who was not sure why she'd uttered these words. Her relationship with Stephen had changed, but she wasn't sure it was for the better.

CHAPTER 39

Joan told herself that she needed to go to the casino to do some shopping. Her mother-in-law's birthday was coming up, and the only place to find something for someone who really did have everything was the Gallery of Shops. She thought she might be able to find a gift that Sandi would not buy for herself or did not already own, either in the Coach store or at Tiffany. And, she told herself, it was a good idea to pay for whatever she purchased in cash. Stephen was on a cash kick, as he called it, using paper money for everything from gas to dinner out. He had five hundred dollars in his wallet at all times and told Joan that using cash instead of a credit card was the best way to actually spend less. They didn't need to spend less— Stephen was making more money now than he had in his other banking job—but he was also on one of his periodic Spartan kicks, giving away things to the Salvation Army, eating less, living frugally. These phases didn't last long, Joan had learned over the years, so she always played along. The added benefit of paying for every-thing in cash was that Stephen would not know how much she spent on the gift for his mother, or how much she spent on other things. Satisfied with her reasoning, Joan stopped at the bank on her way to the casino and withdrew five hundred dollars.

Because the easiest way to get to the Gallery of Shops was

through one of the gaming floors, Joan decided to make a quick detour to the roulette tables, just to see what was happening. Her footfalls were silent on the plush, patterned carpeting. But everything else around her made noise—conversations people were having at tables she passed; the slot machines dinging; dealers calling cues to patrons; ice cubes hitting glassware at the bar; and, as she got closer to the roulette tables, the ball skipping in the wheel. She smelled cigarettes, in spite of the casino's air filtration system. She smelled warm beer and Scotch, perfume, cologne, deodorant, and sweat. And as soon as she saw her table, she knew she wanted to sit down, had wanted for days to sit down and play. She lifted herself up onto the padded seat and leaned back against the smooth, curved wood backrest. It was as if the chair had been custom made for her, so perfectly did it fit her body—more so than any seat she could think of, including her family room couch and the cushioned chairs in her doctor's office. The casino chair was better: firm enough to support her back and soft enough in the seat to please her bottom. One of the omnipresent "Indian Princess" servers was at her side within seconds, asking Joan if she'd like a vodka with soda or vodka straight up. Feeling in control, Joan proudly declined the offer, and then turned to her purse. She took the money from the paper envelope given to her by the bank teller and handed it all to the croupier, named Traci. Two hours later, it was all gone, every dollar, every chip.

She told the croupier that she'd be right back—and she was, with three hundred dollars, the most the nearby ATM would give her. And in another hour, that was gone, every dollar, every chip. Traci told her she could write a check at the bank tellers' window and get more cash. She felt sure, Traci did, that Joan's luck would change. But Joan had heard Traci's pitch before and decided to leave the table and the gaming area and do what she had come to the casino to do, even though, if she were honest with herself, she had to admit that she had already.

She walked into Tiffany and strolled alongside the cases, looking at the gemstones, the silver, and the gold. Her eyes landed on a pair of gold ball earrings, and she knew she had found the perfect gift. She asked for help from a sales associate, who smiled her way through explaining the properties of the earrings: 18-karat gold, 8-mm sizing, part of the legendary bead collection started in the 1950s, with a very affordable price point of six hundred dollars. Joan asked to try them on, and they were, indeed, stunning in her ears. When the sales associate was called away by another customer, Joan spun slowly in place, so she could look around the room; all the other employees were occupied, either on their phones or helping other customers. She casually walked to the case closest to the exit, lingering there, pretending to look at silver chains. She counted to ten, glanced over her shoulder to find no one paying attention to her, and walked out of the store.

She had just about reached the casino floor when she heard someone call her name. She stopped walking, already feeling sick to her stomach, already searching for the words to explain her actions, for an excuse. But when she turned around she was met not by the Tiffany's salesperson but instead by a family friend. They chatted for a few minutes about the unusually warm weather, Sandi's upcoming birthday, summer plans—all the while Joan glancing over Betty Goldstein's left shoulder to see if the sales associate who had given her the gold bead earrings was emerging from Tiffany with a panicked look on her face. When Betty checked her watch and announced that she had to meet a friend shortly, Joan gave her a bright smile and told her how nice it was to run into her.

"And I must say," Betty said, "that your earrings are exquisite. Tiffany?"

Joan put her fingers to her earlobes. "Yes," she said. "Stephen gave them to me."

"Beautiful. He is good to you." Betty's grin revealed a lipstick stained front tooth.

"He is indeed," said Joan, turning away from Betty, smile instantly dropped. She scooted into the closest women's room and sat down in an upholstered chair, putting her legs and feet up on the ottoman in front of it. She leaned back and closed her eyes. She had not done anything like this, taken something that didn't belong to her, since high school. Back then, it had not felt like this. It had been fun, a kind of game that she and her friends, also living in low to middle income households, played when their mothers refused to buy them the article of clothing that was being worn by the girls living in middle to high income households—the sweater, usually, which was often the article of their most fervent desire, other than boys. They would fan out in the mall, the five or six of them who were allowed to meet there after their Saturday morning chores had been done, wearing discount department store blue jeans and shapeless sweatshirts that would easily fit over a sweater or shirt. They would try on whatever they wanted and then cover it, conceal it with their own clothing. And they would walk out of the dressing room, hand the salesperson the other items they had brought in with them as decoys, and casually meander out of the store, sometimes stopping to look at one last item, daring the store employees to catch them. Afterward, they would meet in the parking lot, drive to one of the girls' houses, lock themselves in her bedroom, and compare their bounty. They could not wear their ill-gotten gains at home, so on school days they stuffed them into their backpacks and changed into them in the girls' locker room before the first period bell rang. Those of similar sizes often traded clothing for the day—and then met back in the locker room to change back into whatever they had worn to school before heading home.

Joan looked at herself in the mirror—her eyes going immediately to the gilded lobes of her ears. Instead of the thrill she had felt in high school, sneaking a T-shirt or pair of shorts out of a department store, Joan felt empty. And she knew what she had done was wrong, just as she had known but justified in high school. Only now, she could not keep what she had taken. She slowly stood, reached for her purse, and walked out of the bathroom. Within minutes, she was inside Tiffany, looking for the woman who had trusted her with a pair of six-hundred-dollar earrings, due to the way Joan looked and dressed. When Joan found her, chatting with a couple interested in an engagement ring, she waited for five minutes without being acknowledged. She took the earrings out of her ears and set them down on the glass case in front of her. Only then did the woman look in her direction.

"What do you think?" she asked. "They are beautiful, aren't they?"

This was the confirmation that the salesperson had not noticed

Joan's absence. She had not seen Joan walk out of the store, had not sprinted after her, had not threatened Joan with shoplifting charges. She therefore had not seen Joan walk back into the store, had not realized Joan had been having a conversation in her head about whether or not she could keep the earrings. The salesperson—Suzannah, her name tag indicated—would not thank Joan for her honesty. And she would not, for all of these reasons, make the sale.

"They are," said Joan, giving Suzannah a slight smile before turning away. She walked quickly along the corridor of shops and through the casino to her car, telling herself that she was done with all of it—gambling, midday drinking, shoplifting, floundering. In spite of what her husband and the rest of the Howard family would think, she was going to get a job.

JULY

Chapter 40

As Joan talked, Ellie got out of her seat and hugged Joan from behind. "I knew you could do this," Ellie said. "I am so incredibly proud of you."

"And I am," said Joan, reaching back with her hands to rest them, momentarily, on Ellie's arms, "still in shock! I know nothing about teaching. I know nothing about working. I have no idea why they hired me."

"Because they desperately need instructors?" asked Alice.

"They are definitely desperate," said Joan.

"No, no," said Ellie. "Nutmeg Community College enjoys a fine reputation and is not—in any way—desperate. My neighbor's son and daughter went there, and they both had very good experiences. And, I will add, they are both successfully employed and living independently."

"When do you start?" asked Alice. "And what is your schedule?"

Joan laughed. "I start now—right after lunch! I've ordered the textbook, so I can read it front to back as soon as it comes in. I've got to design the course and come up with a syllabus by the end of August."

Being hired as an adjunct instructor at Nutmeg had happened very quickly. Joan had called the math department and been told that two adjunct positions were available. When Joan told them she didn't have a teaching degree and that she had no experience, the woman on the other end of the phone, to whom Joan had e-mailed her updated resume, had stated, *You've got a master's degree. And that's all any of us had when we started here.* The very next day, Joan had an interview with the head of the department, who told her she was impressed with Joan's academic record—and with her ideas for structuring a macroeconomics class. If Joan wanted to work full-time, she could teach up to four sections in the fall semester. She could teach two sections if she wanted to work part time, which Joan decided was the better way to start. She would have to submit her syllabus for faculty review, and she would be observed several times over the course of the semester by a member of the department, who would pop in unannounced. When Joan had called Stephen to tell him about the job offer, he told her he was pleased.

She and Stephen had talked about it ahead of time, and he had been very supportive, enthusiastic even, which surprised Joan. He told her he thought it would be beneficial for her to get out of the house and into the working world. A job would help her put the casino behind her, he said. And it would give her a purpose in life, now that both girls were no longer living at home. He told her he would pave the way with his parents, but he was hoping that Joan's decision to work would create less of a stir than either of them thought. Sandi, his mother, had wanted Joan to stay home to raise the children, Stephen explained. But he thought she would accept Joan's working outside the home now that the girls were gone.

"No kidding," said Alice. "And to think that you've been saying since last fall that the Howard family would never let you work."

"I had no idea," said Joan.

"Maybe it's just the right timing," said Ellie. "If you had tried to land this job last summer, when Liz was still at home, there might have been more pushback."

"Well, there's that, and the fact that I wasn't an inveterate gambler last summer," said Joan. "I think my casino experience turned Stephen's head in another direction. He told me he would be lost without his job and could certainly understand why I wanted one."

"Talk about a one-eighty," said Alice.

Joan gave Alice a tight smile. Criticizing the husband of a friend, Joan thought, was in poor taste. She had not ever openly criticized Alice's husband, Dave, even though Alice had given her and Ellie ample ammunition. Joan had asked Alice questions about him, perhaps leading questions, but she had never insinuated that he was out of line.

"Hey," said Ellie. "I have an idea. It's such a pretty day, let's drive to the beach and soak up the sun for twenty minutes. I have chairs in the back of my car."

"I am totally in," said Alice, reaching for the check. After studying it for a moment she said, "It's fifteen dollars each."

Because they were Southwood residents, they all had beach stickers on their cars. They drove the short distance to the public beach and parked next to one another. The parking lot, full by ten in the morning on the weekends, was almost empty. It was midafternoon, and the high school and college kids had gone home to shower for their summer server and host jobs at the area restaurants, and the young mothers had taken their children home for naps. Ellie really did stay only twenty minutes because she had a three o'clock meeting with a new client. And Joan, anxious to run to Staples for teaching supplies, left the beach right after Ellie. Alice lingered. She had completed her errands that morning, and she had already decided that she would run just before dinner, when it had cooled down. She lay back in the sand chair that she had promised she would drop at Ellie's house before the weekend and shut her eyes. She had the kind of skin that could take an hour or two of sun without burning, and she was the kind of woman who liked the look of tanned skin, who thought it looked healthy, no matter what the dermatologists said. She had changed her face cream to one that included sun protective agents, which she used as rationale to sit in the sun. She sat up in her chair and pulled her phone out of her pants pocket to text Linda. *What r u up 2?*

Hanging out with Stella

Want to come to the beach?

Is that where u r?

Yes. Beautiful afternoon
How long will u b there?
Another half hour maybe
No can do. On our way to DQ!

Alice ended the electronic conversation with a smiley emoticon and put her phone back in her pocket. She had just leaned back in the chair and closed her eyes when something cast a shadow on her face. She opened her eyes to find Greg Anderson standing over her. "You want to take those pants off now?"

A half teaspoon of the Italian dressing Alice had on her salad at lunch shot up from her stomach and sat, soured, in the back of her mouth, and her heart, seconds ago at rest, pushed, pushed, pushed against her bra and her T-shirt, a wild animal trying to escape from its cage. She pressed her hands against her belly, confirming what she already knew. Her gun, normally tucked into the wide belt underneath her shirt, was in the glove compartment of her car. She had put it there before lunch, in an effort to avoid one of Joan's sarcastic comments about the chances of getting accosted at High Tide at one o'clock on a Wednesday. Alice looked to her left and to her right and saw no one for a couple hundred yards. No one who wouldn't avert his eyes, thinking she and Greg were having indiscreet but consensual sex on the beach.

Hands still gripping the wood arms of the canvas chair, Alice rocketed upward. As soon as she was standing, she launched the chair backwards, away from her body, allowing her to turn and run. She lumbered through the sand, which filled her shoes. Greg Anderson pursued her. "Not this time!" he called to her from four feet away. "You're going to take those pants all the way off!"

When Alice's feet hit the cement boardwalk, she was able to quicken her pace. She thrust her fist into the front pocket of her jeans, grabbing for her car keys as she ran. She did not call for help as she bolted past the snack bar; she would do it by herself; she would do it right this time. Alice sprinted into the parking lot that hosted only a half dozen other cars. If she could get to the car with five seconds to spare, she could get in and lock the doors behind her. Thirty yards away, she kicked up her pace to a speed she knew she could not sustain for long. Keys in hand, she used her fob to unlock the driver's side door, and, gasping, shaking, she yanked it open, launched her body into the car, and pulled the door closed behind her. She clicked the lock, just as Greg Anderson's body slammed into the door, violently rocking the car. She lunged at the glove compartment, grabbed her gun, and twisted her body to point it at him. Either he didn't see it, or he didn't care; he was pounding on the glass, yelling at her to open the door. Alice hit the unlock button on her fob; Greg pulled the door open. He reached for his belt buckle. Screaming, Alice fired.

CHAPTER 41

Ellie was driving home from her meeting with a woman who had recently opened a jewelry store on one of the side streets in town when she heard the text message signal on her phone ding twice. A supporter of the "It Can Wait" campaign against texting while driving, Ellie continued to focus on the road, not on her phone. She did wonder, however, if the text was from Diana. They had started talking again—and had even met at the dog park, twice, for face to face conversation. When Ellie had told her how much their conversation on the phone had hurt her, Diana had been genuinely apologetic. *I want to be friends,* she had said, during their first walk at the park. *And if things progress from there, I will not fight it.*

Ellie drove her car into her garage and walked into the kitchen. Before she filled the cappuccino maker with water, she set her accounting notebooks down on the table and rooted through her purse for her phone. The text, to Ellie and Joan, was from Alice.

Come when u can

This was the second message. The first message that read *I shot Greg Anderson at the beach* had been received twenty-eight minutes earlier, when Ellie was still in her meeting. Ellie had forgotten to check her phone afterward.

"Shit!" said Ellie, running back out to the garage and hurrying into her car. She backed out of the driveway and headed for the beach, hoping Joan had been able to respond immediately, that she might be there already.

The parking lot was still relatively empty, except for the three police cruisers, an ambulance, and a fire department vehicle. There were several people lined up on the edge of the pavement, twenty yards or so from the activity. A young man in shorts and a T-shirt and carrying a Frisbee was talking with an officer. Ellie steered toward the edge of the asphalt, jammed her transmission into park, and rushed out of the car. She ran toward the police cars, calling Alice's name as she went.

"We're over here, Ellie." It was Joan's voice. She and Alice were sitting in the back of a police cruiser, the engine running, the air conditioning blasting, the rear doors wide open.

Ellie got into the backseat beside Alice and wrapped her arms around her. "Are you okay?" she asked. She pushed back slightly, holding Alice by the shoulders and looking into her red-rimmed eyes. "Alice, tell me you are okay."

The flow of tears that Joan had been trying to stem with soothing words for a quarter hour instantly regained momentum and purpose, racing down Alice's cheeks, swollen rivers racing to the sea. "I don't know," she finally said. "I don't know if I'm okay."

"Tell me what happened," said Ellie.

Alice turned to Joan. "Will you tell her?" she asked quietly. "I'm too tired."

Joan explained that Greg Anderson had shown up at the beach after she and Ellie had left. And that he had approached Alice and told her, essentially, that he wanted to pick up where they had left off on the running trails. Alice had managed to escape, even though he was blocking her, threatening her. She ran to her car for the gun and before she knew it, she had shot him.

"Is he dead?" asked Ellie, looking at Joan.

Joan shook her head. "No. He's in that ambulance," she said, using her right pointer finger to indicate what Ellie had already seen. As all three women looked in that direction, the ambulance started to move. The lights spun, the sound of the siren splitting through the hot silence. Greg Anderson and whoever was attending him were on their way to Southwood Hospital. Officer Marilyn Walsh watched the ambulance leave and then turned her attention to the back of her police cruiser and the three women inside. They all looked at her when she squatted beside the open door and asked how Alice was doing.

"I'm okay," Alice said after a brief pause. Ellie, Joan, and Officer Walsh knew she was not; it was a question that needed to be asked. And while Alice's answer was two seconds late for what would be called an automatic reply, it was what was expected. It was how polite Southwood residents answered when people they met in the community asked how they were doing.

"How is he?" asked Ellie, everyone knowing she was referring to Greg Anderson.

"We'll know more later," said Officer Walsh. "He's lost a lot of blood. But the paramedics think you somehow managed to miss his stomach, liver, colon, and pancreas."

Alice wiped her cheeks. "I know."

Officer Walsh removed her cap. "What do you mean?"

"I shot him where I did to stop him, to hurt him," she said. "I shot him where I did so he would survive."

"How did you know that?" asked Ellie.

"Because I've done my homework," said Alice. "And I'm a very good shot." There was nothing boastful about this remark; her tone was neutral, matter of fact.

"Well, you must be," the officer said. "To shoot that well in a panicked situation is extremely unusual. As you might imagine, we see very few gunshot wounds in Southwood. The two I've seen were accidental." Joan looked at Alice, but didn't say anything. This was not the time to talk about the topic she and Alice disagreed about the most. "I'm going to need to get a statement from you. Are you feeling up to it? If not, we can talk tomorrow morning."

"No, it's fine," said Alice. "I'm up to it."

"I don't want you to drive," said Officer Walsh. "Do you want to ride with me?"

"I'll take her," said Ellie.

"Dave is on his way," said Alice, looking at a text that had just arrived. She started typing with her thumbs. "I'm telling him to meet me at the station."

"Do you want me to come to the station, too?" asked Joan.

Alice shook her head. "Dave's on his way. I think I'll be okay."

"Okay. Don't worry about your car—Ellie and I can take care of it," said Joan. "As soon as Ellie gets you situated at the police station and Dave has arrived, she can come and get me. Give me your keys. I'll leave them on your kitchen table after we deliver the car to your house."

Joan exited the back seat on one side, and Ellie got out on the other. Alice sat still in the middle. Joan ducked her head down. "No rush."

"I'm coming," said Alice, feeling unable to move. Several seconds passed. She leaned forward and then began to slowly scoot her bottom over to the seat just vacated by Joan. Joan held her hand out, and Alice took it. Alice squinted in the bright sunlight. Her sunglasses had fallen off somewhere.

Ellie walked around to join them. She could see that Alice was trembling, and she put her arm around her waist. "My car is just over there."

"Alice," said Joan. Alice looked at her. "Call me if you need something. I can be at the police station in five minutes."

"I will be okay," she said. "As soon as Dave gets there, I will be okay. Would you mind looking for my sunglasses?"

"No, I'll do that right now," said Joan. "Ellie, call me when you are ready to get Alice's car. I'm available anytime."

After telling Officer Walsh that she would have Alice to the station in ten minutes, Ellie guided Alice to her car and helped her into the passenger side. Alice continued to move haltingly, as if she had been physically damaged in an accident. As soon as they were both inside, seatbelts on and ignition started, Alice said to Ellie, "I could have killed him."

"Yes," said Ellie, letting the car idle.

"I wanted to kill him."

Ellie hesitated a moment, in case Alice wanted to continue talking. And then Ellie turned the car around and drove out of the beach lot. As soon as they were on the main road, Alice said, "I opened the doors, so he could get in, thinking I would kill him with my weapon. But as soon as the door was open, I knew I could not."

"What do you mean you opened the doors? I assumed you didn't have time to lock them."

"I had time," said Alice. "I got to the car before he did. I unlocked my door, jumped in, and locked the door behind me, a split second before he slammed into the car."

Ellie turned the car onto Route 1. "And then you opened the doors?"

"Yes," said Alice. "I opened the doors to let him in, so I could kill him."

"And then you didn't."

"No," said Alice, shaking her head slowly.

"Why?"

"I don't know."

They drove without speaking for a few minutes until Ellie turned her car into the parking lot of the Southwood police station. She pulled into a space, switched off the ignition, and then turned in her seat to face Alice. "Have you told this to Officer Walsh?"

"No," said Alice. "Once she knew I was okay, she focused her attention on the ambulance personnel."

"You don't have to tell her what you just told me."

Alice unbuckled her seatbelt and then turned to face Ellie. "Why wouldn't I tell her that?"

Ellie looked out the windshield at the front doors of the police station. "Because they might take it the wrong way."

"What wrong way?"

"That you were safe in your locked car, and you could have simply driven away."

"But then I opened the doors, putting myself in danger, only so I could shoot him," said Alice, taking hold of Ellie's line of thinking, grasping her warning. Ellie didn't respond. "But he will tell them. Greg Anderson will tell them."

"And who are they going to believe?" Ellie asked. "Greg Anderson or you?"

Just then Dave arrived. He parked his car and ran to the front doors of the police station. Within seconds, he had disappeared inside.

"He looks pretty concerned," said Ellie.

"He is," said Alice, opening the car door. "He's been talking; we've been talking."

"Good," said Ellie, opening her door. "Let's get you inside, so he can see that you're okay."

Alice wiped fresh tears from her cheeks with both palms. "I don't feel okay."

"I know," said Ellie, who felt at that moment like she didn't know anything. "It will take time, Alice, but I know you will be."

CHAPTER 42

Alice played with instead of ate her salad, using her fork to move arugula, grape tomatoes, and slices of red pepper from the center of her plate to the rim, creating space for the scoop of chicken salad that she sometimes ordered, but had ten minutes ago declined. Greg Anderson was out of the hospital and in jail, awaiting trial. The bullet from Alice's gun had severed his small intestine, which a local surgeon had reconnected. The bullet missed his spine and everything else that could have caused a serious problem. He was in some discomfort. But his digestion process would return to normal over the next several weeks. And a couple months from now, Greg Anderson would be as good as if he had not been shot, the impact of his encounter with Alice at the beach erased. She looked up from her plate to find Ellie and Joan, their lunches partially eaten, looking at her. "What?" she said.

"What indeed," said Joan. "Talk to us, Alice. You have not said a word since you ordered that salad you are not eating."

Alice pushed her plate toward the middle of the table. "I don't know what to say."

"Say anything," said Joan. "Start anywhere."

"Even if he's found guilty," said Alice, "he'll only get a year in prison."

Ellie looked at Joan and then Alice. "How do you know that?"

"Because it's a misdemeanor," said Alice. "Because he did not actually rape me, it's a misdemeanor in the state of Connecticut."

"Yeah, but he beat the shit out of you," said Joan. "That's worth some jail time."

Alice closed her eyes for a moment and then opened them. "What happens after his year in prison? Will he find me again?"

"I agree with Joan," said Ellie. "What about the fact that he is a repeat offender? Officer Walsh said two other women have come forward to identify him. And there's his escape from police custody. He's not going to get out in a year, Alice."

"I should have killed him," Alice said. "All I had to do was shoot six inches higher. I could have done it. I knew what I was doing."

Joan picked up the second half of her grilled cheese and bit into it. "You did know what you were doing," she said. "That's why you shot him where you did—so you wouldn't kill him."

"Yeah, well, I've changed my mind."

"Have you really changed your mind," asked Joan, "or are you back in cahoots with the Well Protected Women?"

"Do you always have to be so direct?" asked Ellie, looking at Joan. "Do you have any filter whatsoever?"

Joan took another bite of her sandwich and set it back down on the plate. "Alice, you are not a murderer. You would not want to be saddled with that label for the rest of your life—no matter what Greg Anderson did to you. You shot him. He knows you shot him. When he gets out of prison five, ten years from now, he's not going to go looking for the woman who shot him. He knows, just as you know, that if he confronts you again, he's a dead man."

Alice reached for her water glass and took two sips, both of which failed to ease the constriction in her throat. "I'm afraid for my daughters," she said, looking down at her plate instead of into the faces of her friends.

"Of course you are," said Joan. "I am afraid for my daughters, too. But they are better than we are at this. Their generation is much less trusting. Women in their twenties are much less likely to run on their own than women in their fifties."

"Meaning I'm an idiot," said Alice.

"No," said Ellie, reaching across the table to take hold of Alice's wrist. "We live in a safe place. This shouldn't have happened. You had every right to be running on those trails on your own. People do it all the time."

"Then why did it happen?" asked Alice. "Why did it happen on that day to me?"

Joan shook her head. "Don't go there," she said. "Sometimes things happen for a reason, and sometimes they don't. There is a randomness to life, Alice. What matters more than what happens to us is how we deal with it afterward, what decisions we make moving forward."

Alice folded her arms across her chest. "That sounds good, Joan. And it probably looked good in whatever article you read. But it doesn't feel right. I find your righteous words and tone off-putting."

Joan shrugged her shoulders. "I'm sorry if I'm offending you," she said. "Personally, I think you did everything right. You got away from him the first time, and you sent a serious message to him the second time. He now knows that any violent crime he is thinking about committing could have very undesirable consequences. Plus, maybe the guy will learn something in prison."

Alice looked at Ellie.

"You need to get through this trial," said Ellie. "Joan and I will help you. Your family will help you. Greg Anderson will be sentenced and will go to prison, and you will be able to live your life without worrying about him."

Alice reached for her plate, pulling it back toward her. She speared a pepper and put it in her mouth. "There will always be something to worry about."

"Are we talking about Dave?" asked Joan.

"It's better with Dave," said Alice. "He's better, in terms of his attentiveness to me. But I still don't think he gets it. I know he loves me, but I also know he has no idea who I am. Sometimes I am incredibly frustrated by this, by his inability to see that I am not the same person he married thirty-three years ago. And then other times I realize that I can't really blame him because lately—since Linda left the house—even I don't know who I am."

"You're a mother," said Ellie.

"And a runner," said Joan.

"And an incredible cookie baker," said Ellie.

"And a loyal friend," said Joan.

"And an activist," said Ellie.

"And a damn good shot," said Joan. Alice allowed herself the smallest of smiles. "You just need to find your next best thing."

"How am I going to do that?" asked Alice, chewing lettuce leaves she had put into her mouth.

"I don't know," said Ellie. "But we'll help."

Alice speared another pepper and then said, "I'm so glad my parents and my sister and her family were here before all this happened."

"Do they know?" asked Joan. "Have you told them what happened?"

"No," said Alice. "It would upset my parents and annoy my sister."

"Why would your sister be annoyed?" asked Ellie.

"She's one of those people who thinks everything happens to us because we initiate it, because we ask for it. So she would be irritated that I let him attack me—and she would use those words—and she would be furious that I shot him."

"Wait a minute," said Joan. "Is this where your insecurity about this comes from, from what your sister would say?"

"She's always right, and I'm always wrong."

"I don't think so," said Joan.

"Me neither," said Ellie.

"Well," said Alice, "they're out of my life until next July."

And because neither Joan nor Ellie knew how to respond to Alice's comment without doing more harm than good, they said nothing.

"It's okay," said Alice. "It's been like this for a long time. We had a pretty good visit, actually."

Ellie and Joan opened their mouths at the same time and said in unison, "Good."

CHAPTER 43

It started as a quick thought as Alice ran errands. It was buried by the time she got home from an unusually long wait at Valvoline and a trip to three grocery stores to find miso, the key ingredient in a recipe given to Alice by a neighbor. But it resurfaced later that afternoon, just before Dave walked through the back door into the kitchen. She didn't say anything, either to her husband or to Linda, who, freshly showered, walked through the kitchen on her way to her car parked outside. "I'm delivering until ten," she said. "And then I'm heading over to Melany's house for some serious partying." Both Alice and Dave looked at their daughter. She flipped her long blond hair, the same shade and style as her mother's, over one shoulder. "I'm joking! I just wanted to see if you guys were listening to me."

"We always listen to you," said Dave.

"Yeah?" she said, grabbing one of her mother's oatmeal raisin cookies from the wire cooling rack on the counter and biting into it. "So that thing we were talking about, when you were watching the Sox game last night, Dad," she said, chewing. "What do you think, yes or no?" Dave closed one eye in an effort at concentration. "You don't remember?" asked Linda, taking another bite as she grabbed her purse from a kitchen chair and slung its strap over her shoulder.

"Was it something about this coming weekend?" he asked. "It was definitely something about the weekend, wasn't it?"

"Dad," said Linda, one hand on her slim hip. "I didn't ask you anything last night. The only time I initiate a conversation when you are watching baseball is when I want a quick yes."

Alice laughed.

Linda put the rest of the cookie in her mouth and grinned at her parents. "See you two later," she said as she walked out the door.

Dave was thankful that Linda was home, had been home all summer. She had the same sense of humor as her mother and often made Alice laugh, which is what Alice seemed to need most right now. He turned to Alice and said, "I love having her home."

"I do too," said Alice. "But it's really different from when she was in high school, isn't it?"

"Yes, it is."

"A year ago, we knew everything she did—or we thought we did anyway—from the moment she got up in the morning until the moment she closed her eyes at night. We knew what she was involved with at school. We knew all her friends. We knew all her friends' parents. And now she breezes in and out of the house, sometimes telling us what she is up to and sometimes not."

Dave picked up the newspaper that was sitting on the table. He glanced at the headlines on the front page. "She's turning into an adult."

Alice held up her hand. "Not quite yet. The other day she had a complete fit about how rudely she was treated by a customer the night before."

"Well, thank God she's not done with meltdowns," said Dave. "What in the world would we talk about?"

Responding to the beeping timer, Alice opened the oven door and extracted a baking sheet holding nine perfectly browned cookies from the oven. She set it down on the stove top and then moved the still warm cookies from the cooling rack to a plastic serving platter sitting on the kitchen table. In one minute, she would transfer the hot cookies on the baking sheet to the rack, a ritual that hadn't yet failed to produce a cookie with a firm circumference and a chewy center. Dave took a cookie from the platter. "How about getting a dog?" Alice asked. Dave stopped chewing, put the paper back down on the table, and looked at Alice, one eyebrow raised. "I know what you're thinking—that this is crazy. And it is crazy. All the kids are gone. Why now, right? Because I have time now. And I love dogs. And I really miss having one. It's been two years since Shasta died."

Dave put his hands on his hips. "What about getting a job? I thought you were anxious to get back to work?"

Alice closed the oven door. "I do want to get back to work, at some point. But if I were anxious, I'd be working already. I don't know what I want to do, Dave, and I don't want to do just anything. You don't seem to need me at either store. And training a dog would not take more than six months or so. I could think about what I want to do while I'm hanging out with our new dog."

Dave scratched his head. "What kind of dog do you want to get?"

Alice shrugged. "I don't know. I'll have to see what the dog pound has to offer."

"A mutt then."

Alice smiled. "Yeah—a big lovable mutt who will run with me."

"Alice, you know how busy I am," said Dave, his forehead creasing.

"I do know," she said, holding out her hands to stop Dave from continuing. "This will be my dog. I will do everything, from training her to walking her to taking her to the vet. She will be my responsibility."

"Okay. Under those conditions, how can I say no?" said Dave. He looked at his watch. "When's dinner?"

"In about an hour."

"Good," he said, already moving toward the hallway. "I'm going to squeeze in a thirty-minute run."

Alice waited until he was gone before she shook her head. He was getting better at processing Alice's feelings, at talking about Alice's feelings, but he was still a long way from showing he understood.

* * *

The next morning, Alice drove to the Southwood Animal Control Center, arriving when they opened at eight o'clock. After a brief interview with an officer, Alice was ushered back to a large room with cages around its perimeter. The dogs immediately started barking. "These dogs come from all over town," the officer shouted over the deafening din while strolling toward the far wall, where large, mature dogs were housed in individual crates. "Some of them are stray dogs that we pick up when people call us. Some of them, like this one here," he said, pointing to an overweight collie mix, "are dropped off in the night. There is a kennel out back where people can leave dogs when we aren't open."

"That seems kind of mean."

"Well, it's far meaner for people who don't love them to keep them in a home where they will not be properly cared for."

"What do you do when you run out of space here? Do you euthanize them?" Alice had never yelled the word *euthanize* before. Doing so made the definition of the word visible in her head.

"We try to find good homes for the dogs," the officer shouted in response. "That's our goal." Alice followed him around the room, looking at each dog as she went. Many of them had a pit bull look about them, which, while not surprising, was still startling to see in the faces and body shapes of one dog after another. "I know you said you're interested in a large, mature dog. But I do have some puppies in the corner crate if you want to see them."

Alice looked in the direction the officer was pointing. "Sure," she said. "Let's have a look." And a second after they stopped in front of the cage, Alice knew she'd found her next dog. There were six of them, all brown and white, with the squared off heads of Labrador retrievers, and the soft, pink bellies of most puppies. "Tell me about them."

"They were dropped off a few nights ago. As far as we can tell, they're about ten weeks old. The people leaving them knew enough, I guess, to keep them with their mother that long," said the officer, unlocking the crate door. "Would you like to hold one?"

Alice smiled at this question, knowing, as the officer knew, that if she held a puppy, she would most likely be taking her home. *Get the merchandise into the hands of the customer* was one of the golden rules of sales. Whenever she walked into the bookstore downtown and asked for a particular item, she was led to it, where she then watched as it was pulled from its place on the shelf and placed in her hands. When Alice had worked at their running store, she had always put the shoe in the buyer's hands. Alice accepted the warm and furry bundle of moving legs. She held the puppy up to her face, touching her dry nose to its wet one. As if to correct this, to make them the same, the dog licked hers.

"She's a beagle mix," the officer said.

"A beagle? She looks nothing like a beagle."

"I thought the same thing. But the people who dropped her off said in their note taped to the fence that the mother was a beagle."

"Will she be able to run with me?"

The officer smiled. "You ever hear of a fox hunt?"

"I'll take her."

AUGUST

CHAPTER 44

"She is so much fun!" said Alice, biting into a veggie burger. "Dave calls her my fourth daughter. And Linda calls her my third, telling me the puppy has definitely replaced her on my list of priorities."

"Ha!" said Joan. "I love that."

"When do you start puppy school?" asked Ellie.

"Next week. I can hardly wait."

Joan poured more ketchup onto her plate for her sweet potato fries. "Have you found your next best thing?"

"The box is definitely checked," said Alice. "I feel ten years younger."

"And you look it too, my friend," said Joan, raising her hand for a high five, which Alice enthusiastically administered. Joan moved her hand, stopping it in front of Ellie's face. Ellie looked at her. "Give me some skin, sister."

Smiling at Joan, Ellie slapped her hand and said, "Someone's in a good mood today."

"Oh, I take exception to that remark," said Joan, "because it implicitly means that I am typically not in a good mood."

Ellie cocked her head. "That meaning was not intended."

"Well then, yes, I *am* in a good mood. I finished my syllabus last night. I've got my first six classes totally mapped out. And both sections of my macroeconomics class are full."

"Someone's on fire," said Alice.

"I hope so," said Joan, chewing the two fries she had just put in her mouth. "We went to Stephen's parents' house last night, and he announced my job to the entire assemblage."

"And?" asked Alice, hers and then Ellie's full attention on Joan's face.

"My mother-in-law? She actually clapped her hands."

"She was three drinks in at this point?" asked Alice.

"No, no," said Joan, shaking her head. "Stephen was right. Sandi is absolutely fine with her daughters-in-law working once the children are out of the house. She'd rather have me devote more time to volunteer efforts. But what she is adamantly against are women who let work take them away from raising children."

"Thank God for that clarification," said Alice.

"I know," said Joan. "Not particularly forward thinking, my mother-in-law. But I was amazed that she seemed legitimately happy for me."

"Well, I'm glad you told her," said Ellie. "And I'm even more glad that she accepted this new stage in your life."

"Me too," said Joan. "I thought that I was going to have to hide the fact that I had a part time job from Stephen's entire family."

Joan's words struck Ellie like a slap on the face. She sipped her water, and then, looking away from their conversation, away from Joan and Alice, said, "It's not easy hiding things from family."

Something in the way Ellie made this remark told both Joan and Alice that she was no longer talking about Joan's teaching job and the reaction of the Howard family to the news.

"No, it's not," said Alice.

Joan ate a fry and then said, "Are you hiding something, Ellie?"

The tears that Ellie was so tired of shedding returned, pooling in her lower eyelids. She opened her mouth to speak, but her bottom lip shook so violently that she was unable to say the words she now wanted, needed to say. Alice, who was sitting next to her, wrapped her arm around Ellie's shoulders and pulled her in for a hug. "What is it, El?"

Ellie pulled back and used her napkin to wipe the water from her eyes. "I'm gay," she said. "And I need to start making some changes."

"Okay," said Joan immediately, more as an affirmation of Ellie's ability to reveal something so personal than as an indication of complete comprehension.

Her quick remark surprised Ellie. "Okay what?"

"I don't know," said Joan. "It's just okay."

Ellie set her elbow down on the table and rested her head in her hand. "I'm not sure it really is going to be okay."

"What kind of changes?" asked Alice.

Ellie used her finger to wipe a tear from her cheek. "I think I need to start living in a way that is true to who I am."

Joan took a sip of her water and then said, "Meaning you need to end your marriage of twenty-five years."

Ellie whispered, "Yes." Ellie was now openly weeping. Alice and Joan both covered Ellie's hands with theirs.

"Does he know?" asked Alice. "Does Chris know?"

"No one knows, except you two," said Ellie. "And Diana McGuire."

"Who's Diana McGuire?" asked Alice.

"The woman who owns the pet store," said Ellie. "I do her books."

"You told her you're gay?"

"Yes," said Ellie. "She's gay, too."

"Are you in love with her?" asked Joan, handing Ellie a package of tissues from her purse.

Ellie blew her nose and took a long drink of water. "I don't know," she said. "I have feelings for her. And I will say that the fact that Diana was married and left her husband and was able to salvage her family life did give me some hope that I might be able to do the same."

"It sounds like you are moving too quickly, Ellie," said Alice. "Are you sure this is what you want to do?"

Ellie shook her head. "I am sure of nothing, except of who I am."

"When did you know?" asked Joan.

"In some ways, I've known my whole life, since elementary

school anyway. I didn't know what it was, but at nine years old I knew I was different from the other girls in my class. As I got older, I knew—but I fought it, and then I repressed it. I met Chris, who is a very nice man, and I thought I could be happy with him. But I've reached a point in my life where I feel I need to be honest with myself. But I am terrified."

"What are you most afraid of?" asked Joan.

"Of deeply hurting Chris and Tim and Brandon. Of being disowned by my entire family. Of giving up the married life I've been living for twenty-five years. Of alienating friends who don't understand. Of being alone. Of everything." New tears appeared in Ellie's eyes.

"How can we help?" asked Joan.

"You are already helping," said Ellie. "If everyone I have to tell is half as understanding as the two of you, I will be okay."

Alice audibly inhaled and then said, "I'm not sure I'm quite as understanding as Joan."

Joan said, "Alice . . ."

"I understand you're gay. What I'm having trouble with is why it's critical to come out now, when you've gone this far without coming out."

Ellie nodded her head. "That's a fair question. Some of it has to do with the fact that gay rights have come so far. This means that being gay is much, much more acceptable now than it was twenty or thirty years ago. And I find this incredibly encouraging. But you're right, Alice. The fact that being gay is easier now than it was when I was growing up will mean nothing to Chris."

"I shouldn't question you. . . ."

"You have every right to question me. I do it all the time."

"Has Diana advised you?" asked Joan.

"A bit. Mostly, she's told me that this is not a decision to be taken lightly, and that it's complicated. She has a good relationship with her ex-husband and children, but that is only because she has worked very hard at it."

"So what are you going to do?" asked Alice.

"I don't know," said Ellie. "I've told you two today, but I need to think more about Chris and my boys. About the entire Kilcullen family. I don't know how to move forward."

"This may sound like a foolish question," said Joan, "but do you want us to be with you when you are ready to tell your family?"

Ellie offered Joan a slight smile. "That is a very kind offer, Joan. But this is something that I need to do by myself. I just don't know if I have the strength to do it."

CHAPTER 45

Every August the Howard women went on a back-to-school shopping trip. They called it that out of habit, a reference to the days when they had children in elementary school needing clothes and shoes, as well as construction paper, crayons, and colored pencils, for the start of the academic year. The term made them all laugh now, as all of their children were long out of elementary school at this point. The day started as it always did, with Jill, married to the oldest Howard boy, Raymond, picking everyone up in her Cadillac Escalade, and then driving through Dunkin' Donuts for coffee. When they arrived at the Amtrak station, the women emerged from the car, all of them looking like they were headed into the city for a day of shopping: black pants, white tailored shirts, and colorful scarves galore. Sandi, every bit the matriarch at eighty-four that she had been when Joan first met her, led the way. And all the Howard women fell in behind her.

On the station platform, Sandi bought the business class train tickets from the automatic dispenser, proud of herself for her ability to master modern technology, and then handed them out to her daughters-in-law as carefully as if they were passes to a Broadway show. They dutifully took them and then slid them into the outside pockets of their brightly colored handbags, ranging in size from something just large enough for a wallet and a cell phone to a satchel roomy enough for the clothes and accessories needed for an overnight stay. When the train arrived at the station, they all followed Sandi to the first car behind the engine, business class, which was always, she said, less crowded than the others. They sat in seats close to one another, retrieved their tickets from their bags for the conductor who would be making his way down the aisle shortly, and set their bags down beside their crossed ankles. The train lurched forward, startling Sandi, who put a flat palm to her chest. This was something she did often, in reaction to good news or bad news, surprises, touching family memories recounted by one of her sons, lots of things really, as if there were a spring in her elbow that operated on a timer, moving her hand to her bosom every half hour or so. Sometimes, after a drink or two with Stephen, Joan imitated this motion, along with its companion, the O-shaped mouth, which always brought a smile to her husband's face.

The chatter on the train stopped the minute they arrived at Penn Station. Sandi was all business until everyone was out of the train, off the platform, through the cavernous lobby area, and seated in a large capacity cab that could comfortably transport five women. "To Bergdorf Goodman!" she announced, prompting the daughters-in-law to repeat the words *Bergdorf Goodman!* as was their custom at the outset of the yearly clothing pilgrimage to New York City. From there, they always walked down Fifth Avenue to Saks and ended their excursion at Lord & Taylor. During the cab ride, Sandi gave each daughter-in-law an envelope containing twenty hundred-dollar bills to spend as she wished; the only string attached was the expectation of a timely thank-you note, which Joan always wrote and mailed the day afterward.

Of her three Howard sisters-in-law, Joan was closest to Gretchen, who was married to Elliot, the second oldest. Jill, Raymond's wife, was an oldest child like he was and could be as driven and stubborn. She was prone to making what Joan called absolute pronouncements—that the quiche she was eating was the best in the city, or that the heels she was wearing were the most comfortable pair of shoes she had ever worn. Sometimes Joan sought Jill's company during holiday gatherings, especially when she was wrestling with a question—because Jill would always have a ready answer. Plus she could be very funny, especially after a martini. Joan hardly ever spent time with Sylvia, who was married to Peter, the youngest Howard. Sylvia, also an oldest child, was very much like Jill, minus the sense of humor. Sylvia had smiled exactly four times in the thirty years Joan had been a Howard. Joan sought Gretchen's company because she and Gretchen were the same age and like-minded, at least around the Howard family. They both paid enough attention to Sandi to be warmly welcomed by their mother-in-law each time they arrived at her house. They both shared stories at the dinner table that seemed to amuse the others. And they both helped Sandi clean up the kitchen after the meal. Jill and Sylvia, forever citing other obligations—whatever they might be at eight thirty on a Friday night—locked eyes with their husbands as soon as the meal was over, which caused Raymond and Peter to announce their imminent departure. Over the years, Joan and Gretchen had found each other's eyes too, as they silently counted the seconds between the last bite of key lime pie and the scrape of Raymond's chair pushing back from the table. One thousand one; one thousand two; one thousand three—*Great dinner, Mother,* he always said. *Jill and I have got to scoot.*

Joan and Gretchen paired off as soon as they all walked into the store, citing an urgent need to visit the ladies' room. Jill and Sylvia, mission minded, declined, considering bio breaks an unnecessary time suck, and Sandi always "powdered her nose," her term for urinating, before lunch. Joan and Gretchen knew these idiosyncrasies, which was the reason behind their annual suggestion. Once rid of the others, Joan and Gretchen, both lipstick freaks, could take as long as they needed in cosmetics to peruse and sample the new fall shades. On their way to the beauty department, Joan looked at her watch. With a noon departure time for their one o'clock lunch reservation at Saks, she and Gretchen had almost sixty minutes.

"It's so good to be able to spend some time with you," said Gretchen. "I always mean to call you for coffee, but it somehow never happens. I'm sorry about that."

"No worries," said Joan, reaching for a tester tube of Chantecaille, her current favorite brand. "I haven't called you, either. Let's both write it down and make it happen."

"Good plan—although you are going to have less free time very soon. I am so excited about your job. I think you are going to be a fantastic teacher. I've learned a lot from you over the years."

Joan smiled broadly at Gretchen. "You have no idea how much I need to hear that. I have never been this nervous in my life—and that includes on my wedding day!"

Gretchen laughed. "Of course you are," she said. "Didn't somebody once say that if you weren't nervous about starting a new thing, then why bother?"

"You just did," said Joan. "What do you think of this color on me?"

"I like it. But I think you could go a shade darker."

They solicited the help of a sales representative wearing a white coat, as if she were in the medical department of a large university rather than in cosmetics at Bergdorf Goodman. She gave them each a handful of Q-tips and tissues. Her practiced eye told her these women might try a dozen shades before making a decision. But she could also tell they were buyers.

"What about you?" asked Joan. "Do you ever think about working?"

"Doing what?" asked Gretchen. "The last time I had a job, I was just out of college."

Joan closed one eye. "You worked in a library, right?"

Gretchen nodded her head. "I was thinking about getting a master's degree in library science—and then I met Elliot."

Joan had set three tubes of lipstick aside and was still searching for what she was calling her "Saturday-night shade," as if she and Stephen went out to an event or dinner every weekend; as if, even if they did, she didn't have a variety of lipsticks at home that matched whatever she wanted to wear. "Would you want to do that now?"

"I don't think so. Libraries are such different places from what they were twenty years ago."

"How so?"

Gretchen shrugged. "They're more like community centers now, busy and noisy, at least the public libraries are. The Southwood Library is private, funded mostly by an endowment and current donors rather than the town. So it still has the feel of the libraries of days gone by."

"So work in a library like that."

"Those jobs come up every half century," said Gretchen. "I'd get the degree and then have to commute seventy miles every day to use it."

"Not an option, right?"

"Definitely not an option," said Gretchen. "But I have to find something to do."

"It sounds like the empty nest is a challenge for you, too?"

They purchased two lipsticks each and then moved on to the eye section. Joan had black, thick lashes that matched her hair, so she hardly needed mascara, a feature all the Howard women had at one point or another remarked about and openly envied. Gretchen picked up a silver Bobbi Brown mascara case. "It's more the papa bird," she said, unscrewing the top and brushing her lashes.

"Elliot can be pretty high energy," said Joan, a smile on her face in case the remark needed softening. "Is something new happening?" She picked up a case of gray and taupe eye shadow promising a smoky look, which reminded Joan, like many things did, of the casino. She put the case down.

"He's high energy, and he's high maintenance," said Gretchen, studying her eyes in the mirror on the glass countertop. "He says that I can devote all my time to him since the kids are all gone."

"What kind of devotion is he looking for?" asked Joan.

Gretchen looked at Joan. "Let's see. He wants all his meals made from scratch using organic ingredients," said Gretchen, using the index finger of her left hand to push back the pinky of her right hand, counting. "He wants the house to look as neat and ordered as a museum. And, he's thinking I should put in a garden next summer, now that our neighbors are dropping off squash and tomatoes. He doesn't have enough to do in his life? He has to dictate what I do with mine?"

"It sounds like you've moved from Southwood to Stepford," said Joan, laughing. "What's brought on this change?"

Gretchen gave one of Sandi's hundred-dollar bills to the cashier. "Who knows? But he is up in my business, and I don't like it."

"Who would?" said Joan. "But now that I think about it, Raymond Senior is kind of like that with Sandi. He likes everything just so."

Gretchen gasped. "You think Elliot's turning into his father?"

"No, no," said Joan, reassuring her sister-in-law. "But he might be less invasive if he knew you were out of the house and working at something you both found interesting. It might mitigate his urge to control you."

"You really think so?" asked Gretchen.

"Maybe," said Joan. "When Stephen was out of a job, he was like that for a while."

"And you think my getting a job would change this behavior?"

"It's worth a shot," said Joan, paying the cashier.

"Maybe I will," said Gretchen.

Joan knew that very second—even though Gretchen didn't—that Gretchen would not explore this option. And as much as Joan liked Gretchen, this was the reason, she instantly realized, that she hadn't called Gretchen to have coffee—because Gretchen was afraid to voice her own opinion, to break out of the mold for Howard women. Underneath her layers of fine, fitted clothing and perfectly applied makeup, she had no confidence, in herself or in her ability to do anything that she was not told to do. How different she was from Alice and Ellie. Sure, Alice's grandstanding routinely annoyed Joan, but at least she stood for something. And Ellie, who had her own bookkeeping business and was considering coming out at almost fifty, was an inspiration. They, and women like them, were whom Joan wanted to spend her free time with. Joan removed the silk scarf from around her neck, similar to the scarves worn by Jill, Sylvia, Sandi, and Gretchen, and tucked it into her handbag.

CHAPTER 46

Alice suggested they go to the beach for lunch. She had been just once since the shooting, and she wanted to get back, to reclaim what she thought of as her territory. After they ordered their foot long dogs, the Wednesday special at the beach snack shack, they pounced on the last table on the deck of the pavilion, Ellie scurrying back to the crowded food window to ask for a washcloth to wipe up the dribbles of mustard and ketchup. Table cleaned, they all settled in under the large umbrella that provided the only available shade. Five minutes later, their number was called, and both Joan and Ellie stood to retrieve their order. When they left, Alice shifted her chair into the sun and closed her eyes for a moment, picturing Daisy. The puppy had been just what she needed to keep her mind away from the fact that she had pumped a bullet into another human being whom she had decided at the last possible moment not to exterminate. The events of that afternoon sometimes visited her in the night. More than once, she had awoken with a drenched nightshirt. She had not talked about it much, after the first rush of filling in the details for everyone she ran into in town who had read about it in the newspaper. And at this point, Ellie and Joan talked about it only when Alice brought it up.

Their conversation that day was, instead, about their youngest children returning to school, and the fact that the three women hadn't seen much of them over the summer. Tim had been away at choir camp—visiting just once for a long weekend—but Liz and Linda had lived in their parents' houses. And yet Joan and Alice had not spent anywhere close to the amount of time with their daughters that they had thought they would.

"I expected this great reunion," said Alice, who had returned her chair to its original space under the umbrella. "You know, hanging out, eating dinner together. She was out more than she was in. And when she was in, she was on her phone."

"Imagine that," said Joan, breaking eye contact with Alice briefly to look at Alice's cell phone on the table.

"I was, like, five hundredth on her list of people to be with," said Alice, oblivious to Joan's slight. "And poor Dave was even lower on the list."

"It's amazing what can happen in one year," said Ellie. "We knew that Tim was going to be away, of course. But we thought he'd call once in a while. We got quick texts about how busy he was and how much fun he was having, but not much else."

"Because they're grown-ups now," said Joan, smiling as she sipped a Diet Coke through a plastic straw.

"Oh, you got that grown-up thing, too?" said Alice. "What is that, actually, supposed to mean?"

"It means," said Joan, "that they're mature, independent adults and can make their own decisions. After all, that's what they've been doing all year at school."

"Give me a break, right?"

Joan laughed. "Yes! I've had to stop myself from telling Liz that as soon as she's paying for everything in her life, then she can claim independence."

"And just a year ago, they were still under our roofs and scared to death about the next step," said Ellie, "even though they wouldn't admit it."

"Oh, Linda admitted it all right," said Alice. "She wanted to stay with her mom forever."

"Wait," said Joan. "Did she say that before or after you bought her the car?"

"Very funny, smarty pants."

Joan held up her hands. "You set yourself up for that one," she said, grinning at Alice. "But you're right. The huge transformation in Liz between this summer and last summer was something I didn't expect, even though I'd gone through it with Cassie. I somehow thought the baby would be different. The nice thing though? Now that Cassie is twenty-five, she's circling back around." Joan took a deep breath, which attracted the attention of Alice and Ellie. "And speaking of Cassie—she's engaged."

"What?!" said Alice. "And you've waited how long to tell us? Wow, what great news!"

"It *is* great news," said Joan. "Stephen and I really like her boyfriend, Jay. I guess I was hoping she, they, would wait a little longer."

"They've been dating, what, four years now?" asked Alice.

"Yes, since they graduated from college. Now Jay has been offered a job in Portland, Maine, and he wants to take Cassie with him."

"She wanted a ring to move from Massachusetts to Maine?" asked Alice.

"No," said Joan. "I think she would have gladly moved there with him without a ring. It was his decision. He wanted to give her a ring."

"Well, then, that's kind of sweet," said Alice.

"Congratulations," said Ellie, in a tone that did not match the word.

"El?" said Joan.

Ellie started to cry. "I'm sorry," she said. "I'm really happy for Cassie and Jay. And I'm happy for you and Stephen. But talking about marriage makes me realize what trouble I'm in. I've got to get *out* of my marriage, and I don't know how. And I'm sorry to be such a self-centered idiot to bring this up when you've just shared some lovely news with us."

"It's okay," said Joan, meaning it. "I will be talking about this wedding for the next six months, so we don't need to dwell on it today. We can talk about you. How was your session with the counselor?"

"It was okay," said Ellie. "She is encouraging me to move forward. She thinks it is the only option for me, now that I know who

I am, if I want a shot at true happiness. And it is definitely the only way, in her opinion, to end my stomachaches."

They ate quietly for a minute—Joan concentrating on the large order of French fries that she was splitting with Ellie, who wasn't eating them, and Alice overchewing the bite of veggie dog in her mouth. "Look," said Joan. "I have an idea. What are you guys up to for Labor Day?"

"Laboring," said Ellie. "We'll be cleaning out the garage."

"Any time for socializing?" asked Joan.

"What do you have in mind?" asked Alice.

"A cookout at my house. Cassie and Jay will be home, and I thought it would be nice to have a small gathering. We're doing a big thing with the Howard family on Saturday night. This would be a small gathering on Monday afternoon, with just our three families."

"With our husbands?" asked Alice.

"With our husbands," said Joan.

Alice looked at Joan. "Do we want to do this? Do we want to let them into the club?"

Joan laughed. "You're joking."

"I am joking—but I'm kind of serious, too. I like having my own thing with you two."

"I know what you're saying," said Joan, "and I agree. But Stephen does ask me about you. He's the one who suggested it."

"No kidding," said Alice.

Ellie took a small bite of her otherwise untouched hot dog. She wiped the relish from her lips and then said quietly, "What if I don't have a husband by Labor Day?"

"You will still have a husband," said Joan. "But maybe you will be able to talk to him by then."

"I need to talk to him. I need to let this out," said Ellie. "Things with Diana are . . . progressing, which I love and hate at the same time. I'm so confused."

"Does this mean she wants to be with you, too?" asked Joan.

"Maybe," said Ellie, making eye contact with her hot dog instead of with Alice or Joan. "She told me yesterday that she is open to the idea of dating."

"Oh boy," said Alice.

"Oh boy what?" asked Ellie, looking up from her lunch.

"This is going to sound harsh, especially since I know about all the turmoil you are going through. But, Ellie, you don't want to start dating a woman until you get out of your current relationship with a man."

Ellie sat back in her chair. "Number one: You don't think I know that? And number two: I would have to get out of whatever relationship I was in—whether it was with a male or a female—to start dating again, whether I was interested in dating a male or a female."

"Well said." Joan closed her right hand into a fist and raised her thumb.

"You know what I meant," said Alice. "First things first. You have to tell Chris."

"Of course I do," said Ellie. "I just don't know how to do it."

"There is no good way to tell him, Ellie," said Alice. "You just need to sit down with him one night after dinner and tell him you're a lesbian."

"Just like that."

"I know I'm making it sound easy—and I know it's not easy. But if you are determined to change your life, you need to take steps to actually do it."

Ellie dipped the corner of her paper napkin into her paper cup of water and wiped at a spot of mustard on her shorts. "Maybe I shouldn't let it out," she said, eyes on her stained shorts. "It's going to hurt too many people."

"It will hurt Chris," said Joan. "But he may understand more than you think he will. And the same may be true for your boys."

"What about my mom, my dad, and my brothers?"

Joan shrugged. "Hey, I'm sorry you are part of a homophobic family. But they are just going to have to suck it up."

Ellie smiled at Joan's comment, her first smile since they sat down. "I don't think they know what that means."

"Tell them your secret," said Joan. "And they'll figure it out."

Chapter 47

In spite of the conversations she'd had with Joan and Alice and with Diana, and in spite of the promises she'd made to herself, Ellie had not been able to tell Chris. She had come close that morning, when the two of them were sitting at their kitchen table drinking coffee and talking about the day ahead. Chris worked for Kilcullen & Sons Construction in the summer months, a company owned and operated by Ellie's Uncle Jack. This year, they were building houses in a new subdivision off Route 1. Chris loved the work—two of Ellie's cousins had taught him everything they knew about carpentry in the fifteen years he had been a part of their summer crew—and he loved being outside all day. He came home every Monday through Friday thoroughly worn out, but also entirely satisfied with his day. No bureaucracy. No recalcitrant teenagers. And his good mood carried over into the next morning, which deterred Ellie from doing or saying anything to dampen it. She questioned whether telling him when he was in a bad mood made any sense—and it didn't. Plus he was hardly ever in poor spirits. But confessing her secret to him, which would erase the permanent smile he wore on his face from the end of the school year until the beginning of the next one, was something that Ellie could not will herself to do, no matter what she told herself when she was alone with her thoughts.

She had never been good at confrontation—so unlike her mother, who didn't kowtow to anyone, well, except for her father. Pat Kilcullen was a mostly measured, often quiet man, but he had expectations of his sons and his wife. The boys were to excel professionally, keep their marital bed sacred, and do their messiest merrymaking in private. Public drunkenness, in Pat's opinion, was a sign of weak character. Brigid was allowed to do whatever she wanted to do, as long as it would not disgrace the family or the Roman Catholic Church. Pat was proud of Brigid's fiery spirit and activism. But he came first. He was allowed these expectations because his sons and his wife didn't challenge him. Sure, the boys had found their share of trouble when they were teenagers. But Pat, still six foot, three inches at eighty-two, had always straightened them out, bloodying their noses if necessary. He'd had expectations of Ellie too, but they were softer in nature: find a good man, make a good home, come to dinner when invited. He didn't mind her working. Of course, he didn't view her business in the same way that he looked at his sons' professional lives. But he was pleased with the way that Ellie had been able to help with the household expenses while she raised her sons. Ellie knew that she had won her father's affection mostly because, in one way, she was very much like her mother; they both carried ninety percent of the family weight without ever complaining.

Ellie brewed herself another cup of coffee and put a slice of bread into the toaster. When the toast popped, she covered it with peanut butter and grabbed the yellow legal pad she kept handy for jotting down groceries needed or things to do. She took the pad, toast, and fresh coffee back to the kitchen table, and reached for a pencil from the label-less soup can at its center. The can had sat there since her boys were in elementary school and did their math sheets and book reports under Ellie's supervision while she cooked dinner. Repeating an exercise she had done several times already, she wrote *Pros* on the left side of the paper and *Cons* on the right side and started her list.

Pros:

1. *I will finally be true to myself.*
2. *I can love someone I am meant to love.*

After failing for five minutes to come up with a third *Pro,* Ellie shifted her attention to the right side of the paper, the easier assignment.

Cons:

1. *I will break my husband's heart.*
2. *I will break my sons' hearts.*
3. *I will break every heart in the Kilcullen family.*
4. *I will lose every relationship that means something to me.*

Ellie, realizing that she was weeping, as she had almost every day since she had told Diana her secret, put down her pencil. She was low again, even though she had been high twenty minutes ago when Diana called her. Ellie's mood swings had become drastic and sudden, and she was having an increasingly difficult time hiding her emotions from Chris, Alice, and Joan. Her counselor—what Ellie called her even though she was a psychiatrist—had offered to prescribe antianxiety medication for Ellie. But Ellie had declined, preferring to think that her exercise regime, healthy eating, and adequate sleep would get her through this. But she had not been doing two out of the three for the last few weeks, food having lost its appeal and sleep impossible.

"I cannot do this," she said aloud. "I cannot tell my family, and I cannot hide it any longer. And I cannot continue to do both at the same time." She got up from the table and walked to the far end of the family room for a tissue from the box that sat on the shelf below the television. As she blew her nose, her eyes found the rifles on the wall, sitting in their locked, wood and glass case. She could see her reflection in the front pane, the guns lined up behind it. She looked at them for what must have been several minutes, even though she'd lost track of time. She'd lost track of everything but the guns. A pronounced stillness had entered her body, like a mist through the pores in her skin, magically drying her tears and calming her overworked heart. Her muddled thinking was clearing; here was another option. She walked back into the kitchen and then into the hallway that led to the staircase. She climbed the stairs, two at a time, and then walked quickly to the bedroom she shared with her husband. In the drawer of his bedside table, she opened the leather box that held the keys to the case. She picked them up and looked at them and then closed her fingers around them; she walked back down the stairs, through the kitchen, and into the family room.

She unlocked the case and carefully removed one of the rifles, the one Chris used. These actions were automatic, requiring no thought on Ellie's part, no hesitation in their execution, like auto summing a column of numbers in Excel. She sat on the arm of the couch, put the butt of the rifle on the floor, and then leaned over, so that the muzzle of the rifle was under her chin. She opened her mouth and tilted her head forward, so she was able to put two inches of the rifle barrel in her mouth, tasting the metal and the cleaning oil, the scent of which filled the house after her husband and sons' annual hunting trip, when they cleaned the guns at the kitchen table, all the while talking about their strategies for the following year's boys' weekend. The muzzle was cold and hard against the roof of her mouth. She closed her eyes.

SEPTEMBER

CHAPTER 48

Monday of Labor Day weekend dawned sunny and cool after a thunderstorm in the middle of the night had cleared out the humidity. Joan was up early, drinking coffee and thinking about what she needed to do to get ready for the three o'clock arrival of her guests. She'd cleaned up from the night before, after a quiet dinner with just the four of them—well, five with Jay. And it had been one of the most enjoyable evenings in Joan's recent memory. Cassie and Jay seemed much more than simply happy with each other; they appeared to be *comfortable* with each other—more valuable, in Joan's mind, than happiness, an overrated sentiment, an overused word. Wasn't it more important to be content? Semantics to some, but not to Joan.

Joan had bought all the food the day before, so setting up the backyard, which Stephen had promised to do, and making the pasta salad and the green salad topped the list. Alice had offered to bring three dozen cookies and enough guacamole for a crowd, and Ellie had promised to bring her grandmother's famous baked beans, which, she told Joan, she would transport in a Crock-Pot, so Joan would not feel obligated to clean a very dirty dish at the end of the evening. Ellie also insisted on bringing classy paper goods so the general cleanup would be easier. Finishing her second cup of coffee, Joan stood and walked to the cupboard that held her large pots. She filled one with water from the sink and set it on the stove top to boil. Just as she grabbed two boxes of rotini pasta from the pantry, Stephen walked into the room. "Hello, mister," she said, giving him her best smile.

"You could not have chosen a better day for a cookout," he said, walking to the coffeepot and filling the mug that Joan had set out for him.

"It was your brilliant idea."

Coffee in hand, Stephen kissed his wife on the cheek and then headed for the door to the back deck. "I'm going to set things up outside. What time are they coming again?"

"Three," said Joan. "You've got all day."

"I'm going to get this done—and then head out to do a few errands. I need some gas for the grill and an oil change. Do you need anything?"

"Lightbulbs," Joan said. "If you're going to the hardware store, I could use some fluorescents for the family room lamps."

This banal banter was comforting to Joan. It was an indication of their shared experience, this easygoing conversation. She and Stephen were not discussing gambling, casinos, afternoon drinking, panicked job searches, or challenging syllabus prep; they were talking about gas, oil, and lightbulbs, routine things, letting her know that everything was, at that very moment, okay in their thirty-year marriage. Alice and Dave and Ellie and Chris, she knew, did not enjoy this same level of comfort—Alice and Dave having grown apart instead of together, and Ellie and Chris heading for separate universes.

Just after 3 p.m., Ellie walked into Joan's kitchen carrying a warm Crock-Pot. Joan took the pot from her, kissing Ellie on the cheek as she did. This was a new, undiscussed gesture that Joan offered her friend, partly because Joan, like all the Howard women, greeted guests to her home with convivial affection, and partly because she had become more aware of the closeness she shared with Ellie and Alice. Ellie's quick smile only briefly masked the nervousness in her eyes. Had she said something to Chris? Chris, a six-pack of beer in each hand, had followed Ellie in, and was now standing next to her. Joan quickly turned her attention to him.

"It is so nice to meet you," said Joan, taking the beer from him and setting it down on the counter. She put her hand out for Chris to shake it, but he wrapped his arms around her shoulders instead.

"You feel almost like family," he said. "I've heard all kinds of wonderful things about Joan and Alice all year long—and here we are."

Hair still wet from the shower, Liz appeared from the hallway. She strode over to Tim, who had walked into the kitchen and was now standing next to his dad with his hands in his pockets, and hugged him. Joan followed suit. "It's so nice to see you again, Tim. I hear you've had an adventurous summer."

"Summer choir camp is always an adventure, Mrs. Howard," said Tim, laughing. "I had a blast, but I am more than ready to go back to school."

"Is Brandon here?"

"He's running a quick errand," said Ellie. "I forgot napkins."

"Like I don't have napkins?" asked Joan, her smile trying to coax one from Ellie. "You must be so happy to have him home for the long weekend."

"I am," said Ellie. "He'll be back in a moment."

"Mom, what did you decide about the beer?" asked Liz, running her fingers through her long black hair, an effort, Joan had seen before, to pair casual behavior with a loaded question.

"Chris? Ellie? Stephen and I allow Liz to have a beer or two at home with us, if she is not driving anywhere afterward. I have soft drinks available, too, so whatever works for you works for us."

"We allow the same thing," said Chris.

"Great!" said Liz. She grabbed Tim's hand and pulled him toward the sliding door to the deck.

"You can follow if you'd like, Chris. Both Stephen and the cooler are that way," Joan said, using the index finger of her left hand to point to the back of the house. By the time Chris was out the door, Ellie was close to tears. Joan took her hand and walked her into the hallway off the kitchen. "What's happening, El?"

"I have to tell him," said Ellie. "I realized on the way over here that I cannot wait another second."

Joan put her hands on Ellie's shoulders. "Do you want to tell him here? Now? Alice and I can support you, if you want to do this today."

"I have to do it myself, Joan," said Ellie. "And I have to do it today, before I lose my nerve."

"What can I do to help you?"

"I don't know," said Ellie. "I have to think for a moment." She used her T-shirt sleeve to wipe a tear from her cheek.

Alice, with a basket of cookies, and Dave, a bottle of wine in each hand, walked through the back door, followed by Linda, Hilary, and Cathy, who was carrying her mother's guacamole. Once introductions were done, Joan led everyone outside. Stephen got everyone what he or she wanted to drink and then suggested a game of croquet. He had earlier in the day borrowed two sets from neighbors, so all fourteen of them could play. The duplicate color players, he explained, would simply have to keep careful track of their balls. Everyone laughed when Chris said, "I always keep careful track of my balls!"

Just as they were getting ready to start, Ellie, who had ducked into the bathroom when Alice and her family arrived, emerged from the house and announced that she wasn't feeling well and needed to go home. "I've got a really upset stomach," she said.

The smile on Chris's face faded. "Another stomachache? Oh boy. We can go with you, honey."

"No," said Ellie, shaking her head. "Please stay here and enjoy yourselves. I'm sorry to ruin this beautiful picnic."

"You are not ruining it," said Joan, stepping onto the deck to take Ellie by the arm and lead her back into the house. Once inside, Joan said, "What can I do to help?" By this time, Ellie was crying again.

"I'm an idiot, Joan. I cannot tell my husband, and I cannot continue to live this life."

"Let me drive you home."

"No, no. I can drive myself home. Please, I've done enough."

Joan hugged Ellie and watched her walk through the door to the garage and to the driveway, where Brandon, who had joined the others in the backyard, had parked Ellie's Honda. When Joan turned around, Chris was standing in front of her. "Is she okay?" he asked.

"I don't know," said Joan.

"Do you think I should go home to be with her? She's not been herself lately." Chris looked concerned, helping Joan understand why it would be difficult to tell him, to leave him. "Has she said anything to you?"

Joan looked into Chris's eyes and was tempted, for just a second, to tell him what Ellie could not. "Why don't you follow her home," she said instead, digging in her purse for her car keys. "Just to make sure she's okay. We're not going to eat for a couple hours. If she's feeling better, you can both come back."

"Good idea," said Chris. "You don't mind if I use your car?"

"Not at all. We'll hope to see you later."

As soon as Chris left, Joan took her phone out of her purse. *Chris is coming home to make sure you are ok. Tell him, Ellie. Love you.*

"What's going on?" asked Alice, walking into the kitchen from the deck. "Is Ellie okay?"

"She's sick with this secret, Alice. She has to let it out. I sent him after her, and I texted her that she should tell him. Was I wrong to do that?"

"No," said Alice. "I wish things were different—but I can see that they aren't. And I want Ellie to be happy. She is such a loving, giving person, Joan. She more than anyone else I know deserves to be happy."

CHAPTER 49

Even though Ellie was not available because she and Chris had a meeting with a real estate agent that morning, Alice took Daisy to the dog park. And even though Alice liked to have company at the dog park, she was relieved that Ellie was busy; Alice had spent a lot of time on the phone and in person with Ellie in the last ten days, since she had told her husband and her sons on Labor Day about being a lesbian. Chris had initially taken it pretty well, according to Ellie. He told her he was sad, like she was, but that he was supportive of her and of her decision to come out. Several days later, however, the reality of what Ellie had said and meant must have sunk in; Ellie said he didn't talk to her for two days. And that was not like him; he was not a grudge holder. His mood shifted again a couple days after that. He wanted to get the house on the market as soon as possible, so he could move ahead with his life. He wanted to find someone who would love him as, he said, he was "meant to be loved."

His anger had surprised Ellie, who had thought the Kilcullen family would be her large but single problem. And she and Chris had fought bitterly one night, actually yelling at each other, which wasn't characteristic of either of them or of their marriage. It was this argument, Ellie told Alice and Joan, that had resulted in Chris's not speaking to Ellie. Now that they were talking again—not a lot, but at least some—Ellie knew that Chris was, as she described it, coming around. He was deeply hurt, which Ellie understood, but she also had a feeling he would be okay, because Brandon and Tim had told her that Chris had told them how important it was to be supportive of their mother. He had hidden his resentment from his sons. And for this Ellie was very grateful. Ellie would have to work at finding a new relationship with Chris, at having a friendship with her husband. But she thought he would eventually be open to it, if only for the sake of their boys.

Alice had a different opinion as to why Brandon and Tim were supportive of their mother. Yes, certainly their dad's demeanor and instruction made a difference. But Alice suspected they were good to their mom because they loved her. Ellie had put their needs ahead of hers—Ellie put everyone's needs ahead of her own—and the boys knew the time had come for her to think about herself and what she wanted. The younger generation was much better at embracing homosexuality than Alice and her peers. And, in spite of her reservations, Alice could see that Tim, Brandon, and the rest of the twenty-somethings were onto something. They knew that judging others was a very bad habit.

Daisy had been to the park a few times. She was playful and submissive, qualities that had attracted other dogs. She made friends quickly. On this particular day, Alice and Daisy followed a pack of humans and dogs around the short loop, and then they returned to the meadow. After ten minutes of nonstop jumping, running, and playing, Daisy was exhausted. Alice scooped her up in her arms, kissed her nose, and then set her back down on the ground and clipped on her leash. As they were walking toward the gate to the parking lot, Alice saw Kelly Shulz, James's mother, getting out of her car. A moment later, Kelly's eager yellow labs were jumping at the gate. Alice's smile was met by a blank stare. And then Kelly said, "I read about your encounter in the newspaper."

"Oh?" said Alice, not sure she wanted to have a conversation with Kelly Shulz about Greg Anderson, guns, or anything else.

"I know what happened," said Kelly, unlatching the gate and letting her dogs through. They immediately crowded around Daisy, all tails madly wagging.

"You do?"

"Yes," said Kelly. "You could have killed him, and you didn't."

Alice tilted her head, Kelly's words sitting in the front of her mind. "How do you know that?"

Kelly started walking toward the meadow, and Alice followed her, even though she had only a moment ago been on her way out of the park.

"Because you're a conscientious person," said Kelly. "When the kids were in high school, whatever task you were assigned by the head of the drama department, you did well."

"Thank you," said Alice, responding to the compliment.

"And," said Kelly, "conscientious people who own guns learn how to use them properly. They go to target practice until they can hit a soup can off a fence post at fifty yards—and then they continue to practice." Alice smiled at the scenario Kelly presented. One of the targets at the range actually was the image of a soup can. And Alice had nailed it at seventy-five yards. "So, I know you could have killed him."

Alice chose to join the conversation. "Yes," she said. "I could have killed him."

Their presence in the middle of the meadow—Kelly and her dogs and Alice and Daisy—had scattered the others. Most people in town, Alice guessed, were still uncomfortable with facing or talking to Kelly Shulz. She and Kelly were alone.

"So why didn't you? I heard he tried to rape you."

"He did try to rape me," said Alice. "And I was certainly angry enough to kill him."

The women were walking now, heading for the path near the brook.

"Was it that you had a split second to consider what your life would be like if you did?" asked Kelly.

Alice hesitated only a moment before responding. "Yes," she said. "I think that's exactly why I didn't kill him."

Kelly nodded her head. "I think my James had that same thought," she said. "Only he had that thought after he shot Emmanuel Sanchez and not before."

"I'm not sure I know what you mean by that," said Alice.

"Well," said Kelly, "if you think killing someone might have a negative impact on your life and you have just killed someone, then you have little choice other than to kill yourself alongside your victim. If my James had thought about it beforehand, like you, both he and Emmanuel might be alive right now."

Tears formed at the corners of Alice's eyes. And, to her surprise, Kelly gave her a quick hug. "Don't fret," Kelly said. "I've done nothing but worry and mourn each and every day since the shooting, and it hasn't helped anything." It was Alice's turn to hug Kelly. "I've gotten rid of my guns," she said. "I'm not really sure why I had them. They were a substitute, I think, for the love my lousy husband never gave me. They were also a sign to him that I would tolerate his cruelty no longer."

"I'm sorry I haven't called you or done anything to help you."

Kelly stepped out of the hug and away from Alice. "It's okay," she said. "No one knows what to say or do in this kind of situation. I don't blame anyone but myself." Alice said nothing. Even though this short conversation had helped her to understand Kelly and James Shulz more than she ever had, Alice couldn't help but blame someone for what had happened, and she chose, still, to blame Kelly. "I'm moving away," said Kelly. "It's becoming harder rather than easier for me to live here as the months pass."

"Where will you go?" asked Alice. It didn't occur to her to ask Kelly to stay.

"I have a sister in Ohio," Kelly said. "She's divorced too."

"I'm glad you'll have company."

Kelly turned away from Alice and Daisy. "I'm not so sure it's the company I'll enjoy," she said as she walked, the dogs falling into step beside her. "It will just be nice to be someplace where no one knows me. That's the only way I can start again."

CHAPTER 50

Ellie's eyes were swollen when she arrived at High Tide just after one. This told Joan and Alice that Ellie had, as promised, told the Kilcullen family the night before—and that it hadn't, as she had anticipated, gone well. As soon as Ellie sat down, Joan reached across the table and squeezed her hand. Ellie dabbed at her eyes with a used tissue she took from the pocket of her jeans. "I've cried all night," she said. "I didn't think I had any left."

"What can you tell us?" asked Joan.

"Let's see," said Ellie, slipping the white cloth napkin from underneath her fork and knife and spreading it over her lap. "My mother started crying, something she hasn't done since her mother died fourteen years ago. My father started swearing, something he does only when extremely agitated or upset. And my brothers started lecturing me on the sin of homosexuality, insisting I repent."

"Oh God," said Alice. "Was Chris with you?"

Ellie smiled briefly. "Yes—but he looked a bit shell-shocked and didn't talk much until we were back in the car. We were there only an hour, but it seemed much longer. They gave me the full benefit of their Catholic school educations, beginning with the

Garden of Eden and ending with the one-man-one-woman argument."

"It was as you expected," said Joan.

Ellie took a sip from her water glass. "Worse, I think. While I suspected it was going to be a difficult conversation, I was still hopeful that because they love me they would support me." Ellie shook her head. "They weren't even able to forgive me last night."

"Maybe that's coming," said Alice. "You know how it can be when you get unexpected news. Sometimes it takes a while for it to sink in."

"Maybe," said Ellie. "But my father wouldn't even hug me when we left."

Joan said, "Oh boy."

"Yes," said Ellie. "That was the most hurtful part of the evening." She used her napkin to dry her eyes. "But hey, I want to hear about your first day of class on Monday. You e-mailed us that it went well, but I need the details."

Joan held her hands, palms out, up in front of her chest. "It was incredible," she said. "And I do want to tell you all about it. But I want to talk about you today."

"I agree," said Alice.

Ellie inhaled deeply and sat back in her chair. "I don't know what to tell you. It was the classic 'homosexuality is a sin' argument. The Pope may be softening, but my parents and my brothers are definitely not."

"What do they propose you do?" asked Joan.

"Fight it. They want me to fight it. And if I can't beat it—their words—then I should continue to hide it. They think a Christian counselor can help."

"So they think that someone can talk you out of being a lesbian?" asked Joan.

"Yes," said Ellie. "The right counselor will straighten me out, according to my father. I don't know how to reason with this personality type. He's like that clerk in Kentucky who refused to marry same sex couples, in the name of God. What I want to ask Kim Davis, and everyone just like her, is this: What are the first two commandments? If she's the Christian she professes to be, she knows that the answer to that question is that we should love God, number one, and that we should love our neighbors as ourselves, number two. As ourselves, period. If my dad, mom, and brothers are Christians, then they should love me, no matter who I am."

"Amen to that, sister," said Joan.

"And when it comes to a discussion about genetics, my father would rather close his eyes and plug his ears with his index fingers than listen to my thoughts about being born this way. He thinks it's a choice—a perverted, dirty, unnatural choice."

"Who would choose it?" asked Alice. "Did you hit him with that argument? Who would choose societal ostracism, criticism, mockery, verbal and physical attack? Who chooses this?"

Joan looked at Alice. "Someone's been doing her homework."

"I have been doing some research online," said Alice. "I think I sometimes don't understand things that I don't have enough information about. Ellie, if I ever gave you the impression that I didn't support you, I'm sorry. Linda, too, has shed some light on the topic for me. This year, there is a young woman on their dormitory floor who used to be a man."

"Ellie isn't transgender, Alice," said Joan. "She's gay. Different issue altogether."

"I know that," said Alice. "I've been exploring all kinds of sexuality issues. It's fascinating actually."

Ellie looked at Alice, wondering if she was joking. Seeing Alice was not, Ellie said, "What's fascinating to you?" The server took their orders and refilled their water glasses. Ellie waited until he was gone before she continued her thought. "What have you discovered, Alice?"

"The biggest surprise to me is that sexuality is not black and white the way I thought it was. It's more of a spectrum. So, there are hetero people, of course, who are attracted to other hetero people—but those attractions run the gamut from urgent to mild. We all know those men who seek female companionship for just one reason. But then there are the men who treat women as equals, whose testosterone levels aren't through the roof, who think about sex every fifteen minutes instead of every fifteen seconds." Joan smiled at her friend. "It's a serious issue," said Alice. "If a couple's sex drives and expectations around sexual relations aren't aligned, it can be a battle. But, I stray from the point I was trying to make—and that is this: There are straight people, and bisexual people, and transgender people, and people who fall into other categories that have not yet been named. And who's to say what's normal? Who's to say what is right and what is wrong?"

Ellie let out a sigh. "I needed you at my parents' house last night."

"I would have come," said Alice.

"And if I had known the depth of your knowledge, I would have asked you," said Ellie. "You seem to understand what my parents will never understand. I tried the born-this-way argument because I thought they might be able to digest that. They might be able to equate homosexuality with race or gender. What I would love to tell them someday, Alice, is what you pointed out. That it really doesn't matter. That we can love whomever we are attracted to. That there is no normal. That there is no right or wrong. That there's only one thing that matters, and that is love."

"Wow," said Joan.

"So what do we do now?" asked Alice. "Now that last night has happened."

Ellie slowly shook her head back and forth. "I don't know," she said. "They have the information. I guess we wait until they process it. Either they will accept me as I am, or they won't. I'm not going back now. I'm out. If my family wants to cut me out of their lives, well, it's been nice knowing them."

"Is Chris doing okay?" asked Joan.

"He is better," said Ellie. "He continues to be sad about separating after so many years together, but he is no longer angry. I think he is trying to focus on our friendship, on the fact that we will still have each other—only in a different way. I think he realizes that I am sad, too."

"What about the boys?" asked Alice. "How are they doing? Have you started deciding things like who they will live with when they are home?"

"They, like your children, will increasingly be living away from home," said Ellie. "But when they are in town, for a weekend or for the holidays, there will be a place for them at both houses—and we will get together as a family. There will be some weird, awkward moments, but I'm not sure those moments will be any more uncomfortable than the weird, awkward moments in a heterosexual life."

"You are incredibly strong, Ellie," said Joan, stifling her rising emotion so that Ellie would not need to comfort her. "And I am tremendously proud to be your friend."

"And I am so, so glad to have both of you as my friends," said Ellie. "At times, I feel closer to you than I do to my family, especially right now."

Joan added, "Your mother, father, and brothers? They will come around."

Ellie shrugged. "I hope so," she said. "But today, it's not my problem; it's theirs."

CHAPTER 51

One of the requirements of adjunct instructors at Nutmeg Community College, outside of teaching class and correcting tests and homework assignments, was holding office hours. Since she worked part time, Joan didn't have a designated office. Instead, for two hours after her Thursday morning class, Joan parked herself and her belongings in one of the empty offices down the hallway from her classroom. The offices were meant to be used by the adjuncts, but Joan hadn't seen anyone there other than her students since school had started three weeks ago. It was a quiet space.

Joan hadn't been settled more than ten minutes when she heard the door open at the end of the short hallway. "Miss Howard?"

"I'm down here," Joan called.

A few seconds later, Devon Johnson plopped himself down in the chair next to Joan's desk. "Hey, Devon," said Joan, pleased with herself for knowing his name, for memorizing the names of her forty-eight students in two weeks. "How are you?"

"I'm okay, Miss Howard," he said. "But I'm having a hard time with the homework you assigned on Tuesday."

"Take it out," said Joan. "Let's have a look together."

When Devon bent over to reach into his backpack, Joan saw a handgun in the waistline of his jeans. When he righted himself, notebook in hand, his baggy sweatshirt fell back into position, concealing the gun. Devon set the notebook down on the desk and pulled his chair closer to Joan so that they could look at his work together. "I'm not sure how to go about answering number six," he said. "I think I have it set up right, but I keep getting the wrong answer."

Joan sat back in her chair, putting more space between the two of them. "Before we get started," she said, "I have to tell you that I saw your gun—and it makes me uncomfortable."

Devon squinted his eyes, like he did in class sometimes when he was trying to remember something. And then he looked down at his side, lifted his sweatshirt, and touched the gun. "This gun, Miss Howard?" Joan nodded her head. "I'm sorry," he said. "I'm so used to carrying it, I forget I have it."

"Can I ask why you carry it?"

"You can ask me," he said. "But a smart lady like you ought to know the answer."

"For protection," said Joan. "You carry it for protection."

"Yes, I do."

"What are you protecting yourself from?"

Devon sat back in his chair, sliding his hands between his closed thighs. "Let's play a guessing game, like you do with us in class," he said. "I'm guessing you live in Southwood or Harbortown or Longbay. Am I right?"

"I live in Southwood."

"I've been to Southwood once or twice—with all the big houses, fancy shops, and expensive restaurants. I live in Stannich— with all the abandoned mills, low-income housing, and closed storefronts." Joan lowered her gaze from Devon's eyes to her desk for a moment, feeling suddenly foolish for asking about his gun, before returning her attention and her eyes to his face. "I carry this gun," said Devon, "so that, on my way from my fifteen-year-old, rusted out car that I park on the street because I have no heated, automatic door opener garage, to the small apartment I live in with my mother, my girlfriend, my daughter, and my four younger brothers, I will have an option when the drug addict on the corner wants to relieve me of the cash I get paid under the table working from two until eight in the morning as a custodian at the Starry Night Club."

"I'm sorry . . ." Joan began.

Devon held up his hands. "Don't be sorry," he said. "Just don't make assumptions. Number one, I have a constitutional right to carry this gun. And number two, the people who carry guns are not always the bad guys."

"I know," said Joan. "You make a very good argument for carrying a gun."

"That's because I've been asked before by people like you."

"Who's making assumptions now?" asked Joan.

Devon grinned at her. "You got me there, Miss Howard."

They looked at each other for another moment, and then Joan said, "Let's get back to the reason you're here. The problem you are having trouble with is actually easier than it seems. You just have to turn your thinking around."

"Kind of like we just did?"

Joan smiled at him. "Yes, Devon—*just* like we just did."

OCTOBER

CHAPTER 52

"Any of your other students schooling you?" asked Alice, a smile on her face.

Joan eased a forkful of coleslaw into her mouth. "All of them," she said, chewing. "All of them. Here's another story." And she told Ellie and Alice about the young woman in her late twenties who wore four-inch heels and skintight clothing to school. "Even though Devon told me to be careful about my assumptions, I continue to make them. I am trying to become more aware of when I do this, but I am nowhere close to where I want to be. So, getting back to my student—I assumed this young woman dressed this way because she needed a bunch of male attention, that she questioned her physical, emotional, and intellectual worth, and that she was one of the weaker members of our gender rather than one of the stronger."

"Oh, this is going to be good," said Alice.

"Turns out she used to weigh almost three hundred pounds. She lost close to two hundred of them by having extensive weight loss surgery. And she is now very proud of her new body, which she shows off by wearing tight clothing and towering footwear. She is also, by the way, the most ardent feminist in both of my classes, as well as my most perceptive student."

"Nice," said Ellie. "I love stories like that."

"Yeah, it turns out I'm not as smart as I thought I was," said Joan.

"I'm not so sure about that," said Ellie.

"At some things, I'm clueless," said Joan.

"It's so nice to hear you admit that," said Alice. Joan winked at her friend. Alice reached for her water glass and then turned her attention and her face to Ellie. "How are you doing, El? Anything new with your family?"

"You mean, speaking of support? No," she said, "not a word."

"Your parents still haven't spoken to you?" asked Joan.

"Nope," said Ellie. "They're too busy bending the ear of the priest at St. Mary's by the Sea."

"How do you know that?" asked Alice.

"Because Father Matthew called this morning and told me how worried they are about me," said Ellie. "He wants me to come in for counseling."

"What did you tell him?" asked Joan.

"I told him I thought it was my parents and brothers who needed the counseling," said Ellie. "But I said, if he is willing to counsel me in the presence of my new Episcopal priest, then I would certainly think about it. He told me he'd get back to me, but I don't anticipate hearing from him anytime soon."

"You're going to the Episcopal church now?" asked Alice.

"Yes. It's Diana's church—and they not only don't believe in burning homosexuals at the stake, they happily *marry* gay couples."

"Imagine that," said Joan, arms crossed across her chest in an expression of satisfaction rather than confrontation. "How is Diana?"

"She's good," said Ellie, taking a bite of her BLT. "We don't know where this is going, but we're trying to figure it out."

"Do you want to be with her, El?" asked Alice.

"That's the question, isn't it? In some ways, I can't believe I'm even thinking about getting into a relationship with someone when I am in the middle of drastically changing one that lasted more than a quarter of a century. And in other ways, it seems completely natural, like this relationship is what I've been looking for my whole life."

"How does she feel?" asked Joan.

"She's cautious," said Ellie. "And I like that about her. She has been where I am now, so she knows that I'm going to have trouble committing to anything for a while. Both of us know our relationship has the potential to be a serious one. We are not looking for temporary satisfaction."

"No quick roll in the hay?" asked Joan, smiling.

Alice shuddered. "I know I shouldn't say this," she said. "But I don't like to picture two women having sex."

"Oh," said Ellie. "You'd rather picture your daughter, Linda, screwing the guy from her psych class in her twin bed in her dorm room?"

Joan laughed out loud.

"You're right," said Alice. "I guess I don't like to picture anyone having sex."

"Yeah, well, that's because the carnal knowledge shared by two people is nobody's business but their own, as you so eloquently pointed out, Alice," said Ellie. "I honestly don't understand why people get so upset about it. How does my being a lesbian have anything to do with my father's or mother's or brothers' lives? How do my actions affect theirs? And what about the second commandment is confusing to people? My family goes to church every Sunday, where the first and second commandments are carved into the stone walls that support the building. *Carved into the stone!* This is not a subtle set of mandates. Are they ignorant, or are they hypocrites?"

"It's easy for people to love a neighbor who's just like them," said Joan. "It's a very different story when the neighbor has a different skin color or subscribes to an alternative lifestyle."

Ellie nodded her head at Joan's remark. "My mother loves to feed the poor at the soup kitchen," she said. "But she'd never dream of inviting any one of them to her home for a meal."

"Yeah, I'd probably fall short in that department, too," said Alice.

"We all do," said Ellie. "That's the point. We all fall short of one another's expectations—most of us fall short of our own. We can go through life being critical of those around us, or we can look for the good. If you are not looking for the good, you will only find the bad. And I'm not surprised, but I am very disappointed that my parents and brothers have chosen to focus on what they perceive as bad when they know that I am, essentially, good."

"You are exceptionally good," said Joan.

CHAPTER 53

Their real estate agent told Ellie and Chris that he would put the house on the market just as soon as they got rid of the clutter, as he diplomatically put it. *People like to envision their own belongings in a house,* he had said, *so the fewer of your things they have to mentally push through, the better.* And there was a fair amount to push through, from Ellie's business files and knitting supplies in the basement to her boys' belongings in the attic. Ellie had told Tim and Brandon that she would store their things until they had a somewhat permanent address. Consequently, the attic was jam packed with whatever they had been unable to part with. Ellie was guilty, too, of holding on to too much. She had more of her boys' childhood toys and stuffed animals than a dozen grandchildren could ever find time to enjoy. And even though she and Chris made an annual vow to get rid of what they no longer used, it hadn't happened in years, meaning no one had an accurate picture of the five hundred square foot space that sat atop the second story of their house or an accounting of its contents.

October was a good time to clean out the attic, which was hot in the summer and cold in the winter. After her morning walk, Ellie filled a travel mug with coffee and climbed the two sets of stairs leading to a jumble of cardboard boxes, plastic storage containers, hanging racks of clothing no one wore, board games, and cast off furniture, reminding Ellie that Tim and Brandon's crib was still tucked away in one of the back corners. Would Goodwill be interested in a twenty-year-old crib? Ellie walked around a pine desk that had not been put into service since her mother had given it to her more than fifteen years ago and started in on the plastic storage containers. She spent two hours sorting through clothes, casting every item into keep, donate, or throw away piles. Next came the boxes, some of which were labeled, the first one having the word TROPHIES written in black marker on one of the top flaps. For the next half hour, she studied them, one at a time, trying to recall the events for which they were awarded. They were cheaply constructed of plastic and metal, but they represented past achievements, no matter how meager. They had been cheerfully handed out at special ceremonies and dinners, Brandon and Tim filled, at least on those nights, with pride and optimism.

The next box she came upon was marked with the words SCHOOL PICTURES/CHRIS. Inside were photos Chris had taken at school over the years, as well as faculty pictures, each featuring Chris in a blue blazer and tie, with the same impish grin on his face in each one. Ellie was transported back to college, when she first met Chris and he had given her that same smile. He smiled a lot, more than most, Ellie thought, because he was a happy person—not happy in an ignorant or self-serving kind of way, but legitimately content. Chris was not a deep thinking man, but he was also not a brooder, not a bully, not a pretender, and not a narcissist—and he had every right to be pleased with his reflection in the mirror, with his trim and toned arms and legs, and with his flat abdomen, his full head of blond hair, his square jaw, and that grin. That's what she had fallen in love with, his playful grin and his easygoing demeanor. Seconds later, she was crying. And seconds after that, Chris walked up the stairs. He called on his way, "I can't believe you're actually up here, El. I'm impressed!" But the smile on his face dropped when he saw that she was weeping. "What's wrong, honey?"

"How can you call me honey, after everything I've done to

you?" she asked him, wiping the tears from her face with the back of her thumbs.

"What have you done to me?" he asked, even though they both knew the answer to this question. Ellie moved her head forward and looked into his eyes. "Oh," he said, "you mean the part about leaving me because you're a lesbian?" The grin was back. And Ellie half smiled in return.

"You are good to me," she said.

He shrugged and then sat down next to her on the wood floor. "I've been upset, El. You know I've been upset. But you're right, I haven't felt angry in the last couple weeks," he said. "What I finally realized was something I knew all along. You are such a good person, to everyone in your life. You have always put everyone's needs before your own. How can I be angry with you?"

"Because this is not what you expected," she said. "Because this is so unfair to you."

"What's unfair—that I've been able to spend twenty-five years with someone I love? That doesn't seem to be a hardship. The fact that you've been unable to feel true romantic love with someone for your entire life is unfair, in my opinion. I need to release you so you can do that, Ellie."

Ellie was crying again. "But what about you? Who will you love? Who will love you?"

"Right now I've got Tim, and I've got Brandon, and I got you— and maybe someday down the road, I will find someone else to love."

Ellie nodded her head. "I know you will," she said. "You are a wonderful man."

Chris stood and held out his hand to help Ellie to her feet. "Well, this wonderful man is hungry," he said. "Have you had lunch?"

"No," said Ellie, looking at her watch. "Hey, what are you doing home, anyway?"

"Half day today," he said. "We had an in-service this morning on security and mental health. The metal detectors are going up at the main school entrances this afternoon."

Ellie started down the stairs. "That saddens me."

"It is sad," said Chris. "Necessary, but sad."

At the bottom, Ellie turned to Chris and asked, "Do you think it will make a difference?"

"If you're asking if it will stop someone with mental health issues from doing harm to someone else, then I think the answer is no. But I do think it will deter kids from bringing weapons to the high school if they know they have to pass through a metal detector and that their backpacks can be searched at any time."

They walked down the second flight of stairs, through the hallway, and into the kitchen. "What can I get you?" asked Ellie, opening the fridge door.

Chris removed the blazer he wore on professional development days and hung it on the back of a chair. "I'm making lunch for you today—so what can I get you? Tuna?"

Ellie smiled at him. "I love tuna."

He returned her smile. "I know," he said. "I think there are still a couple English muffins in the bread drawer. How about a tuna melt?"

"Are you kidding me?"

"I," said Chris, taking the muffins from the drawer, "never joke about cheese, even when it's paired with fish."

Ellie laughed, and then said, "What can I do?"

"Sit," he said. "Keep me company."

Ellie pulled a chair out from the table and sat. "Shall we talk about us?"

"Absolutely," said Chris, switching on the oven broiler.

For the next ninety minutes, they talked about their common history, starting with the first day they met, their first date, the first time they slept together—"Did you know then?" Chris asked—moving to their after college dating days, the proposal, the wedding, the birth of their sons, parenthood, and the empty nest. "That's the part that's the hardest for me," said Chris, their plates empty at this point, their second glasses of ice water gone. "I thought this would be our time to rediscover each other. It has been so busy for the last twenty years—I feel like we've barely seen each other. Maybe that's why I didn't know, El. Maybe I wasn't paying attention. I know I've taken you and your love for granted, and I was hoping to make that up to you."

Ellie shook her head. "You've got no making up to do," she said. "I have been just as preoccupied as you. And I have not felt put upon. Yes, I did the lion's share with the boys, but that's what I signed on to do. You told me I could work, and I chose not to until they were in school. And you were also a help around dinnertime and bedtime. You have given the boys no less than a thousand baths. You did not shirk your duties."

Chris reached across the table and squeezed both her hands. "You may be looking through rose-colored glasses."

"That's okay," she said. "I've always liked pink."

They talked about what they would do once the house sold. Chris said he might live in an apartment for a while, until they figured out the next step. But he wanted Ellie to have a house, with enough room for the boys. And while Chris would rent a place with two bedrooms, so he could host them, too, he thought it would be better if they all gathered at Ellie's house for holidays and other family get-togethers.

"What will happen when we start dating?" asked Ellie. "That will be hard for the boys."

Chris shrugged. "It might be harder if we didn't date anyone. They are sensitive, compassionate young men—thanks to you. We will all get through whatever it is we need to get through."

Ellie got out of her chair and walked to the sink with her water glass. She filled it, drank half of it, and then said to Chris, "Have they talked to you about me? Are they confused?"

"They have talked to me a bit," he said. "They're not so much confused as they are worried, about both of us. They worry that your family will never understand—and they know how much the Kilcullen clan means to you, means to all of us. And they worry about me being on my own after so many years of being with you." Ellie started to cry again. The tears that she had been able to hide for so many years were no longer cooperative. They flowed on their own schedule. All Ellie could do was wipe them again and again. "El," said Chris, standing, walking to her, wrapping his arms around her shoulders. "I hate to see you cry."

She wrapped her arms around his waist and leaned her head against his chest. "Will we get through this? Will we emerge as hap-

318 • *Susan Kietzman*

pier people on the other side of this mountain we are trying to climb?"

Chris pulled away just enough so that he could look into her eyes. "Our life is changing, but the deep feelings we have for each other, for our boys, are not. It is the love we have for each other that will get us through this sadness and pain. It is this love that will also—eventually—convince your family that, no matter what it looks like to them or anyone else, what we're doing is the right thing for us."

"You are so brave, kind, and handsome," said Ellie. "How can I leave you?"

"Because you are now on a quest," said Chris, "to find a brave, kind, and pretty partner, and I have made up my mind to do whatever I can to help."

CHAPTER 54

Alice had her phone in her hand when she sat down at the table at High Tide. "Did we actually plan to have this lunch on the anniversary of the shooting?"

"No," said Joan. "It just worked out that way."

"Yeah, but don't you think this means something?" Alice put her phone on the table. "As I get older, I increasingly think things happen for a reason."

"Everything?" asked Joan, wearing the skeptical look that Alice had seen many times before.

"No," said Alice. "I don't yet think there is any cosmic meaning behind a string of green traffic lights when I am in the car and in a hurry."

"Thank you for that."

"But there is something to being together on this day," said Alice.

"I agree," said Ellie. "It was a horrible day that managed to create something good. Consider our friendship—where we were and how far we've come."

"Tell us something good," said Alice. "Tell us the latest in the transformation of Ellie Fagen."

Before Ellie started talking, the server arrived and took their orders. They all ordered clam chowder, side salads, and a basket of warm bread. Ellie then told them that her family was still not speaking to her. "And, I have decided not to live with Diana."

Alice pushed her shoulders back. "I didn't know you were thinking about living with Diana."

"I don't think she knew either," said Ellie. "It was something I was exploring on my own."

"You need time," said Alice.

Ellie shook her head. "I don't know that I do need time. I've had a lifetime of wondering and thinking, if only subconsciously. It's more that I don't want to hurt Chris."

"How is he?" asked Joan.

"He has been incredibly understanding lately," said Ellie. "He has not said a negative word in more than a week."

"You sound surprised," said Joan.

"I knew he could not stay angry in the same way that my mother, father, and brothers are angry. He's not that kind of man. But I didn't expect him to be as sad—or as deep—as he is." Ellie's eyes moistened. "The other day, I found him in our family room, looking at a framed picture of the two of us taken by another hiker when we walked a section of the Long Trail several years ago. Chris and I were covered in sweat, dirt, and bug bites, but we were looking at each other and absolutely beaming." A fat tear fell out of Ellie's left eye. "This is the hardest part. He and I are best friends."

"Maybe you still can be," said Alice. "Maybe not best friends, but you can be very good friends."

The soup and salads arrived. Ellie and Joan each took a piece of bread from the basket, and Alice forked a grape tomato and dipped it into her balsamic vinaigrette dressing.

Ellie nodded her head. "We have talked about this—about how we have to live apart, but how we can try to hold on to some of what we had." Ellie wiped her cheeks with her napkin.

"You are so brave, Ellie," said Joan. "You are a kind, good, brave woman."

Ellie said, "And you always know what to say."

"Ha!" said Alice, looking at Ellie. "I'll grant that she always *has* something to say. Whether or not it's the right thing is up for discussion. Tell her, Joan. Tell her what happened at school the other day."

Joan sighed. "Alice had the good fortune to run into me at the grocery store after class last week, so she got to hear it just a few hours after it happened."

"What happened?" asked Ellie.

"I held my failing students after class for a few minutes and told them they were disappointing me," said Joan. "I told them I expected some degree of academic success from all of them, and that, if they didn't plan on succeeding, then they should simply drop the class and save themselves and me the time and energy of doing it later on in the semester, when the process gets more complicated and the paper work thickens. One of the students went directly to the dean's office afterward, claiming that he had been emotionally battered by his professor."

Ellie's hand covered her open mouth. "And then what?"

"I got a lecture about the power of positive reinforcement."

"Go on," said Alice.

Joan looked at Alice and then back at Ellie. "I told him that I know all about positive reinforcement, and I freely employ it in my classroom. I also told him that there was such a thing as accountability, which seems to be missing altogether in this age of entitlement."

Ellie grinned. "You are awesome," she said. "This is a lecture parents need to hear. Chris tells me all the time about the phone calls and e-mails from parents making excuses for their children."

"Wait a minute," said Alice. "I'm not sure I agree. Parents are involved in their children's lives now, as they should be. My parents were completely removed from my education. They crowed about my sister's report cards, of course. But that was the only thing they commented on. That was the extent of their knowledge about our high school achievements and failures. How can today's parental involvement be a bad thing?"

"Because they, we, are overly involved," said Joan. "We micromanage our children's lives long past the time it is necessary to do so. I know that technology has made this much more possible for us than it was for our parents. But hell, whether I thrived or failed in high school or in college was up to me, not my parents."

"So you think these community college kids are indulged."

"Yes, Alice, I do," said Joan. "Not all of them, of course. But the eighteen-year-olds who giggle through class and don't turn in their homework? They are the targets of my consternation."

"Who's not the target of your consternation?" asked Alice. "You're pretty demanding, Joan."

"Well, right now, you're not the target of my consternation," said Joan to Alice. "But if you pick up that phone to check for random text messages that you could easily look at and deal with after our lovely lunch has reached its natural conclusion, then you might be."

Alice waved the back of her hand at Joan. "Let's not start in on that again."

"Did you also discuss cell phone etiquette at the grocery store? Boy, I missed out on a good one," said Ellie. "What did you decide?"

"Joan told me I need to be present where I am," said Alice. "If I'm expecting an urgent phone call, it's okay to keep the phone handy. If not, the phone should be in my purse and not on the table. When I set my phone down on the table, I am sending the message that the phone is more important than the person I'm with, and that my attention is divided."

Ellie, who never had her phone on the lunch table, but who would also never tell those who did that they were wrong, said, "Interesting!" And then she laughed.

Alice looked at her phone once and then slipped it into her purse. "There," she said. "Are you all happy now?"

"We are very happy," said Joan, smiling. "Tell us about Daisy. How is your training going with her? Is she enjoying your runs together?"

Alice smiled back at Joan. "She is such a good dog. She stays right with me, whether she has a leash on or not. And she's very protective of me."

"Are you still running with your gun?" asked Ellie.

"Sometimes," said Alice. "But I don't take it every time. And I don't take it on the weekends because Dave has started running with me again."

"What?" Joan's eyebrows met with her trimmed black bangs. "You have not said a word."

"Don't get carried away," said Alice. "It has just been the past two Saturdays."

"What brought this on?" asked Joan.

Alice shrugged. "I don't know," she said. "We've been making more time for each other. And I think everything that has happened and everything I have said has finally worked its way through his brain and opened his eyes to how he has been treating me. I have no doubt that he loves me, but for many years, he simply put me at the back of the line. And this is partly because, as soon as my daughters were born, that's exactly where he fell in my world. We are working on putting each other first—or at least closer to the top."

"And how does that feel?" asked Ellie.

Alice smiled. "Pretty good," she said. "It feels pretty good. Plus, he told me yesterday that he's fully covered at both stores for the trial next month. He said he wants to be with me every day of it."

"That's great news, Alice," said Joan. She spooned some chowder into her mouth, swallowed, and then said, "And you know I will be there as often as I can be."

"Me too," said Ellie.

"Look," said Alice. "You two have been with me all along on this. You have jobs. You have lives. You"—she looked at Ellie—"have romantic relationships to pursue. Come when you can, but know that when you can't, I will be okay."

"You are already okay, Alice," said Ellie.

Someone's phone rang; Joan assumed it was Alice's. "You can check your phone, Alice," she said.

"It's not mine," said Alice. "Mine's on vibrate."

"Oh—that's my phone," said Ellie, reaching for her purse. Alice and Joan looked at her, wondering who was calling. Ellie's phone had not rung once over the course of a year of biweekly lunches. Ellie studied the screen and then looked up at her friends. "It's my mother," she said, just before she answered.

EVERY OTHER WEDNESDAY

Susan Kietzman

About This Guide

The suggested questions are included
to enhance your group's
reading of Susan Kietzman's
Every Other Wednesday.

DISCUSSION QUESTIONS

1. Alice, Joan, and Ellie know one another from their children's participation in the high school drama department—but they do not become friends until after their children have graduated. Does this timing affect the nature of their friendship?

2. Why is running again so important to Alice, especially since she has been pursuing other forms of exercise?

3. Joan keeps her gambling habit a secret from both Alice and Ellie, as well as from her husband—which indicates that she knows gambling is not something they would advise her to continue. And yet she does. Why does she persist?

4. Ellie and her husband, Chris, have not spent one night apart from each other in their entire marriage. Is this typical? Is this admirable or unhealthy?

5. The women meet for lunch every other Wednesday. Is getting together every week too often and once a month not enough, as Joan suggests, to build and then sustain a friendship?

6. What do the parents of Joan, Alice, and Ellie have in common—and what effect has their parenting had on the three women?

7. What changes Alice's mind about her commitment level to the Well Protected Women?

8. What event makes Joan finally decide that enough is enough? Why is this the moment she knows she needs to change her behavior?

9. How and why is Ellie able to suppress her true feelings for so long?

10. What makes the three friends often able to speak honestly and also to confront one another when many people are more likely to hold their tongues rather than risk offending a friend?

11. The husbands of the three women occasionally move to the foreground, but they are more often in the background. Why?

12. Is the search for self-identity ever over? Where are Alice, Joan, and Ellie on this path when the novel ends?